the Will *of* Wisteria

Other novels from Denise Hildreth include:

Savannah from Savannah
Savannah Comes Undone
Savannah by the Sea

Flies on the Butter

the Will *of* Wisteria

denise hildreth

THOMAS NELSON
Since 1798

NASHVILLE   DALLAS   MEXICO CITY   RIO DE JANEIRO   BEIJING

Published in Nashville, Tennessee, by Thomas Nelson. Thomas Nelson is a trademark of Thomas Nelson, Inc.

Thomas Nelson, Inc., books may be purchased in bulk for educational, business, fund-raising, or sales promotional use. For information, please e-mail SpecialMarkets@ThomasNelson.com.

ISBN: 978-1-59554-209-0

CIP has been applied for.

Printed in the United States of America
07 08 09 10 11 RRD 6 5 4 3 2 1

Dedication

This book is dedicated to those who remain moldable.

May we realize that often yielding our wills
creates a far more beautiful life.

part 1

August

chapter one

The streets of downtown Charleston were deserted, almost silent except for the redundant racket of the occasional cicada. Dim street lamps hummed overhead, and the humidity of the August night wrapped everything in its thick presence. Elizabeth Wilcott's feet held to the steady rhythm as her running shoes connected with pavement still soft from the heat of the day. Her ponytail slapped against the back of her wet T-shirt, keeping time with her pace.

Elizabeth liked to run at night; that way she wasn't limited to sidewalks. She didn't like limitations. At night she could run in the middle of the street without the nuisance of vehicles or horse-drawn carriages or camera-laden, plaid-shorts-wearing tourists. Besides, no woman had ever been more determined to silence her demons, and fighting the ones that lurked in dark places was a commitment she had made to herself years ago.

At least that's what she thought running at night proved.

Her mind pounded with the rhythm of her feet. Tomorrow. The reading of the will. Her father, Clayton Wilcott, dead. She was an orphan. Siblings didn't count—not hers anyway. She was alone.

Yet her father's death also brought with it another redefining for her. His fortune. For her entire thirty-three years, his money had sifted to her through *his* fingers. Soon her own fingers would determine how it would filter into her world.

Elizabeth envisioned her inheritance, saw it piling up in places predetermined by her alone. From such a position of power she could control everything around her. She had known influence and success as a commercial real estate lawyer. But more satisfying than that was the respect that followed her, and she had done it all without plastering her face on a billboard or a television commercial. The real estate market in Charleston was strong—the second largest industry in the city, next to tourism. She didn't suffer for work. The money was good, the authority satisfying.

But money like her father had—well, money like that could accomplish almost anything.

Yet still something nagged at her. A premonition, maybe. A pressure in her gut every time she thought about tomorrow. She had felt it since the funeral a week ago. The foreboding feeling that somehow, as good as it all sounded, it might not turn out the way she expected. And in the thickness of the hot, salty darkness she almost felt as if she were wearing the uneasiness.

She tried to shake off her pessimism—a futile effort. She had been shaking at it for years, and still it clung to her like the sweat hanging on her brow. She wiped the sweat away with the sleeve of her T-shirt, her own salt mixing with the brine from the harbor air. The shirt clung to her chest and stuck to her back.

Elizabeth stopped running and slowed her pace for a cool-down walk. She paced along the narrow pathways of what the Charleston guide books called White Point Gardens, but to the locals it was the Battery. Her breathing steadied as she let the familiarity of the city she loved soothe her anxiousness.

She walked through the Williams Music Pavilion, erected in the center of the historic space. Tourists flocked here during the day to hear its history, both real and make-believe. Tour guides loved to add their own local flavor to their narratives, and some of the stories had been repeated so often they had become part of the city's history, as real as the water bugs that scurried on sidewalks or lurked in bedrooms.

During the day many of the natives sat on their porches offering warm smiles and innate hospitality—and sometimes a glass of sweet tea—to passing tourists who had come to take a peek into their gardens. Later in the evening, when the tourists had wandered off to find some "taste of Charleston" or returned to their bed-and-breakfasts,

the locals would come out to tend their immaculate garden court-
yards and reclaim the sidewalks as their own.

But few were ever out doing what Elizabeth was doing at this time
of evening. At least not alone anyway. She continually had to remind
her fear who was boss, and on most occasions it agreed. Her father had
admired her tenacity, had actually helped develop it in her. Yet he
had never really understood where the fear she fought so hard to hide
had come from. She never told him. A father should know.

That same tenacity explained why Elizabeth Wilcott was so good
at the law firm that bore her name—and hers alone. She had a couple
of attorneys working with her who wanted to become partners, but
she wasn't ready to carve out space on her placard. Besides, none of
them would do it quite like she would, and sharing accolades wasn't
one of her strengths. She had never really played well with others.

Nor did she willingly share space in her bed, at least not space
that included a bag and a toothbrush. Commitment held the desire
of unsweet tea. None. Sharing her bed meant sharing closet space
and bathroom space. She needed her *own* space.

She had been independent since she was eleven, the year her
mother, Rena Wilcott, died. That was the year her life changed. She
went from being her mother's little girl to surrogate mother and surrogate wife. Her baby sister clung to her, her father depended upon
her, and her little soul aged. The year she turned fourteen, when she
realized no one had taken care of her the way she had taken care of
them, she turned her back on them. If she was going to have to fend
for herself, so would they.

But in spite of how she had come to regard her family, there was
still the name to protect. Her pathetic excuse for an older brother,
who should have shouldered more responsibility, had turned out to
be a total failure at commitment and an embarrassment to the family name. Someone had to uphold the Wilcott name with the respect
it was due. She was the only one capable.

Elizabeth ran her hands down the still-warm wrought iron railing as she descended the steps from the gazebo toward a nearby park
bench. She sat back and tried to yield her body into its metal. It

didn't give. She didn't mind. She leaned her body over, resting her elbows on her knees, placing her head in her hands.

Her mind reviewed the last years of her father's life and the senility and oddness that accompanied him. Those years had only made her more certain that she needed to get out from under his influence—in business as well as her personal life. Five years ago she had set out to build her own firm, even though she had to use every penny of her annual $200,000 trust to do it. She didn't need that trust fund anymore. She was making it nicely on her own. She only took it because it was the least she deserved for what it had ultimately cost her.

She had cried a couple of times since her father's death. Maybe some Wilcott blood still flowed through her veins after all—even if the tears were more self-pity than grief. But still she had cried.

Elizabeth raised her head and extended her arms across the back of the park bench. She could hear the lapping of the river as it hit against the stone barrier wall built to create a peninsula for South Battery Street. She closed her eyes, lost in the soothing rhythm of the water's sound.

The rough hands seized her from behind. As a black bag was jerked down over her head, she caught a glimpse of a white van parked in front of one of the stately mansions on South Battery. She must have run past it without noticing.

The hands lifted her from the park bench and dragged her toward the curb. But she didn't make a sound. Any scream she might have uttered died at the base of her throat, stifled by her own willpower.

Even the one who had heard her scream years ago had paid no attention, and he was supposed to have loved her. Why would strangers care?

———

Dr. Jeffrey Wilcott pushed the button on his laptop and watched as the computer screen went black in front of him. The silence was absolute. No phones, no voices, no opening and closing of doors—

all activity in the office had ceased hours ago. He moved the two invitations to upcoming social galas to the other side of his desk. He'd have his secretary send the RSVPs tomorrow.

Jeffrey smiled to himself. Being the top name on the Charleston social calendar had its perks. As the eldest sibling of one of the richest families in Charleston and now the *real* heir—as far as he was concerned—he would be invited to everything from galas to birthday parties to baptisms. He'd probably end up as godfather to most of the children born this year.

Maybe he'd be better at being a godfather.

He pulled back the French cuff of his white shirt and looked at his watch. Ten, and he hadn't called home. It hardly mattered. His current bride of two years was probably at a club with her friends while the babysitter watched the kids—his eight-year-old from his last wife, and his ten-month-old from this one.

Theirs was an amicable enough marriage, at the very least a smart business move. He repaired her drooping parts, and she hung on his arm as an example of his fine work. He had chosen plastic surgery a little over a decade ago, right about the time Southern women were catching on to what women in New York and L.A. had known for ages: the body you came into the world with didn't have to be the body you went out with.

Jeffrey picked up his cell phone and slipped it into the pocket of his suit coat. He locked the office door, closed it behind him, and headed for the elevator. It dinged and opened immediately, then slid shut, leaving him smiling at his own reflection in the polished glass.

He did love his job. Not only because it gave him a wonderful living—even if he didn't need it, given his large trust fund—but because he enjoyed the sculpting process: uplifting breasts, trimming thighs, tightening stomachs. Making noses daintier, cheekbones higher, lips poutier. He enjoyed the women who submitted to his scalpel. Why not? He had found his last two wives that way, after all.

Not his first though. He had met Claire in college, been crazy about her and certain it would last forever. But then a kid came early, and the first woman who came into his office wanting a boob job had been a welcome diversion to a new baby at home and a hormonal wife. No one had ever warned him of the dangers of such distractions.

Claire now lived on James Island with their son, Jacob. The boy had contacted Jeffrey a time or two. Jeffrey would always ask if he needed money, but he never did. So, what else was there to offer him? Claire hadn't been interested in his money either. He couldn't understand it, but he didn't argue with her over it. Nor had he shed any tears over the loss of his marriage or his child. Their absence, in fact, made life less complicated.

His second wife, Priscilla, made up for that. She could drink her weight in Jack Daniel's and ended up trying to knife him one night in a drunken rage over his affair with wife number three. He had gotten out of that with their kid, Matthew, and no alimony. Unfortunately, prison didn't provide child care, but he had to consider himself lucky anyway. He had come out alive, and the kid had turned out to be a rather unobtrusive add-on to his life. Jennifer, wife number three, had signed a prenup as tight as her recently Botoxed forehead and given him his first daughter, Jessica.

He rarely saw Jennifer or the kids. Jeffrey spent his days at the office and his nights—well, most of those were spent with Pamela, the exotic publicist he had hired for his recent ad campaign on the new hair-removal cream. Half the billboards around town had her face on them—reason enough for any woman with peach fuzz to head straight to his office. He had seen an almost 20 percent rise in sales since the campaign started. And even though Pamela's flawless Portuguese beauty didn't require any improvement from his professional skills, he had managed to convince her of his personal ones.

The bell dinged and the elevator doors opened at the parking garage. A stale smell struck him at the entrance—he had never been sure whether it was mold or just what a garage smelled like. An unidentified hum, possibly an air-conditioner compressor, provided the background white noise to the slap of his own soles against the pavement.

This had been Jeffrey's first day back to work since his father's death. He had taken a week off for the sake of his image, to show a semblance of grief. Only he would have to know any feelings for his father had taken a week off years ago. The work had piled up. And he'd be gone most of the day tomorrow with the reading of his father's will.

Tomorrow would officially change his life. With all the wealth he was about to inherit, he might never show up again. He could get rid of wife number three and the baby she'd had, send his son off to a nice boarding school up north, and travel the world enjoying good wine and good food and—well, the delicious Portuguese Pamela.

But there was something else that money would buy him. Respect. He'd no longer just be the son of the man with the money. After tomorrow, he would simply be the man.

And for some reason that respect mattered. His mother had always seen his potential, but she died when he was thirteen, and something died inside of him too. His father had been too consumed with his own success to care about a grieving teenage son. And so Jeffrey created his own kingdom, one that never merited his father's attention or approval until about five years ago.

But by then it was too late. There had been no reconciliation.

He reached his car, pushed the remote, and extended a hand toward the unlocked door. But before he caught hold of the handle, he heard the roar of an engine and the squeal of tires. Footsteps sounded behind him. A black hood was thrown over his head. He grabbed for his cell phone, but it slipped from his fingers and fell to the floor. A powerful grip subdued his struggling and flung him into the waiting van. He heard the metal doors slide shut.

Jeffrey was not accustomed to fear, but at the moment his heart was hammering so hard it threatened to burst. He took a deep breath, trying to calm himself. It would have worked had such a situation not perpetuated honesty. And that honesty let him know that not a soul in the world would even care if he came home tonight or not.

And then he smelled it. Cologne. Expensive. Familiar.

But he couldn't place it.

Mary Catherine wiped the spaghetti sauce from her army green tank top and inspected her jeans for any more thick red dots. Her husband, Nate, had run out to grab a box of spaghetti. It was nearly ten, and they hadn't eaten yet. But they hadn't recovered from European time since they returned to the Isle of Palms from their honeymoon, and then with her father's death, her whole system had been thrown off kilter. Now her internal timer thought dinner was better at bedtime.

The sheer white curtains rustled slightly in a breeze from the open French doors. The scent of salt water came off of the ocean and mixed pleasantly with the rich smell of her sauce. From the stereo Michael Bublé was singing "Try a Little Tenderness." Mary Catherine sang along, doing a shuffling little dance with the wooden spoon. Coco, her chocolate Lab, lapped up the stray sauce from the hardwood floors beneath her bare feet.

The sheer pleasantness of the evening brought a tender aching for her daddy. Mary Catherine was the only one of his children who really spent any time with him. She had checked in on him often during his last stages of cancer, had sat at his bedside remembering her mother with him, even though her own memories were few. She had been so little when her mother had died.

Now her father was dead too. And though she hated to admit it, his passing did do one thing that his living would not have accomplished. Her trust fund was nice, but she could spend that up in a month. With what she was about to inherit tomorrow, she and Nate could spend the next year traveling the world—the only real desire she had in this life.

The others in her family thought Mary Catherine was obsessed with travel. They had never understood. She didn't care. Let them be responsible; she wanted to see the world, appreciate its food, its architecture, its beautiful treasures. She wanted to make love with Nate in exotic countries and unexpected places, and when they returned home open up a surf shop for him and an antique store for her. She would sell all the amazing things she had purchased on her travels, then travel more to acquire new things. They could do what they wanted, and she wouldn't have to worry about using that education her father had insisted upon.

Every one of Clayton Wilcott's children was required to go to college. It wasn't an option. To get your trust, you had to go to school. Her older two siblings had taken the whole school thing to the extreme—one a doctor, the other a lawyer. Mary Catherine had resigned herself to study education with an emphasis in literature because she figured it would be easy. As many books as she consumed, it seemed practical.

But Danielle Steel hadn't been a good segue into Updike and Hemingway, so five years and two summer schools later, she had barely passed. Then came the torturous student teaching semester, and again she scraped by, doing just enough to convince her supervisor that children wouldn't be harmed under her care. She had met Nate her final year of school, and after two years of living together— much to her father's disapproval—they figured it would take, and went ahead and got married. Nate quit his job, and she had taken him to surf all the great oceans of the world. It was the perfect life.

Mary Catherine sang quietly as she picked up the wooden spoon to taste the spaghetti sauce. But the spoon never made it to her mouth.

Without warning, someone jerked a hood over her face. There was a noise. A bark. A scuffle. The scent of salty night air. The slamming of a van door.

As the van squealed away into the night, Mary Catherine began to pray. She wasn't sure why she prayed, or whom she was praying to. But somewhere, ingrained in her memory, her mother's prayers rose to the surface of her mind. And if there ever was a time for prayer, this was probably it.

———

Will closed the door of his new Porsche and let the crumbs from the hamburger he had just eaten fall from his weathered jeans. Two boys hollered from the window of a passing car. He gave them a wave, their music still reverberating long after they were gone. He fingered the soft leather strap of his key ring and blew upward, trying to shift his tousled brown hair out of his eyes. He could smell his own alcohol-laden breath as he headed across the street to the fraternity house. Poker with the boys usually got started around ten. They'd be waiting for him.

His frat brothers loved having him around; his trust fund gave him deep pockets. And they would be even deeper come tomorrow after the reading of his father's will.

Will wasn't sure if he missed the old man or not. He had pretty much stayed drunk since the funeral. But it didn't matter. It had never mattered.

He had never mattered. His birth, he knew, had been unplanned and unexpected. His mother had died when he was three. His father had never been available. None of his multiple caregivers had ever— well, cared.

Nothing mattered. So he just enjoyed living his life. No responsibilities, just school at the College of Charleston. As a senior for the second year at age twenty-three, he figured he could milk at least three more years out of college. Just last year he had told his father to consider his first year like redshirting on the football team. He'd be eligible awhile longer.

His fraternity kept him on as president for reasons he was certain had everything to do with his charming personality. He took them to his family's plantation and to the beach for an oyster shuck. Fine food, fast women, endless alcohol. It was the perfect life. Good buddies. Good beer. Good fun.

Yet Will had found one conquest not readily attainable. She had caught his attention last year, but she wouldn't have anything to do with him. Said he had a reputation for things she wasn't interested in.

She was the only one who wasn't interested. Other women hounded him like a dog to a bone. She never even sniffed.

That drove him crazy. *She* drove him crazy. He had made a bet with the boys that he would have her by summer's end. It didn't happen. They offered him an extension until Christmas. At the rate of the wager, it was worth the risk.

His key ring slipped from his hand and jingled as the keys hit the pavement. Maybe he'd had one too many before he left his condo on Laurens Street. His knuckles brushed the warm asphalt as he reached down to pick them up, but before he could get to them somebody threw a black hood over his head and began to drag him away.

Will laughed. He loved it when the frat brothers pulled a prank. Last one ended up at a strip club. Who knew what they had up their sleeve tonight? He didn't put up a fight, didn't struggle. Why should he? He'd just go along for the ride.

chapter two

"Get your hands off of me!" Elizabeth jerked and screamed underneath the hood, her wrists bound uselessly behind her. Her Nikes flailed out, striking what seemed to be someone's leg, but she couldn't be sure. Not in this blackness. Four strong hands dropped her into a chair. As soon as they released her, she jumped up. "Sit down!" a voice boomed.

The voice sent a shock of fear through her—fear she hadn't experienced in years. She sat immediately and heard the sounds of thrashing and cursing coming into the room.

"Do you know who I am?" The man's voice seemed vaguely familiar, but muffled. Elizabeth couldn't quite place it.

"Who is it? Who's there?!" She kicked her feet from her chair.

"Ow!" The man cursed again. "It's none of your business who I am. Who are you?"

More screams filtered into the room. A woman's voice this time—a very young woman, by the sound of it. "Help! Oh God, help!" The sobbing girl was pushed into another chair and continued to wail.

Then Elizabeth heard the strangest sound of all—laughter.

"You guys are whacked. Where are you taking me? We've been driving forever."

The inane laughter and the woman's sobbing continued. Then another voice spoke.

"Remove the hoods, gentlemen, and leave us for the moment."

Elizabeth's hood was pulled roughly from her head. She squinted against the bulb that swung brightly overhead and waited for her vision to adjust from darkness to light.

The stranger slowly came into view, waiting silently and stoically in front of them.

Elizabeth turned to survey her companions and gave a little gasp. Jeffrey. Mary Catherine. Will.

What was going on?

Mary Catherine began to wail again. "God! Oh, God! Oh, God, help us!"

"Shut up, Mary Catherine!" Jeffrey snapped.

"We're about to die here, Jeffrey!" she screamed back. "Someone better start praying—and quick!"

"Mary Catherine . . ." Elizabeth's mothering instincts from years ago came back to her in a rush. "Mary Catherine, look at me."

Mary Catherine's lips were still moving as she turned her head toward her sister.

"I need you to get a grip for a moment here. No one's going to die. But we have to remain calm."

Mary Catherine nodded. Large tears fell on her tank top, which was splattered with what looked like spaghetti sauce.

Elizabeth studied the sparse warehouse, empty but for a wooden desk and chair and the four metal chairs occupied by her and her brothers and sister. She turned toward the man in front of them. "Do you mind telling us what we are doing here?"

"I *know* what we're doing here!" Jeffrey blurted out. "This man has come to kill us to get all of our father's money!"

Elizabeth transferred her glare to Jeffrey. He matched her with one of his own.

"You guys are so stupid." Will laughed. "This is one of my fraternity brothers' pranks. Before you know it, they're going to be rolling a big old cake out here and a really hot babe's gonna jump out of it. Ain't that right, old man?" Will gave the stranger in front of them an inebriated wink.

"You're drunk, Will." Elizabeth shot a glance at him. "Shut up."

"Actually, if you'll all be quiet, I shall end your speculation," the

man said in a calm British accent. He walked around in front of the
wooden desk and sat down, then picked up a manila envelope and
held it up for them to see.

"What's that?" Jeffrey demanded.

The man opened the envelope and pulled out a stack of white
papers. "These, my friends, are your father's last wishes."

"I told you, Elizabeth!" Jeffrey said. "This *is* about Dad's money.
Everything has *always* been about Dad's money!" He turned back to
the stranger. "What do you want? You plan to kill us all so you can
get your hands on a fortune?"

Mary Catherine moaned.

Elizabeth leaned her head around Jeffrey to catch Mary Catherine's
eyes. "Breathe, Mary Catherine, breathe." Mary Catherine began to
pant like a woman in the twentieth hour of labor.

The stranger continued, "As I said, Jeffrey . . ."

Jeffrey gaped at him. "How do you know my name?"

"Mary Catherine has been screaming your name," Elizabeth
interrupted.

"As I said, Jeffrey, if you'll be quiet for a minute, I will tell you
what is going on." He crossed his legs casually in front of him. "No
one is going to die. In fact, you are here because this was part of your
father's plan."

Will shook his shaggy sun-streaked brown hair. "No, I told you,
this is my fraternity brothers'—"

"Shut up, Will!" Elizabeth and Jeffrey said in unison.

"No, Will." The gentleman rose and walked over to Will. Will's
blue eyes seem to register slightly more clarity as the man approached
him. "This is about your father and his will." He paused and looked
around. "Your father knew each of you pretty well."

"Yeah, right." Jeffrey half laughed, not even trying to hide the
sarcasm in his tone.

"Laugh if you wish," the gentleman responded, removing his
gold-rimmed glasses. "But he did. And it was his decision to bring
you here tonight to have the will read."

Elizabeth and Jeffrey traded glances. Mary Catherine was still reminding herself to breathe. Will kept tossing his head, trying to get his bangs out of his face.

"My name, for our purposes here together, shall simply be Mr. Smith. Your father planned this because he knew that once you discovered the contents of his will, you might not appreciate his . . . shall we say, requirements. He also knew that money and power can be both a blessing and a curse. Tonight I will read this will, I will stand as its executor, and you will be returned to where you were picked up. I will be taken to a place where you cannot trace me, thereby preventing any tampering, either legal or illegal, with the express desires of your father's will."

"Why don't you just get on with it then?" Elizabeth's icy words filled the room, but she was listening intently to try to gauge whether this accent of his was truly British or just a really bad Hugh Grant impersonation.

"What do you mean, *requirements?*" Jeffrey asked.

The Executor replaced his glasses and walked around to the other side of the desk. He pulled out the wooden chair and sat down, laying the papers neatly in front of him. Then he began to read.

All distractions ceased. Four pairs of eyes gazed at him—two brown and two blue. Even the bloodshot pair never wavered. He spoke distinctly, and they hung on every word. Waiting . . . waiting for the part, the only part they really cared about.

"And to my children," the Executor read.

For the first time it felt as if their father had actually entered the room. Elizabeth's jaw remained set, but she fought back unexpected tears.

"For the course of one year after my death, your inheritance will be kept in a secure trust controlled by the Executor. Each of you has one week to tie up your respective business and place it in someone else's hands for the next year."

"What?" Jeffrey's face went red, and the veins in his neck throbbed visibly. "The sick son of a—"

"Jeffrey, I'm not finished." The Executor, still completely composed, cut him off.

"There is no way I'm going to throw away a business I have worked years to build, for a man who is lying six feet under!"

Elizabeth narrowed her eyes at him. "Jeffrey, would you please just be quiet so we can get this over with?"

"I have this friend named Stephanie who has had more plastic surgery done than anybody you've ever met," Will offered. "I bet she could help out while you're gone, with all she probably knows."

Jeffrey didn't even bother to look at him.

Mary Catherine's hyperventilating slowed to a slight gasping sound. Maybe now that she realized she actually wasn't going to be killed, Elizabeth thought, she might try to listen to what this man was saying.

"You are to spend the next year working pro bono in a position of your choosing."

Elizabeth kept her gaze locked on the man.

"You may choose a related field, or pick one that is outside of your area of expertise. But you may not in any way, once this first week is over, have any connection with your present work. You may not contact your patients, clients, or customers after you have left, nor may you contact your employees. Every aspect of your career must rest in the hands of someone else for the duration of the year."

The muscles in Elizabeth's jaws pulsed. "You sick son of a—"

"Would you please be quiet so we can get this over with?" Jeffrey mimicked.

"I have a friend who has been arrested so many times his attorney has already told him he should practice law," Will said, leaning toward Elizabeth. "Since he already knows so much about being in the slammer, I could hook you two up if you want. I hear he's pretty competent in defending people."

"I'll bear that in mind." Elizabeth kept her eyes fixed on the Executor. "Do you have any idea what you are suggesting here, Mr. Smith?"

"Furthermore, you are not to travel, unless your new position requires it, and you are to spend no money, except for necessities, for which funds will be supplied to you—if, and only if, you adhere to the preceding requirements."

Mary Catherine's breathing began to increase rapidly again. Will opened his mouth to speak, but she cut him off immediately. "I don't want to hear one word about any of your friends, Will!"

"Well, that's a shame, because one of my best friends owns an antique store downtown."

Mary Catherine's shoulders began to shake.

"At the end of one year," the Executor went on, raising his eyes above the top of his glasses, *"those of you who have successfully completed the task will divide the inheritance in equal shares, and the plantation will be given to one of you. If you do not complete your task, you will receive no inheritance. Those who do not participate will lose both their present annuity and any future inheritance."*

The Executor removed his glasses, folded them, and placed them in his inside coat pocket. He picked up the will and began to walk toward the warehouse door.

"So that's it?" Jeffrey spat. "You kidnap us like a second-rate hoodlum—"

The Executor stopped and turned his gaze upon Jeffrey. "I wouldn't call this second-rate. I think we surprised you pretty well."

"You think you can just turn our lives upside down and drop us back on our doorsteps? Well, I'll have you know something, Mr. Smith. You may think you're walking into the dark night and we'll never find you, but keep looking over your shoulder, mister."

"Thank you for bringing that up, Jeffrey." The Executor turned to face them again. "Please be aware that all of your actions this year will be observed. Who knows, when you least expect it, I might just show up for coffee." He gave a slight smile and turned again to leave.

"I want to see the document," Elizabeth demanded. "I want to see the document *now*."

"Tell me it's not real, Elizabeth," Mary Catherine whimpered.

"I have a friend who—"

"Shut up, Will," the Executor said before any of the other three could beat him to it. "You will each receive your own personal copy of the will tomorrow. I assure you it is authentic, perfectly legal, and perfectly binding." He offered a brief nod, the consummate British gentleman. "I can tell you what your father's estate was worth, however. If you like?"

"We know. He was *our* father," Jeffrey said.

"Do you really?" The Executor moved toward the door. "I thought it was a well-kept secret that your father was worth a billion dollars."

"A what?!"

Elizabeth managed to keep her mouth from speaking, but she couldn't keep her brain from spinning. She knew her father was worth well over a hundred million. She had worked with him for years, knew about his investments. She had handled a large majority of them. But she had no idea he was worth this much. How?

"He invested wisely," the Executor responded as if reading her mind. He gave her a wink and strolled out the door.

Immediately the four black hoods were snapped back on. Elizabeth had not even realized their abductors had returned.

The Executor's voice entered their darkness. "Oh, and one more thing. Your father also requires that you meet once a month at Wisteria Plantation to have dinner together." He chuckled. "Good luck."

The sound of Will's singing was the last thing Elizabeth heard.

chapter three

Elizabeth didn't even turn around to try to catch a glimpse of the anonymous men as they dropped her back on the black wrought iron bench at the Battery. The dampness of dew seeped into her thighs. She jerked the hood off. For a few minutes she sat motionless, waiting to see if there was a second act to the evening's events.

But she was alone. When the realization hit her, she lifted herself off of the bench and ran. She wasn't sure her legs could keep up with the pace she was inflicting on them, but they would have to give way before she'd slow down. The drone of the cicadas followed her pounding footsteps. She ran as if the hounds of hell were chasing her, back to her town house on East Bay Street.

Elizabeth knew how to repress fear. She had done it most of her life—so well, in fact, that no one who remotely knew her would believe she had ever been afraid of anything.

This was different. Tonight the threat was inside her.

Her feet thudded loudly on her front steps as she fumbled for the house key stuck inside the tiny pocket of her running shorts. The brass door handle felt cool beneath her touch. She steadied her hand and tried to do the same with her breathing as she placed the key into the lock.

She flung the door open, flinching as the alarm began to beep. She shut the door quickly and locked it firmly, then stood staring at the illuminated buttons of her alarm pad while the beep counted down the seconds until the siren would blare. She had known the code when she left. What was it? A blaring alarm was the last thing her nerves needed. Her hand rested on the keypad, tapping at the plastic numbers lightly until instinctively her fingers entered the code. Silence. Not necessarily what she wanted now either.

Her feet began their frantic pace again as she walked through the foyer turning on every light, including the small lamp that sat on the antique chest underneath the stairwell. Her hand shook as it turned the small rolling switch on the cord. Continuing her campaign of illumination, she headed toward the kitchen, turning on every light along the way, and then opened the refrigerator door wide. She guzzled down half a bottle of water before she even thought about closing the refrigerator door.

On the black granite kitchen island, the little blue light on her Bluetooth earpiece blinked. She wrapped it around her ear and held down button number three on her phone.

"Aaron, you awake?"

"No." The word came flatly over the phone.

"Aaron, please, I know it's late."

"It's beyond late, Lizzy; it's like tomorrow." He yawned through most of his answer.

"I know, and I wouldn't ask you if it wasn't really important. Something—well, something odd just happened, and I really need to talk through it. Could you come over?" She hesitated. "Please."

She could hear him moving. That was a good sign.

"I'll be there in a few minutes. I doubt traffic is too bad at *two* in the morning."

The line went dead. Two a.m. She had been gone four hours.

She paced, closing all the shutters and turning on even more lights. The perspiration from her run had cooled her, and she was shivering. She found a University of South Carolina sweatshirt in the hall closet and pulled it on. Then she began to pace back and forth across the hardwood floors, never pausing until she heard the knock on the door.

Aaron Davis stood there, his hair disheveled from sleeping. He kissed her on the top of the head and then walked past her into the kitchen, his flip-flops slapping against his heels and his baggy navy blue sweatpants hanging loosely from his hips. This attire was a far cry from the suits and ties he wore as her father's right-hand man. He had stayed on with the old man even after Elizabeth's abrupt and rather nasty departure.

She closed the door, locked it quickly, and turned to follow him.

"So what's this all about, Lizzy?" He opened her pantry door and looked inside. "Please tell me you have at least one cereal that doesn't contain bran."

She turned the corner into the kitchen. "I have oatmeal. It helps cholesterol."

His head stayed buried in the pantry. "So does sleep, I'm sure."

"Do you really have to eat now?"

He pulled the pantry door toward him so he could see her face. His brilliant blue eyes stared at her. "It's morning, Lizzy. That means it's time for breakfast." He let out a sigh. "Next time you invite me over for breakfast, I'm bringing my Frosted Flakes."

She slid a wooden stool out from underneath the counter and sat down in its scooped seat while Aaron rummaged for a bowl and spoon and retrieved milk from the fridge.

"It's about my father's will, Aaron."

He let the spoon fall dramatically on the counter. "Please tell me you didn't call me over here to talk about your father's will. Quit obsessing, will you? You'll know soon enough. The reading is today. Surely you could have waited just"—he looked at his watch—"eight more hours." He slapped his forehead with the palm of his. "Right," he said. "I forgot. You *always* obsess."

"I already know what is in the will," she said flatly.

He paused, a spoonful of bran flakes halfway to his mouth. "How? Wills are supposed to be sealed until the reading."

"Tonight *was* the reading, apparently." Elizabeth stood up and began to pace again.

"Please don't pace. I hate it when you pace."

She kept on pacing. "I was running tonight, you know, like I always do. I stopped at the Battery just to rest for a minute before I headed back home, and two men grabbed me from behind and threw a sack over my head." She replayed the highlights, then added, "And that's when I called you."

Aaron had lost interest in his cereal about the time she mentioned the black hood. He jumped down from the counter and took her face in his hands. "They didn't hurt you, did they?"

She patted his hands and tried to laugh. "No, I'm fine."

Aaron took her by the hand and led her through the kitchen to the sunporch. "Sit down." He pulled her onto the sofa. "What are you going to do?"

"What do you mean, what am I going to do?"

"Okay, you're tired and stressed. How about I try this another way. *What are you going to do?*"

"Well, I'm not being a part of this charade, I'll tell you that. I have a business that my father couldn't get his hands on. If he thinks he's going to control me from the grave, that just confirms he knew absolutely nothing about me."

"He knew more than you think."

She ignored this. "Anyway, I own a law practice that I've made successful. My clients respect me. I've proven to be completely capable of taking care of myself and providing myself with a substantial living. I don't need my father's money. Not his trust fund, not any of it!"

"You're not even going to *think* about this?"

"You have got to be kidding me."

"This is your inheritance we're talking about, Lizzy. Your father worked hard to build this estate so he could leave it to his children. Don't you at least want to *try* and see if you can do it?"

She looked at him incredulously. Aaron had always loved her father. And her father had loved him. She got up from the sofa and glared down at him. "Did you know about this, Aaron? Did you know this was what my father was going to do?" She didn't wait for an answer. "Of course you did. You'd have to. You're his right-hand man. I can't believe I called you." She was already headed for the door.

Aaron stood up and grabbed her arm. "Lizzy, quit being paranoid. I knew nothing about this. I am as surprised as you are. I thought your father told me everything too."

Her eyes raked over him, trying to see into his soul.

"He didn't tell me anything about this. I swear. Apparently no one knows anything but this Executor. Lizzy, you know me. You've known me for almost fifteen years. I wouldn't let anything happen to you, and I don't keep stuff from you. Come on, sit." He tugged her back down onto the sofa.

"Then who witnessed this will?"

"I have no idea. But it wasn't me."

"Sorry. This whole thing is just so ludicrous. It has me acting completely insane. You'd think I was Mary Catherine." Her body succumbed to exhaustion as she sagged into the sofa cushion. She turned her head slightly toward him. "You're the best friend I have in this world. You're right, this whole thing probably has me a little paranoid."

"It's okay." He wrapped his arm around her. She leaned her head into the crook of his arm. "Why don't you have any girlfriends? I mean, most women would call their girlfriends at two o'clock in the morning."

"You know women hate me, Aaron."

"Oh, that's right. I forgot. The beautiful long legs, the striking good looks, the charming personality, the money. Of course women hate you."

She nudged him in the ribs. "This is serious."

He laughed. "Yes, it is. Very serious. That's why we're not just going to throw this out the window. Your father loved you, Lizzy, despite what you may believe. If he has required you to do this for a year, then he must have had a good reason. And if you can't trust him, you need to trust me."

She looked up at him. "You *do* know something, don't you?"

"You don't need to worry about what I know. You need to worry about what you need to *do*. And before you go off trying to do this by yourself—"

"If I find out you had anything to do with this . . ."

"I had nothing to do with this, Lizzy. Now sit here and be quiet and let's just think this through for a while."

⌒

It wasn't long before her weight grew heavy against him. He kissed the top of her head again, then laid his cheek gently against it.

Every shutter in the house was closed. She was afraid, and he hated the idea that she feared something he couldn't find, couldn't deliver her from. He had tried. Tried to rescue her, tried to rescue himself. His heart kept telling him to let her go, but she kept pulling him back in with her need, the very need she adamantly denied having.

She never knew. Never knew he loved her. But there were many things Lizzy didn't know, even if she thought she knew everything. Maybe tomorrow she would consider what her father might be trying to accomplish from the grave. For now, he'd just sit here and enjoy the sound and the feel of her next to him.

⁓

Will stood in front of his condo on Laurens Street. He'd get his car tomorrow; apparently his kidnappers hadn't wanted him to drive.

The smell of burnt macaroni and cheese, a fatal attempt at cooking earlier in the day, greeted him as he came through the door. He shuffled to his bedroom and climbed between the cool rumpled sheets fully clothed. This was why he never made the bed.

The buzz from his drinking binge was fading, and his head throbbed. He hoped his fraternity buddies would come up with a better prank next time—preferably one that didn't involve Mary Catherine.

He scrunched two pillows up underneath him and flipped the television on for the noise. Before the control made its way back to the nightstand he was headed for never-never land.

But somewhere in the middle of his dreams he remembered that he needed to set his alarm clock. The reading of his dad's will was at ten o'clock in the morning, and whatever he did, he sure didn't want to miss that.

⁓

Jeffrey tapped the steering column impatiently as he waited for the gate of the oceanfront community on Kiawah Island to open. His kidnappers had dropped him off at his car. The entire thirty-mile drive

home, he had been shaking with fury. Thankfully the hour-long com-
mute had proven much shorter in the early hours of the morning.

On the way home he checked his cell phone. No missed calls.
Not even from Pamela. She was so different from his other con-
quests. He was on her mind only when he was in her sights.

He pulled the Mercedes SL500 coupe into the driveway of the
massive stone-and-cedar-shake home. His Mercedes. His home. His
prizes for a life well lived.

He parked in the first slot of the four-car garage and entered the
kitchen through the mudroom. He could still smell the remnants of
Chinese food. Takeout, of course. His latest wife hadn't cooked a day
since they had been married. A few plastic-wrapped fortune cookies
lay on the marble countertop.

"I'd have better luck with one of these as my inheritance," he
muttered, tossing one across the counter. The plastic made a scraping sound as it slid across the marble and onto the floor.

Jeffrey opened the refrigerator and studied its contents. Six Slim-
Fasts, five yogurts, a package of peaches, and two shelves full of
bottled water.

He slammed the refrigerator door shut. "Why did I come home?"

He dragged himself heavily up the stairs, wishing he could come
down and start the day over. But no amount of wishing could change
what had happened.

He opened the bedroom door and was greeted by heavy chainsaw
snoring coming from across the room. He grabbed a pair of pajama
bottoms out of the closet and retreated to the guest apartment over
the garage. At least the guest quarters had a well-stocked liquor cabinet; he poured himself an enormous glass full of top-shelf vodka. He
studied the clear liquid through the clear glass and thanked God for
man's many achievements.

As each swallow burned its way through him, it coated and
numbed the events of the evening. His body sank onto the white
linen sofa, and he studied his sterile surroundings. His current wife
liked the crisp look. He had never really cared up until this point,
but now it irritated him that there was hardly any color in his house.

The kitchen was white; most of the furniture was white. The walls were white. Come tomorrow he was hiring painters.

"Each wall will be a different color," he muttered, taking another long burning drink. "One blue, one yellow, and one a brilliant shade of orange. Maybe that will get rid of her." He fell silent, concentrating on finishing the last drop in his glass.

"I hate being told what to do," he said, his speech starting to slur. His imaginary audience offered no response.

———

When Mary Catherine arrived back on her front doorstep, she was still praying profusely. She stumbled into the foyer feeling like a woman who had been beaten for three weeks straight, a feeling confirmed when she caught a glimpse of her face in the hall mirror— smeared mascara and skin as pale as paper. She could hear the sound of the television coming from the family room. The smell of her spaghetti sauce still hovered thick in the air.

She held on to the wall as she made her way through the kitchen. That was when she saw the second horror of the night. Her new husband lying in front of the television. Laughing.

At that point her patience officially ran out. She dashed into the family room screaming at the top of her lungs. "Why in the world didn't you come and find me?!"

Clearly she scared the heebie-jeebies out of both her husband and the dog. Both looked up wide-eyed.

She headed straight for Nate, arms flailing, tears running down her face. Coco jumped from the sofa and parked herself in the chair on the opposite side of the family room. Close enough to watch. Far enough to avoid.

"What are you doing?" He jerked his hands up, trying to shield himself from her attack.

"Did you not even notice I was gone?!"

"Calm down!" Nate grabbed both of her wrists and held on. "Have you lost your mind?"

"Have *I* lost *my* mind?" she yelled. "Did it not one time seem strange to you that your wife was gone for . . . for . . . *for half her life*!"

He held on tighter. "It's two a.m. You've been gone four hours." He stared at her, dumbstruck.

Mary Catherine grabbed the remote control and punched the off button, then threw the control across the room. "I was gone for four hours, Nate. Four hours! Did it not occur to you when you got home and I wasn't here and there was no note and my car was still here and the sauce was still on the stove that something might have happened to me?" She finally took a breath

He scratched his head.

"I was kidnapped! Kidnapped! By at least ten horrible men dressed in black and they took me to a dungeon and they handcuffed me and tormented me! I've been defiled, Nate! Defiled, I tell you!"

"I didn't know, MC. I just thought maybe you had gone for a walk on the beach or something."

"For four hours? Did you think I took a walk to Florida? And don't call me MC! My name is Mary Catherine. Not Mary! Not Cat! Not MC! Mary Catherine!"

"Okay, okay . . . calm down. Let me get you a glass of water." He stumbled to the kitchen and fumbled in the cabinet, finally retrieving a glass. "Come on, baby, now sit down and tell me what happened."

"It was . . . these men. They snatched me from . . . from . . ." She held her shaking finger up and pointed to the kitchen in front of the stove. "They snatched me from right there." She gasped for breath. He made her take a sip of her water.

"They threw a black bag over my head," she went on, "and they drove me around for at least an hour. Then they put me in a dark room, and when I got there my brothers and sister were there. And some strange man that looked like the bad guy in that movie we saw— you know, with Mel Gibson and Julia Roberts. The one where Mel Gibson bit the guy's nose."

"*Conspiracy Theory?*"

"Yeah," she shivered. "He looked like the man in that movie. And he read Daddy's will. And . . . and it was *awful!*" Her whole body heaved.

"But your dad's will isn't supposed to be read until this morning."

"I know," she wailed. "But they read it and it was . . . it was *horrible*!"

Nate stood up, his bare feet pacing the sea grass rug. "What did it say, Mary Catherine?"

"It said that I've got to go back to work—" She started hyperventilating again. "For free!"

Nate frowned. "Stop crying for one minute, Mary Catherine, and tell me what is going on!"

Her blue eyes widened at his tone.

"I'm sorry, baby, it's just, well, this is all real stressful."

"Stressful? Stressful for a man watching television, or for a woman whose head was wrapped up in a hood?!"

"I'm sorry! Now, just tell me what it all means."

"It means, Nate, that for one year I can't travel, can't shop, can't do anything! All I can do is go to work for nothing, and if I don't, there is no inheritance!"

Nate rubbed his head as if trying to push this information inside. "So you have to do this for a year?"

"That's what I said."

"Or no inheritance?"

"*Zero. Zilch. Nada. Niets. Nichts. Niente.* I can say *nothing* in ten more languages, if you want. All countries I won't see for a *year*!"

"It's just a year, Mary Catherine!"

She gaped at him. "What do you mean, it's just a year?! You don't think there is any way this side of the very fiery gates of hell that I am going to spend a year *working*!"

"MC . . . uh, Mary Catherine, baby doll, listen to me. Listen to me." He started rubbing her arm and trying to ease her rigid body back onto the sofa. "Baby, just think about it. Would you give up everything we—you—have planned for your life, just for a year? You can do anything for a year."

Rigor mortis had set completely in by this point.

He rubbed harder and faster.

"Quit rubbing me!" She slapped his hand. "I'm not a genie!"

"You can do this, Mary Catherine. Just think about it. What does the rest of your family have to do?"

"The same thing—work for nothing! But they don't care about traveling and buying things. They *like* to work!"

"Well, think about it. Think about Elizabeth. She'd hate giving up control of her law practice, with all that she's built and slaved over."

Her head cocked slightly. She could tell he was trying to cheer her up.

"And what about your brother. George?"

"Jeffrey."

"Yeah, what about him? He's a plastic surgeon. He'd have to give up fine women for a year. He'll never be able to do that. And your little brother, he isn't good for anything. He wouldn't work if his life depended on it."

She studied the face of the man next to her. She had been with him for a long time and thought she knew him. Yet something was different about him tonight. He was halfway making sense. "I can't do it for a whole year either. It's too much to ask of one person."

His mouth twitched slightly. "You could have the entire inheritance to yourself, Mary Catherine."

"You think?"

"I'm certain. Your brothers and sister—they're a bunch of wusses. They'll never do this. But you, my sweet Mary Catherine." He bent down and kissed her firmly. "You can whup every single one of them. It's just a year."

"It might be a good idea to quit saying the *year* word."

"Okay, no more *year*."

She leaned into his shoulder. "You really think I can do it?"

"I'm certain you can, baby doll."

Her eyes scanned the bar in the kitchen as her head rested against him. She noticed the empty spaghetti plate sitting on the counter. He had eaten. She had been abducted and tormented while he sat in front of the TV eating spaghetti. She got up from the sofa, reached over, and slapped him upside the head, then headed into the bedroom, slamming the door behind her.

chapter four

Elizabeth woke to find herself on the sunporch sofa. She smelled bacon and heard the sounds of Beethoven's "Für Elise" wafting through the house as well. Sunlight warmed her face as she stretched. This was her favorite time of day, early morning, the brightness of the morning sun refusing the shadows a place to hide.

Yet the shadows crept back, the memories of last night, filtering in as the sun filtered through the windows. She cursed the fear that had overtaken her last night, compelling her to close all the shutters; apparently Aaron had opened them.

The scent of bacon drew her into the kitchen, where Aaron stood at the stove in an olive green linen apron.

"Morning, sleepyhead."

"Morning." She rubbed her eyes. "Nice skirt."

"You think olive suits me? I wasn't sure."

She laughed and pointed toward the frying pan. "Smells like grease."

"Tastes better." He set his plate down at the bar and motioned her over.

She studied the plate. Two eggs over easy, cheese grits, home fries, and two perfectly crisp pieces of bacon on the side. "Where'd you get all that?"

"Not from your fridge, that's for sure." He grinned. "I went to the store while you were out cold."

She pulled the bar stool out, and he slid a bowl of granola toward her. With a side of orange juice. "*Your* breakfast." He grimaced.

"Sure you don't want some of mine?" He picked his plate up and ran it under her nose.

"Not on your life."

"All right then. Eat your heart out." Aaron picked up a fork and began to shovel it down with gusto, the morning stubble on his face prominent as his jaw moved. "So what's running through your head this morning?"

She furrowed her brow at him. "I'm supposed to be thinking already?"

"Well, you've got that look."

"What look?"

He wrinkled his forehead in imitation of her. "*That* look. Your concentrating look. I think you must have come out of the womb with it."

"Aaron, it's too early to think." She crunched her granola. "Even for me."

"Well, *I've* been thinking, even if you haven't." His curved fingers ran down the small juice glass, pushing the condensation down around its base. "It's your father's will, Lizzy."

"It's my father's manipulation. It's what he always did."

"It's what he *used* to do. He wasn't that way anymore. You just didn't take time to get to know him."

She wiped her mouth and turned in his direction. "I gave my father twenty-eight years to get to know me. He never made the effort. All his effort went into protecting his investments, his reputation. He just wanted someone with the Wilcott name to take over his company, and I'm the only offspring he produced that is worth anything."

"If he wanted you to do this, Lizzy, I know he had a good—"

The doorbell interrupted him.

Elizabeth's eyes widened. She raced to the front door and opened it. A stranger stood there, holding out an envelope. She jerked it out of his hands and ripped the envelope open.

Aaron came up behind her. "Your father's will?"

She nodded, flipping through to the last page. All that mattered were the names. The ones she found didn't surprise her.

Without a word Elizabeth dashed back through the kitchen to

the sunporch with Aaron flip-flopping behind her. Elizabeth thrust her feet into her running shoes, grabbed her keys, and took off toward the garage. When she opened the door of her Jeep Commando, she could see the top of Aaron's head on the other side. "Wait here," she said. "I'll be right back."

She left him standing in the garage. He was a speck in her rearview mirror in less than ten seconds.

When Elizabeth reached the home of Harvey Jefferson, she wasted no time with the doorbell but simply began banging on the heavy front door. Harvey was the oldest of her father's friends, and keeper of all his secrets. He had worked for her father for almost fifty years. They had been army buddies together.

Harvey opened the door, his tie hanging unknotted around the collar of his starched white shirt.

"Elizabeth, what are you—?"

She shook the papers in front of him, yet her voice remained perfectly calm. "What did you make him do, Harvey? What did you and Lester make him do?"

Harvey squinted. "What is that, Elizabeth?"

"It's my father's will, Harvey. The one he changed. The one you signed."

He stood back from the doorway. "Would you like to come in?"

"Only if you're going to tell me the truth."

"I'm an army man, Elizabeth. I don't lie."

She stepped inside. Harvey closed the door behind her and stared into her eyes. He had always remarked on how she had her father's eyes, and now she wondered if he were seeing the reflection of his old friend in her face. "I did sign a new will, Elizabeth. I gather from your reaction that it had some significant changes to it. But your father wouldn't let me read it. Lester and I only witnessed that it was a new document, signed by your father."

She started to pace the foyer. "That's crazy."

"We didn't ask him any questions, Elizabeth. He was adamant. He only said that it was what had to happen."

She turned to study the crystal blue eyes of her father's friend. "He told you nothing."

"He told me nothing. And your father tells me everything. He said it would be best if no one knew; that way when his children came to question us, we could honestly say we didn't know. Obviously he was right."

Elizabeth stopped pacing. "Why would he change his will?"

"Your father never made any decision without great thought. That may not be much consolation, but it is the best I can do."

She looked up to study Harvey's eyes one more time. If his soul was as pure as the blue of his eyes, Harvey didn't know a thing.

By the time Elizabeth reached home, the idea had formulated itself in her mind. It was less an idea than a revelation, and Aaron always said her revelations weren't exactly trustworthy. She had, in his words, too many "issues." But she was confident in this one.

She walked back through the kitchen without so much as speaking to Aaron. He untied his apron, laid it on the counter, and followed her into her office. She was already rummaging through the drawers of her large burled walnut desk.

"I can't believe that I didn't think of this in the beginning. I'm usually much quicker."

"Think of what?"

She stood up, holding a red folder in her hand. She waved it in his direction. "I'm smarter than this. I should have thought through all the possibilities. Why would my father change his will at the last minute?"

"I don't know. Why?" he asked, sitting down on the sofa across from her.

"Think, Aaron. It's really simple. Think of how strange he acted after I left the company. He was declining rapidly. So with that in mind, is it not possible that someone manipulated him into changing the will?"

He leaned his head back on the sofa and rubbed his eyes. "Your father wasn't declining, Lizzy."

"It's harder to view someone objectively when you are with him day in and day out. It's understandable you didn't see it. Plus, your admiration for him caused you to be far less objective, I'm sure."

Aaron raised his head, the furrow of his brow deepening. "Don't analyze me, Elizabeth."

She felt herself flush but wasn't about to apologize. "If you were able to see it from my vantage point, you'd know he was making very irrational decisions."

She sat down at the desk and opened the file. Her fingers scanned down the sheet, her eyes brightening as the name she was looking for rested beneath her finger. She'd used him in a case trying to prove illegal activity for a purchase of some land downtown. She picked up the phone and dialed the number.

"You've reached James Cavanaugh. Please leave a message, and I will call you back."

She waited for the beep. "James, this is Elizabeth Wilcott. I was the attorney for Hawthorne Building Group when they were working on the Chapel Street property a couple of years ago. You and I worked together on that, and I need to talk with you about another matter. If you could call me at your earliest convenience, I would greatly appreciate it." She left her number and hung up, closing the file in front of her.

"Well, that will be productive."

"Yes, it will." She leaned back, and her chair squeaked slightly. "Wonder where I left the oil can?"

"Don't try to change the subject," Aaron said. "You really think there is something suspicious going on with this?"

"We'll see." She cocked her head.

"You're completely paranoid. Who? Who would try to manipulate and control your father?"

"Jeffrey," she said flatly.

Aaron laughed out loud. "Jeffrey?"

"Yes. I wouldn't put it past him. You know how much the prestige of money and fame mean to him. He wants the position that our father held, and he thinks his money could afford him that."

She chewed on a hangnail, then stopped herself and forced her hand away from her mouth.

"Jeffrey probably got to him when he was weak. Talked him into this craziness after he had already found some kind of pro bono job he could do for a year. He's probably taken care of every detail to make sure his business runs perfectly. Even down to that charade last night. If I ever saw anybody overacting—"

She paused, waiting for Aaron to confirm or deny or argue. When he remained silent, she want on. "He's so self-absorbed he wouldn't even consider the possibility that any of us would do it. I'm sure he thinks he has this entire inheritance sewn up. We both know neither Mary Catherine nor Will is capable of pulling off a challenge like this. But he is very foolish in thinking that I couldn't."

Aaron gave her a curious look. "Is that enough to motivate you?"

She ran her hands across the leather inlay on the desktop. "Jeffrey beating me at something? Especially something this big? Sadly, I think it might be."

He wasted no time. Aaron jumped up from his seat. "Then go get dressed so you can go to the office and get to work on making sure your business is taken care of for the next year."

She stared at him, and her mind spun. Finally she shook her head adamantly. "This is absurd. I can't do this. I have clients. An entire practice. This really is insane, Aaron."

"Have you ever just thought about taking a leap, Lizzy?"

"I took a leap the day I left my father's business."

"When? The day you left his business with a $200,000 annual trust fund?"

She raised her right eyebrow. "What's your point?"

"My point is a *real* leap, Lizzy. A leap you can't control. A leap so big that you have no idea what is on the other side. Don't you wonder what is on the other side of life?"

"I love my life."

"Of course you do, because you can *control* your life." His blue eyes studied her. He walked over to where she sat and reached his hand out to her. "I want you to take this leap."

"A leap formulated by a sick brother? That's not a leap. That's insanity."

He grabbed her hand and pulled her from the chair. "Yes, it is. It is completely insane. But I don't think your father was crazy. I don't think Jeffrey has anything to do with this. And as crazy as it may sound, I think there is something in this that you might find amazing."

She looked into his eyes and leaned toward him, and could feel his warmth. For a minute she almost believed him.

He tugged her to him. "You have capable employees, Elizabeth. You make me a list of all the essential information that they need, and I will personally make sure your law practice runs the next year as if you were there every day."

She tilted her head back slightly and examined his face. His eagerness for her to accept the challenge of the will might mean that he was really a part of all of this. And now he was willing to take care of her business. The question lingered, but her brother Jeffrey seemed the more likely suspect.

Besides, the way he was holding her didn't feel like a man who was out for her money. It was more like—

She pushed the thought aside. "Aaron, this is crazy."

"Ludicrous," he confirmed. "Let's do it."

chapter five

Jeffrey!" The nasal voice penetrated the guesthouse.

Jeffrey didn't move. Everything about her irritated him. Especially today.

"Jeffrey! I've been looking all over for you. You've got to get up. We're already going to be late for the reading of your daddy's will."

Her perfume stung his nostrils. The woman wore more perfume than a pig wore stink. He twitched his nose and cracked one eye open. There she stood, her bleached blonde hair sticking out from underneath a floppy black hat, her manufactured breasts straining at the plunging neckline of a skimpy black dress.

"We've already had the reading of the will." He rolled over and stuck his face in the sofa cushions, wishing the ostrich move could work for him.

She shook his arm, hard. "Jeffrey! I'm serious! Get up!"

He jumped off the sofa, startling her and not doing himself any favors either. At his feet lay an empty vodka bottle, a reminder of why his head was pounding. The room began to spin.

"There is no reading of the will today, Jennifer!" Jeffrey yelled. The yelling wasn't such a good idea either. The noise made the room spin faster, and he had to sit back down on the sofa.

"Do they cancel will readings?"

Jeffrey rubbed his temples. "No, it's all a joke. The whole will is a joke! Dear old Daddy is getting the last laugh from his grave."

"What are you talking about?"

He turned to look at her. She was paying him absolutely no

attention; instead, she was peering into the mirror, rubbing lipstick from her teeth. Had she been watching him, she wouldn't have missed his eyes rolling. "There is no will."

That took her attention off herself. Literally anyway. "You mean we aren't getting your daddy's money?" She sank down onto the edge of the sofa, looking stunned.

"*We?*"

"Well, you know what I mean."

"No, *I'm* not getting Daddy's money. Not unless I follow along with his ludicrous scheme for the next year, which I have entirely no intention of doing."

Her Botoxed brow would have furrowed if it had been capable. "Jeffrey, you're confusing me. Tell me what you're talking about."

"I'm talking about a father who wants to pawn his self-righteousness off on his children after his death instead of caring about them while he's alive. That's what I'm talking about. And if he thinks he's going to get me to become some soft-hearted do-gooder like he decided to do the last couple of years, even though he couldn't take good enough care of himself to keep doing it, he's got another thing coming."

"You can pawn your emotions now?"

He looked up at her fake green eyes. "What are you talking about?"

"You said he had pawned his self-righteousness."

"Are you an idiot, Jennifer? Honestly, are you a complete idiot?"

Her bottom lip began to quiver. "Jeffrey, I've told you not to call me names."

"Well, you have to be. You have to be completely stupid. No, I'm the idiot! I'm the one who married you." He got up from the couch, the tail of his white shirt swaying against his pajama bottoms as he paced.

"You're a really, really mean man," Jennifer said through her tears. She tottered slightly on her three-inch heels as she stood up from the sofa. "I don't have to listen to this. You can just get your stuff and stay over here until you learn how to treat me."

"Me?!" He stopped pacing to stare at her. "I'm not going any-where. You, however, can get your things and get out of *my* house!"

"Jeffrey!" She gasped. "You're just stressed, baby." She reached out her hand to touch his face, her fake fingernails coming at him like tiny bayonets.

"Don't touch me, Jennifer. I mean it. You need to pack your stuff and go." He waved his hand toward the door. "I'll get you an apartment. A condo. Whatever. But you're not staying here. This relationship is a joke, and we both know it. You can get what we settled on in the prenup. That should keep you perfectly satisfied, and then you won't have to wait around on *my father's* money."

He saw the blotch of red start at the base of her pale neck and work its way up to the top of her pristinely shaped eyebrows. "It's *her*, isn't it? You're seeing that foreigner, the one with the big bazookas that you claim she arrived on the planet endued with. Enparted."

"It's *endowed*, Jennifer."

"I knew it! Well, don't think for a minute you can get rid of me that easy! Besides, I have an appointment next week with you for liposuction! Let's just see what you do when I show up at your office!" she shouted and then stormed from the guesthouse.

He didn't care what she knew or thought she knew regarding him and Pamela. He'd give her a liposuction vacuum in the settlement if that would keep her happy. From now on, she could suck out her own fat.

Half an hour later, Jeffrey made his exit from the oceanfront golf community. He had successfully avoided the children and Jennifer as he left the house. Hopefully she'd be gone by the time he got home, but for now all he wanted to do was feel the wind blow through his hair and forget about this unbelievable game his father was trying to play with his emotions.

The salt breeze came off the ocean as he headed toward downtown Charleston and watched the golf course fade in his rearview mirror. He had never liked golf; he bought the house for its prestige. But he did love the story told by Charleston Carriage Tour Guides. When the Scots immigrated to America, the guides said, they brought with them religion, scotch, and golf. There are eighteen holes of golf because there are eighteen shots in a bottle of scotch.

It worked for him. And since Charleston was the home to the first golf course in America in 1786, he thought it only fitting he should live on one.

On the radio, Shania Twain was singing "It Only Hurts When I Breathe." Jeffrey wondered briefly if the song was about having a heart attack. With the pain in his own chest, the lyrics seemed rather fitting. The DJ came on and assured him that there would be five more in a row. That would get him to the office. The office would get him back to normal. Whatever normal was. Truth be told, he wasn't sure he'd ever known normal.

The phones were buzzing like a plague of locusts when he opened the back door and stepped into the office. The geometrical pattern on the carpet made him dizzy even when he didn't have a hangover. But the interior designer he had hired, briefly slept with, then fired because she had charged him for those hours, too, had assured him it would hide dirt.

He spotted a stain in front of the door and cursed the woman under his breath as he continued down the hall to his office. He unlocked his door—an unresolved issue, his office manager, Helen, had informed him. "If you can't trust me after I've worked for you for the last five years, then you've got far deeper issues than a locked door."

He had locked it every day since, mostly to prove a point. He walked behind his desk and moved his mouse so that his screen would come up. He never turned his computer off—something else that drove Helen crazy. His calendar popped up. Monday and Tuesday were his days for seeing patients, and he did surgeries the rest of the week. But it was technically his first day back since his father's death, so he had appointments back to back. He sat down behind his desk and closed his eyes. His body ached everywhere. He'd enjoy not sleeping on the sofa tonight.

Pamela tapped lightly on the door. She entered with a beautiful tan and an even more beautiful smile. "Hello, handsome." Her exotic black eyes sparkled as she locked the door behind her and headed in Jeffrey's direction.

He was so tired he could hardly muster the energy to act excited. "Hey, beautiful."

Her sleeveless taupe silk dress shimmered in waves against her perfect figure—one he hadn't helped sculpt a lick, despite what Jennifer thought. Her black hair fell gently across her shoulders and glistened as she walked toward him. He had always had a thing for brunettes. His first two wives were brunettes, another reason he had never really figured out why he married Jennifer. She thought it was destiny because both of their names started with *J*. That should have been his second clue.

Pamela pulled his chair out from under his desk and sat across his lap. She bent down and kissed him with all the passion and fire that belonged to her heritage. She reached for his tie and began to remove it.

"I didn't hear from you last night," he said through their kiss.

"Sorry, darling. A new campaign had me tied up last night."

As her fingers grazed his neck, all Jeffrey's nerves came alive, along with a terrifying thought. His eyes opened as they kissed, and he scanned the room frantically. Someone could be watching—when they least expected it, the Executor said.

He reached up quickly, placing her hand in his own, and stopped her before his tie was completely removed. He hadn't done that, in— well, ever. "Pamela, I'm sorry, I can't." He removed her arms from around his neck and helped her get back to her feet. He didn't perform for crowds.

"What's wrong with my darling?"

"It's just, well, something strange happened last night and with my dad's death and all and . . ." He shifted his mouse again. The computer screen came back to life. "With all these appointments today, I'm just trying to get caught up here at the office. I just need a few days to regroup and get myself together."

She walked over and pressed herself against him, her arms wrapping around his waist. "What's really going on, Jeffrey?"

He kissed the top of her head. Her smell alone was intoxicating. He still didn't know how someone could be this beautiful without his assistance. It seemed downright otherworldly. And holding her there in his arms, he told her all the events of the previous evening.

He saw her nose crinkle. That meant she was thinking.

"What?" he asked. "What is it?"

She smiled at him. "You know, as crazy as this may sound, we might be able to use this to your advantage."

He puffed and walked back to his chair and sat down. "You're right. It sounds crazy."

"Seriously." Her accent thickened as her excitement grew. "We could use this as the perfect opportunity to get a press release out on you and market you to areas outside of Charleston."

He propped his feet up on the edge of his desk and leaned his chair as far back as it would go. "How would leaving a practice I've spent years building to go work for some nonprofit boost my career? Anyway, have you met my clients? There are few so demanding."

She seated herself in a leather chair opposite his desk. He tried to remove his attention from the thigh-high slit that had just exposed her perfect leg. "What person wouldn't admire a man who felt led to go help a needy organization for a year? This could get you more media than you could imagine. *Charleston Magazine* would finally give you that cover you've been longing for."

"Make a publicity stunt out of this?"

"Call it brilliant marketing."

The thought made him smile.

"My boy is smiling. It's good, no? You spend a year having this entire city come to think you're one of the greatest heroes since Oprah."

He wouldn't have picked Oprah. "This is crazy."

She smiled that insanely inappropriate smile. "This is a gift."

chapter six

Mary Catherine slipped into the shower and turned the water on so hot the steam had fogged the glass door before she could even get her body soaped. She wanted all remnants of last night gone. She wanted to forget it all.

Her fingers massaged her scalp trying to work out the dull ache of little sleep. Her index finger felt some foreign object underneath it; she pulled at it frantically until the black burlap string was hanging in front of her face. She dropped it like it was a flying cockroach and pounded it down the drain with her foot.

This was a nightmare—the abduction, the terms of the will, everything. But she needed her daddy's money. She'd really rather have him back, but if he was gone, then his money was the only way to afford the lifestyle she wanted.

And now she was supposed to *work*? The only real job she'd ever had was student teaching, and that wasn't even a paying gig. Besides, she had never really liked kids. She probably shouldn't have majored in education, but she hadn't taken into consideration that she might actually have to come in contact with the germ-infested, runny-nosed, whiny little creatures.

Fifteen kindergarteners. They had tormented her for a solid year. Driven her to Prozac. Of course, there had been one or two . . .

She pushed the thought aside and shut the water off. She heard the doorbell and the sounds of Coco sniffing at her bedroom door and whining. When she opened it, Mary Catherine found Nate sitting by the door waiting too. He was holding the copy of her father's will that had just been delivered.

She talked to Coco and ignored Nate. "Sorry, baby girl, Mommy shouldn't have left you out here with this mean old man." Coco slipped in beside her, and she slammed the door again and locked it.

"Come on, Mary Catherine!" Nate pounded his fists on the door. "You've got to talk to me, baby."

"Are you sorry?"

"Very."

"Sorry, sorry?"

"In triplicate."

She opened the door and peered at him through the crack.

"We've got to talk about this, Mary Catherine."

"I don't want to. I'm traumatized. I'll probably need therapy for a decade after what I went through last night. And another decade after that just to deal with the fact that during my torture you were snarfing down spaghetti and watching sitcoms. Wonder what a judge would say to that?"

"Now, baby . . . baby." He pushed the door open and wrapped his arms around her before she could slam it again. "You just need to calm down. And don't even speak the word *judge* or *divorce*. This is forever." He kissed the nape of her neck. "Now, come on. Sit."

He led her into the bedroom and eased her down onto the bed. "You have to think through what happened last night. And not just the horror of it all, but what you're going to do."

"I don't know what to do. I can't do something pro bono."

"What about just going to work for an antique store or clothing store or something? You could do that for a year free."

"Are you crazy? Every antique dealer I'd be willing to work for would talk trash about me all over town if I asked them for a job without pay. Besides, I think pro bono means doing something good for the community. You know, like helping people. Like a nonprofit organization. Not just working at Dairy Queen."

"What about using your education?"

She tilted her head.

"Yeah? You've been thinking about that?"

"Well, I know how to do it. Kind of. At least I know Prozac can get me through it."

"You'd be a great teacher."

She crinkled her nose, and he laughed and leaned over to kiss it. "You would. A great teacher." He released her and stood up. "That's it, then! You'll teach for a year, and then you'll have all of your daddy's money! Because you don't have another sibling who'll ever be able to do what my Mary Catherine can do."

"You *want* me to work, don't you? You *want* me out of the house."

He knelt down and took her hands. "I want my baby to get what she deserves. You're the only one who even paid your father any attention over these last few years. He'd want you to have it all for that reason alone."

"I did take care of him." She sniffed.

"I know you did, baby." He kissed her again. "Now, you get dressed and we'll figure all of this out."

"Me and you, Pookie?"

"Me and you."

———

Will jumped from the bed. The clock read twelve thirty. He hoped that meant midnight, but the sun streaming in from outside was a pretty good indicator that it was afternoon.

He swore under his breath as he ran to the bathroom and studied his appearance. Still dressed. That would save time. He breathed into his hand. Not too bad. He'd keep his distance. He slid his feet into his flip-flops and headed to the door, grabbing his car keys and wallet as he went. The suction from under the door sent a white envelope fluttering down the hall away from him. No time. He'd get it later.

The car wasn't in the parking garage. His hands ran through his hair as if that would awaken his memory. It worked, because a brief flashback of his buddies' prank the night before came alive.

He'd let them have it about not getting his car back to him. He'd also let them know how lame this prank had been compared to the last time.

He jogged down Laurens Street and went up Anson until he hit George, where he cut over to the College of Charleston.

His car was right there where he had left it, across from the fraternity. He slid into the silver Porsche his dad had bought for him after he had totaled his other one. Of course his father refused to buy the more expensive one, so he'd had to settle for the eighty-four-thousand dollar model. But not for long.

He sped through the streets of downtown Charleston to his father's office on King Street. He muscled through the rotating doors, pushing them harder than they were willing to go, and waited impatiently until the elevator arrived. On the third floor, Tabitha sat behind the large reception desk and gasped as Will came bursting through.

"Will, what in the world is going on?"

"How late am I? Is anyone else still here?" He couldn't hear her response because he was already halfway down the hall. He jerked open the door of his father's office. All that stared back was an empty chair and his father's wall of books. He ran through the office and swung open the door on the far side that led into the conference room.

Three men in dark suits stared back at him. "The will. I'm here for the reading of the will."

A balding man with a fringe of gray hair stood from his chair and removed his glasses. Will recognized him. He was the attorney for his father who had gone to college with his dad and been a part of his business since the beginning. "Will, I was informed that the reading took place last night."

"What?" Will laughed. "That? That was nothing but a prank by my fraternity brothers. So tell me, what's up? What did the old man leave me?"

The attorney scratched his forehead and looked at the other two men in the room. They offered no help. "Your sister came to see me this morning and told me that the reading was held last night. The reading of a new will that I witnessed your father sign. I was not the executor of it, nor have I been given any details of it. It's apparently sealed for a year to anyone but his children. All I can prove is the authenticity of it."

Will ran his hands through his hair. "This is crazy. This is so crazy."

The elderly man put his hand on Will's shoulder. "If I can do anything else, just let me know."

"Yeah, uh, sure. Well, I guess I'll just go, then."

Once he was out of the building and back in his Porsche, Will dialed Mary Catherine's number from his cell phone. She didn't answer. He dialed Jeffrey's. No response there either. Then he dialed Elizabeth.

———

Elizabeth stood in front of her bathroom mirror, her wet hair still dripping down her back. Her cell phone sat ringing on the edge of the stone countertop. She studied the caller ID, shook her head, and debated answering. Finally, reluctantly, she slipped on her earpiece.

"Hello?"

"Elizabeth, what's going on? I just left Dad's office and nobody's reading the will."

"You were there last night, Will."

"Would y'all quit talking about last night? That was nothing but a dumb prank by my college buddies. They do stuff like that all the time. Please don't tell me that the attorneys think that was real and now aren't even going to bother reading the real one."

She listened to his naïve and pitiful voice. *This is what my father has created—a child who can do nothing on his own.*

"Okay, little brother, why don't you just sit back, then, and wait until someone contacts you about the real will?"

"Well, duh. What did you think I was going to do? Go do pro bono work for a year?"

She hung up the phone while he was still laughing. The way he said it reiterated just how absurd it really was.

Jeffrey closed his office door behind him. After all the body parts he had seen today, he just wanted a drink. He poured some amber liquid into a small glass and drank until he could see one eye staring back at him from the bottom.

The white envelope sat in the center of his desk. Other than to pull out the invitations, he had been so busy yesterday that he hadn't even looked through his mail.

But this hadn't come through the mail.

Gingerly he opened it, as if it might explode. His father's will. He read through it, studying the names of the two witnesses. His father's closest friends. That didn't surprise him. He didn't even care.

He tossed the papers back on his desk and turned to look out the window. The sun was starting to set, and the churning in his stomach reminded him he hadn't had lunch. The events from last night raced through his mind. In spite of Pamela's desire to exploit the situation, he still felt something was off about this whole scenario.

Elizabeth's stoicism. Her unabashed calm. Fear was inbred in Elizabeth. And a situation like that would have had it oozing out of her.

He slapped the palms of his hands down on the desktop. Of course she wasn't afraid. Why would she be afraid? She had planned this entire thing. "She thinks she is going to run off with Dad's inheritance to get back at me. To get back at him. I can't believe I didn't realize this earlier!" He stood up from his desk, propelling his chair so hard that it bounced off the walnut credenza behind his desk.

He grabbed the receiver and went to dial, then instinctively pulled the receiver away from his face. If Elizabeth was behind this, he wouldn't put it past her to have his phone tapped. In the movies, people always unscrewed the mouthpiece, but the new kind didn't screw on. He studied it carefully, tugging at the bottom of it, trying to see if he could get it to come apart. He lifted it up and studied its underbelly. No signs of tampering there. He replaced the phone and ran his hands around the edges of his desk. He felt stupid for checking but too suspicious to stop.

He inspected the full circumference of the desk, then climbed onto his leather chair and reached up to feel inside the light fixture.

The door opened. Helen raised both her eyebrows.

"I'm changing a lightbulb." He pretended turning a bulb. His hand hit the scorching bulb and instinctively retreated.

She flipped the wall switch to cut off the light. "How many doctors does it take to change a lightbulb?" she muttered as she closed the door behind her. Obviously simply saying "good night" wouldn't have been half as amusing.

His examination of the light fixture turned up nothing. He went back to the phone and pounded in the numbers. "You can bet your five-hundred-dollar-an-hour fee that I'll find out who this Executor is and who you're in cahoots with, little sister. I'll bring this pretense crashing down around you. I will officially beat you at your own game."

The call went through, startling him. "Littleton Investigators."

"Oh, um—sorry. Wasn't sure anyone would be answering this late."

"This is my cell phone. I'm still working," came the flat response.

He paused a moment wondering if he should give a false name; he decided it might be best, then figured it might not help to lie if he actually wanted to get information. "This is Jeffrey Wilcott."

"Wilcott?"

Jeffrey wouldn't help him try to figure it out. "Yes. I—I'm kind of in need of some help."

"What can I do for you?"

Jeffrey thought the man sounded like he was eating something, but he didn't ask. He offered him the essential elements of the previous evening's activities. "I want you to find out the location and identity of this so-called Mr. Smith. The Executor. And see what his connections are with an Elizabeth Wilcott."

"Didn't you say *your* name was Wilcott?"

"No relation."

They ended the conversation with a few housekeeping items—a retainer, Elizabeth's address and phone numbers. By the time their conversation was over, Littleton Investigators had potentially one of their more lucrative assignments in years.

He disconnected the line only to punch in seven more numbers. Pamela answered. "Game on," Jeffrey said.

"I'm home if you'd like to discuss the details."

By the time the clock struck midnight, they had the entire game plan laid out. A late-night call to one of Pamela's acquaintances netted him a one o'clock meeting tomorrow with one of the leading reconstructive surgeons in the nation—who just happened to be at the Medical University in Charleston.

Then they played their own familiar game.

When Jeffrey arrived home, not a single light was on in the house. The only illumination came from the streetlight that filtered through the front windows. He went upstairs in the dark and opened Jennifer's closet door. That light came on automatically.

It was empty. He breathed a sigh of relief and rested his weight against the door frame. She had finally gotten it. Now he just needed to call the credit card companies and see exactly how much she had charged. When Jennifer got angry, she spent money. His money.

She had come into this marriage with nothing but a fake Louis Vuitton and eight thousand dollars of debt from cosmetology school— a school she never even finished. Fortunately she had access to only one of his bank accounts, and he determined how much money was in it. This morning he had deposited enough for her to secure a place to rent until they could sort through their financials and she could be on her way.

He turned the faucet on and took out his toothbrush. His hand felt like lead as it approached his mouth; the day had been absolutely exhausting. He caught a movement out of the corner of his eye and turned to see a slight figure standing in the doorway.

"Matthew, son, what are you doing here?"

Eight-year-old Matthew looked confused and disheveled. His T-shirt and baggy pajama bottoms hung from his skinny frame.

"You didn't think she'd take me with her, did you?" The boy walked over and sat on the edge of the tub.

Jeffrey obviously hadn't thought about it at all. He studied his son through the mirror. "Well, no, of course not. I guess I just thought she would have sent you to someone's house to spend the night."

"Yeah, well, no such luck. I'm still here. But I'll tell you this much, I sure am glad she's gone. That woman about drove me crazy."

Jeffrey laid his toothbrush down and turned around. "Yeah, me too."

"Gretchen will come get me from basketball camp, but you know how she is about working after five. So that means you'll have to be here, or else I'll be staying by myself."

"Gretchen?"

"Gretchen. She's my nanny, Dad."

"Oh, yes, Gretchen." Jeffrey nodded his head and slapped his leg as if he and Gretchen were old friends. They'd met twice. "Well, don't worry. We'll figure it out." Jeffrey looked him over. He looked pretty unscathed for his evening alone. "I mean, you could probably stay by yourself."

"Yes, I probably could. But I'm only eight."

"Yeah, I know. You should have called me tonight when you were here alone."

"I did call. Three times. You never answered."

Jeffrey remembered now. He had figured if it was the home number, it might still be Jennifer. "My phone has been acting up. Sorry about that, son." He walked over to him and pulled him up from the tub. "Now, get back in bed so you'll be ready to go in the morning."

Matthew walked to the door.

"About Gretchen—she picks you up for basketball too?"

Matthew never turned around. "Yeah, Dad, you won't have to worry about doing that either."

Jeffrey would deal with finding someone to watch Matthew tomorrow. Right now he would just enjoy the silence of Jennifer's absence.

Will left the frat house around 2 a.m. Instead of trying to figure out what in the world was going on with the reading of his dad's will, he had decided just to drown himself in the fraternity's pre-initiation parties. Most of the new students had already arrived, but rush didn't start until next week, so he hung out with the regulars and washed the night away.

Registration was next week too. The late evenings would come to an end soon enough. Still, five years of college had taught him never to schedule classes before noon.

Besides, none of it mattered—or wouldn't, at least, once he got his hands on his inheritance. He could quit this stupid archeology degree. He had never liked rocks much anyway, and had gotten into it his freshman year when he heard about a class called "rocks for jocks" and figured he'd fit in pretty well. None of it made much sense to him, but the program worked well with his social life and he had a couple of girls who were willing to help him study, even take his tests and write his papers.

Getting the degree had always been his father's stipulation for receiving a house. College graduation meant college gift. College gift was a paid-off mortgage. But his father had purchased the town-home he lived in, so he guessed he owned it now since his dad was dead. The power of the Porsche's engine vibrated beneath him.

"My pitiful family," he mused to himself. "Not a one of them with enough sense to know when they've been hoodooed."

chapter seven

In the still darkness of the early morning, Elizabeth made her way through the back gardens and past the recently remodeled carriage house toward the garage. The floodlights flicked on as they detected her motion and brought into focus the head of a rose from one of the rose bushes. The aroma lay heavy and pungent on the predawn air.

She raised the garage door and the overhead light came on, harsh and artificial in the blackness. Her ringing cell phone proved there was actually someone else other than herself awake at such an hour. She fumbled for the earpiece, stuck it in her ear, and clicked on the phone. "Elizabeth Wilcott."

"Elizabeth Wilcott. This is James Cavanaugh. I got your message last night. Good to hear from you. What's going on?"

She had tried to plan out what she would say when he called back; now that he was on the telephone, she hesitated. But Elizabeth never hesitated long. "Well, James, this is actually something more on the personal side." She climbed into her Jeep and began to back into the alley.

"Your husband cheating on you?"

She didn't laugh. "I'm not married."

"Boyfriend?"

"No. If you'll quit trying to guess, I'll tell you."

He waited while she related to him as discreetly as possible the events of the previous evening. "And to be perfectly honest, this Executor's accent could be as phony as half the breasts in Charleston."

"So let me get this straight. You want me to find out who this man is and where he is?"

"Yes. And one more thing."

"Could you give me the one more thing, then? It helps to know what you're looking for when you're an investigator."

"I need you to do some checking on a Jeffrey Wilcott as well."

"Jeffrey Wilcott, the big-time plastic surgeon?"

"That's the one."

"I thought you said you weren't married."

"He's my brother."

"And what am I checking on for Mr. Wilcott?"

"I want to know if he and this Executor have had any interactions. Check bank records, phone records—shoot, check birth certificates too. I've always wondered if Jeffrey and I were really related. I believe they are conspirators in will forgery."

Cavanaugh gave a low whistle. "That's a big accusation."

"I've got a big checkbook."

"Excellent. Because I've got plenty of time and resources."

"I expected as much. Are you always up this early?"

"I do a lot of my job in the dark."

Elizabeth pressed the disconnect button on her earpiece and exhaled loudly. The streetlights began to flicker off as the first rays of the sun channeled their way through the darkness. A single ray illuminated the tall white steeple of St. Michael's Episcopal, the oldest church in Charleston.

The intersection of Broad and Meeting Streets, where St. Michael's called home, had been cited by *Ripley's Believe It or Not* as "The Four Corners of Law." The historic church, attended by both George Washington and Robert E. Lee, resided on one corner and represented God's law. City hall took up another corner, representing municipal law. The county courthouse, originally the statehouse, represented state law. And the federal court and post office, built on the site of the old town guardhouse, represented federal law. The locals called the corner *jail-bail-hell-mail.*

Thinking of the courthouse reminded her of the waiver she needed to get for one of her clients at the Register of Mesne Conveyance, or the RMC. Maybe she'd simply call Campbell Harris, daughter of her father's old ally Judge Harris. Campbell was on the planning commission and might be able to get it pushed through without Elizabeth having to bother. At the end of the day, knowing people was often the best way to get work done.

Elizabeth drove down Meeting Street savoring the beginnings of morning rush. Jeffrey and Mary Catherine had retreated to the privacy of offshore islands, but Elizabeth had enough of islands growing up at the plantation on Edisto. She didn't need wide-open vistas, tourists riding bicycles, manufactured ambience like she saw on Kiawah, or forgotten spaces like Sullivan's Island. She needed clustered, contained structures. Historical beauty merged with twenty-first-century appreciation. The eclectic mix of new and old.

She pulled into the small gravel parking lot next to her office. Parking space was a precious commodity in this area of prime Charleston real estate. Parking tickets, on the other hand, were passed out like beads at Mardi Gras. People still wondered how she had been so fortunate to get both the building that housed her law practice and a parking lot to boot.

Elizabeth picked her way over the uneven gravel, looking up with pride at the ivory-painted brick building. The truth was, her father had infused the treasure of this city and its islands into her blood. He had made his wealth in Charleston real estate, but it wasn't just a business to him. He loved every square inch of it. And so did she. It was one thing, at least, that he had shared with her.

She climbed the staircase at the front entrance, the wrought iron railing already warm beneath her touch. She preferred to enter through the front doors so she could make sure her clients' first impression met with her approval. She opened the large wood-and-glass-paned door, closing it and locking it behind her. Visitors had to be buzzed in.

On a marble inlaid coffee table, one magazine lay slightly askew. She straightened it, stood back, and nodded, then climbed the oak plank stairs to her office on the second floor.

The scent of an amaryllis candle still hovered in the air. She set her briefcase and purse down and removed the Bluetooth from her ear. She ran her hands along the back of her chair, letting her eyes take in everything, inhaling the flowery scent. She felt, oddly, as if she were seeing everything in her office for the first time.

Or the last.

Elizabeth knew this place as well as she knew her own soul—or better. Every floorboard, every pane of glass. The location of every file folder, every client's name, how they liked their coffee, or if they preferred iced tea. She remembered the details of every pending deal. She felt safe here. This was her world. Perfectly controlled.

A tightness began to constrict in her chest, but she pushed it down. This was where she belonged, and the thought of having to spend a single day at this charade her father had cooked up—let alone a year—seemed utterly ludicrous. She didn't need her father's money. She had enough of her own. Life wasn't about money anyway. It was about respect.

It was hard work for a woman to gain respect in a man's world, particularly in her world of developers and real estate. She was determined to be the woman who got the job done, the woman who helped change the Charleston landscape. Her father had received his recognition for it. Now she wanted hers. As much as she loved the historic aspects of her city, there was a place for the new urban development as well. And she was the one capable of making that happen.

Elizabeth pushed back her doubt and tried to steady her resolve. She would make a name for herself, but apparently it would have to wait for a year. Jeffrey had left her with no other choice. He wouldn't beat her this time.

She needed coffee. Now. She walked over to the wet bar in the back corner of her office and smiled as the perfect cup poured out of her Miele Whole Bean Coffee System. The machine for the coffee connoisseur. The aroma pierced through the clutter of thoughts, and for one brief moment she was back in her mother's arms, sitting on her lap sipping from a white china cup covered with baby blue flowers. Her mother shared her "special" coffee with Elizabeth every morning. Elizabeth would drink from her own pretty cup—more milk and sugar than coffee. But when her mother had died and

Elizabeth had become the mommy, she graduated to straight black, the way her mother always drank hers. It had become her therapy ever since.

She took the coffee back to her desk, sitting down in her leather chair, allowing her body and mind to savor the moment.

The tap at the door sliced the moment in two. "Can I come in?" It was Aaron, looking quite different today than he had yesterday morning—his suit and tie immaculate, the stubble of beard shaved clean.

"What are you doing up so early?"

"Thought I'd come see you before I went to my own job." He sat down on the linen sofa. "So, have you changed your mind?"

"Changed my mind about letting my brother manipulate himself into an inheritance he has no right to? Changed my mind about not stopping until I uncover who is at the bottom of this? Changed my mind about getting the best legal representation money can buy and suing his French cuff shirts right off his back?"

"I gather that's a no."

She sipped her coffee. "It's a definite no. In fact, I've got my investigator on top of it, and as long as I have to play along with this little charade, I'm going to make this year work for me. Ever hear of the Benefactor's Group?"

"The one that helps heirs get their property back from big development corporations? I did some work for them with your dad."

"Then you know they're my competition. My clients are the development corporations. My clients are the 'bad' guys."

"The Benefactor's Group is a really great organization, Lizzy. I hear they have a new lead attorney—I can't remember her name, but I hear she's something of a character. And she's very capable. She's really turning the place around."

"Well, she's soon going to have some help."

"What do you mean?"

"I've thought it all out. It's a piece of cake. I work for them for a year, and then"—she wrapped her hands around her coffee cup and smiled—"with the information I gather, corporate clients will be beating down the doors to pay me even more than they already do. I'll need to hire you to be my assistant."

"What do you think you're doing, Lizzy?"

She turned on him. "Don't give me the self-righteous act, Aaron. I'm simply planning to take advantage of a situation that is taking advantage of me. You think that's not acceptable. You can't imagine how I sleep at night. Okay, how is this for your moral compass? I've worked every day of my adult life for the betterment of this city, to take it into the twenty-first century. I've given nights, weekends, holidays, and every other day of the week to keep Charleston on the map, not just for our past history, but for the history that we are creating now. I'll play out this charade—for a month, six months, however long it takes for me to find this Executor and put a stop to this craziness. And if in the process I can better my knowledge of the competition in order to benefit my clients and my firm, then I would say that makes me the real winner."

"Does it?" He fixed her with an intent, focused gaze. "Or does it simply mean you don't like to lose? Say what you want about your life goals, but at the end of the day this is about childhood competition for you. It's about beating Jeffrey. I don't think that's exactly what your father had in mind."

"How would you know what he had in mind? You said you knew nothing about it." She set her cup down and picked up a brown filing box, letting it plop with a thud on the top of her desk. "These are my current projects, A–F anyway. I need to get organized if I'm going to leave here in a week. Are you going to help me or not?"

———

"There's no way it's time to get up." Jeffrey's hand slammed down on the snooze button. The sun was already streaming through the tiny cracks of the plantation shutters. He rolled onto his back and wished for two more hours. But the meeting he added last night to his schedule forced him to go in early this morning and get his staff busy rescheduling a few clients.

The bathroom tile was warm beneath his feet, heated by coils set on seventy-five at all times. He stared at his own bare chest in the mirror. By all accounts, according to the women who seemed more than willing to tell him, Jeffrey was a fine specimen of a man. He liked his strong jawline, his thick black hair and dark eyes. This was what television doctors were made of. He studied his abs and flexed them slightly in the mirror. Next to Pamela, working out was the only other regular activity he had.

Jeffrey turned his chin and ran his hands across his morning stubble. He had never had any plastic surgery done on himself. *Charleston Magazine* had named him one of its "Ten Most Beautiful People" last year. He didn't need improvement.

He sniffed the air and caught a whiff of the faint remnants of Jennifer's perfume. How long would it take, he wondered, to get that stench out of his house? He climbed in the shower and turned on all six heads, hoping the water would wash away the last of her scent.

When his shower was done, he dried off and went to the closet to dress. He pulled on a fresh white pair of briefs and stood there for a moment, feeling an unexpected breeze. He looked down. Someone—and he was pretty sure he knew who—had cut out the crotch of his underwear. He reached in the drawer for another pair. No crotch in this pair either. Cursing under his breath, he went through every pair of briefs in the drawer. Jennifer hadn't left as dutifully as he had originally thought.

Then he noticed his gym bag sitting in the middle of the closet floor. With all of the commotion over the last few days, he had never gotten to the gym, but he was certain he had put a clean pair of underwear in there. Sure enough, there they sat, folded neatly in a square. Thankfully he wouldn't have to go loosey-goosey today.

He opened his sock drawer, unrolled a pair of dark grey dress socks, and stuck his foot in. His toes kept right on going.

He cursed again, this time at the top of his lungs. Not only had she sadistically removed his undergarments of their necessary compartments, but she had maliciously folded them neatly back up. He grabbed another pair of socks, also toeless. There was no need to continue looking. He'd go sockless if necessary.

Fortunately she had left his expensive Italian suits and white shirts alone. But every necktie on his necktie holder was cut in half. Where were the missing pieces? There was not so much as a scrap of fabric on the closet floor.

He didn't have time to bother with it. At the moment he had the daunting task of going to work with no socks and no tie. A suit with no tie was worse than underwear with no crotch. He'd have to send Helen out to get him one when he got to the office, but he still had two appointments before any stores opened.

His four-hundred-dollar shoes clicked on the hardwood floor of the upstairs hall as he made his way to Matthew's room. Jennifer obviously hadn't figured out how to destroy shoes. He supposed he should be grateful for small favors.

He cracked open the door to Matthew's room. The bed was perfectly made, the shutters were open, and the room was immaculate.

"The kid's a neat freak."

Jeffrey slipped into Matthew's closet and studied the ties of a second grader, all of which would hit him about midchest. He puckered his lip as he stood in front of the wooden mirror attached to the wooden dresser and lifted the pink and blue striped one first, then the green and blue striped one. A far cry from the beautiful ones in his closet. He'd take that out of her alimony.

"Who bought you these ties, kid?" he muttered to no one in particular.

The pink and blue striped one more or less blended with the gray suit and white shirt. He rigged it so that it fell just slightly below the top button of his suit coat. He'd just have to make sure he didn't wear his white doctor's coat open.

The garage held one less car. That was a good sign. His Mercedes sat next to the Range Rover—a vehicle he had purchased just in case he ever had to actually take the kids somewhere. He slid behind the wheel of the two-seater convertible, opened the garage door, and pushed the start button on the car. The Mercedes struggled to start, choked, and lurched beneath him, then died. He cursed and tried again. Nothing.

"This is the last thing I have time for today." He popped the latch and raised the hood. The chrome Mercedes letters shimmered. The black plastic coverings were as pretty as the day he first studied them on the showroom floor. Too bad he didn't know what any of them were for or what to do with them. He found what he thought might be the oil stick and pulled it out. It had black grease running slightly up the stick. "Well, that shouldn't be the problem."

Finally, he gave up and shut the hood, then walked around to the passenger's side. The gas tank cover was opened slightly. He pulled the cap back and saw fabric protruding from the opening. There had been an intruder on the premises last night.

He tugged on the fabric. A piece of a silk tie. The toe of a sock. The white cotton crotch flap from a pair of briefs. Now he knew where all of his missing parts had been stored.

chapter eight

Elizabeth tried to push her reservations aside and made the call she had been delaying all morning.

The voice that answered the phone sounded like it belonged to a twelve-year-old. "The Benefactor's Group. How may I help you?"

"This is Elizabeth Wilcott. I would like to speak with your head council, please."

"One moment, Ms. Wilcott."

Elizabeth didn't even get obnoxious Muzak on the other end. "Guess that costs money," she muttered to the silent receiver.

The prepubescent girl came back on the line. Elizabeth heard voices and commotion in the background before the girl spoke again. "Um, Ms. Wilcott, our, um, our, um, she's not available at the moment, but if you'd like I could tell her what this is regarding."

Elizabeth rolled her eyes. "I wanted to see if she could meet me for lunch. I have something I'd like to discuss with her."

"You'd like to meet her for lunch because you have something you'd like to discuss with her?" The background commotion started up again.

She spoke more slowly, certain the child had cognitive issues. "Yes, tomorrow at one at Anson's, if she is available."

"Tomorrow at one at Anson's?"

"Do you always repeat everything back to people when they say something to you?" Elizabeth demanded.

"Huh?"

"Never mind. Just ask her to call me back."

"Um, no—wait, um, actually I'm looking at her schedule. Yes, I'm looking at her schedule right now and tomorrow is packed."

"Oh, well . . ."

"But she could do today at one."

Elizabeth cringed. She was expecting a day to acclimate to the thought.

"Are you available today?"

"Um, yes, sure. Today at one will be fine." Elizabeth hung up. Then she made herself another pot of coffee.

———

When eleven thirty rolled around and she hadn't heard anything from her private investigator, Elizabeth called the phone company. They assured her that her telephone and voice mail were working perfectly, but she wasn't convinced. She had less than one week to stop this mechanical bull before it tossed her through the air and landed her on her backside.

She parked across the street from Anson's, in the public parking at the Old City Market. This was one of her favorite restaurants in the city. The entrance, with its stucco-over-brick facade, was flanked by two sculpted holly trees in concrete planters. They had effectively endured the cruel summer that had scorched the entire eastern seaboard this year.

Elizabeth stopped and studied the group of tourists lined up around the parking lot. They waited and chatted while the next group of horse-drawn carriages offered another ride in the blistering sun, their drivers telling stories that were true and stories that were almost true.

A woman on the back of the buggy raised her camera in Elizabeth's direction, pointed, and clicked. Then she gave Elizabeth a wink as the carriage rounded the corner and out of Elizabeth's sight. Either Elizabeth had just had her first proposition from a woman, or it wasn't just the Executor who was watching her. A chill crawled through her veins and up her neck. She stood at the door at Anson's trying to push the feeling back down before she went inside.

A tall blond man opened the green wooden door, the etched glass shimmering as it caught the early afternoon sun. "Good afternoon, Ms. Wilcott. I didn't know you would be joining us today."

"Hey, Craig. It wasn't actually on my agenda either." She stopped in front of the wooden hostess counter. "I'm not sure who this is I'm meeting, so just bring her to my table when she arrives. She has my name."

"No problem. Follow me. I'll seat you at a booth in the back."

Elizabeth followed him across the stone-tiled floor.

"Here you go, Ms. Wilcott. Your server will be right with you. Can I get you something to drink while you wait?"

Elizabeth hesitated. "Water, please." She felt like having a real drink, but she had always believed that drinking was a sign of weakness. Her father hated the stuff. *Hard liquor is for people who can't handle their stress,* he always said. *Nobody drinks hard liquor because it tastes good.*

She agreed with him except in the case of martinis.

"I'll be right back with your drink." Craig unfolded her linen napkin and placed it across her lap.

Elizabeth let her gaze wash over the other people in the restaurant. Most seemed engaged in enjoyable conversation, oblivious to the fact that her father had, in less than forty-eight hours, turned her world completely upside down. They went on their merry way, enjoying good food, good drink, and seemingly good conversation. She despised each of them.

"Get a grip, Elizabeth," she muttered under her breath. "Your life is fine, and you do not have to do any of this. You can go right on living just as you are and be perfectly happy." But the bite in her gut, no matter how hard she tried to ignore it, reminded her she hadn't been perfectly happy in years. She hadn't been perfectly happy since, well . . .

She pushed the memory down. It would not surface here. Now was not the time to let weakness show.

Through the frosted glass partition that separated the booths from the bar, Elizabeth saw someone else enter the restaurant. She caught a glimpse of spiky orange hair and an ample figure in layers of black. It couldn't be. She took in a breath and began to cough.

Walking straight toward Elizabeth was her old law school nemesis, the woman who had plagued her for three years.

Ainsley Parker.

The professors at the University of South Carolina School of Law loved Ainsley. Elizabeth despised her. Every day of law school she thought about how she could have been accepted at Harvard or Yale. But no, her father required the Wilcott children to attend a state school—he insisted on supporting the state's economy. And for that principle, Elizabeth had to endure three years of laboring in Ainsley Parker's shadow.

And a substantial shadow it was.

To make matters worse, she was a Yankee.

"Well, who would have thought I would be having lunch with Elizabeth Wilcott?" Ainsley's voice boomed out halfway between the front door and their booth. By the time she reached the table, half the restaurant was staring.

Elizabeth decided it best to act polite. She stood to shake Ainsley's hand.

Ainsley laughed—the same loud, irritating laugh she'd had in law school, the one that had always made Elizabeth twitch.

"I haven't seen you in almost eight years, and all you're going to offer me is a handshake? I don't think so." She grabbed Elizabeth and hauled her into a lung-crushing hug. Suddenly she wished she had ordered that Jack Daniel's.

Ainsley finally let go, only to pull Elizabeth back toward her. "Elizabeth, you're too thin. You were always too thin." She patted her hard on both shoulders and laughed. "But, sit. Sit."

Elizabeth sat.

"We'll have a bottle of the Heitz Cabernet Sauvignon," Ainsley told the waiter without even looking at the wine menu. "Martha's Vineyard 1996, if you have it."

Elizabeth tried not to let her irritation show. Elizabeth wanted fish, and she didn't like red wine with fish. Besides, she resented

Ainsley's attempt to impress her by ordering a three-hundred-dollar bottle of wine. Ainsley would stick her with the tab, just as she always did whenever a group of them would go out to eat in college.

"They pay you that well working for a nonprofit?" Elizabeth couldn't resist.

Ainsley didn't miss a beat as she scooped up a piece of bread from the basket that had just arrived. "Actually, they treat me pretty well, but my husband gets treated *exceptionally* at his job." She waved the bread, buttered it, and began to chew.

Elizabeth studied her. So Ainsley was married. Proof that everyone has someone out there to love them. Her eyes ran across the woman's face. She had barely aged. Still the same in almost every way. And still obnoxious.

"But I do what I do because I love it," Ainsley went on. "You watch the smile on those people's faces when they finally become the owners of the land and home they've lived in for years, and you just can't help enjoying it." She grinned. "I bought the wine because I thought it would be nice to celebrate the reunion of old friends."

Much to Elizabeth's relief, the waiter came and took their order, sparing her the necessity of a response.

"So what about you, Elizabeth?" Ainsley asked as soon as the waiter had gone. "Your family still got as much money as God?"

The wine steward appeared, popping the cork and pouring a small amount for Ainsley to approve. She swished, sniffed, and sipped it. "Perfect."

He poured Elizabeth's first. She swigged it down before he even finished pouring Ainsley's. The waiter eyed her empty glass, then refilled it. Ainsley chuckled.

Elizabeth took a calming breath and decided to go for broke. "I'm here, Ainsley, to find out more about this program of yours. See if there is some way I can assist you in achieving your goals."

Ainsley lifted an eyebrow. "Liar."

"I beg your pardon?"

"There's no pardon to beg, sunshine. I know you too well. This isn't about any 'wantin' to know what my program's about.'" She mimicked a fake but rather good Southern drawl. "So what's really up? You in trouble with some deep pockets? You must have a client who needs information really bad to come down in the slums with the likes of us."

Elizabeth inhaled every last drop of wine that her glass held. She battled to keep her voice calm. "For your information, I'm not in trouble with anyone, Ainsley, and I resent your insinuation."

"I wasn't insinuating, honey. I was asking."

The waiter laid their plates down in front of them. Ainsley sliced into her filet and began to eat, her gaze never leaving Elizabeth's face.

Elizabeth studied her roasted halibut. "Well, I have been doing research on your organization and found it rather inspiring."

"Liar," Ainsley said again.

Elizabeth forced a smile. "I'm not lying. I've heard wonderful things about your organization."

"Liar," Ainsley repeated, taking another bite. "Your big corporate developers probably have very little to say about my organization, and anything they do say doesn't come close to *wonderful*."

Elizabeth laid her fork down. "Quit calling me a liar."

"Well, quit lying. Look me straight in the eye, Elizabeth, and tell me why you give a rat's rear end about what we're doing. Does this have anything to do with your father's death?" Her voice lost a bit of its belligerence. "I was very sad to hear about that, by the way. Your father was a great man."

"Leave my father out of this," Elizabeth said through her gritted teeth.

"Down, girl. Down. I wasn't trying to offend you, just trying to get you to be honest with yourself."

Keep calm, Elizabeth reminded herself. *Remember the goal of all this.* "Okay, you want me to be honest. It actually *was* my father's death that got me thinking." That much, at least, was true.

She had Ainsley's full attention now. The woman stopped eating, placed her elbows on the table, and settled her chin in her hands.

It was working. Elizabeth's composure returned. "I know that my father's organization has done some work with yours. I've heard how

well you lead your team." She swallowed down the bile that threatened to come up. "I'm considering what I'm going to do at this point,
whether to stay in the line of law I'm in or possibly return to my
father's company."

Now, that was a bald-faced lie, but Ainsley didn't bite. "Anyway, I
think it would be good to take a mental break from all of it," Elizabeth
continued. "Get into something new and completely different; find
out what I really want to spend the rest of my life doing. Your area is
so diametrically opposed to mine, and I find it extremely fascinating."

She stopped. She had almost convinced herself.

Ainsley wrinkled her nose and shook her head. "I don't buy it,
Elizabeth. We don't make your kind of money, so this has to be about
something else. You in trouble with the IRS?"

"It has nothing to do with money, Ainsley. I don't need the
money." She paused for dramatic effect. "You want me to prove that
my intentions are pure? Fine. I am willing to spend the next year
working for you *for free.*"

Ainsley picked up her wine glass and sipped slowly. She said
nothing. She simply stared at Elizabeth. Elizabeth stared back.

At last Ainsley spoke. "We've got an amazing program, Elizabeth.
And we've got a great team. Frankly, I have suspicions about this sudden interest of yours, but I don't really have to know why you're considering this. I'll let you have a job with us for a year. If nothing else,
I'll enjoy watching you be tortured for twelve months. Because I'm
certain that if you actually make it through a year, the truth behind
your motives will reveal itself."

She pushed her plate back and leaned in toward Elizabeth. "But
what I won't tolerate is someone coming into this wonderful organization with a bad attitude, thinking they can restructure our program or
change the way we do things. It's working and working well. Let me
be completely honest, since no one else at this booth wants to be.
Unless you can find an ounce of decency in you to actually care for
someone other than yourself, I don't want you anywhere near my company. We have to fight enough external battles. We don't need internal
wars as well. But I'm too ornery to walk away from a challenge."

Elizabeth breathed in deeply. "Are you saying you'll let me spend a year with you?"

"I'm saying you can stay until you give me reason to fire you. That could just as easily happen on your first day."

Elizabeth felt her brow furrow. Her father's will had mentioned no provision in case of firing. She wasn't sure she was that good of an actress. "I'd like to start on Monday."

The waiter offered dessert. Ainsley graciously declined. He brought the check, and Elizabeth reached for it.

Ainsley pushed her hand away. "This one is on me, Elizabeth. Even God's money needs to take a vacation every now and then."

As they walked out into the sticky August afternoon, Ainsley turned in Elizabeth's direction. "I'm giving you one last chance to change your mind. Because I really don't think this is what you want. But if you show up, you will work and you will work hard."

"Hard work has never scared me."

"No, I never believed that work was the ghost that haunted you. But whatever it is, you apparently have yet to shake it." Ainsley grabbed her and hugged her again, never saying another word as she left Elizabeth on the sidewalk in front of the holly tree.

chapter nine

Dr. Rajesh Nadu had been chief of Restorative Surgery at the Medical University in Charleston since shortly after Jeffrey's residency. Dr. Nadu specialized in birth deformities, burns, and reconstruction after severe trauma or cancer. His medical expertise and his humanitarianism had been touted in so many medical journals and honored so often that Jeffrey almost regretted having chosen him. He didn't want all of Dr. Nadu's fame and respect to overshadow the press and prestige that Pamela was planning for him.

As Jeffrey walked through the hospital corridors, the heavy odor of antiseptic and illness assaulted him. He hated hospitals. He might have to visit one every now and then, but he didn't want to be there every day.

Jeffrey found Nadu's office in the far wing of the hospital on the seventh floor. An attractive nurse, a redhead, greeted him as he walked into the waiting room.

"New patient?"

"Actually, I have an appointment with Dr. Nadu."

"May I have your name?"

"Jeffrey Wilcott. *Dr.* Jeffrey Wilcott."

"Well, *Dr.* Jeffrey Wilcott, I'll tell him you're here."

In a few minutes the same red-headed flame led him down a corridor and into a rather sparse office. "He'll be with you in a few minutes." She smiled at him coyly.

Jeffrey knew he was in bad shape when he couldn't even return the smile. He hadn't been himself since the kidnapping, although he was apparently still enough of himself to attract the usual female attention.

The receptionist closed the door, leaving him alone. A smoky scent, like a recently snuffed candle, lingered in the air, and the sounds of some orchestrated piano music filtered through the room. The furnishings were spare and a bit shabby, nothing like the elegance of Jeffrey's own office. "Obviously trauma doesn't pay like elective," he muttered under his breath.

On the far wall, a floor-to-ceiling bookcase was filled to overflowing. He ran one hand along the spines. Many of them had nothing to do with medicine. Clearly, if the man had read half of these, he had never discovered golf.

The remaining walls were adorned not with tasteful artwork but with photographs—most of them pictures of Dr. Nadu himself. Jeffrey gazed at the dark chocolate features of the Indian doctor as he smiled from each picture. A seemingly genuine smile, showing real care for each child, each man, each woman in the photographs with him. Jeffrey leaned in closer. He could see no duty. Only pleasure. Authentic pleasure of a kind totally foreign to his experience.

The door opened behind him. "Dr. Wilcott, welcome," Dr. Nadu said. His accent was heavy but precise. Nadu placed an armload of files on the desk and extended his hand.

Jeffrey shook it. "Um, yes, sir. I appreciate your being willing to see me on such short notice."

He removed his wire-rimmed glasses and stared directly at Jeffrey. "How may I be of service?"

"Oh, well—" Jeffrey hesitated. "I'm just . . . just figuring out exactly what it is you do."

"I see you have looked at the pictures. It should be quite clear." Nadu seated himself in his scarred black leather chair and motioned for Jeffrey to take the chair in front of him. "We give to people what they wouldn't have otherwise, Dr. Wilcott. We mend their broken places, so to speak. It truly is a rather enjoyable job, I must say."

"You must get tired of always seeing such pathetic people." Jeffrey laughed nervously.

"Obviously you and I have different perspectives of what consti-
tutes pathetic."

Jeffrey suspected it wasn't a compliment.

Nadu went on. "Dr. Wilcott, I am aware of your reputation around
Charleston. I hear you are quite a good plastic surgeon, but I am not
altogether certain I understand the nature of this visit. Do you need
my help in some way?"

Jeffrey felt the pulsing in his jaw. "No, actually I came here to
offer you my services."

Dr. Nadu's expression never changed. "And how is that?"

"Well, I have to, ah—to be honest, I've been thinking through
exactly what I want to accomplish this next year in my life. I feel that
there is a part of me that's just not—" He paused for dramatic effect.
"Not completely fulfilled doing what I'm doing. I have a great practice. I really do. But there is the possibility of learning more. And
with my gifts and training, there is also much I can offer. I want—"
He paused, groping for words. "I want to give something back. So I
would like to offer you my services for the next year. Free."

Dr. Nadu laid his glasses on the top of the desk. "You want to
work with me. For a year. For free."

Jeffrey swallowed. Loudly. "Yes. I honestly think I could fill in
some of your cracks. Offer you my expertise. Think of it like this:
with you and me working together, we would pretty much make up
the ultimate plastic surgeon."

"The ultimate plastic surgeon," Nadu repeated.

Jeffrey licked his lips. "Yes, that is what I honestly believe. I could
start on Monday. Together we could accomplish things in the coming year that would turn this city on its ear."

Dr. Nadu rose from his chair. He was a small man, but his presence seemed larger than his stature, and Jeffrey felt uneasy. His
father was the only other man that had ever made him feel that way.
"I've never really had a desire to—what was your phrase? *Turn this
city on its ear*? All I have ever wished to do is accomplish what you
see in those pictures up there. Do you understand what I'm saying,
Jeffrey?"

"Of course. You want to reach as many people as you possibly can. That's every doctor's goal. We want maximum impact."

Dr. Nadu came around to sit on the edge of his desk. He leaned in closer to Jeffrey. "No. Not every doctor. Not me. My only ambition is to make one person smile. At the end of the day, that is all that I am after. One person." He waved a square brown hand in the direction of the photographs. "If I never touched anyone else other than the people on that wall, it would be enough. Because my purpose for being a doctor was accomplished in each life. Each one."

Jeffrey stared at him. False humility was the last thing he had expected from a doctor of Nadu's reputation. It wasn't exceptionally attractive on him.

"You do not believe me."

Jeffrey said nothing.

Nadu smiled as if absorbed in some private joke. "Well, Dr. Wilcott, I do not believe you either. I suspect that coming to work for me was not your idea at all."

Nadu might be a fool, Jeffrey thought, but he was perceptive. He scrambled to regroup. "Dr. Nadu, I have a very well-established practice already. Coming here would be a sacrifice for me *and* for my clients. But it is a sacrifice that I believe—"

"Then why come? Why get your hands dirty with, ah—how did you put it? Pathetic people?"

"I didn't really mean pathetic. I just meant . . . challenged."

"The same question applies. Why leave your world to come work with challenged people?"

Jeffrey shifted in his seat nervously. The Executor had not specified whether he could tell anyone about his father's challenge. He judged it might not be such a good idea. "Let's just say it creates a rare opportunity."

"And you are looking for rare opportunities?"

Lord have mercy, this man asked a lot of questions. "I'm just wondering if it might not be a good idea for my future and the future of plastic surgery in Charleston as a whole if two of its most renowned surgeons come together and increase the . . . the smiles."

Jeffrey stumbled into silence, and for a long time neither of them spoke. Dr. Nadu returned to his desk chair and sat there, pressing his fingers to his lips and gazing at the photographs that lined his wall. At last, as if he had been in deep conversation with someone Jeffrey couldn't see, he gave a resigned sigh, shut his eyes, and murmured, "All right."

Finally, he looked up. "Dr. Wilcott, taking you on for a year might possibly be one of the most reckless things I have ever considered. And I am not a reckless man. I do, however, take risks. Every day when I place that scalpel between my fingers, I take a risk. I— what is the American idiom? I trust my gut." He raised an eyebrow and stared Jeffrey down. Jeffrey squirmed slightly in his seat. "You may come to work with me."

Jeffrey rose. "Thank you, Dr. Nadu. I—"

Nadu cut him off. "Dr. Wilcott, let me be perfectly clear. Our patients come first. If anything in your behavior or attitude leads me to believe you have not represented yourself candidly, you will be released. Immediately. I am not a man to make veiled threats, nor do I endure deception or arrogance. Do we understand one another?"

"Perfectly."

"Then I will expect to see you tomorrow."

Jeffrey stood up, about to protest.

"You will start tomorrow, or you will not start at all. That will be all, Dr. Wilcott."

Jeffrey Wilcott had been dismissed.

———

Jeffrey snatched his phone from his suit coat pocket as he made his way to his car, fuming as he went. He had missed three calls, the first one from his private investigator. He didn't even listen to the message but dialed him back immediately.

"Frank Littleton."

"Frank, it's Jeffrey Wilcott. Tell me what you know or I'm going to have to fire you, because there is no way I am going to start working for that pompous—"

"Did you listen to my message?"

"Tell me what it said."

"Well, I think I've gotten a lead on our elusive Executor."

"What kind of lead?"

"We've been doing some digging on your wife, and—"

"My *wife*? First of all, I never even told you I was married."

"Dr. Wilcott, you are paying us to be investigators, aren't you? We've been on this case twenty-four hours. If you want us to be good at our job, then you should hope we know everything about you by now."

Jeffrey stopped in the middle of the parking lot. He couldn't be angry at the guy for doing what he had paid him to do. He rubbed his temples as he continued on to his car. "If you'd met my wife, you'd know she isn't smart enough to come up with something like this."

"Well, no, but you'd be surprised how many times in situations like this—"

"I highly doubt you've ever had a situation like this. Get to the point."

"Well, there are multiple phone calls to an overseas number. We're looking into those now."

Jeffrey climbed into his car and leaned his head on his steering wheel. "This is crazy. She was probably ordering something off an infomercial. What about my sister?"

"We have begun an initial search into her as well, starting with her bank records. That will be most telling."

"If you don't give me something concrete by morning, the medical practice I've spent years building will be history. Do you understand that?"

"Sir, I understand you were kidnapped by men smart enough not to leave a trace of themselves in your parking garage or on any surveillance camera within a fifty-mile radius of your office. The only other thing that could track them would be the CIA and satellites. If you have that kind of money, more power to you. If not, then you are going to have to do whatever you have to do tomorrow and smile. Because this is going to take longer than a day."

Jeffrey hung up the phone. He'd do the dismissing this time.

chapter ten

Visiting the Middleton Place Plantation—though still in Charles-ton and so not technically "traveling"—had been just the reprieve Mary Catherine needed. She sat on the first of five rolling levels that led down to two mirroring lakes framed by lush green grass—the Butterfly Lakes, they were called, because they had the look of butterfly wings. Beyond the lakes lay the scenic Ashley River.

It had been a wonderful day. She'd had lunch at the Middleton Place Restaurant, serving the Southern fare that she loved most: col-lard greens, Hoppin' John, she-crab soup. Now she looked out over the peaceful river that during the eighteenth and nineteenth centuries had served as the "main highway" to the plantation.

She lay back on the smooth, manicured lawn, turning her head slightly so she could smell the freshness of the grass She had toured most of the sixty-five acres of landscaped havens, walked, kayaked, sat by the river—in short, spent the entire day trying to force the looming dread of tomorrow out of her mind.

A tiny face peered over hers. "What you thinkin' 'bout, lady?"

Mary Catherine jumped up.

The little boy's mother retrieved him quickly. "Sorry about that. He doesn't meet many strangers. Which might be a good thing."

Mary Catherine smiled. "No, it's a nice diversion."

"So, what you thinkin'?" the boy repeated.

"I'm thinking there's too much to do around here for just one day. I'm pooped."

"I poop too!" The little freckle-faced toddler giggled and clapped his hands.

Mary Catherine felt her face flush. His mother laughed.

"No, I meant I'm tired."

"You want to take a nap?"

"I think I might go home and do just that."

"I hate naps. They're for sissies," he informed her.

"That's not nice," his mother scolded.

"Sometimes they're for old people too," Mary Catherine said.

The little boy peered into her face. "Are you old?"

"Ancient."

And with that he tossed his tiny hand in front of her and took off toward some man Mary Catherine only hoped was his father.

His mother whispered something as she passed by Mary Catherine.

"I'm sorry, did you say something?" Mary Catherine asked.

"Oh, I was just saying a year goes by quickly." She motioned toward the child. "They grow up so fast."

Mary Catherine sighed heavily as she made her way back to the main house. Breathtaking manicured gardens led to the top of the hill where the Middleton House, now a museum, sat surrounded by hydrangea and crepe myrtles. This hill had been the backdrop for some of Hollywood's biggest epics and most beautiful period pieces. The home itself was more reminiscent of an English manor in the countryside than a Southern plantation home like the one she grew up in.

It would have been a perfectly lovely day had she not passed by the museum store. She froze at the entrance to the store, her knees going weak. She wrapped her hand around the door frame of the entrance.

"Can I help you with something?" the girl behind the sales desk asked.

"Oh, no thank you," Mary Catherine managed. "I'm just . . . just looking."

The girl cocked her head the way Coco often did. "You're more than welcome to come *in* and look, if you'd like."

Mary Catherine would have closed her eyes if it would have helped, but she would have still been able to smell the "stuff." She gripped the door frame until her knuckles turned white. She squinted her eyes as if not being able to see the items inside the store quite as well would diffuse the heart palpitations.

No such luck. She had only one option left. Run.

She ran.

———

Elizabeth slid the glasses from her nose, shut her book, and laid it on the edge of the tub. The doorbell rang—once, twice, three times. She knew it was Aaron; he'd be the only person concerned with the fact that she didn't come back to work. She picked up the bottle of water and ran it across her forehead, its wet condensation cooling her face, while the sounds of Chopin's *Berceuse* in D-flat major cooled her remaining frustration.

Tears stung her eyes. She opened the bottle and took a long drink. She would keep drinking until the bathwater grew cold, and she'd deal with Aaron tomorrow.

———

Jeffrey drove through the streets of downtown Charleston in a fog of desperation. The questions pounded inside his head: How would his practice survive a year without him? Where would his patients go? What would his staff do? How would he ever have a clinic of his own again?

He tried to reassure himself that with the money he'd inherit by being the only one to complete this insane challenge, he could start an entirely new practice if he had to. "But your reputation will be toast," he muttered aloud.

On the stereo, the soulful Toni Braxton tried to soothe him. He thought of Pamela's perspective: tell them he'd been working for children in need, and they'd think he was a hero. But that argument had yet to stand up against the temperaments of people addicted to his talents. His clientele wouldn't care about anything other than the fact that he wasn't there to tuck their bellies or lipo their thighs.

But did he really have an option? Did he really want to suck out fat and pump up breasts for the rest of his life? Didn't he want what his father's money had to offer?

He drove his car back to the office and pulled into the parking garage. A part of him simply wanted to cry—it would feel good, and he knew it. But the day his mother died, his father saw his lower lip quivering and informed him that men didn't cry. He had been a man ever since.

He picked up his phone and punched in the speed dial for Pamela. "You need to get over here immediately. Your publicity prowess is going to have to get into action sooner than you think."

"Laura!" he barked at his secretary as he came through the door. Laura was a stately redhead and more beautiful now than when she had started working with him. Neither her elegant nose nor her trim, firm thighs were original. "Get Dr. Frederick Peterson on the phone and see if he can meet with me today at four. Then call that new Jordan McAllister. The one Dr. Jefferson mentioned I might want to look at bringing on as a partner. I'd like to meet with her at five. Then call my attorney and tell him I need him here by 5:30 and not to plan on going home anytime tonight."

He went into his office and punched the intercom button. "Helen?"

"Yes, sir?"

"I want to see a list of everything that is on the books for the coming year."

The door flew open, and she stood there with one hand on her hip. "What?"

Helen handled all of his scheduling. She was sixty and only working to reach retirement and the benefits it provided—a fact she reminded him of daily. She hated plastic surgery and had spent her first six months working for Jeffrey scaring his patients away. He let her know her only chance to reach retirement with him was to keep her mouth shut. It had worked—at least with the patients. With him, keeping her opinions to herself seemed an impossibility. "Do you know how many that is?!"

He stared at her. "No. I don't have to know how many it is.

That's your job, and that's why I asked you to get it. And I want it quickly. Because this afternoon you have to pick up Matthew from basketball practice."

"What about the nanny? Gertrude?"

"Gretchen. She doesn't work past five. And tell Sheila to get me a drink."

Helen closed the door behind her. Jeffrey could hear scurrying on the other side. His nurse, Sheila, brought him his drink.

By the end of the night he had successfully brokered a deal to have Dr. Frederick Peterson handle all his surgeries. The new Dr. Jordan McAllister would handle the day-to-day activities of seeing patients. And the contract agreement his lawyer drew up for Dr. McAllister to sign stated clearly that there would be no staff changes and no restructuring of the business.

He had done all he could to protect his business. He just hoped it wouldn't have to go on too long.

Pamela came by to help him write a letter to his patients and work on a press release that was effective without crossing the line. Dr. Nadu had made clear that "exploitation" wasn't on the list of acceptable behavior.

As he finally crawled into his car and headed home, Jeffrey realized he had forgotten one thing—checking the actual patient references of one Dr. Jordan McAllister. He and Frederick Peterson had been colleagues for years. Jordan was an unknown.

But she wouldn't be doing surgeries anyway. What could go wrong in a year?

Will stumbled along the path to the student center and collided with someone in his way. He cursed, then looked up and saw who it was. "Oh, sorry . . . hey, Olivia, what are you doing out this late?"

"Hey, Will. Looks like you've been having a rough evening." She pushed past him and entered the lobby of the Student Center.

He followed. "Yeah, well, I've been at the frat house for a little while. I'm headed back home now."

She opened the door to the small food court and walked over to the Chick-fil-A counter. It didn't close until 11 p.m. on weeknights. "Can I have an eight pack of nuggets and a medium sweet tea, please?"

Will had barely noticed the hunger pangs that had stabbed at him over the last two hours. Booze and poker tended to distract him. But smelling the aroma of the chicken brought him around. He ordered two chicken sandwiches, a large order of waffle fries, and a large Dr Pepper. He and Olivia reached the register at the same time.

He pulled out his wallet to find only a five-dollar bill. He laughed sheepishly at the young girl who stood behind the cash register. Olivia noticed and handed the girl another five to cover what he lacked.

"Thanks. I'll pay you back. Can I sit with you?" He didn't wait for an answer but began following her with his tray.

"I really came to do some work for my sorority, Will."

"Yeah, yeah, I won't bother you. I just wanted to talk." His speech was still coming out slightly slurred.

She sat down at a table by the wall. "Talk? I'm not sure that would be in your best interest this evening."

He sat down across from her. "You're so cruel to me." He leaned over and did a bad imitation of Elvis: *"Well-a don' be cruel . . . to a heart tha's true."*

She didn't respond.

He went on, taking a bite of his chicken sandwich. "Why do you hate me?"

She looked up at him. "I don't hate you, Will. I just don't have any interest in you. I think you're sad."

He almost blew out half his sandwich. "*Sad?* Do you know that I'm the president of my fraternity?"

"Do you know *why* you're the president of your fraternity?"

He frowned. "Huh?'

"My point exactly. You don't have a clue, and that, Will, is very sad. Now if you'll excuse me, I think I'll just take this back to my room."

He would have protested had he not been so hungry. Instead, he let her go, vowing that she would be his in multiple ways before this year was over. And seeing as the year hadn't even officially begun, he had plenty of time to make that happen.

chapter eleven

The phone on the night table woke Mary Catherine from a fitful dream of toddlers and topiaries.

"Hello?"

"This is Frances Bordeaux from the Charleston County School District."

Mary Catherine sat upright in the bed. Her eyes scanned the room for a camera, someone watching her, plotting out her life without her willingness or participation.

"I'm looking for a Mary Catherine Bean."

"This is she. How did you get this number?"

"Well, a Nate Bean contacted us, and—"

"My *husband*?" She punched Nate, nearly knocking him off of the bed.

"Yes. Apparently he called yesterday telling us about you and your qualifications and wanting to know if we have any positions available. He said it was very important that you find something by the end of the week. He was quite convincing, I might add."

Nate turned over and groaned, rubbing his side. Coco simply relocated herself at Mary Catherine's feet.

"I called so early," the woman went on, "because there is a position available, and we need someone to start right away. We thought we had the post covered, but at the last minute our new teacher was unable to fulfill her commitment. A substitute is taking the classes for the time being, but the principal has asked for a meeting immediately. Preferably this morning, before classes get started for the day."

Mary Catherine rubbed her eyes and scratched her head as if that would somehow give her the brainpower necessary to make such a ridiculous decision.

"Mrs. Bean? Could you make it there by eight o'clock?"

"Eight o'clock?" Her eyes tried to register the numbers on the green florescent clock across from the bed. It didn't work. "What time is it now?"

"It's six thirty."

"Where am I going?"

"The school is in North Charleston off Rivers Avenue."

"North Charleston?"

"Mrs. Bean, do you or do you not want to take this meeting? I doubt that anything else will come up before the Christmas holiday. We're already two days into the school year. All other positions are filled."

Mary Catherine gave a huff. "Yes, I guess so. I'll go and see what they are wanting. What grade, do you know?"

"It's a middle school."

"I don't do middle school. I only do kindergarten."

"I'm sorry to tell you, Mrs. Bean, but you won't find a kindergarten teaching spot available in this city. You're lucky to get this offer. Would you like the directions or not?"

She clenched her teeth. "That will be fine."

When Mary Catherine finally hung up the phone, she turned on Nate. "So you didn't think I was capable of getting a job on my own?"

"I was just trying to help. I know you've been so stressed, and I thought maybe this might take some weight off of you, me contacting them for you and all."

She cocked her head at him.

"Really, I just want to make this as easy as possible for you."

She dropped her head into his chest. "Could you make me some eggs?"

"I'll make you bacon *and* eggs."

Elizabeth woke up completely refreshed, almost as if yesterday had never happened, but she suspected that her compartment of denial was almost full.

The phone rang while she was in the shower. Caller ID showed *unknown number,* but whoever it was had left a voice mail. It turned out to be James Cavanaugh, the private investigator. "I've got some information," the curt message said. "Call me."

When he answered, she didn't even bother to say good morning. "What do you know?"

"I know your brother is headed to a new job today."

"Just like I thought. He's going to play along with his own charade."

Cavanaugh grunted. "It could be that he has no more to do with this than you do."

"He *has* to know something about this. This simply reeks of Jeffrey."

"Well, whatever it reeks of, he is reshuffling his entire office as we speak. He starts his new job this morning."

"But we don't have to start until Monday."

"Looks like he wants you to know he's serious."

Elizabeth's brain spun, trying to make sense out of this information. "Anything else?"

"Not now. I'll get back with you as soon as I know more."

Elizabeth snapped the cell phone shut. She was in the closet, half-dressed, when curiosity got the best of her. She hurried back into the bathroom and grabbed her phone.

Mary Catherine's number rang twice, and then Nate answered the phone. Elizabeth despised him. She had tried to warn Mary Catherine that he was only after her money, but Mary Catherine would hear nothing of it.

"Yes, um, Nate. This is Elizabeth. Is Mary Catherine there?" Elizabeth had no idea what she was going to say to her sister. She just needed to know . . . *something*.

"No, actually Mary Catherine is at a *job interview*." He placed special emphasis on the words.

"She is? Well, just tell her I called."

"Anything particular?" The words hung in the air—laced, Elizabeth was certain, with dual meaning. Nate was a snake.

"No. I just had her on my mind. I know she went through a lot the other night, and I wanted to make sure she was okay."

"Well, I'll tell her you called. Of course with her *new job*, she'll probably be very busy."

"That's okay," Elizabeth lied. "It's no big deal."

She closed her phone, then opened it again and dialed Cavanaugh's number once more. "Check out one more person. His name is Nate Bean. He's my sister's husband."

"Your brother-in-law."

"No, my sister's husband."

Elizabeth disconnected the line and walked back into her closet to finish dressing. What did you wear on a day like today? A day when you had to begin the complete rearranging of your life? She chose a soft baby blue blouse and tailored white slacks. Blue made her peaceful. White made her feel clean.

An old memory fought its way to the surface of her mind, and she pushed it down. Blue and white. She needed both today.

———

Mary Catherine let the top down on her VW convertible so she could take in the rush of the palm trees as the ocean breezes swept past. She had lived on the Isle of Palms, a barrier island just northeast of Charleston, for the last four years. After college and a year of travel, she had moved out here and liked the small community atmosphere. Fewer than five thousand people lived on the island. It had recovered beautifully from the ravages of Hurricane Hugo, even though the live oaks with their draping Spanish moss were just now coming back to life almost twenty years later. The azaleas had already blossomed and gone, but all along her route crepe myrtles bloomed in shades of pink and white and purple, and gardenias emitted a powerful and lovely fragrance.

As she headed down I-26 and the commercialized landscape of North Charleston came into view, Mary Catherine felt as if she might as well be driving into a foreign country. She'd lived all her life here and never exactly *been* to North Charleston. For years the area had a reputation for being a rough blue-collar area that had gone further downhill after the shipyard closed. Families abandoned it, leaving it to crime, poverty, and the ever-growing drug community.

She had heard that over the past few years North Charleston had experienced a revitalization of sorts—renovated cafés, antique stores, and banks. The artsy crowd had taken over some of the run-down historical homes and brought them back to life. But she didn't see much of that as she drove, and however eclectic and interesting the place might be, she didn't belong there. This was beginning to feel like the first day of the worst year of her life.

She found the middle school without too much trouble and parked parallel to the curb. The building was long and narrow, a dull gray brick two-story surrounded by patchy grass and red dirt. It couldn't have been drearier if it had been a federal penitentiary.

An assembly of children shuffled around the walkway, obviously waiting for the bell to ring. A few of them noticed her, pointed, and got the attention of their friends. Soon everyone was watching.

Mary Catherine took in a deep breath and tried not to lose her bacon and eggs. "You can do anything for a . . . for a year," she murmured to herself.

Her feet felt like lead, but she forced herself to make the long walk, a prisoner lumbering toward the cell block. She tried to smile as she passed a student. The snickering that followed as she passed proved that smiles weren't worth much around here.

The door was metal, institutional, painted a dark charcoal gray. Just inside to the left, reinforced glass walled off the front of the principal's office. Another cluster of students stared at her as she walked by.

"You're just here to talk," she reminded herself. "Nothing more. Just to see what the position is. That's it."

She pulled open the glass door and walked inside.

A woman behind a large counter was giving a young girl a

tongue-lashing, and she didn't look up. "Mr. McClain is not going to let you get by with your shirt knotted up like some two-year-old incapable of buttoning her buttons, with your little navel showing." The woman swatted at the girl's knotted shirt. "Now get it down and get it down *now*."

"But, Mrs. Gerald . . . ," the girl whined.

"I don't want to hear it, and trust me, you'd rather get it from me than from Mr. McClain. Now go."

The girl untied the knot, buttoned her blouse, and slunk out of the office. The woman looked up. "Hey," she said. "Be with you in a minute."

Mary Catherine tried to busy herself reading all the flyers lying neatly on the counter. One laid out the dress code: khakis for all grades; red shirts for sixth grade, blue shirts for seventh, and yellow shirts for eighth. The knotted-shirt girl was a sixth grader.

The woman went back to tapping on her keyboard. The placard on her desk read, "Myrtle Gerald, Secretary."

Mary Catherine waited. Myrtle Gerald didn't budge. Finally Mary Catherine coughed and said, "Excuse me."

"I said, hang on." She finished her typing, exhaled a heavy sigh, and looked up. "Can I help you? Are you a new student?"

On any other day Mary Catherine would have loved such a compliment. She had always liked being petite and looking younger than she was. But some of the middle schoolers in the hall and on the sidewalk outside towered over her like a pine tree over a peony bush. That wasn't exactly in her best interest when she needed to be the pine.

"Uh, no, ma'am. I'm actually here for an appointment. With the principal."

"Lord have mercy, I'm so sorry. You must be the new recruit. I'm Myrtle Gerald, Mr. McClain's secretary. Come right on through here, and we'll just see what Mr. McClain is doing." She stood up and opened a half door in the counter, gesturing Mary Catherine to follow her.

"Mr. McClain," she said as they rounded the corner of the principal's office, "this young lady says she has an appointment with you."

The man looked up, stood courteously, and smiled. "You must

be Mary Catherine Bean. I'm Derrick McClain." Mary Catherine tried to stifle a gasp. The principal was at least six-three, a powerhouse of a black man with dreadlocks spreading across his shoulders. He held out a hand twice the size of Mary Catherine's and shook hers pleasantly yet firmly.

"Have a seat, Mrs. Bean." He motioned toward the aged blue leather chair in front of his desk.

"Please, call me Mary Catherine."

The principal settled himself on the edge of his desk. He was neatly dressed in black slacks and an off-white cotton polo shirt. He seemed nice enough, but even seated, he was intimidating.

"You graduated from Columbia College?"

"Yes, sir." She hesitated. "Five years ago."

He returned to his chair, and he picked up a pair of tortoise-shell glasses and a manila folder. A shiver ran through Mary Catherine. The last manila folder she had seen caused her to end up here. She hoped this one had better results.

"I've looked at your resumé."

"Resumé?" Mary Catherine repeated stupidly.

Mr. McClain peered at her over the top of his glasses and held up a neatly typed sheet of paper. *Nate*, she thought. *He has gone and typed me up a resumé.*

"You haven't taught since your student teaching semester," the principal continued. "Any reason you got your degree and have never used it?"

"Well, um, I just wasn't really sure that teaching was what I wanted to pursue." She shifted in her chair.

"And what makes you think it is now?"

She laughed nervously. "I just thought I might want to try it on for size. No time like the present."

He removed his glasses and laid them on the desk in front of him. "There is something you need to know, Mary Catherine. I run a tight ship. I expect performance from my teachers and my students. We aren't into 'trying things on for size' around here. We're about charting the course for the futures of these young men and women. It isn't an easy job. They come from tough environments and challenging circumstances."

"Yes, sir."

"Teaching at this school is not for the weak at heart. It's for the serious and the diligent. If you're not serious about this position, then you and I have nothing further to discuss."

"You might want to get serious about changing that paint color in the hall, then," she murmured to herself.

He narrowed his eyes. "Excuse me?"

"I understand, sir." She breathed heavily. "I am serious."

"All right." He patted both hands on the top of his desk. "Then let's get back to your resumé."

After thirty minutes of questions he finally stood up and gave her an odd, penetrating look. "I've got two other interviews today, but there's something about you I can't quite identify. I have the feeling you need to be here."

Mary Catherine couldn't tell if this was a compliment or not. "Thank you, sir."

"Would you like to see the classroom before you leave?"

An actual classroom had never crossed her mind. "Yes, that would be nice."

He walked her to the door. "Let's go see where young lives are shaped for the future."

They made their way out into the hall, now crowded with jostling students. "Stop running, Terrance," Mr. McClain said as a group of young boys came hurtling toward them. They slowed immediately. "And what's that in your hand?"

Terrance's black eyes peered up at the principal. "It's, um, a magazine, Mr. McClain."

Mr. McClain took it and studied the scantily clad woman on the cover. "Are you supposed to have magazines like this in my school?"

"Uh, no, sir. I don't believe we are, sir, but actually it's not mine." He shrugged and started toward the trash can near the door.

"Hold on, Terrance," Mr. McClain said. He extended a huge hand. "We wouldn't want any of your classmates finding that, would we?"

"No, sir."

"Then hand it over. I'll dispose of it."

The young man gave a meek nod and surrendered the magazine. "Sorry about that, Mr. McClain."

"Now get on to your classes. And, Robert, you need to tuck your shirt in pronto."

Robert followed Terrance, scurrying and tucking as he went.

Mary Catherine accompanied the principal past a brightly painted cafeteria and down a long drab corridor. The mint green tiled floors allowed every sound to reverberate through the halls.

"Sarah Jarvis left us because she gave birth to twins over the summer," Mr. McClain explained as they proceeded down the hall. "She had been with us for six years but needed some time with her little ones. Ms. Bordeaux might have told you we had someone else lined up, but her husband died suddenly and unexpectedly. So sad." He turned the corner into a classroom.

Mary Catherine surveyed the room. Sterile gray walls. Gray lockers. White dry-erase board. Black metal teacher's desk. Royal blue desk chairs lined up in five rows of five.

She hated royal blue.

"Do all your rooms look like this?" Mary Catherine asked.

"Well, our teachers have the freedom to make the rooms their own."

"How much their own?"

"As much as they like."

"No limits?"

"There are always limits, Mrs. Bean. This is a school."

She lifted her eyebrows. "Who can learn without artwork and culture and color and, well, just plain ambience?"

Mr. McClain gave her a perceptive glance. "As I said, Mrs. Bean, you do whatever you like with this room—assuming you end up being chosen for the job."

He grinned broadly at her. Her heart lifted—not much, but just a little. Enough to set her redecorating glands pumping.

And for now, that was sufficient.

chapter twelve

This is where you will spend your day, Dr. Wilcott." Dr. Nadu
pointed to the conference table in front of them. Three enormous
stacks of files lay on the table, neatly aligned in front of the center
chair. "These are the current cases that we are dealing with. I think
it will be beneficial if you familiarize yourself with all of them. You'd
be wise to write down any questions you have, as many of these may
be, shall we say, outside of your area of daily familiarity. I'll be back
to check on you this evening."

Jeffrey stood dejectedly in the center of the room. Nadu's refer-
ence to "this evening" was all too familiar. All doctors kept ridiculous
hours . . . until eventually they no longer felt ridiculous. Unfortunately for him, Gretchen left at five, and he hadn't arranged an
evening sitter for Matthew. He'd call Helen. She was too old to have
anything else to do anyway, and she had always had a fondness for
Matthew.

Jeffrey hadn't been under anyone's authority since the day he finished his residency. To be ordered to go through case files made
Jeffrey's skin sting as if a case of the shingles were setting in.

A young man in a white lab coat poked his head through the
doorway. "Could I get you a cup of coffee or anything, Doctor?"

Jeffrey looked through him. "Yeah, sure, coffee. That would be nice."

The young man stared at him. "You okay, sir?"

"Yeah, I'm okay."

But he wasn't okay. Just last night he had his own office. Today he
was in the middle of a stranger's office. Looking at a stranger's files.
About to walk in a stranger's world. For a year. His loathing for his

father began to rise like bile in the back of his throat, followed closely by anger at both Elizabeth and Jennifer.

He took off his suit jacket and slipped on a white coat, but it couldn't cover up his rage. He cursed his father under his breath. This entire thing was simply absurd. What kind of father reached up from the grave and uprooted his children's entire lives?

The young man returned with the coffee, and Jeffrey reached for the top folder off the first stack. The picture on the front page caused him to recoil: a gaping hole the size of a plum in the middle of a patient's cheek. Not exactly how he wanted to start the day.

The hole was caused from a desmoplastic melanoma—something Jeffrey had only seen on one patient that had come through his office. He had referred the patient elsewhere.

He returned his attention to the file. Apparently a surgeon in another state had botched the reconstructive job, and Dr. Nadu was working on repairing the cumulative damage. It was a deep and invasive wound, and considering the change from the original pictures to the most recent, the transformation Nadu had already accomplished was extraordinary.

As he sipped his coffee, Jeffrey studied every aspect of the patient's chart in front of him. By the time he closed it and reached for the next one, he knew more about desmoplastic melanoma than he had ever bothered learning in school or his own practice.

———

"Dr. Wilcott?"

Jeffrey lifted his head to see Dr. Nadu standing in the doorway. He hadn't even heard the man come in.

"Have you been sitting there all day?"

Jeffrey rubbed the back of his neck and stretched. "Yes."

"Did you get some lunch, I hope?" Dr. Nadu asked as he came around to the other side of the table and pulled out a chair.

"Yeah. That young resident checked in on me a couple of times and grabbed me a sandwich."

Dr. Nadu raised his eyebrows. "So you never left this room?"

"I went to the men's room twice. Does that count?" Jeffrey put his head in his hands and laughed. "No, Dr. Nadu, I never left this room. But I didn't get through all of these charts." He pointed to the charts that remained—three-fourths of them.

"I would have been surprised if you had." Nadu chuckled. "Those files will take you a week."

Jeffrey kept quiet. Surely this man didn't intend to keep a surgeon of his caliber holed up in a room looking at grotesque pictures for a solid week.

"What did you think of what you saw?"

Jeffrey paused, trying to process the mountain of information he had collected. "I think you have a lot to remember."

"Is that all?"

Jeffrey hadn't the faintest idea what Nadu was after, or how to respond. "Yeah, I guess for today that's all."

Dr. Nadu nodded. "Very well. I trust you will discover more as you spend the rest of the week finishing the remaining charts." He stood to leave.

"You aren't serious, are you? You expect me to spend an entire week doing nothing but looking at charts?" Jeffrey glared at Dr. Nadu. "I'm a very experienced surgeon, you know."

"What we do is about more than surgery, Dr. Wilcott. It is about people. Now go get some rest, and return in the morning. I will be making rounds with my surgical residents and interns tomorrow, so I will not be here, but you already have your task. Have a nice evening." He closed the door behind him.

Furious and exhausted, Jeffrey jerked his suit coat off the coat rack and muttered imprecations at both his father and Dr. Nadu. The nerve of Nadu, treating him like some green intern! And the nerve of his father, acting as if he were a rebellious child who needed to be taught a lesson!

Anger surged within him like a wave, threatening to overwhelm him. Then a terrible thought occurred to him, and he panicked. What time was it?

He glanced at his watch. Seven thirty. He had forgotten to call Helen! How had he forgotten to call Helen? And where in the world was Matthew?

He fumbled in his coat pocket and dialed his home number as he ran to his car. Much to his relief, his son's voice answered on the third ring.

"Hey, Matthew." Jeffrey tried to slow down his breathing. "You home, son?"

"Yes, Dad. I'm home." A pause. "I answered the phone, didn't I?"

"Well, yeah, I get your point. Ah, how exactly did . . ."

"How exactly did I get home after basketball practice because you didn't come to get me?"

"Don't get smart, Matthew."

"I called Helen, and she came to get me."

"You called Helen? Well, that was good thinking, son. Very wise of you. So, you okay there? I mean by yourself?"

"Yes, Dad. I've already fixed my dinner, taken a shower, done my homework, and now I'm watching television."

"None of that trash stuff, I hope?" he said, trying his best to sound like a father.

"I don't watch trash, Dad. I watch sports."

"Right. Sports. Okay, then. I'll see you when I get home, and I'll tuck you in or something."

"I'll be fine, Dad."

"Okay, well, I'll see you shortly."

"Bye." And the line went dead.

Jeffrey let out a sigh. He might not be able to do anything right with Dr. Nadu, but at least he had raised a son who knew how to take care of himself.

———

Aaron lay stretched out on the sofa in Elizabeth's office, watching her work. She sat on the floor, her legs tucked underneath her body, her hair poking out from all ends of her ponytail holder. Like a woman obsessed, she sorted through file boxes and made notes on yellow Post-it notes, which she placed on each client's folder.

"You've got all week," he said.

"This is two years' worth of work, Aaron. It's going to take longer than a week."

The room was filled with the aroma of Chinese food, much less appealing now than it had been when it was delivered an hour ago. Elizabeth hadn't eaten anything.

"Did you say that you're going to the plantation for dinner on Sunday?"

She slapped a file folder down onto the stack with more violence than was absolutely necessary. "Can we talk of more appealing things? Say, oh, Ainsley Parker, maybe? Even Ainsley would be more appealing."

"Why do you hate going there, Lizzy?"

She leaned back against her desk. "I don't hate it."

"Liar."

She opened her eyes and glared at him. "Don't call me a liar. You sound like Ainsley Parker. I'm not lying. And don't ask me questions that you know I don't want to answer. Then you won't be forced to hear an answer you obviously don't want to hear."

"You wouldn't be defensive if you weren't lying."

"I wouldn't be defensive if you weren't calling me a liar."

"Your father loved that place, you know. Every part of it. The land, the house, the heritage. He always wanted his children to love it the way he did. But none of you even went out there."

"I'm glad he loved it, Aaron. I'm so glad he loved his precious land and his precious house and his precious heritage. Unfortunately, most people I know protect what they love."

Aaron thought about pressing further. The hint, the insinuation, was as far as she ever went in articulating her feelings. The last time she came back from the plantation, she withdrew into her own world of isolation and anger for two weeks. He felt that if he could just find the right string and pull it, the knot would unravel, and she might find some healing and restoration.

Unfortunately, Lizzy never let anyone get close enough to find that string.

———

Mary Catherine opened the front door of her home and slipped the leash from Coco's collar. It was well past eight, and she still hadn't heard anything from Nate. She and Coco had gone for a stroll up Front Street, where they could listen to the music streaming from the bistros and mingle with the sunburned tourists. Her cell phone was lying on the counter, its message light blinking.

She picked up the phone.

"Mrs. Bean, this is Derrick McClain. I wanted you to know that I'm willing to offer you this teaching position. I'll need you to start on Monday morning. If you could call me back first thing tomorrow, I would appreciate it."

Mary Catherine closed the phone and placed it back on the granite countertop. She went into the bedroom and started pulling rolls of fabric from under her bed. She had six days to make draperies and a slipcover for the sofa she wanted to put in the reading nook. The tan chenille would be perfect—

Then she remembered exactly what was happening. A year. No money. No travel. Working with inner-city children. An entire year.

Her stomach churned. The fabric dropped from her hands, and within fifteen seconds she was in the bathroom with her head hanging over the toilet.

chapter thirteen

Friday was the official registration day of the new semester at the College of Charleston. Will parked on Calhoun Street and headed toward the Lightsey Center, where the registrar's office was located on the second floor.

Just as he passed the bookstore, a campus police officer rode by on a bicycle and nearly ran him over. Will lurched out of the way, swearing under his breath. Rent-a-cops on bikes. How much more hopelessly out-of-date could this place get?

Faculty and administrators were always ragging on the students to appreciate the heritage and beauty of the school, founded in 1770 and reigning as the thirteenth oldest college in South Carolina. He remembered that much anyway—it had been drilled into him often enough. But the buildings people fawned over and took pictures of and touted as "historic" felt more like musty old tombs to him, and the wandering, so-called "scenic" pathways designed to show off the architecture and flowering plants just made it take twice as long to get from point A to point B.

The only thing Will appreciated about college was that it kept him from having to get a real job. If he actually showed up for classes this year, he might graduate. Not that graduation was a huge issue to him either. After all, college was mostly about enjoying the life he had grown comfortable living. He wasn't in any big hurry to leave.

Just beyond the glass doors at the entrance to the Lightsey Center, students were milling about everywhere. People he barely knew greeted him, patted him on the back. Girls whispered about him to their friends. Who would want to rush all of this?

The elevator took him to the registrar's office, and he greeted the registrar's secretary. "Lucy, you're looking beautiful today, as always." Will grinned. Laying on the charm always worked to get him what he wanted. He was on a first-name basis with almost every staff person at the college.

Lucy flushed slightly. "Hey, Will, I was wondering if I'd see you today." She typed on her keyboard and then stopped suddenly. "Will?"

Distracted by the shapely coed who had walked up to the window next to him, Will turned his attention back to Lucy. "Yeah, what's up?"

Lucy peered over her glasses at the computer screen and shook her head. "I'm not sure what the problem is, but it says here that your account is due in full."

"What do you mean? My account is always paid by my trust."

"Yeah, I know." And she did. They'd been doing this same song and dance for years. "But the computer is saying that it isn't paid. Do you have a credit card on you or something?"

"Um, no. I didn't bring anything with me. It's got to be a computer error or something. Why don't you go talk to Nancy and see what she can find out?"

Lucy nodded and headed to the back toward her supervisor's office. In a minute she returned. "Nancy placed a call to the bank regarding your trust. They informed her—" She leaned in closer and whispered the rest. "They informed her that your trust was frozen and that you would have to pay for this semester yourself, up-front."

Will leaned back, trying to reconcile this information. He didn't get it. "Oh, Lucy, everything has been so mixed up since my father died. But don't worry, I'm going home Sunday, and I'll get this all figured out. I'll catch you on Monday."

He gave her a reassuring wink and headed back toward the door. He might have worried more about it, but a group of the new freshmen girls looked like they needed help in locating their dorm.

He walked them down the street. As they made their way, a lost-looking boy, obviously a freshman, came their way with a crisp new book bag draped across his shoulders. "Come here," Will said, motioning to him and giving the girls a wink. "See that little flag in the middle of the street?"

The boy nodded, his eyes following Will's point toward a small pink flag attached to a red ball weight.

"Well"—Will grinned over his shoulder at the girls—"those flags are for the new freshmen. Kind of a souvenir, you know? Everybody who's anybody has got one."

The bright-eyed freshman ran out into the street and picked up the flag, cradling it in the palm of his hand and then stuffing it into his pocket. "Thanks, man," he said, and jogged off in the direction of the registrar's office.

The giggling girls watched the boy go, and Will reached out, putting his arms around the two prettiest ones. "What that kid doesn't know," he told them with a laugh, "is that the little pink flag he's carrying is actually a marker for the sanitation department. They put those down when a horse on the carriage tour relieves himself in the middle of the street."

Most of the girls laughed, all but one. "That was a mean thing to do," she said. "You told him it was a souvenir."

"It is a souvenir—kind of," Will said. "The tourism department loses about a hundred and fifty of them every year."

———

On Friday evening around seven o'clock, Jeffrey finally closed the last file. He rubbed his eyes and leaned back in his chair. Each day he had entered this room furious and frustrated at the turn his life had taken, and each evening as he closed up another folder, he had to admit that these cases were remarkable, to say the least. There were so many different types of traumas that Jeffrey had never even seen before.

He stood up, pushed the chair back under the table, grabbed his briefcase and suit coat, and opened the door.

Dr. Nadu stood within inches of Jeffrey's face.

He jumped back. "Sorry, Dr. Nadu. You startled me."

"I apologize for the intrusion. Are you finished?"

Jeffrey nodded. "All done. My first week of initiation is officially over."

"So, what did you learn?"

"I'm guessing you're looking for a different answer than the one I gave you the other day?"

"That is correct."

Jeffrey laughed softly. "You want an honest answer?"

Dr. Nadu narrowed his eyes. "Are there others?"

Obviously this man didn't live in Jeffrey's world. "Well, I can honestly tell you I've seen a lot of different cases come through the doors of my practice, but I've never seen anything like what I've seen going through your files this week."

Obviously this appeased him. Dr. Nadu sat down in one of the conference room chairs and removed his glasses. "I will see you on Monday, then."

"See you on Monday."

Jeffrey walked to the garage, his step a little lighter. But when he reached his parking space, a haze seemed to be rising from the hood of his car—the car he had just had inspected to make sure it wasn't bugged.

Acid. Someone had poured acid all over the hood of his beautiful Mercedes—obviously some nutcase who had rented *Fatal Attraction* recently. He cursed himself, cursed his life, cursed his father and his sister and his crazy wife.

He called a tow truck and a taxi, and while he waited, he called Littleton Detective Agency. "Don't worry," Frank Littleton assured him. "We've got a lot more digging to do. We should have some solid answers for you by the end of next week."

Jeffrey slammed the phone shut. By the end of next week there could be far more to investigate.

———

Elizabeth clipped her Bluetooth on her ear as she walked out the front door, then paused on the stoop. The new paint job on the pink stucco looked good, even if it was hard to see in the dark. She hardly ever saw it in the daylight.

The night air was invigorating. She'd been closed in and working like a dog all week. Getting out for a run would do her good, even if she didn't look forward to what she had to do first.

She dialed her client's number, then hooked the phone safely back at her side once the ringing came through her earpiece. It was only seven o'clock in L.A. She had dreaded this call all week, and so she had put it off until the latest possible hour on Friday.

"Elizabeth Wilcott, you work too much."

"Hey, Mr. Everett. Getting ready for the weekend?"

"Of course not. I work too much too. I'm still at the office."

"I figured you would be." She paused.

"Something going on with our land acquisition?"

"No, no. That's all running smoothly, actually. We should have a counteroffer by the end of next week. No, there's something else I needed to talk with you about."

"Something I need to come to town for?"

"No, nothing like that. Mr. Everett, you know there is nothing I desire to do more than to service my clients as effectively as possible."

"You've never disappointed me, Elizabeth. You're like your father in that regard."

She tried to remain focused, even though any mention of her father's sterling reputation made her want to jerk him up from the grave and shake him into reality. "Well, thank you, sir." She breathed deeply.

"Elizabeth, are you all right? Are we running into trouble here?"

She laughed. "Thankfully, no. But I'm just going to have to shoot straight with you and ask you to trust me. I'm taking a leave of absence from the firm for the next year." She slightly rushed the next part. "But before you jump to conclusions, I need you to hear me out."

"I'm listening."

"I have the opportunity to work for an organization for a year that could offer us great insight into what you and I are trying to accomplish together. I have people who are more than capable of handling your contracts while I'm gone. The whole operation will be managed by Aaron Davis."

"From your father's company."

"Yes, sir, that's him. Everyone understands that my absence is only temporary. I promise you, sir, in the long run it will make what we do more effective."

"Can you tell me what it is?"

Elizabeth was dreading this question the most, but it would be all over the city by the end of her first day. If she told it, she could maintain some control over the information.

She felt the unevenness of the cobblestones under the soles of her Nikes and suppressed the desire to start running. Now. Run and run and never look back.

"I'm going to spend a year working for the Benefactor's Group."

"I see."

"I know it sounds insane, but I haven't gone off the deep end. I've actually seen an opportunity, and if you will trust me, keeping this in confidence, I believe this will give us insight into what we are dealing with in the majority of our land acquisitions."

"There's no other reason than the fact that you're going to acquire information."

"No other reason." *That he would ever know of.*

"You're a great lawyer, Elizabeth, but you're not replaceable."

She paused, balancing herself on a cobblestone, trying to manage her anger so that she didn't lose before she had technically made it to the field. "I have the best people in the country working for me, Mr. Everett. And if you're not taken care of, I'll pay you back personally."

"Do you know how much that is?"

"I wrote the contract."

"I like you, Elizabeth, you know that. You've worked hard for me, but I'm not in business to lose money."

"Neither am I, sir."

She could hear him pacing. "Well, if you're convinced this Benefactor thing will reap us some rewards in the future . . ."

"Thank you for understanding, sir. And as in all things, I ask you to hold this information in confidence."

"Well, I'm not legally bound, but there's no reason for me to do otherwise. I'll look forward to hearing from your team next week."

"They'll have the counteroffer on your desk by Friday."

"Can I call you if anything happens?"

She felt the sweat running down her back, and she hadn't even started running. "No, sir, I'm sorry, but I can't be in touch with any of my clients during this period that I am working for the Benefactor's Group."

"This better be worth every day."

"Yes, sir, it better."

chapter fourteen

A storm had swept through on Saturday night, bringing a break in the hot and muggy summer weather. Esau Brown welcomed the change.

He didn't welcome what he knew he was going to face this afternoon.

He loved them kids; he really did. But nothing had been the same since Mrs. Rena passed, and now Mr. Clayton was gone too. Life kept going on, he reckoned, and death along with it. But sometimes the changes just seemed too much for a body to bear.

He stood on the front porch and shaded his eyes, waiting to see the rolling dust that signaled a car coming down the long dirt driveway. Lining both sides of the drive, the wisteria Mr. Clayton loved so much still bloomed and gave off that sweet fragrance, like they were honoring his memory.

Esau was well-nigh eighty years old, and there was a limit to what he could do these days. He tried to keep the wisteria pruned so they'd bloom all summer long, but he couldn't reach the high places anymore, and the plants were beginning to look a tad scruffy in the upper regions.

He chuckled and rubbed a gnarled hand over his head. He reckoned lots of things around here were getting pretty shabby, himself included. But as long as he had breath in his lungs and blood in his veins, he would take care of this place the way his daddy had done, and his daddy before him.

Esau had often talked about the slavery days with Mr. Clayton—what life had been like for Esau's granddaddy, and what possessed old

Colonel Wilcott, three generations ago, to be so different. When everybody else was running their plantations on slave labor, the Wilcotts had never owned a single slave. According to family legend, Colonel Wilcott had said, "As long as a man knows he's free, he'll have a heart to serve anyone."

And he was right. Esau's family had worked faithfully for the Wilcotts all these years because they knew they were free to stay or free to leave. Colonel Wilcott gave them dignity, and that heritage was passed down through all the generations.

Esau had been born on this plantation, played here as a boy, worked here as a man. It was the only home he'd ever known. When he grew up and married Bernice Clark, she came to live and work here too.

Esau and Bernice had both been devastated when Mrs. Rena passed. Before she died, she had made them promise to spend the rest of their years looking after her husband. She believed if he could be salvaged, then so could her children.

But Esau thought maybe she had been wrong. Mr. Clayton was dead, and from what he knew and saw and had been told, the children's lives were in shambles. Even the successful ones had no real character. What kind of people would they be, he wondered, if he had tended to them with the kind of love and devotion he gave to Mr. Clayton?

But it was too late now. Too much water over the dam. All you could do was play with the hand you were dealt. And Esau meant to do that. And now that hand required monthly dinners together.

Over the years Mr. Clayton had treated Esau more like a brother than an employee. He'd built Esau his own fine house right on the grounds. Gave his wife the funeral of a queen. And now had put him in charge of the plantation during the interim year before the inheritance would be divided.

Even dead, Mr. Clayton still had a few tricks up his sleeve.

———

Jeffrey was grateful for last night's storm and the lower humidity; it was the only positive aspect to what he was certain would be an otherwise torturous day. His week had already been a nightmare. Nothing much felt like his anymore—including his life.

He had pawned Matthew off on a friend for the afternoon. He had really wanted to bring him, for the sake of adding more parties to the conversation, but the guidelines of the will hadn't made it clear.

He leaned his head back and let the warm wind blow through the sunroof. Returning to Wisteria Plantation always called up memories of the life he once knew.

Jeffrey had always appreciated the plantation—its rich heritage, the heritage of Edisto Island. He would come back each year when the house was on the Edisto Island plantation tour. That was about the only time he and his father would even see each other, but he had once thought of this as home.

At least until his mother had passed away. Sunday was her favorite day. She'd dress them all for church, and when they returned, she and Esau had a big Southern dinner waiting for them. Dad wouldn't go to church, but he always sat at the dinner table with them. They'd talk about their week, their lives, their joys and challenges.

It was the only time Jeffrey ever felt as if they were a family.

Jeffrey cast a glance toward the Presbyterian Church on Edisto Island and grunted. But as he eased across the Dawhoo River and "Edisto time" set in, his tension eased as well. Edisto held something for him he couldn't explain.

He pulled onto the old dirt road that led to the driveway of his family home. A nondescript sign announcing "Wisteria Plantation" hung at the base of the black iron mailbox. He had tried to tell his father a more ornate sign would be fitting for the majesty of this land and home. But his father didn't do grand. He simply did business.

There was no gate—another source of conflict with his father. Jeffrey pulled into the drive, its pathway overhung by a canopy of live oaks and hanging moss. Wisteria was always the most popular home on the tour. He loved to hear the whispers, see the dazzled expressions and childlike wonder as visitors took in the beauty and wished the place was part of their heritage, their memories.

At last he emerged from the tunnel of live oaks and onto the circular driveway. The sun broke through again, illuminating the wisteria that ringed the driveway. Even before Jeffrey's birth, his father had begun cultivating it, binding it on large stakes until eventually each woody stalk was able to stand on its own. On the spring garden tour, when the blossoms first filled the air with fragrance and color, he charmed all the ladies with his knowledge of the beautiful vine. It was the beauty of the wisteria that had finally given this place a name other than the Wilcott house.

And it was the possession of this house that helped give Jeffrey a name in this sleepy city. When his friends from Porter-Gaud would laugh that he lived on an island and not in the heart of the city, he packed them in his car and brought them to this place. They never laughed again.

Elizabeth opened the sunroof of her Jeep. Her head throbbed—she didn't know if it was because she had slept so hard last night during the storm or because of the torture of having to go home.

Elizabeth hated the plantation. Everything about Edisto Island had always felt so unrefined, so rural. Attending Ashley Hall School for Girls in the city had made her declare that one day she would be an SOB—the common nickname for the truly wealthy, those who lived south of Broad.

Her father had money, of course. He just didn't care if anybody knew.

She didn't necessarily care either. She just hated the dirt, the smell of the pluff mud in the marsh.

Once she was finally able to leave and go to college, she never returned to Edisto Island to live. All the other island kids returned home during their college summer breaks to ride the horses, surf the waves, enjoy the marsh. But not Elizabeth. For her all the plantation held was the torment of her past. The only good memories she possessed were the Sunday dinners her mother had made for them when she was alive.

But that was a long time ago. Too long.

She drove past the Presbyterian Church and wondered briefly why not one of her siblings ever expressed any desire to go to church. They had to go while their mother was alive, but once she was gone, not one of them ever went back. Sunday became just another day.

As she crossed the Dawhoo River, Elizabeth felt the old fear creeping into her bones. She fought it all the way to the dirt road that led to her childhood home. She cursed the dirt as it blew up around her car, cursed the fact that no one had cared enough to pave it, cursed the reality that she would have to get the car washed to rid it of the dust and smell.

Elizabeth removed her sunglasses as she entered the tree-lined path. The live oaks hung with moss had always freaked her out, especially when storms would blow up off of the Atlantic. The trees would sway and the moss would move like some terrible creature out of horror movies, out of nightmares.

At last she came back into the sunlight and squinted. The wisteria brushed against her car, and again she cursed under her breath. Her father had poured all his attention and affection on those demanding vines, and if they had scratched her car, she'd cut them down herself.

———

Mary Catherine was nursing a sore back from all of the boxes she had been packing up to take to her new classroom. Once she had decided that she really was going to take the job, she was almost excited. She couldn't wait to see the expressions on those kids' faces when they walked into an environment that begged them to learn. The other teachers would be asking her to do a makeover in their classrooms by the time the week was over.

She hadn't been quite as thrilled about today's event though. She had begged Nate to go with her. He had assured her it was better if she spent this time with her family alone.

But it wouldn't be the same. Daddy wouldn't be there. She hadn't been back to the house since the day of the funeral, when half of

Charleston had descended on the hundred acres Mary Catherine called home.

She had hated leaving home, hated leaving her daddy. In those final years he had started to say, "I love you." He had actually been available to her. She would have moved Nate into that house in a heartbeat, but her father told her that in order to start a new life with a new husband, she should have a home and life of her own.

Mary Catherine had left early enough to stop for a few minutes at the Presbyterian Church. She had always thought it funny that it wasn't called the First Presbyterian Church or Edisto Island Presbyterian Church, but the Presbyterian Church on Edisto Island.

This was the church her mother had attended—the church all the siblings attended before their mother's death. It was an old structure—almost two hundred years old, she thought—with white clapboard siding and tall white pillars and carved wooden pews. Mary Catherine had fond memories of this church, memories only she and her mother shared. Memories that she had never forgotten, even though most of the time she lived as if they happened in another life, or to someone else altogether.

She had picked up some flowers on her way into Edisto, as she always did, but this time the flowers weren't just for her mother. She might have pitched a hissy fit or two over her father's will, but he was still her daddy. She skirted the front porch and walked around to the cemetery. There was his grave, still fresh and lumpy.

The funeral home told her it would be another couple of weeks before the footstone with her father's dates would be back, and then it would take its place next to her mother's. She placed the flowers in the bronze plate attached to the large Wilcott headstone.

She wiped some wet mowed grass from atop her mama's marker and told her how much she loved her. She scolded her daddy for the craziness he was forcing her to endure. Then, when there was nothing more to say, she kissed her palm and laid it on the flowers, and took her leave. As much as she wanted to resent her daddy for what she was enduring and how her life had been turned upside down, she missed him more than she could hate him.

She passed The Edisto Bookstore and momentarily had to catch her breath. She'd never not gone inside. Her foot pressed the the accelerator . . . Hard.

When she turned on to the dirt road that led up to the plantation, Mary Catherine found herself thankful once more that, even though her daddy had as much money as God, he still hadn't paved this road. The rawness of it made the character of her home that much more majestic.

The beautiful plantation house came into view, inspiring the same awe it had always brought her. No wonder movie directors used these old Southern homes as the setting for a bygone era. A house like this begged people to immerse themselves in its story: the large wraparound porches that surrounded the first floor, the powerful white columns, the crispness of the white wood siding against a backdrop of green. Even portions of *The Notebook,* her favorite movie, had been made on this land.

Mary Catherine turned her car into the driveway and smiled at the beautiful blooms still hanging on the wisteria in the late summer. Her father took such care of that wisteria—pruning it after the first bloom so that it would continue to bloom all summer long.

Before the final stages of cancer confined her to bed, her mother had loved to get out and walk in the sunlight. Mary Catherine remembered how she trailed the petals of the wisteria through her fingers as if she were trying to memorize them for the moment when she wouldn't be able to touch them.

She had touched Mary Catherine's face in much the same way.

———

Will decided it might be best if he took a shower before he went down to his folks' place. His mother had always insisted on them dressing up for Sunday dinner. That was one thing he remembered. And one thing he always did. Even if he was going out to a bar with the guys, if it was Sunday he put on a tie. It might look like an accordion, but he'd have a tie on nonetheless. He slipped on a moderately unwrinkled pair of khakis and a pink button-down shirt.

He hadn't drunk as much yesterday, so he felt relatively normal, whatever normal was. And relatively in control. It was a good thing; he had thirty minutes for an hour's drive.

The Porsche hummed beneath him as he sped past the Presbyterian Church in record time and across the Dawhoo River. He did slow down slightly so he wouldn't completely destroy his front-end alignment as he swerved onto the dirt driveway. Then he hit the accelerator again and flew past the live oaks, past the draping moss, past the gardens, past the wisteria in front of the house, at last careening to a stop in a cloud of dust next to Mary Catherine's Volkswagen.

He jumped out and took the stairs two by two, grateful that he'd get a good meal and some cash.

———

"Come on, children, dinner's a-ready," Esau announced in what was left of his singsong Gullah, the Geechee dialect. It was a Creole language, beautiful and musical and still widely heard in the Low Country. As a little girl, Elizabeth had loved it and tried to imitate it, and even now it still had a way of bringing her a brief fondness for her childhood. Esau had Americanized his language through the years, but he could still break into a mean Gullah when he was with his friends. Elizabeth loved to listen to him in those moments, hearing the flow of the language, feeling the pleasure its familiarity brought.

She followed her siblings into the dining room, and everyone took their usual seats, as if their parents still existed. Jeffrey at the head of the table—or the tail, depending on who you asked. Will on Jeffrey's left and Esau on the right, with Mary Catherine next to Esau and Elizabeth on Will's side. The deeply etched habits of life were not easily erased.

Her father had always insisted that Esau eat at his table. In the deep South, in the early years when the Ku Klux Klan was still burning crosses on yards, Clayton Wilcott paid no attention to the social expectations of his class and status. "If you're good enough to prepare it, Esau," Daddy would tell him, "then you're good enough to sit at this table and enjoy it with me."

Esau grinned at them as he took his own seat at the table. "Now say you some grace and get filled up with you some ba'becue."

Elizabeth bowed her head awkwardly. The others followed suit. No one spoke. The silence lengthened. Someone coughed.

"My Lord, mercy, mercy. Ain't nobody know how to pray?" Esau shook his head. "Lord, thank you for your blessings this day. Bless this food and these here chi'ren. Amen."

Will snatched the barbecue from the center of the table and scooped out a serving big enough for an entire congregation at a covered-dish dinner.

Elizabeth glared at him. "Will, quit acting like you're from a third-world country and have never eaten."

Will bugged his eyes at her as he spooned up a big helping of rice and covered it with hash. "You know, I've got some friends who actually went to a third-world country one time. They said they couldn't find any food to save their life. Said they nearly starved to death." He sucked down a forkful of rice and hash.

"So, Will, what are you going to do? Work for Habitat for Humanity or something?" Jeffrey was baiting him, and Elizabeth knew it. She found his transparency irritating.

Will, however, seemed clueless. He laughed, took a mouthful of barbecue, and still managed to answer Jeffrey's question. "You mean that Jimmy Carter group that builds houses for poor people? No way. I've got a couple more good years of school, I figure—except that something's gone screwy with my trust. I've gotta get it straightened out next week so I can pay my tuition and register. But after school, who knows? I might get a *real* job."

Elizabeth felt a string of barbecue lodge itself in her throat. She might need the Heimlich maneuver before this dinner was done. "You? Get a real job?"

"Yeah, I've got a hookup with some fraternity brothers who are working on this big deal with somebody at Microsoft or something like that. And once this whole farce is over, and I get my inheritance, then I'll be able to give them the funding to create something bigger than even Bill Gates could imagine."

"*I've* got a new job," Mary Catherine interrupted.

Elizabeth saw the shock register on Jeffrey's face. Obviously he hadn't thought Mary Catherine would play this game.

"What kind of job?" he asked.

"I'm going to be teaching. Actually *using* my degree."

"So you're going along with this too?" Will asked through a mouthful of cornbread.

"You really don't think Dad's telling the truth?" Mary Catherine shot back. "You just said yourself your tuition isn't paid for. *Of course* I'm going along with this, Will. I don't have another choice."

"You're an idiot, Mary Catherine. You're going to get to the end of this thing and be kicking yourself around the block for throwing away a perfectly good year on what? Some underprivileged snot-nosed brats?"

Mary Catherine's lower lip began to tremble. Nobody paid any attention.

"What about you, Elizabeth? What are you doing?" Jeffrey asked.

Will shoveled another mound of hash into his mouth. "Yeah, Elizabeth, how are you making it through?"

Elizabeth turned her gaze to Jeffrey. "Everything is working out fine, exactly according to plan. How about you, Jeffrey? What's it like not being able to Botox something?"

"Don't worry about my practice. It's in exceptional hands, and I've already been at my new position for several days. I can't wait to see how many lives I impact through this *incredible* experience."

If it were Oscar night, Jeffrey would have walked offstage with a little gold naked man. Elizabeth turned on him. "You're such a pathetic liar. How are you really doing, working with Dr. Nadu?"

His cornbread stopped midway to his mouth. "Perfect. He's an exceptional physician."

Mary Catherine interrupted them both. "Has anyone wondered if someone put Daddy up to this?"

Jeffrey turned pale. "What makes you think that?"

"It's just odd. I came out here a lot on Saturdays to spend time with him, and it seems—well, unlike him. What if he was black-mailed? What if he had a love child or something?" She whispered it, as if that would make it more believable.

Nobody responded to this ludicrous idea, and after a minute of silence, Mary Catherine got the message. "Well, Tony Randall had a baby when he was in his seventies. Disgusting, I know, but no less doable."

"It's not totally crazy," Will chimed in. "I have a fraternity brother who has a five-year-old sister that's his daddy's love child. I hear it happens all the time. Didn't think our old man had it in him, but who knows about people nowadays?" The great philosopher dug back into his coleslaw.

"But couldn't it be possible?" Mary Catherine looked straight at Elizabeth as if she expected a response.

"You know what, Mary Catherine," Elizabeth snapped, "you may want to worry less about our father's phantom love child and more about what that husband of yours is up to."

Mary Catherine's face registered the blow, and her voice went up half an octave. "Don't talk about my husband."

"Quit your whining, Cat!" Jeffrey said, throwing his napkin down beside his plate. "You need to just grow up. If you want to be whining or crying to somebody, why don't you go out there to that grave of your dear old sweet daddy and cry to him! Because I frankly don't give a flip about hearing it."

Elizabeth took note of Jeffrey's anger. She hadn't expected it from him. He was a better actor than she thought . . . or else he wasn't behind this at all.

"You know, I have a friend whose dad is a family therapist. It might not be a bad thing for all of y'all to consider," Will said. He reached over for another whopping spoonful and let the barbecue splatter across his plate.

———

Esau started to chew at the inside of his jaw. He didn't have to know the details to understand what was going on. The competition around his dinner table was enough to prove that boundaries and conditions had been set on their daddy's fortune.

At last he'd had enough.

"Get up!" he shouted as he pushed his chair back. "Get up each one of ya!"

Mary Catherine's whining ceased. Will's fork fell to the side of his plate. Elizabeth's eyes widened, and Jeffrey stared in shock.

"Get up and out that door and away from this table. I'm gonna take you ungrateful children on a trip."

chapter fifteen

"What is this place?" Elizabeth asked.

It was a tiny blue house all the way on the other side of Edisto Island, facing Highway 176. Dozens of vehicles were parked all around it, at odd angles, and Esau wedged his car in, just barely, between an old pickup and a battered Chevy.

"This here, Elizabeth, is where me an' you chi'ren's daddy would come most every night of the week, but 'specially on Saturday nights and Sunday afternoon for dinner."

A tattered sign out front read "Gullah Home Cookin'"—a redundancy, Elizabeth thought, to anyone who knew what Gullah cooking was.

Jeffrey slammed his door. "What's this about, Esau? I've got things to do today."

Esau's coal-black eyes stared through Jeffrey as he spoke. "This is about learning somethin' 'bout your daddy. Somethin' you never took time to do. Believe it or not, you don't know everything. Now get to steppin'."

"Esau!" a heavy black lady hollered as she came out of the kitchen, still carrying her spatula. "Haven't seen you since Mr. Wilcott passed, God give rest to his sweet soul."

"I know. Haven't felt much like getting back to the normal."

She patted his lean back. "We misses him too, Esau. We misses him so much."

Elizabeth stared at the stranger and was struck by her apparent intimate knowledge of their father.

"This here is Miss Mae Jacobson," Esau said. "Mae, these is Mr. Wilcott's chi'ren." He sat down at a long table covered in a white vinyl tablecloth. "Can you get us some of that there delicious cobbler you fix?"

"Gotcha fives a-comin'!" Mae headed back toward the kitchen.

"There is somethins you chi'ren need to know 'bout your daddy. Your daddy wasn't selfish like you fours have turned out to be. The way your mama raised you, I can't believe you come out this way. But apparently this here is how you are. Your daddy was a fine man. I know he didn't dote on you like you deserved after your mama died. But he loved each of yous. And I'm not gonna let you disrespect him no matter what you think he's done to you."

Elizabeth tried not to roll her eyes. She folded her hands and placed them on the tablecloth, where they stuck fast to the vinyl.

"What about our daddy?" Mary Catherine asked.

"Your daddy came here ever' Saturday night. He'd get up in here and play the saxophone of his for these here sweet people."

"Our father never played the saxophone," Jeffrey said. "He didn't even like instruments in the house. After Mom died he got rid of the piano."

"Your daddy didn't hate music, Jeffrey. And despite what you've all gone to thinkin', he didn't get rid of that piano to go and torture you either. He got rid of it because every time he looked at it he saw your mother. He heard her hands running across them keys, and it made his heart ache so."

Elizabeth felt the pang of a long-forgotten memory rushing back to the surface. Esau turned in her direction. "And every time he saw you sitting there playing them keys with your pretty little fingers, he saw your mother."

He cut his eyes back to Jeffrey. "So, when I tell you something, don't you go sassin' me. If I tell you your daddy played the saxophone, then he played the saxophone."

Mary Catherine scooted her chair closer to the table. "Who taught him?"

"One of the fellas that went with me to church started coming over a couple nights a week and teachin' him. Your father told me how sorry he was for taking that piano out the house. He knew how much that hurt you, Elizabeth."

She turned her head and stared out the window. "Well, he never told me."

"You can't tell people things when they don't care nothing 'bout talking to you."

Elizabeth kept her mouth shut and her eyes averted. She wouldn't give him the satisfaction of a response.

"So your daddy would come down here every Saturday night and try out what he'd gone and learned that week," Esau continued, laughing at the memory. "They was some forgiving souls, let me tell you. He'd always pick on little Macy Simmons over there and lean down to her and say, 'How you like it, Macy?' And she'd just blush as much as a black person can, and he'd go to playin' again. He'd play for two or three hours."

"Why do we need to know this?" Elizabeth demanded.

Esau's response was interrupted by Mae returning with five enormous bowls of peach cobbler. When Mae had gone, he picked up his spoon and waved it at them. "Because not a one of you 'preciate nothing 'bout your daddy."

Elizabeth glared at him. "Right now, Esau, the issue isn't how we appreciated our father but how he appreciated us."

"I can tell that will has all you chi'ren fit to be tied, but whatever your daddy gone and done, he done for your own good. And if you got trouble remembering that, then try to visualize him down here on a Saturday night doing nothing but makin' folks happy. No matter what you think bout your daddy, that is all he tried to do for you. Maybe he shoulda whipped your butts more and given you less. Then you might be able to 'preciate a little more than you do."

They all sat in silence as Will and Esau ate. Nobody else seemed to want any dessert. Mary Catherine played with hers until the ice cream melted into a puddle. Jeffrey sat and fumed, the muscle in his jaw working overtime.

Elizabeth ignored them all and tried to process this new revelation about their father—a father who had no concern for his own children but enough for strangers to give them music every Saturday night.

———

Esau picked up the ringing phone from the edge of Mr. Clayton's walnut desk.

"I just saw them all leave. How did it go?" The British accent made Esau smile. It sounded so . . . elegant.

"Lord have mercy, if they survive this, the heavens ain't yet run short of miracles."

"Elizabeth and Jeffrey already have private investigators. I don't want them suspecting anything about you."

"The only way they'll go and find things 'bout me is if you slip up. You got to be makin' sure all your tracks been covered."

"That is what they pay me to do. Good luck in your part to play."

"My part ain't so hard. Same part I've always played with these chi'ren. Protecting their father's interests."

The line disconnected, and Esau went back to what he knew. Taking care of Wisteria Plantation.

chapter sixteen

Nate cursed underneath his breath.

"I heard that," Mary Catherine said. She opened the rear gate on the small U-Haul. "Don't forget you're the one who got me this job."

She had dragged him and one of his friends out of their beds almost before the sun was up. She needed time to renovate her class-room before the kids got there. She wanted to take their breath away as soon as they entered the room.

Nate and his buddy unloaded a beautiful carved antique book-case, the sofa she had made the slipcover for, and a leather ottoman she had put in storage. She arranged each one neatly in the back cor-ner to make a reading room and put huge throw pillows on the floor for extra seating. She hung children's artwork she had purchased from a charity event all around the room and a bulletin board collage of book jackets from all her favorite childhood books. When that was done, she arranged valances made from leftover throw pillow fabric and brought in an antique chair to sit by her desk just in case any of them needed extra attention.

Grumpy and sweaty and still half asleep, Nate left her with a peck on the cheek.

Mary Catherine was surprised at her own excitement. She laid her lesson plans for the week in front of her on her desk. Over the weekend she had done research on appropriate reading lists for middle schoolers and gone over the curriculum that Mr. McClain had sent her. She even gave her best shot at lesson plans, but hoped no one would ever see them.

A deep, rich voice filtered in from the hallway. "Good morning, ladies."

"Good morning, Mr. McClain," came the singsong response. Three young girls entered the classroom giggling, with the principal right behind them.

Mary Catherine's pulse began to race. She breathed in and out several times, then stood up, straightening her skirt and running her hands through her ponytail.

"This is your new teacher, Mrs. Bean," Mr. McClain said.

The threesome didn't even notice her. They were too busy taking in all of the new decorations that had appeared overnight. "Is this like *Extreme Home Makeover* or something?"

"Nice job," the principal said. "Hope you didn't bring anything too precious."

"Thank you, sir."

"What did you say your name was again?" one of the girls finally asked. "Bean? Like butter bean?"

Mary Catherine was suddenly certain that changing her name to Nate's was the biggest mistake she could have made. She should have kept Wilcott. Elizabeth would keep Wilcott if she ever got married.

"You mean somebody named you *bean?*"

"How about you just call me Mary Catherine."

Their eyes widened.

"Um, Mrs. Bean, I'm sorry, but we don't allow our students to call their teachers by their first name. It's a matter of respect." He turned his gaze on the three girls.

"Yeah, we have to show respect to our elders," one said grudgingly.

Mary Catherine had officially become an elder.

"Mrs. Bean, I'll leave you now," Mr. McClain said. "We'll talk later about your lesson plans." He turned to go, then looked back. "Oh, one more thing. We teach the children here respect, Mrs. Bean, but it's not something that can be forced. You have to earn it. Good luck."

He left her there standing in the doorway. The three children eyed her oddly, then simply abandoned her as they went to the back of the room to check out the books in the bookcase.

Other students began to file in. She recognized Terrance, the boy whose girlie magazine had been confiscated. "What happened to this place?" he asked as he tossed his books on his desk.

She tugged at the edges of her denim jacket, as if straightening it could make her more of an educator. "I did some redecorating."

"I'd say. This place doesn't even look like a classroom."

"Well, it's supposed to make you feel more at home. You know, relaxed. I think you'll learn better that way."

"Lady, I don't come to school to relax." He plopped down on the sofa, tossing his hands behind his head and putting his feet up on the ottoman. "You got a name?"

She began writing today's lesson on the dry-erase board. "Uh-huh."

His two friends came in through the door and stopped at the entrance. He laughed at their expressions, but he didn't lose track of his conversation "So what is it?"

She kept her back to him. "Mrs. Bean."

"Mrs. Bean?" One of Terrance's buddies hooted with laughter. By the time the rest of the class entered, she didn't have to repeat her name again.

"Class, I want you to get out your English books and turn to page 45."

She heard the commotion of the turning pages and felt a small sense of accomplishment already. Mrs. Bean or not, she was still the teacher.

But when she turned to face the class, an auburn-haired girl in the middle of the room sat slumped in her desk, blue eyes glaring at Mary Catherine, her book closed and her expression daring Mary Catherine to say a word.

Terrance's voice interrupted the flutter of pages. "We already done these pages."

"Excuse me?" Mary Catherine asked, turning her attention to Terrance's interruption.

"I *said*, we already read this. With that substitute woman who filled in before you got here. We ain't going to waste our time rereading a bunch of stuff that was stupid the first time." He flipped his book shut.

"Yeah!" others around the room echoed.

Mary Catherine tried to collect herself. She had done practice teaching, but it didn't prepare her for anything like this. Kindergarten kids only talked back to each other, never to their teacher. These kids were like a pack of circling animals, and she was sure they could smell her fear.

"You're not suppose to say ain't," a girl's voice spoke from the middle of the room

"Shut up, Charmaine! You ain't the teacher." He emphasized the *ain't.*

The auburn-haired girl stood up from her seat and approached Mary Catherine's desk. The child had to be at least five foot six. What kind of fertilizer were these kids fed anyway?

"You know, lady," she said, "if all you gonna do is waste our time with stuff we already learned, we ain't going to sit around here just staring at you." The girl laid her pale hands on top of another's student's desk in the front row and tossed her hair to one side.

"Leave her alone, Nicole!" Charmaine said.

Nicole flung her head around. "Charmaine, you need to mind your own business and quit trying to be such a suck-up! Mrs. Jarvis ain't here this year, so your days of being the teacher's pet are over! You got that?"

Charmaine's steady and confident gaze never left Nicole's glaring look.

"*Isn't,*" Mary Catherine corrected. "Mrs. Jarvis *isn't* here this year."

Nicole cut her eyes in Mary Catherine's direction. She put her hand over her mouth and said mockingly, "Oh, *excuse* me. *Isn't.*" She turned a sneering gaze on the decorations in the classroom. "You bring all this stuff from your house?"

Mary Catherine took a step toward Nicole. "That 'stuff' is antiques. And, yes, it is from my house."

Nicole ran her hand across the carving at the top of the antique bookcase. "So you don't want it messed up, right?"

"You need to get your hand off of that."

"What? I can't touch our new stuff?"

Now Mary Catherine remembered why she hated teaching. Her eyes darted to the red Magic Marker in Nicole's hands, but she couldn't stop it. As if in slow motion the red marker made its way across the first row of books, down the matte finish of the bookcase, and back up again. Every ounce of air was sucked from Mary Catherine's lungs.

Nicole snapped the cap back on the marker and strode toward the front of the class like a commander addressing her new recruits. "Now, *I* say we all go make the best of a lovely morning."

A groan escaped Mary Catherine lips.

"What's that?" Nicole scooped her hand around her ear. "Ladies and gentleman, our little butter bean has spoken. We are to go explore the day and have us a free period."

And with that, every single child but one exited the room and made haste to the playground.

Mary Catherine never even turned her head toward the door. She simply walked over to her bookcase and stood there, running her hand over the marked spines and ruined wood,

Charmaine came over and stood beside her. "Mrs. Bean, don't let the uniforms fool you. We're not a nice clean bunch of prep schoolers. You're going to have to get a grip if you're going to control this group of kids."

Mary Catherine tried to respond, but couldn't. The tears were too close to the surface.

"Let me tell you about Nicole," Charmaine went on. "That girl's been through more foster homes than you can count. She's hard and mean and ornery. You've got to show her who is boss. And Terrance? Trouble follows him like cockroaches to dark places. But his mama and daddy are tough on him. I promise you he doesn't talk like that at home. Just tell him you're going to call his parents—it will scare him to death. And if you keep a tight rein on the two of them, you won't have to worry about the rest. They don't have minds of their own anyway."

Charmaine patted Mary Catherine on the shoulder. "And don't you worry about your name, Mrs. Bean. Eventually they'll find somebody else to make fun of. But when they come back in here—and trust me, they'll come back, because once Mr. McClain finds them, they'll all be serving detention for a week—you'll need to take charge pretty quick. The longer you let them control this classroom, the worse they'll be."

Mary Catherine looked up into the girl's dark, intelligent eyes. If she only had a few more Charmaines, she might get through this year without running out of Prozac prescriptions. But she had her doubts.

Elizabeth sat at a small table in the Starbucks on King Street, waiting. She had to see Aaron one more time just to make sure he was ready. By the time he arrived she already had two large cups in front of her.

"What did you order?" he asked, giving her a kiss on the cheek.

"I got you a regular old Joe Schmoe coffee. I got a double espresso."

He laughed. "I can only imagine why. So how was the family dinner yesterday?"

"I've had pap smears more enjoyable."

"Spoken like a true Southern lady."

"I can get past Jeffrey and his pompous attitude, even past Will and his ignorance or Mary Catherine and her miserable personality. But what I can't get past is how my father had time to make other people's lives enjoyable, play music on a saxophone, but he had no appreciation for me. Did you know this? Did you know that every Saturday night my father would go down to the Gullah restaurant with Esau and play for the people while they ate?"

Aaron took a drink of his coffee. "Actually, I did."

She stared at him. "You did not."

"Yes, I did. I went to see your father quite often on Saturdays. Then he, Esau, and I would go to the Gullah place and eat some of the best shrimp you've ever put in your mouth. Usually finished it off with either peach cobbler or blackberry cobbler. Mae Jacobson is one of the best cooks in the Low Country, you know."

Elizabeth's mouth dropped open.

"What? Elizabeth Wilcott is speechless?"

"You *knew?*"

"I believe that is what I just said."

"How did you know? Why did he let *you* know?"

She hadn't intended it to come out as if Aaron wasn't good enough to know, but that's how it sounded. He didn't miss the insult. His face flushed and his eyes shifted, but he did not comment on the slight.

"You want to know how I knew, Elizabeth?" He leaned in across the table. "Because unlike you, *I* took time to listen to your father. And unlike *you,* my life doesn't revolve around me. That's how *I* know a thousand things about your father that you don't."

Since the kidnapping and the reading of the will, Elizabeth had felt a red-hot fury simmering just below the surface. Now it threatened to erupt. With some effort she pushed it back down.

Aaron went on. "Do you remember that your father would call you every week, Lizzy?"

She raised an eyebrow.

"That's okay, you can sit there and pretend you don't remember. It was on Saturday—every Saturday morning, as I recall. Why do you suppose he called you on Saturday, Lizzy? You think maybe your father might have wanted you to go with him? Show you what he had learned? Maybe try to make up for some of the lost years in the process? But you never took his calls, did you?"

He stood up and gave her a peck on the cheek. "Now, I'm leaving you to sulk because that is what you're best at. You might not want to waste a great deal of time on it, because you do have a new job to start tomorrow. And who knows, if you let yourself, you might learn a thing or two in this process. Becoming less self-absorbed might be a good place to start. Because it wasn't your father who never had time for you, Lizzy. You never had time for him."

She watched him walk away knowing they hadn't covered one thing. Not one thing of importance anyway.

Elizabeth fumed on the way to her car. She flung her briefcase into the passenger's seat. It was much lighter than usual—another reminder of all that was missing. Gone were the folders filled with pending cases. Gone were her beautiful office and her parking lot. Gone were her employees and her developers. Gone . . . gone . . . gone.

She *had* to find the Executor and his cohort and get this fraud of her father's will revealed and reversed. None of it made sense. Jeffrey was playing his own game. And because Jeffrey was playing, she was forced to play.

She wished she could put it all aside, empty her mind the way she had emptied her briefcase, and let it all go.

The Benefactor's Group was housed in a mud-colored brick building that offered no welcome at all, no invitation. It also offered no parking. Elizabeth left the Jeep on the street and waded through the papery grass to the sidewalk that led to a chipped and faded front door.

She took a deep breath, opened the door, and stepped inside. The scent of grapefruit overwhelmed her—the odor of a cheap candle that didn't even begin to mask the musty, mousy smell. Gray Styrofoam partitions divided the office into cubicles, and everywhere stacks of law books overflowed rickety wooden bookcases and spilled over onto a floor covered with shabby navy blue carpet.

"Well, well, if it isn't Elizabeth Wilcott."

Elizabeth bristled at the sound of the obnoxious voice.

"I see you've made your decision."

Elizabeth turned and faced Ainsley Parker. "I'm here to work."

"Well then, work you shall. Come on, I'll show you around."

Ainsley started walking through the maze. Elizabeth assumed she was to follow.

"These are our offices. Hopefully we will get larger ones later, but right now we're trying to conserve our funds for more important purposes."

Ainsley slid a stack of books to the other side of a desk and cleared another stack from the seat of a black armless office chair. She plopped them on the floor behind the chair. "These are the staff attorneys' cubicles. You can take this one. My office is back there, the one with the glass wall. That way I can keep my eye on you." She pointed behind.

Elizabeth swallowed down a sarcastic response. Who did that surprise?

"The office is pretty quiet at the moment. Everyone is already out in the field—interviewing clients, filing motions. All those sort of things we lawyers do. You'll notice there is no receptionist."

"Is she out in the field as well?" Elizabeth muttered.

"No, she doesn't exist. *We* are the receptionist. We take turns. Cover what needs to be covered. Do what needs to be done. It keeps us humble."

Humble wasn't exactly a word Elizabeth would apply to Ainsley Parker, but she kept her mouth shut for the moment. "So who was that who answered the phone the other day, a law clerk?" She narrowed her eyes. "You do you have law clerks, right?"

Ainsley let out a piercing laugh. "Of course we have law clerks. But they're out in the field today too. Everybody hits the ground running on Monday. And most of our work is done outside the office anyway."

Well, Elizabeth thought, at least that was one thing to be grateful for. If it didn't matter where she worked as long as things got done, she might even go back to her own office. She wondered if the provisions of the will would allow for that.

"To tell the truth," Ainsley said, "I'm kind of surprised you showed up. I didn't know if you'd really come get your hands dirty with the likes of us. But since you're here, I'm going to head out as well. You can play receptionist today and get yourself acclimated."

Ainsley grabbed an oversized black tote bag from a desk chair and threw it across her shoulder. She gave Elizabeth a hard slap on the arm. "I'm really glad you're here, Liz. I think this will change your life."

"It's Elizabeth."

"Yeah, yeah, get over all that prim and proper stuff, sweetie. We're all just family around here. Oh, but if it makes you feel better, we have one amazing coffeemaker in this office. And if you're still the

coffee snob that you were in college, I know you'll appreciate him."
And out she walked.

Elizabeth watched the door slam shut. When Ainsley was gone,
she stood motionless in the middle of this strange, confined, and
rather pungent environment. Once her eyes caught sight of the
offensive fruity candle, she walked right to it and blew it out, then
went on a mad search for the person, whoever he was, who made
such fabulous coffee.

The small kitchen was located in the back of the office building
across from the restroom. She tried to ignore the proximity. Kitchens
too close to restrooms gave her the creeps, and coffeepots in hotel
bathrooms made her gag reflex go into overdrive.

A lime green dish drainer sat on the top of the counter filled with
about ten coffee cups. Apparently most people in this office had the
same addiction.

No one was back there. Elizabeth scanned the tiny kitchen and
found nothing. Apparently this "amazing coffeemaker" guy Ainsley
had referred to hadn't done his job this morning. She searched
around, hoping to find a system like she had in her own office.

Then she saw it, and the mocking irony of Ainsley's words made
the blood rush to her face: *If you're still the coffee snob that you were
in college, I know you'll appreciate him.*

An old black plastic Mr. Coffee machine sat in one corner, with
a glass pot that looked to have been used for the better part of the
current decade.

"Coffee snob, huh?" she muttered under her breath. "Forget this,
Ainsley Parker. I don't have to live with your snotty little—"

The telephone rang. She left the kitchen and went to the receptionist counter, staring down at the phone as if she had never laid
eyes on such a contraption. In her office, calls were put through *to*
her, not answered first *by* her.

"Hello, Benefactor's Group," she said, refusing to say her name.

"Just making sure you know how to answer a phone." Ainsley's
voice was grating even when she wasn't in the room. "Did you find
the coffeemaker to your satisfaction?"

Elizabeth snapped. "Go to—"

"Now, now," Ainsley chided. "Let's not burn any bridges with the boss on the very first day. Glad to know you're a part of our team. Have a great day, Liz." The line went dead.

"My name's not Liz!" Elizabeth screamed into the receiver. The pulsing tone of the disconnected call sounded a great deal like chuckling.

chapter seventeen

As Jeffrey pulled into the Medical University physician's parking lot, he hit redial and got the investigator's voice mail. Again.

The man was not returning his calls. His mind raced out of control. For all he knew, the investigator was in cahoots with the Executor. What if the investigator had found something, and the Executor paid him off?

It was possible. Jeffrey knew he was being watched. He could feel it. Sense it. Besides, the Executor had told him he would be under constant scrutiny. If the Executor knew every move Jeffrey made, then surely he was aware that Jeffrey had hired an investigator to find him.

He felt the sweat gather in the armpits of his starched white shirt. He hated sweat-stained shirts. They never looked the same again.

Dr. Nadu was waiting for him, surrounded by a swarm of residents and interns. "Good morning, Dr. Wilcott. I hope you are ready to get your hands dirty this week."

"Yes, sir, I certainly am. I do my best work in the operating room." Jeffrey looked forward to teaching these young students a thing or two.

"I'm glad to hear that. Follow me, please."

Dr. Nadu set off, his white coat flowing behind him, his black sneakers squeaking on the tile floor, the residents and interns following in his wake like baby ducklings. Jeffrey picked up his pace as his expensive Bailey Florsheims drew even with Dr. Nadu. One way or another, he had to stake out his territory, let people around here know he was Nadu's equal.

When they finally reached a door marked Research Lab, Jeffrey hesitated. He knew from his own med school days that much of an intern or resident's education took place in the lab, though he had always preferred hands-on experience. He stepped back, letting the students enter before him. He'd just wait for Dr. Nadu out here until he had given them their assignments for the day.

But apparently Dr. Nadu had other plans. When the last student had filed through, Dr. Nadu gave him a curt nod. "After you." Jeffrey smiled awkwardly and proceeded through the door.

The smell of formaldehyde was overwhelming. In the center of the room lay a stainless steel autopsy table and a cadaver.

"Dr. Wilcott, this is Dr. Randall," Nadu said, indicating the young resident at his elbow. "You and the interns will be working with him this week. The rest of the residents will be with me."

The resident offered him a sheepish smile. Jeffrey offered none in return. "You're leaving me in here with a bunch of interns and researchers?"

"You can go home if you wish, Dr. Wilcott. No one is holding you here. But if you are to work with me, then you will respect Dr. Randall, listen to what he has to say, and learn from him." And with that Dr. Nadu left as if nothing else needed to be said.

When Nadu was gone, Dr. Randall turned to Jeffrey. "Do you know how good that man is, Dr. Wilcott? He is one of the foremost authorities on face transplants in the world."

"Yeah, well, I do face transplants too," Jeffrey muttered. "I move them back about ten years."

Dr. Randall did not laugh. Instead he turned to the cluster of intense young interns. "Who can tell me what the major cause of death is in the first four decades of a person's life?"

One student raised her hand. "Severe trauma, sir. It outnumbers even cancer and heart disease."

Jeffrey didn't know this, but he refused to act impressed. He wouldn't give Nadu—or this infantile Dr. Randall—the satisfaction.

"You did *what?*" Nate shouted.

Mary Catherine lay on the sofa with her feet propped up on a pillow, a cold washcloth stretched across her head. "Don't yell, Nate. It makes my head worse."

"You just *left* when you were supposed to be watching those children?"

"*Children?* They aren't children! Children are human. These are beasts. Mongrels! Horrible little creatures!" She sat up, and the washcloth slid awkwardly down her face. She jerked it up and slapped it back onto her forehead. "They *mocked* me. They slithered around like little snakes waiting to devour me as their prey. And you don't even want to know what they did to me at lunch."

"It's only a year."

"It will take a year to recover!" She threw her head back on the pillow.

He sat down on the end of the sofa and began to massage her feet. "Pookie, you've got to remember the goal. It's only one year. I'm certain you can do this. Just remember your brothers and sister. I wonder if they've started their jobs."

He moved his hands up to her calves. "You just go in there and let them know who's boss, and I'm sure it will be perfect." He lay down beside her and kissed her softly on the neck. "I know you can win them over just like you did me."

She returned his kiss. He *could* be rather convincing, when he tried. She smelled a foreign fragrance on him. It distracted her, just briefly.

"I *can't* go back," she wailed. "I *can't.*"

He moved his kisses to her cheek, and then to her mouth. "You *can.* You can do this, baby doll. You can do it because at the end, you'll be the last sibling standing."

⁓

At a quarter to six, Elizabeth was crawling down Meeting Street in a snarl of brake lights. She had never seen this kind of traffic; she was at work before most of them woke up and didn't leave the office until most of them were three drinks into happy hour at their favorite bar.

The traffic came to a standstill in front of the Charleston County Courthouse. With a surge of rage, Elizabeth realized that her next trip there would not be as Elizabeth Wilcott, respected attorney at law, but as Liz Wilcott, no-account receptionist for Ainsley Parker. The very thought made her honk irritably at the car in front of her and swear under her breath.

Elizabeth had arranged to meet Aaron at the FIG restaurant—an acronym for Food Is Good. She loved the bistro atmosphere, the eclectic menu, and Chef Michael Lata's fanaticism for organic foods. And the coffee. Good coffee.

She had already downed most of a pot before Aaron made it to the table. She ran her hands across the white tablecloth and leaned back in her chair. "Is my business still afloat?"

Aaron sat across from her and ordered a glass of sweet tea for himself. "Nice to see you too. And how was your day, Aaron?" He answered his own question in a mocking singsong: "My day was wonderful, Lizzy. And yes, your business is fine. However, you look like crap."

"The same to you, thank you very much. I'm thrilled that you had such a wonderful day. I, however, am just having my first cup of coffee, and it's almost 6:15 p.m. For the last eight hours I've sat with a phone glued to my ear, answering questions regarding legalities I have absolutely no interest in. So looking like crap is a rather fine achievement, I'd say."

Aaron ignored her and opened his menu. "Mmm, the hanger steak with bordelaise sounds delicious. What are you thinking about?"

"Two of everything."

The waitress returned with another refill of coffee before she took their order. Aaron ordered the hanger steak for himself and the pepper-seared tuna for Elizabeth. It was her favorite, but she was too obsessed with Ainsley Parker to have the grace to thank him.

"That woman's going to make her point no matter what."

"And what point is that?"

"The point she's always had to make with me—that she is in control. She's a control freak, you know."

He rested his elbows on the table, placing his head in his upright hands. "You don't have to go back, Lizzy."

"Nice try, Aaron. But I wrote the book on reverse psychology. I will go back, and you know it. Because you know me."

He leaned back in his chair and waited.

"The thing that gets me more than anything," Elizabeth ranted, "is that fake sweet act of hers. Honestly, the whole thing just reeks."

"You went to her for the job, remember?"

"And as I recall, you're the one who thought I should take up this ridiculous challenge. It's a—" She stopped midsentence. "No. It can't be."

He leaned forward. "What?"

"You don't think *Ainsley* could have anything to do with this, do you? I mean, out of the whole country, why would she pick Charleston? Why would she pick the one organization that's the greatest obstacle to *my* clients? I can't believe I haven't thought of this before."

He opened his mouth to respond, but she shushed him. She was already on the phone. "Ainsley Parker. Investigate her," she barked, then slammed the phone shut and laid it on the edge of the table. "That man has *got* to get an assistant!"

He palmed the phone and slid it to his side of the table. "I thought she told you not to even show up."

"My defenses are down. My mind isn't sharp. She wanted me to show, all right. And I went, and so she won that one too." She threw her hands ups in the air and reached for her coffee cup as her left hand came down. She blew and then sipped. "She's two for two. I'm losing by the hour."

The waitress arrived with their dinners.

"Eat, Lizzy," Aaron said. "Just eat."

⁓

And eat she did, never stopping to say another word.

As Aaron sat and watched her, he saw the child she worked so hard to hide, the child she never admitted was there. She tried to be so strong.

But he could no longer protect her from herself. If she chose to squander an opportunity that could possibly change her life, that might actually *give* her a life, he was not going to stop her. He was through playing her rescuer. Until she was willing to admit she needed rescuing, he was going to quit saving her from herself.

He kissed her good-bye on the sidewalk and headed home. No matter what she said, she would go back tomorrow. He knew she would. That was perhaps the only good thing about her competitive nature. It would keep her playing just a little longer.

Or until she won.

———

Will hit the eight ball into the corner pocket.

"You really think this whole college payment thing is just a mistake?" Tate asked. Tate and two of the new pledges hovered around the pool table, cues in hand.

Will racked a new set of balls. "I already called my dad's attorney, and he's getting right on it. Should be settled by tomorrow."

Tate went to Will's fridge, cue stick in hand, and peered in. "There's only half a pack of hot dogs in here. Where's the beer?"

"I haven't even had time to get any."

Will lifted the triangle from around the perfectly racked balls. Tate set down his cue stick and motioned to the other two. "We gotta get going. Got a few last minute things to pick up at the bookstore."

"What? We just got started."

"Yeah, but we've still got things to do at the fraternity house."

Will frowned. "Well, okay, I guess. I'll be over there later."

"You're bringing the keg right?"

"I got it all under control."

They closed the door behind them. Will chalked his stick, aimed at the cue ball, and popped it viciously. His cue stick slipped and stuttered across the surface of the table, leaving a ragged gash in the felt.

Under control. Right.

He had a bad feeling that things were just beginning to spin out of control.

chapter eighteen

Mary Catherine let her bare feet slide into the cool damp sand. She hadn't been able to sleep, so she and Coco had slipped out for an early morning walk. Seagulls chattered overhead, and sand crabs scurried away at Coco's lumbering paws. Coco ran ahead and circled back again, energized by the clear predawn air.

The sky was just beginning to lighten as they approached the house. Mary Catherine's pulse accelerated when she saw a dark figure silhouetted at the bottom of her steps that led down to the beach. The hairs on the back of her neck stood up.

Coco, of course, was useless. The Lab ran headlong toward the dark stranger, never barking, wagging her tail wildly.

Then she recognized him. It was Mr. McClain. If he was coming to her house at this hour of the morning, she was in deep trouble.

He stood up and shook the sand from the cuffs of his khaki pants. "Hello, Mary Catherine. Sorry to stop by unannounced like this. But we need to talk."

"Oh, it's no problem, really." The escalated treble in her voice gave her away. "Would you like to come inside for a minute?"

"I'd appreciate that."

She led him across the small wooden bridge into their backyard, around the pool, through the French doors, and into the kitchen. "Could I offer you something to drink?"

"No, thank you. I grabbed a biscuit and some juice on the way. I won't be here long, I promise."

She turned on lights and pulled a bottled water from the refrigerator, downing half of it before she was even willing to look at him again.

"You've got a beautiful home here, Mary Catherine." He ran his
hands across the walnut armoire in the breakfast room. "This carving is extraordinary."

She walked over to admire it with him. "I got that a couple years
ago on a trip to France. It's nineteenth century."

"I love the symmetrical precision of the French Empire pieces."

She tilted her head at him. "You know antiques?"

"Antiques, architecture, art—all passions of mine. If I hadn't
become a principal, I probably would have ended up selling fine
antiques and art."

Mary Catherine felt a little breathless. "Oh, me too. I love everything about antiques: the lines, the history, the styles. Every piece
tells a story—where it came from, who created it, what they were
feeling." She pointed to the painting over the fireplace. "Like this
Chagall here . . ."

"Is that a real Chagall?" His dark eyes widened as he moved
closer.

"They make fake ones?"

He laughed. "They make *prints*. Reproductions."

"That's appalling!"

He was still staring at the painting: the magnificence of it, the
sweeping drama of the colors, the varied images. "It's not appalling;
it's wonderful. It allows the magical work of this artist to be in more
homes, for others to enjoy the beauty of what he has created."

She hadn't quite thought of it like that. "I see your point."

"Can we sit?" He motioned toward the breakfast-room table.

She sank into a chair across from him, clutching at her bottle of
water.

"Mary Catherine," he said, "I like you. I hired you because I felt
it was the right thing to do. Now, I know our students can sometimes be difficult. But you left your classroom unattended, and that
is simply not acceptable, no matter what the circumstances. For that
alone, you should be fired on the spot."

He watched her with those calm dark eyes, letting this truth sink in. Mary Catherine said nothing. She couldn't speak past the lump in her throat.

"Now," he went on after a minute or two, "I am willing to give you one more chance." He held up an index finger. "Only one. And you have to come in with a different game plan, or you're never going to make it. Our teachers actually have to *teach*. That's what we pay them for."

"Yes, sir."

"Do you really want this job?" He narrowed his eyes at her.

She didn't tell him why, or what her ulterior motives might be. She simply said, "Yes, sir, I do."

"And you understand that things have to change. Starting now."

She nodded. "Starting now."

His expression grew distant and meditative. "You know, Mary Catherine, when I was in the second grade, a teacher called me retarded. I spent years thinking that was who I was, until one day another teacher looked me in the face and said, 'Don't you ever let what anyone says about you define who you are.'

"That statement changed my life. That is the power a teacher has. She can convince a child he is stupid or convince him he can rule the world. I see something in you, Mary Catherine. Something that you obviously don't see in yourself. You can do something important here, make a difference in the lives of these students, if you want to. But you can't do it for me or for any other reason. You have to do it because you believe that you have something to impart to these kids' lives."

He paused and got to his feet. "I'm asking you not to come back today unless you can believe that for yourself. These kids deserve that. And if they were honest, and didn't have to pretend to be cool, they would tell you so themselves."

———

The school was still quiet at seven thirty in the morning. Mary Catherine stood over the lesson plan book and ran her finger down

the lessons she herself, a certified teacher, had actually written. She
pulled the desk chair underneath her and scooted toward the desk,
and for the next thirty minutes she read over those lesson plans like
a teacher. A real teacher.

She was determined to try this all over again.

The warning bell rang, and students began to file into their
classroom.

"Well, looky, looky," Nicole said in her sneering drawl. "Mrs.
Butter Bean has graced us with her appearance once again." The girl
began her slow, cocky, and lumbering stride in Mary Catherine's
direction, advancing until they were almost nose to nose.

"You staring at me, Mrs. Bean?"

And in that moment something snapped. All movement in the
classroom ceased, and everyone turned to look.

Mary Catherine took a step forward, and her fear vanished. Nicole
took a step backward. With that one small step, Mary Catherine knew
she had control. No one spoke. No one even breathed.

"Nicole, despite what you may think, I'm the teacher of this
class." She took another step forward. Nicole's chest sank slightly.
"And it will be best advised for all of you"—she cast her gaze around
the room—"to remember that."

She turned back to Nicole. "You will sit down."

Nicole stood, still facing her.

"Now."

Nicole sat.

Mary Catherine walked to the front of the class and gave the
white erase board in front of her a rather substantial smile. Had she
not thought they'd notice, she'd have given it a high five too. Then
she turned around.

"Now, you are at school. And when you are at school, you learn.
So I suggest you open your English books."

A snickering laugh came from Terrance's direction.

She walked straight to Terrance's desk and stood in front of it.
"Something funny, Terrance?"

"Uh, no, ma'am. Nothing all that funny."

"Then find your English book." She turned back toward her desk and could hear the shuffling of books, the flipping of pages.

The sound of victory.

⁓

Elizabeth opened the door to be greeted by utter pandemonium.

The offices of the Benefactor's Group swarmed with bodies. Telephones were ringing everywhere. A young man who looked like a college student sat behind the receptionist's desk. For one brief moment she almost wished for the controlled chaos of yesterday.

A hand protruded into her space. "Ward Bennett," the kid at the reception desk said by way of introduction.

She studied his face, then scanned the rest of the group. Suddenly she felt ancient. She and Ainsley were the oldest people there.

"Elizabeth," she said. "Elizabeth Wilcott."

"Oh, I know." He flashed a goofy smile. "I know all about you, Ms. Wilcott. You and your family are famous in this city." He pushed his glasses up, scrunching his nose as if to hold them in place. "So, how did you like your initiation day?"

"My what?"

"Your initiation day. Yeah, it was Ainsley's idea. Let you have the place all to yourself. Answer the calls. Of course, she did transfer two of the office lines off-site so it wouldn't be like it is today." He gave a snorting laugh.

"Will you excuse me, um . . ."

"Ward, ma'am. It's Ward."

"Yes, Ward. I need to see someone." She turned her back on him and headed straight for Ainsley Parker's door. She didn't bother knocking; the door hit the doorstop and bounced back slightly.

A gray-haired woman was seated in front of Ainsley's desk and darted her head toward the door. Ainsley shifted a stack of papers and looked up.

"Well, Elizabeth! You joined us for another day, I see." She stood up. "I'd like you to meet—"

"Excuse me, ma'am." Elizabeth nodded to the woman and then returned her attention to Ainsley. "I wondered how long it would take you to prove that this 'little miss nice' role of yours was nothing but a pile of—" She cast a glance at the older woman. "Nothing but a charade. One day. It took one day."

"Elizabeth, I don't know what—"

"Save it, Ainsley. You hated me from the moment law school began. You thought you'd make my first day here miserable enough that I wouldn't have the guts to return." The gray-haired woman shifted slightly and looked in Ainsley's direction.

"Well, let me tell you something," Elizabeth went on, "you just got stuck with me for the next year whether you like it or not. I'm not going anywhere. And there is absolutely nothing you can do to get rid of me."

Ainsley leaned her weight against the edge of her desk and folded her arms. "Anything else?"

"Yes, I'd appreciate it if you'd quit pretending that you are something you're not. You've competed with me for years. Why pretend this isn't all about competition now? Go ahead, Ainsley, be the little boss. I'll follow your little rules, and we'll see who ends up on top when this year is all over with."

"Does that mean you're staying?" Ainsley asked with an annoying smile.

Elizabeth fumed. "That means the game you thought you won back in law school isn't over."

She turned to leave the office and heard behind her an exchange. The elderly lady said to Ainsley, "This will be interesting."

And Ainsley responded, "It always has been."

———

Will climbed into his Porsche and noticed the tank was on empty. He had to get back to the registrar's and get his tuition taken care of, and then he had to arrange for pizza and a couple of kegs for the frat house beer bust tonight. He was a genius at squeezing the last drops out of a tank, and he could probably wait until after the party, but he didn't want to take the chance of running out of gas at 2 a.m. and having some cop find him drunk along the roadside, rather than taking ten minutes now to fill up.

He pulled into the gas station two blocks from the fraternity house and chose the premium grade. You didn't fill a Porsche with cheap gas.

He stuck his MasterCard into the slot on the gas pump, leaned against the car, and waited for the pump to kick on. Nothing happened. The screen said, "Insert card again."

"Give me a break." He inserted the card again. This time the message said, "See attendant."

"You have got to be kidding me." He tried three more cards, including the American Express, which didn't have a limit. Same message.

Will slammed the car door and marched into the gas station, where a bleary-eyed college student jerked his head up from the counter. "Listen, you need to get out there and do something to that pump. It won't let me use any of my cards."

"Um, well, why don't you try using another pump? Maybe it's just got a short or something."

"That ever happened before?"

"Not that I know of."

Will moved his car, tried again, got the same message, and didn't even bother trying the other cards. He marched back into the gas station.

"All your pumps are broken."

"Huh, well, sorry about that. Want to pay with cash?"

"Cash?" The thought hadn't even occurred to him. He found two twenties wadded up in the side pouch of his wallet, pulled one out, and threw it on the counter.

Twenty bucks' worth wouldn't get him very far in a Porsche. First thing tomorrow he'd call Harvey at his father's office about his credit cards. This shouldn't have happened to him.

He was a Wilcott, after all, and Wilcotts were never out of money.

chapter nineteen

Ward the Geek slipped a document in front of Elizabeth. She raised her eyes, and he stepped back and withdrew his hand from the paper he had just laid on her desk.

"Ward, I'm not going to bite you."

His eyes didn't reveal that he actually believed her. "It's just— well, this will be your first case. Honestly, it may be your only case."

She looked down at the document in front of her.

"The client is Hazel Moses. But she's going up against one of the big guns. It's a company out of California that does a lot of developing around here."

Elizabeth scanned the yellow form rapidly. Then she saw it. *Everett and Associates.* Her client. Her company. She felt her morning coffee begin to work its way back up.

"You okay, Ms. Wilcott?"

"What?" She looked up and saw him still standing there. "Yeah, I'm fine. No problem. Sure you want to trust a newbie with an opponent this big?"

"Mrs. Parker said you would be the perfect one to handle it."

Elizabeth closed her eyes. She breathed in and out steadily, trying to calm herself. When she lifted her head, Ward was gone. The only one in her view was the red-headed she-devil behind the glass.

Elizabeth was certain she smelled smoke. Because she knew she had just landed in hell.

Will left the fraternity house and headed over to the ATM machine in the lobby of the Stern Center. After the fiasco with the credit card at the gas station last night, he thought it might be a good idea to keep a little change in his pocket.

The young-looking kid in front of him pulled out a pristine brown leather wallet and inserted his card.

"Just get that shirt?" Will asked, eyeing the starched and crisp Izod shirt.

The kid raised his head in a half nod. The alcohol from Will's breath filled the space between them.

"It looks nice on you. Really," Will said. He tugged a stray piece of thread from the frayed bottom of his ragged polo. "You a freshman?"

"Yeah," the kid said, pulling his money from the slot. "Just got here yesterday."

"Well, if you need anything, my name's Will," he said extending his hand. "I've been around awhile. Know just about everything there is to know. Just ask for Will, and people will know who you're looking for."

The kid opened his new wallet and tried to wedge his card back into the stiff slot. He stuck his cash inside and folded it back into his jeans pocket.

"Thanks. I really appreciate it."

Will turned his attention to the ATM in front of him. He reached into the front pocket of his torn jeans, retrieving his credit cards, which were held together by a large black paper clip. He pulled out the top one and stuck it into the slot. The noise assured him the machine was accomplishing something. He punched in his request, then his pin code, and waited. Then a terrible sound came from the guts of the machine—a grinding, tearing noise. The screen flashed a message: *Your card has been destroyed. Please notify your bank immediately.*

———

Jeffrey had never cared whether it was a Monday, a Wednesday, or a Friday. He had always set his own schedule, controlled his own life. Now, Friday had become his day of salvation.

A couple of residents stared at him as he strode down the hall to the boardroom. He didn't even bother to return their stares. He wasn't here to win friends and influence people. He was here to get what was rightfully his.

Dr. Nadu sat at the conference table.

"Hello, Dr. Nadu."

"Jeffrey. Sit, please."

Jeffrey still hated the arrogance of this man, continually telling him what to do, but nevertheless he sat. Dr. Nadu pushed the morning newspaper across the table. Jeffrey immediately recognized himself looking back from the front page. Even upside down, it was a pretty good picture.

He smiled. "I had completely forgotten this was coming out today." He picked up the paper and opened it. It was a long article touting Jeffrey's new venture at the Medical Hospital and his work with Dr. Nadu.

"I'm going to have to ask you to get your things and leave, Dr. Wilcott."

Jeffrey looked up sharply. "You're asking me to what?"

"I told you the first day we spoke that I would not allow what we do here to be exploited. Your work here is not some mission of mercy to further your career."

"But that's not what—"

Dr. Nadu stood. "I've made my decision, Dr. Wilcott. Your presence here is no longer needed or desired."

Jeffrey felt a foreign panic seeping into his blood. This couldn't be happening. This was a good day. It was Friday. He was on the cover of the newspaper. With a phenomenal picture, he might add. Pamela was a PR genius. He could pump this puppy for at least six months.

"Dr. Nadu, please let me explain."

Dr. Nadu paused.

Jeffrey fumbled for a lie that would sound believable. "This isn't what you think. I have this publicist see, and she's worked for months for this article. It just happened to be coming out at this time. What do you want me to do, tell these people no?"

Dr. Nadu's bushy black eyebrows twitched. "Get your things, Jeffrey." He opened the door to the boardroom. "I do not tolerate dishonesty."

Was this man psychic? Jeffrey walked over to the door and closed it. "What do you want from me?"

"I want the truth. And unless you are willing to give it, you will leave immediately and not return."

Jeffrey let out a sigh and sank into one of the conference chairs. "All right. You win. I have to be here. I can't tell you why. But I *have* to be here. And, yes, that article was all about me. It was about me wanting my face on the front page of the paper. Are you satisfied?"

Dr. Nadu didn't respond. He remained standing by the door as if he were waiting for more.

"And there is another article coming out on me in the *Charleston Magazine.*"

"You will stop it."

"It's the cover!"

"You will stop it."

"What kind of man are you?" Jeffrey demanded. "All doctors want the spotlight! We're like gods to people! We shape them. We mold them. We sculpt them. We *heal* them!"

Dr. Nadu walked over to Jeffrey and leaned over him. "A man who believes himself a healer is a very foolish man. A man who believes himself to be God is a man to be feared." His eyes went hard, glittering like marbles. "You will not play God with my patients."

Jeffrey knew he had made a serious error—perhaps a fatal one. All the life went out of him. "I'm sorry. You're right. Please, I'm asking you. I'll do whatever you want me to. I'll stay in the lab. I'll sit in this room doing nothing but research. I won't touch a patient the entire time I'm here. Please, just let me stay. I'll be quiet. I'll listen. I'll learn." The sigh came out louder than intended. "And I'll cancel the cover of the *Charleston Magazine.*"

Dr. Nadu pressed his lips together and lifted his chin toward Jeffrey as if he were peering into his very soul, measuring the purity of his heart.

"They're waiting for you in the lab," he said. "Do not make me regret this."

———

The Executor stood before Will, close enough for Will to catch the faint smell of fish on him. Will wouldn't have taken him for a fishing kind of man. "What's up? My boys still have you on retainer?" Will chuckled.

The Executor extended a white envelope.

Will leaned against the door frame and opened it, letting the envelope fall to the floor. *Notice to Quit.* He scanned the bogus eviction notice, caught sight of the number sixty in there somewhere, and then returned his eyes to the Executor's face. Will wasn't quite sure what he saw in the piercing eyes of the stranger. He laughed, nervously. But he still laughed.

He handed the letter back to the Executor and would have offered him a beer, but considering his momentary lack of funds, he didn't feel quite as generous as he had in the past. He gave the Executor a pat on the shoulder and closed the door.

part 2

November

chapter twenty

Mary Catherine pulled her robe around her tighter as she sipped her coffee and listened to the pounding of the surf in the distance. She stretched out on the lounge chair next to the pool, taking in the first remnants of morning, thankful for the peace and quiet. She'd been a teacher—or more accurately, hellion director—for barely three months, and she was exhausted.

By the time she got home every evening, it was all she could do to eat dinner and crash. Fortunately Nate wasn't hounding her all the time for sex, and for that she was grateful. But it did worry her slightly, since they'd only been married for five months.

After the initial standoff with Nicole, the victories had come slowly, but they had come nonetheless, and brought with them a sense of accomplishment unlike anything she had ever felt. Nicole still hated her, but the rest of the class was shaping up. Mary Catherine wasn't sure they quite respected her yet, but they at least paid attention most of the time.

She laid her head against the mesh of the lounger and shut her eyes. She had come to count on these few moments of solitude every morning to gather the strength she needed to face the day.

Nate's voice penetrated the quiet. "What you doing out here?"

She kept her eyes closed. "Just relaxing."

She heard his bare feet pad over to the lounge chair and felt his weight shift the chair as he sat down on the edge. "I'm going out to the beach to surf. I'm not sure when I'll be back. Later this evening sometime."

She reached out and stroked his leg—a fine leg, muscular and tanned and covered with soft hair. Pretty soon he'd be wearing his wet suit and she wouldn't be able to admire those legs. "I might come join you later this afternoon when I get home, then. I thought maybe we could go out to Old Towne tonight and get some dinner."

He stood up and headed toward the garage. "You don't have to meet me. In fact, I think we're going out to Kiawah today. They say the surf has been a little stronger over there lately."

Her eyes were open now. "I know I don't *have* to. But I *want* to. You've been gone late every night for the last month or so, and I've been so tired. I thought it would be nice just to spend an evening together."

Apparently he heard a change in her tone, because he came back over to her and took her hand. "I know, baby doll, it's been crazy. But if I'm going to turn pro, I have to stay focused. And I really want us to be able to go to Hawaii next year when all of this is over. If I hope to compete over there, I have to work really hard." He leaned down and began to kiss her neck, talking through his kisses. "You know it's hard for me to concentrate out there when you're in that hot red bikini of yours."

"It's too cool to be in a bikini."

"It will be in the upper seventies by afternoon."

He was right, she knew. Mary Catherine remembered once, when she was still in grade school, leaving for Christmas vacation wearing shorts. "But I want to spend the evening with you," she said. "I'll make it worth your while."

A creepy feeling washed over her before the words were even out of her mouth. Was she really sitting there trying to manipulate her husband into spending time with her?

An expression passed over his face—a look she couldn't quite decipher and wasn't sure she wanted to. "I know, baby doll," he said. "How 'bout tomorrow evening? Just me and you. No one else."

He leaned back down and kissed her lips softly. Maybe she was mistaken about him. Maybe she hadn't seen what she thought she saw. She wrapped her arms around his neck and returned his kiss,

and after a minute he released himself and jumped up, heading back
to the garage.

"Don't wait up!" he hollered back to her.

"Don't wait up," she mimicked to his disappearing form. "Why
would we wait up?" She rubbed Coco's head and drank the rest of
her lukewarm coffee.

———

The parent-teacher conference schedule sat on the desk in front of
her. A blessing and a curse. On the one hand, most of the students
were on their best behavior, fearful of what their parents might hear
about them. On the other hand, the conferences themselves were
exhausting.

Mary Catherine was amazed how many parents didn't even
bother to show up. One mother specifically asked not to be called
again. A few cussed her out, and a couple others just hung up on her
altogether. Out of twenty-five students, she had successfully booked
ten parent meetings, and of those ten, only one where both the
mother and father were going to come. Terrance's parents. That
should be interesting.

The one parent she was most eager to meet was Charmaine's.
The child had more than intelligence and talent. She had the wisdom of an old soul. But for some reason Mary Catherine never could
get anyone to answer the phone.

"Well, Mrs. Bean, how are you this morning?" Terrance asked.
He nodded respectfully and went straight to his seat.

Mary Catherine tried to hide her smile. "I'm fine, thanks. And
you, Terrance?"

"Oh, doing just fine on this lovely day."

She turned her back and began to pin up a new poster on the
bulletin board. "You seem exceptionally glad to be here for a
Monday."

"Of course. It's school. I love school. I love to learn. And I love
tests. Have I ever told you I love tests?"

She turned toward him and laughed out loud. "No, Terrance, for the past three months you've managed to hide that little detail from me."

Other kids began to enter, but their presence did not deflect his determination. "Oh, yes. I know you think that Charmaine is probably the only one who loves tests, but don't you forget that old Terrance here just loves to learn."

"I'll do my best to remember that."

The final bell rang. As usual, Nicole entered on the last clang, not a second before. And as usual, she was chewing gum.

It was a daily ritual by now. Mary Catherine walked over to her holding out the trash can. Nicole spit her wad into it, glaring.

Mary Catherine took a book from the side of her desk, the book *Whirligig*, by Newbery Medal winner Paul Fleischman. She had tried to introduce the kids to reading—not just textbooks, but fiction, novels that took them out of this small classroom for a while and transported them to different places. This current novel was a story of guilt, forgiveness, and self-discovery. And whether they admitted it or not, most of them liked it. She had heard them talking about it over lunch when they didn't know she was listening.

She held the book up. "Okay, let's review for your test on Wednesday."

The class groaned in unison. Mary Catherine smiled.

"Blame Terrance," she said. "He loves tests."

———

On his way back from the bathroom, Will heard some kind of commotion outside his front door. He unlocked the deadbolt and saw the letter attached to his front door. *Summons and Complaint for Unlawful Detainer.* He wasn't sure if this had anything to do with the eviction notice the "Executor" had brought, but his dad's attorneys always took care of stuff like that, and he didn't need a new door ornament. He snatched it off of the stained wooden door and crumpled it in his fist. Then he locked the door behind him, tossed the

paper ball in the general direction of the kitchen garbage can, and
headed back to bed.

———

"Follow me," Dr. Nadu had said to Jeffrey as soon as he walked through
the door.

The last time Dr. Nadu had spoken those words, Jeffrey had
been confined to three months of perpetual purgatory in the lab, and
even though he had been obedient, he still wasn't happy to be here.

"Where are we going today, a body farm?"

Dr. Nadu pushed a large square metal button, and a set of double
doors swung open. His Nikes led him to the emergency room.
Better, at least, than autopsying cadavers and smelling like formaldehyde.

A stout, no-nonsense nurse pointed with a stubby finger. "Dr.
Moss and his team are working on the patient right over there."

Jeffrey turned, his Florsheims clicking loudly as he did. The
activity behind the white curtain was fast and fierce. A man in green
scrubs—Dr. Moss, he assumed—barked directions to his team.
Jeffrey could make out nothing of the patient except a pair of faded
jeans and battered Reeboks.

"How old?" Dr. Nadu asked.

Dr. Moss responded over the commotion and beeps of the
machinery, yet he never faltered from his work. "Young male. Thirteen, fourteen, maybe. House fire. Went back in to get the dog." He
addressed his staff again. "Gentle with the clothes, everybody. Let's
get him rinsed off."

Jeffrey craned his neck but still couldn't see much. The tennis
shoes hit the floor, followed by the jeans and a singed rag that could
have been a T-shirt.

The boy moaned.

"Get that IV started *now*," Dr. Moss said.

Jeffrey kept his eyes focused on the tennis shoes, the Reebok
insignia still readable. A nurse began to hang different bags of fluid

on the IV cart, then went to work on getting the IV started. "I can't find a vein, Doctor."

"Why can't she find a vein?" Jeffrey muttered. "It's not brain surgery."

Dr. Nadu turned a scathing look on him. "She can't find a vein, Dr. Wilcott, because in extreme burn cases the blood vessels can be destroyed altogether."

"What I can see of his legs looks okay."

Dr. Nadu took Jeffrey by the shoulders and pushed him forward. Most of the young man's face and upper torso were charred beyond recognition. Even his parents wouldn't have known him.

"He's shivering. We need to get him wrapped, people."

When the team had done all it could, Dr. Moss spoke to Dr. Nadu. "So, if he makes it through this, you have any hope for his body?"

Dr. Nadu patted him on the back. "There's always hope, my friend. And as young as he is, he should be resilient. You make him better, and then I'll do my part."

"He'll never look the same."

"But he will look good," Dr. Nadu assured him. "We will work diligently to make him look good."

"That's why I called you." Dr. Moss motioned in the direction of the family waiting room. "Now, will you go with me to see his mother? We need to talk to her about intubation."

"Come with us, Dr. Wilcott," Dr. Nadu said over his shoulder.

The last thing Jeffrey wanted was to have to console a bereaved family. This was one reason he did boobs and butts and facelifts. He never had to tell some hysterical woman that her kid was going to look like a freak for the rest of his life.

But Dr. Nadu's words sounded more like a command than a suggestion. He trailed the two doctors down the long hall and into the waiting area. A woman paced near the windows, her back turned to them.

"Are you Mrs. Webber?" Dr. Moss asked.

"My son! How is my son?"

"He's alive. We're doing the best we can. Could we speak over here?" Dr. Moss and Dr. Nadu took her gently by the arms and led her to an adjacent room. Jeffrey had always avoided the "family room." It was where the bad news was delivered, where people screamed and cried and raged and tried to deal with their trauma.

Jeffrey watched her from the back, her shoulders slumped and shaking. A long brown ponytail hung down the back of her black shirt.

Dr. Moss opened the door and let the mother go inside. As she reached the other side of the room, she sat down and looked up. Her tears had left visible streaks down her olive cheeks.

Jeffrey felt his knees go weak. She stared at him.

"What is *he* doing here?" Her voice rose as she stood up and headed unsteadily in his direction. "I want him out of here. I want him out of here *now!*"

Jeffrey began backing toward the door. The name hadn't registered with him; he had forgotten she had changed it. He had forgotten *her*.

Until he saw her.

So the boy in that bed was . . .

"Ma'am, calm down! Please! Dr. Nadu, could you get him out of here?"

Nadu grabbed Jeffrey and pulled him out into the hall. "Dr. Wilcott, what in the world is going on here? How do you know that woman?"

Jeffrey felt the coolness of the wall as he leaned against it; it was all that was holding him up. He put his head in his hands and rubbed hard, hoping somehow that would make all of this make sense.

"Who is it, Jeffrey?"

"That's my . . . my ex-wife." He slid down the wall to a crouch, resting his elbows on top of his knees. "And that means that kid in there is my son."

chapter twenty-one

Elizabeth inhaled the fresh air, grateful for a moment without Ward Bennett up her tailpipe. The kid had shadowed her for three solid months. Three months that had proved torturous, because not once was she allowed to contact her new client or deal in any way with their lawyers. Everett and Associates, she was told, had put the project on hold.

This was the way Ainsley operated: bait, hook, and wait. The woman was evil.

Meanwhile, Ainsley had sent Elizabeth to at least twenty workshops and let her spend the remainder of her time as Ward's law clerk.

Aaron was keeping her office running smoothly—at least that's what he told her. So far she hadn't been served with any lawsuits; that was, she supposed, a good sign. But Aaron hadn't been available for much more than a weekly update lately. They never had dinner together anymore. He was always too busy.

It was probably for the best. After Elizabeth's first week of "initiation," she began going into the office before seven and rarely got home before nine or ten. She had long been accustomed to such hours, of course, but when she was working for herself, she had hardly noticed. Now, as each night enveloped her, fatigue became her constant companion. She felt as if she were digging ditches rather than practicing law.

The private investigator didn't seem to be getting anywhere either.

Driving toward her appointment this morning she called him again on the cell phone. "Please tell me you found out more over the weekend."

"I wish we could say we have, Elizabeth. But this Executor of yours is good. I've never run into so many dead ends. We have found some interesting activity in your brother's bank account though."

"What kind of activity?"

"Large withdrawals. All being wired to the same account. We should have more on that in the next couple of days."

"I need something *now*."

"Well, I can tell you that your friend Aaron is exactly what he seems to be. He's working hard for your company and for your father's company. There just isn't anything on him anywhere."

"And Ainsley?"

"She isn't as squeaky clean as a lawyer should be. A couple of years ago she had an investigation into some questionable activity that brought her before the Law Review Board. Came close to being disbarred."

"What were the charges?"

"Embezzlement."

Elizabeth pulled up in front of the house on Smith Street for her appointment and put the car in park. She stared straight ahead.

"Embezzlement?" No wonder Ainsley could afford Heitz Cabernet. It had nothing to do with her husband. She was a crook.

"Yes, that's all we know right now. We just found it late Saturday. Prescott's working on the details of it today."

"I expect an update by this evening."

"It might not be until—"

"This evening." She clicked her earpiece off.

She racked her memory, trying to recall any time Ainsley Parker had met her father. Two occasions, that she could think of. Ainsley had been desperate to meet him and ingratiatingly charming when she finally did. But the way Ainsley talked about him with such affection was odd. Overly familiar.

She got out of the car and stood on the sidewalk surveying the house—a rambling, run-down frame home with light blue siding. It was her first meeting with this client, the client who could end her career if Elizabeth couldn't talk her into letting Everett and Associates take over the place.

As the warm breeze swept over her, she realized it was going to be a pleasant November day. You never could be certain with Southern winters, when they would start or when they would end. Fall could tease you with cooler temperatures in mid-October, and then vanish again until late December. Winter came when it pleased and left at its own whim. It could be an ornery visitor, sometimes even thumbing its nose at you in late March.

She closed the Jeep door and carefully negotiated the cracked sidewalk. The yard was a patchwork of red dirt and crabgrass. Some of the siding was hanging off the house, shifting in the wind, and the wrought-iron railing that led up the steps had come loose at both ends.

The porch boards slanted precariously, but two fresh white rockers sat on each side of a small wicker table. The wooden front door was also neatly painted, and the screen door seemed to be brand-new. She tapped on the side of the door.

A tiny black woman appeared, eyeing the new arrival curiously. Her graying hair was cut close to her head, and her eyes were an almost translucent light brown shaded with flecks of green.

"I suppose you're from the Benefactor's Group?"

"Yes, ma'am. I am. I'm Elizabeth Wilcott. You're Hazel Moses?"

"I am indeed." The woman opened the screen door. "Come in, young lady. Come right on in."

Elizabeth stepped inside the old house, its aged wood floors creaking under her step.

"Don't mind those." The woman chuckled, the small gold hoops in her ears dangling as her head moved. "That's just one of the things that needs to be replaced. Truth is, *I'll* probably be replaced before we can get all of this settled. Come sit down on the sofa and rest awhile."

Elizabeth sat obediently.

"Let me get you a glass of sweet tea."

Elizabeth shook her head. "Oh, really. That's not necessary. I'm not—"

"Now, now. My mother always taught me that if guests come to your home, you serve them something to drink whether they want it or not." Her voice trailed away as she headed toward the kitchen.

Elizabeth looked around at the shabby house. This wasn't her life. She took meetings in elegant restaurants and opulent offices, over expensive meals and fine wine and rich coffee. Not a place like this. Not Elizabeth Wilcott.

Elizabeth's eyes caught two small chairs in the corner of Hazel's living room with stacks of children's books nestled by each one. The one on the top was recognizable to Elizabeth immediately. It was *The Secret Garden*, her favorite book from childhood.

Hazel Moses returned bearing two glasses of iced tea—one in a small Mason jar and the other in a dazzling piece of crystal stemware. She handed the crystal glass to Elizabeth and motioned to the sofa. "Have a seat, please. My son, Willie, will be here shortly. He's been helping me handle all of the issues that have arisen since we found out that we have no legal claim on this property. Had these developers not come in here to take it from us, we would have never known."

"I'll look forward to meeting him." Elizabeth took a sip of her tea, just to be polite. It ran down her throat smooth and thick like Esau's. It was very good.

"Would you like me to show you around until Willie gets here?"

"I'd like that very much."

The front room ran shotgun-style straight through the dining room and into the kitchen. Clearly the house was aging not so gracefully, but the rooms were open and spacious, and everything was neatly placed and immaculately clean.

"My ancestor, Willamina—that's where Willie got his name— she was brought to Charleston and sold here as a slave at the Old Slave Mart in 1859. This house was deeded to her and her family once emancipation came to Charleston. She passed it down to her children; then they passed it down to theirs, and it ended up with me. Awhile back I discovered there wasn't a piece of paper this side of eternity that had me as the rightful owner of this home or land. I always felt it was mine, even though there isn't a law that would agree with me."

Elizabeth followed Hazel into the kitchen, where a capturing aroma emanated from the oven. "Are you making bread?"

"Yes. My Willie loves homemade bread with pear preserves."

"My mother used to make bread," Elizabeth blurted out. Until this moment, she had forgotten.

Hazel patted Elizabeth on the arm. "All good mamas make their babies homemade bread."

Hazel continued her narrative as she showed Elizabeth the dilapidated back porch—the backyard even worse than the front. "When I tried to contact my family members about getting the property deeded to me so I could fight the developers, I contacted all of them, cousins, aunts, uncles. Lord have mercy, you would have thought I was asking them to sell their plasma. They were indignant, mean, and greedy. Not a one of them had given this place a second thought until they got a call from me. But when they thought they might have a right to something they never worked for, cared for, or invested in, they wanted a piece of it anyway."

"I'm sorry this has been so difficult for you."

"My son Willie owns a construction company and would do all of these repairs for me, but I don't want him to put any more energy in it, if they're just going to come and take it away from us. My mother gave me this house. She had all eleven of her children born right under this roof. This is my home. I've worked hard for it through the years. I was an English teacher until I retired five years ago, and I always thought I'd live out my life here. I want to make this home beautiful again. For my children."

Her expression grew distant. "I know a lot of people call your company because they want to sell their land and can't because they don't have the deed. But that's not why I called. I don't want to sell it, and I don't want a developer coming and trying to steal it out from under me. I just want it to be legally mine, and to be free to make it into the home it needs to be."

Elizabeth looked into the woman's eyes. "I think that's a noble purpose, Miss Hazel."

"It's not noble; it's just right. Kids need a heritage. My grand-babies love for me to read to them in a special corner that is just for them. They'll do that with their babies. That's my legacy."

The passion she exuded was contagious, and Elizabeth felt her-self profoundly affected by this diminutive woman and her cause. "If you'll give me the names and numbers of the family you contacted, we'll begin some family mediation for you, and then we'll deal with the developer. Hopefully we can get all of this resolved with as little incident as possible."

Hazel accompanied Elizabeth to the door and cautiously down the steps to the car. "Sorry Willie didn't get here to meet you. You would love him. But I really appreciate it. Next week is Thanksgiving. Every family needs a home where they can get together on holidays, don't you think? I want this to be a place my great-grandkids can come to. A place they'll remember."

Elizabeth opened the car door. "Yes, Miss Hazel, every family should have a place like that."

She climbed in the car and watched as Hazel Moses climbed her lopsided steps one at a time onto her slanted, ramshackled porch. The old woman paused and waved good-bye, then took a hand-kerchief out of her sleeve and dusted off the arms of the rocking chairs.

Elizabeth's stomach rumbled, and her mind called up images of all the Moses clan gathered in that warm, shabby dining room around a table loaded with turkey and dressing and pumpkin pies and Hazel's homemade bread.

Elizabeth Wilcott had no plans for Thanksgiving.

And she had accomplished absolutely nothing she had come here to do.

Dr. Nadu eased Jeffrey into a chair at the boardroom table. "Dr. Randall, get Dr. Wilcott some water, please."

Jeffrey ran his sweaty palms together and tugged loose the knot of his tie. Oxygen. He needed oxygen.

"Jeffrey, I'm sorry," Dr. Nadu said. "I had no idea that was your son. The name Webber—?"

"It's her maiden name. She took it back after we got divorced."

"So you haven't talked with her in a while?"

Dr. Randall returned, setting a bottled water on the table. Jeffrey unscrewed the cap and drank a little while Dr. Nadu paced quietly behind him.

"Perhaps you would like to go and stay with him for the rest of the day . . ."

Jeffrey exhaled heavily. "With the way his mother feels, it might be best if I just keep my distance."

Dr. Nadu nodded. "You might be right. I suspect you are in shock too. Can I get someone to drive you home?"

"No. I think I'll just get out of the hospital for a little while, just to get my head together. Maybe I'll come back later."

Dr. Nadu patted him on the back. "We'll do everything we can, Jeffrey. I promise."

Jeffrey nodded his head. "I'm certain you will, sir."

When Dr. Nadu left, Jeffrey ran for the parking lot and threw up in the shrubs. Leaning against the brick building, he tried to steady himself. But brick and mortar could not steady a life in ruins.

———

One good thing about being a teacher is that you got out of school before rush hour. Mary Catherine pulled onto King Street, parked, and got out to walk. She loved this neighborhood, everything about it—the smells, the sights, the *stuff*.

She intended to go straight to Old Towne. But an English commode in the window of her favorite antique store caught her eye. The inlaid drawers were like nothing she had ever seen. She ran her hands along the glass of the front window and let her feet carry her right through the front door.

The ringing bell gave her away.

"Mary Catherine!" the store owner crooned as she made her way, arms wide open, straight for Mary Catherine. "Where have you been, darling? I haven't seen you in months."

"Hello, Lacy." Mary Catherine returned the hug, feeling the perspiration start at the base of her neck. "I've been . . . ah, busy."

"You are admiring my beautiful chest, aren't you?"

Mary Catherine hoped Lacy didn't go around saying this to everyone. "The one in the window. Yes, it's lovely."

"I'll give you a wonderful deal. Like I always do."

Mary Catherine's heart hammered against her rib cage. "No, really, I need to go. I'm meeting someone up the street for dinner."

"Darling, you've never left my shop empty-handed, and you're not going to start now. Where have you been anyway? Why haven't you been to see me?"

Mary Catherine debated telling the truth. "As I said, I've been busy. Traveling." She rationalized the lie. North Charleston was, more or less, a different world.

"You keep those miles adding up, don't you? Where have your travels taken you?"

Mary Catherine picked up a candle, stalling, trying to think of something else to talk about. It didn't work. "I've gone back to teaching, actually." She set the candle back down. "Yes, I've gone back to teaching."

"You have a *job*?" Lacy uttered the vile word with contempt as if what she had wasn't one. Mary Catherine figured her logic was based around the fact that she owned the store.

"It's what I went to school for."

"Well, isn't that interesting. Mary Catherine Wilcott has gotten herself a job." She used the Wilcott name deliberately, Mary Catherine was certain, and made no attempt to hide her disdain. "So, what can you buy on a teacher's budget?"

Mary Catherine studied Lacy's arrogant face and looked at the carved baroque bookcase next to her. All of a sudden it all felt shallow, superficial. "I don't intend to buy anything, to be honest with you. I have everything I need."

"Well then!" Lacy clapped her hands together. "Oh my. Would you look at the time? I better scurry back there and finish doing . . . well, whatever it was I was doing. Do come again."

She hustled Mary Catherine out the door without so much as a good-bye. And Mary Catherine felt something inside of her bend. Something that had never bent before.

———

Elizabeth had no choice but to request Ainsley's assistance. The lying swindler Ainsley. She hated to admit it, but if she were to completely understand the legal undertakings of her new case, she was going to have to go to the head.

For the last three months she had dealt with Ainsley only when necessary. And Ainsley's manufactured civility only frustrated Elizabeth more. But after years of pretending real life wasn't what it really was, Elizabeth figured she could handle this as well. She pushed herself back from her desk and willed herself to move in the direction of Ainsley's door.

"Do you have time for dinner tonight?"

Ainsley took off her glasses and rubbed her eyes. It was already eight o'clock. She sighed heavily.

"I'm not asking for a date; I'm asking for dinner."

Ainsley chuckled. "I know. It's just that this brief is due before the judge Wednesday morning, and it will probably take me until then to get it finished. How about Wednesday night? I'll be all yours. You can wine and dine me until dawn." She laughed.

Elizabeth didn't.

"I'm not brushing you off. I've really got to get this brief in by tomorrow night, or I'm going to have to fire myself."

Elizabeth raised an eyebrow.

"Ah. I see the prospect of my imminent departure pleases you."

She apparently wasn't as good an actress as she had thought. "Sure, Wednesday's fine," she said. She reached to close the door.

"Hey, Elizabeth?"

Elizabeth turned back around. "Yes?"

"Thanks. I know you're working a lot of hours, and I really appreciate all of your effort."

Elizabeth averted her face to hide the smirk. "It's all part of the job."

Ainsley nodded. "Yes, it is all part of the job. But thanks anyway."

Jeffrey sat in his car, staring out the front windshield. He had driven around all day going nowhere. But stalling offered no alternative to what awaited at the hospital. Now he had come full circle and sat in the parking lot, staring at the sign that read "Physician's Parking." The car idled quietly, but his thoughts were shrieking.

All he had really wanted to do was to find Pamela and pretend none of this had happened. After all, he hadn't so much as seen this kid since his wife left the house with him over ten years ago.

Claire had left when she found out that Priscilla, his soon-to-be second wife, was pregnant with Matthew. She walked out the door that day asking for nothing, so he had offered her nothing.

Dr. Nadu had expected emotion from Jeffrey. For God's sake, this was his son. Fathers cried over wounded sons. Fathers ached over them. That's what normal fathers were supposed to do.

His hands twisted against the leather of the steering wheel. He hated what this might bring to the surface. This would probably be the tide that brought in Claire's greed. She'd probably expect him to pay for everything. Worse than that, she would probably expect him to *care*. Expect him to help. Expect him to . . .

A voice inside finished the thought: *Be a man. Be a father.*

Long gone was the warmth of the Carolina sun. The parking lot—indeed, his whole world—was now illuminated by artificial light.

He didn't want to be here. Wanted to be somewhere else, anywhere else. Any*one* else. But he had still felt the need to return. As fast as he drove away, something inside was tugging at him, pulling him, drawing him back. As much as he had tried to ignore his moral compass, it had spun him around and made him follow its direction.

He entered the bustling halls of the hospital, seeing the entire spectacle from a completely different perspective this time. Now he wasn't the doctor, in control and in charge. The patient was no longer just a nameless stranger, a list of symptoms on a chart.

He opened the door to the ICU slowly. The nurses moved about quietly. The ICU rooms surrounded a central station, and he scanned the rooms looking for Claire, looking for Jacob.

The older woman behind the nurse's desk paid him no attention. He leaned over the counter. "Could you tell me where Jacob Webber's room is?"

"Sir, no one is allowed in ICU for another hour, and then only for ten minutes at a time. You'll have to wait." Her eyes never left the chart in her hands.

"I'm Dr. Wilcott. I work with Dr. Nadu. This boy is his . . . our patient."

She lifted her eyes apologetically. "Oh, I'm sorry. I didn't realize—" She pulled a chart from the vertical filer on the desk and began to scan it. "Let's see here. I just got on duty an hour ago. I have a Jacob *Wilcott* . . . oh my, that's your name. How ironic is that?" She laughed awkwardly. "He's over there, in Unit Four."

"Is his mother with him?"

"I don't believe so. Not at the moment. I think I just saw her walk down the hall with a couple of people."

"I'm going to check in on him, but would you—" He paused. "Would you just give me a heads-up if you see her headed back this way?"

"No problem." She nodded. "But I'll be in shortly anyway. It's time to re-dress his burns."

Jeffrey entered the glassed-in unit slowly. Monitors attached to Jacob's body surrounded his bed on both sides. The boy was completely bandaged from his face to the top of his thighs, the bandages spotted with oozing blood and plasma. A light sheet lay neatly tucked over his legs.

He scanned the labels of the IV bags. Fluids had to be continually replenished, and morphine administered for the pain.

He stood by Jacob's head and placed his hands on the cold metal railing. The heart monitor beeped lightly, followed by the gentle rhythmic hiss of oxygen from the ventilator and the periodic inflation of the cooling blanket. It was a miracle this kid was alive.

A harsh whisper came from behind him. "What are you doing in here?"

So much for getting warned. He turned to face Claire. "I just wanted to stop by."

The nurse followed on Claire's heels. "Um, she's here, Dr. Wilcott."

"I see that."

"You need to go," Claire said. He nodded and headed out the door. He wouldn't cause a scene.

Just outside the ICU main doors, he heard her following and turned to face her.

"I want you to leave us alone," she said. "This is no time for you to come around pretending to be a father."

"Claire, I just . . ."

"I honestly don't want to hear it, Jeffrey. We haven't needed anything from you before, and we don't need anything from you now. The last thing I want my son to do is wake up and have one ounce of hope that you are coming back into his life."

"I'm sorry, Claire. I don't know what to say."

"Forget the apologies, Jeffrey. It's way too late for that. Just leave."

Jeffrey nodded his head. "Okay. Okay."

She spoke again. Obviously she wasn't ready for him to leave quite yet. "Do you know why he went back in that house, Jeffrey?" Her voice broke.

Dr. Moss's words from the emergency room came back to him, registering with the nudge of her question. "They said it was for a dog or something."

"Yes, it was for a dog. The dog *you* bought him for his third birthday. He kept that dog for more than ten years, loved that dog, Jeffrey, because it was a part of you. He wouldn't even let me change his name from Wilcott when I changed mine. He still wanted to be your son, even though you never called. Never wrote. Never checked on him. So unless you take pleasure in seeing what all your reckless ambivalence has produced, then please, just stay away from us."

She left him with only one option: watching her walk away, again.

———

Elizabeth was soaking in the bathtub when the call came. She recognized the caller ID and snatched up the phone. "Tell me what you know."

"All the charges against her were dropped. The embezzlement claim came from a disgruntled employee who worked under her."

"Charges are dropped all the time. That doesn't mean she wasn't guilty. If she had enough money to pay someone off—"

"Mrs. Wilcott."

"*Ms.*," she corrected.

He paused. "*Ms.* Wilcott. I'm the investigator. You're the lawyer. I'm just telling you the information I received. Whether you choose to believe it is your decision."

chapter twenty-two

Jeffrey rummaged frantically through kitchen drawers. He ransacked closets, emptied dressers, but he found nothing. Finally, as a last resort, he made his way back to the family room and flung open the cabinets underneath the bookcase. A dozen labeled boxes sat there, perfectly positioned and organized by date.

After ten minutes of searching, he found what he was looking for. Standing there by his birthday cake with the big number 3 on top was Jacob, grinning, holding a flailing puppy. Bobo the Boxer.

Jeffrey sank heavily to the floor. Bobo was supposed to be named Bruno, but Jacob couldn't say Bruno yet. So Bobo was as good as it got.

His eyes took in every detail of the picture. The vibrancy of the color, the smile on Jacob's face, his tiny hands grasped around the puppy's stomach. Then he noticed Claire in the background, standing behind Jacob in that pink sweater Jeffrey always said complemented her dark hair.

What he had failed to notice eleven years ago was like the North Star today, pointing straight to his denial. Her eyes were dark, heavy, and tired, and she was only twenty-four. They had married in college at the age of twenty, much to his father's objections. But they didn't care. They were excited, full of life. She was passionate about Jeffrey and everything else. In four years he had taken away her youth.

He laid the picture down in front of him. "My God, what did I do to her?" His mind tried to wrap around the reality. "I made her that way. I'm the reason she was so unhappy."

The revelation brought with it a barrage of memories, memories of the last fifteen years. Torturous memories in which Jeffrey began to see himself as he was—shallow, self-centered, narcissistic. Wanting what he wanted when he wanted it. Not caring about who he hurt in the process.

Jeffrey grabbed an eight-hundred-dollar crystal Lalique vase from the bookshelf and threw it across the room. It crashed against the floor in the foyer, leaving massive chunks of crystal strewn across the marble and shimmering shards in almost every corner.

Then he knelt on the rug and screamed—a primal, guttural scream—as every painful moment of the past thirty-eight years tore through him. He flailed his fists at the ceiling, wanting with all his might to direct this anger at his father, to blame him. But Jeffrey could find no one to blame except himself.

And then the tears came. He wept for his mother. He wept for Claire and the look on her face in that picture. He wept for his son Jacob, for his pain and his burns and his loneliness. For the lost years. He wept over every stupid decision he'd ever made. He wept for the fact that heaven held no answers.

And he wept, for the first time in his life, over his father.

He remembered now, with painful clarity, the phone calls he never returned. The days his dad would pick up Matthew and ask him to come.

Then he wept over Elizabeth and her screams in the barn, and the fact that he'd never told what he should have told. And now that he was weeping for her, he remembered . . .

That was the last time he had ever cried.

Jeffrey heard movement in the hall, slippered feet coming down the stairs, crunching over the slivered glass in the foyer. But he couldn't make himself stop crying. Now that the gates had opened, he couldn't shut off the flood.

Jeffrey felt a small warm hand on his back. Through his tears he looked up at his son, the face of an adult on an eight-year-old boy. He reached up and took his son in his arms, and then he wept some more.

This time he wept for Matthew. And Matthew held on to his dad the way a father holds on to his child.

"Hey! Where do you think you're going with my car?!"

The tow truck driver looked at Will and spit a straight line of tobacco juice between his teeth. Will backed up instinctively. "Just doin' what I've been told to do."

"But this is my car. I wasn't parked illegally."

The man kept his finger on the button. The car continued to rise. He pulled out a wadded up piece of pink paper from the pocket of his overalls. "Says here on my paper that this car is stolen. I'd say you're lucky I'm here and not the po-lice."

"This car isn't stolen. I'm Will Wilcott. And this is my car."

"Well, I'm Potese Goff, and this here's my car now."

"I'm going to call the police!" Will threatened.

"You wanta go to jail tonight, then you go right ahead. But my paper says this here car belongs to an Elijah Clayton Wilcott II."

"That's my dad. But for your information, my dad is dead."

"Your dad is your dad? What's that s'pose to mean?"

Will's voice escalated. "I said he is *dead*. D-E-A-D."

"Oh, well then, I'm real sorry 'bout your loss and all, but that don't change my 'sponsibilities. So you run on and take your issues up with someone else."

Will was still standing in the middle of the street when Potese Goff headed off with his Porsche.

The new day was about to reveal how much her kids had really learned. Mary Catherine walked into her classroom with a stack of test papers in her hands. "Go straight to your desk, put your books away, get out a pen or pencil, and sit quietly until everyone else arrives. Review your notes if you like, but no talking."

Five minutes after the bell rang, Nicole wandered in. "What's everybody so quiet for?" she asked through her chewing gum.

Mary Catherine repeated the instructions and held out the trash can. Nicole spat and sat with a huff and a roll of the eyes.

"Ladies and gentlemen, you will have the entire class period to finish your test. If you finish early, please take out a book to read quietly. If you talk, you will automatically be suspected of cheating, your test will be taken from you, and you will receive a zero." She paused and smiled. "I am confident you will all do well. You know this material. Now, go show me what you can do."

For thirty minutes absolute silence reigned. Charmaine finished first, of course. The child was diligent at everything she did. Mary Catherine gave her a wink as she laid her paper down. Terrance brought his paper to her desk after forty-five minutes, looking tense and sweaty. Nicole remained firmly in her seat, arms crossed, leaning back in her chair. She never picked up her pencil.

When the hour was over and every test was turned in except Nicole's, Mary Catherine made a decision. She made a brief call from the class phone to the gym teacher. He agreed to her request, and she hung up the phone.

"Class, I want to thank you for being so quiet and respectful during this test. You can all go to the gym and enjoy yourselves until I come and get you."

All the kids rose and headed for the door, chattering excitedly. Nicole got up and started out with them.

Mary Catherine held out a hand. "Nicole, you stay here, please."

Nicole turned around slowly, hesitantly. She sucked her teeth.

"I don't believe you're finished with your test. The gym is for those who have completed their test. You need to take a seat."

Nicole took a step forward. "I'm not taking that test. And there's nothing you can do to make me."

"Well, whether you take the test or not will be your decision. However, how long I make you stay in that chair will be *my* decision. Take a seat."

For a moment she wasn't sure if Nicole would defy her and walk out. The girl shifted on her feet and sneered at Mary Catherine. Then she sauntered over to her desk and slumped back into it, crossing her arms defiantly.

Mary Catherine sat back down at her desk. She wasn't sure how long it would take, but she wasn't going anywhere.

———

Mr. Nash, the gym teacher, called around noon. "Send the kids on to lunch, if you don't mind," Mary Catherine said. "There's no change here."

He called again after lunch. "Can you keep them a little while longer?"

A little after two, Mr. Nash called for a third time. "Go ahead and send them to art. That's their last class of the day. They can go home after that. I appreciate your help."

By five o'clock, Mary Catherine's stomach was growling incessantly. She had missed lunch. Nicole still sat in her chair, arms crossed, but she looked about to doze off. That wasn't about to happen.

Mary Catherine opened her mouth and began to sing. She was exceptionally bad at it, and exceptionally loud at it. If ever there was a situation that called for bad, loud singing, this was it.

She turned her back to Nicole and sang away, off-key and with gusto. Mr. McClain walked by her door during her serenade and peered through the glass. He smiled and continued down the hall. As it finally began to get dark outside, Mary Catherine finally gave up.

"Bring me your paper, Nicole."

Nicole picked her paper up and walked over, slapping it down on Mary Catherine's desk. Not even the space where her name went had been filled in.

"You can go home now." Nicole didn't respond; she just headed for the door.

"Ever walked through a graveyard, Nicole?"

The girl turned. "What?"

"Do it one day. Take an hour and walk through a graveyard, Nicole. More lost potential rests in graveyards than anywhere else. Possibilities are buried there every day. The greatest books. The greatest songs. The greatest teachers. The greatest scientists. They can all be found in graveyards, forgotten, anonymous, because they never dared to be what they were supposed to be. It takes courage, Nicole, to be great."

Nicole shrugged and left without a word.

Next time she gave a test, Mary Catherine decided, she would pack a lunch and a Snickers bar.

———

Jeffrey had gone in twice to check on Jacob, after making sure that Claire was out. He had consulted with Dr. Moss on the most effective course of treatment and discussed with Dr. Nadu what the reconstruction options were, assuming Jacob made it through this touch-and-go time. Dr. Nadu had explained the process in detail, and Jeffrey had listened. Really listened.

Jeffrey left the hospital and pulled onto the James Island Expressway. Porter-Gaud, Jeffrey's alma mater, was just off the first exit, one of the most reputable schools in Charleston.

The school had come into being in 1964 when Porter Military Academy, an institution with its roots in the Episcopal denomination, merged with the Gaud School for Boys and the Watt School. The seventy-acre site on Albemarle Point situated the campus right on the banks of the Ashley River.

Jeffrey drove through the pristine grounds and for a moment felt lost. He had never once come here to pick Matthew up from school.

He knew Matthew was playing basketball, so he backtracked and made his way around to the gym, where a line of waiting cars gave him some assurance that students might exit here. A few minutes later Matthew came out of the gym and scanned the parking lot for his ride. Jeffrey still had no idea how he played basketball at his height. But from what Gretchen told him, the kid was actually a pretty good basketball player.

Jeffrey himself hadn't sprouted until he was fourteen. He had spent three years on the sidelines watching his middle-school buddies play football until he was finally big enough to play. Matthew, it seemed, would be a late bloomer as well.

Jeffrey watched as Matthew continued to scan the parking lot, a look of disappointment on his face. And suddenly Jeffrey realized he'd never even think to look for his car.

He got out and waved his hand. "Hey, Matthew!"

Matthew's brow furrowed as he walked slowly toward his dad's car. "What's wrong, Dad? Did somebody die or something?"

Jeffrey could have come back with several smart remarks, but he refrained. The truth was, it was a shame that a child should be shocked when his own father came to pick him up. "I wanted to take my son to dinner tonight, if that's all right with you."

Matthew screwed up his face. "Sure. I guess dinner would be good." He kept staring at Jeffrey all the way out of the parking lot. "You sure there's not something wrong? Have you been diagnosed with something?"

Jeffrey laughed softly and said, "Yeah, probably. Terminally pathetic fathering."

"You could be right there."

Jeffrey looked over at his son and grinned. He reached out and tousled his thick brown hair. "What would you like for dinner?"

"Well, I kind of like tofu."

"*Tofu?*"

"Yeah. Gretchen gets it all the time."

"You mean you wouldn't rather have pizza or hamburgers?"

"Naw, Dad, I really try to eat healthy. I know a great sushi place."

Jeffrey shook his head. He had no idea who this kid was. "Sushi, huh?"

"Yeah, it's really good."

"I don't eat raw fish."

"Not all sushi is raw, Dad. And they have a hibachi grill if you want meat."

Jeffrey followed Matthew's directions to the Japanese restaurant. The waterfall front was surrounded by stone and held a bronzed fish in the middle of the fountain. "Gretchen takes you to nice places, huh?"

"She always says if you were paying, we might as well enjoy ourselves."

They stopped on the sidewalk. Jeffrey took Matthew by the arms and knelt down in front of him. "Did you enjoy yourself, Matthew? Did you really enjoy yourself? I mean, without me in your life?"

Matthew's soft smile disarmed his father. He took both of his hands and laid them on top of his father's shoulders. "Honest, Dad?"

"Honest."

"I like this much better."

Jeffrey leaned over and kissed his son on the top of the head. Matthew's big eyes lit up with a life Jeffrey had never seen before. As they headed into the restaurant, Matthew placed his tiny hand inside Jeffrey's, and for the first time Jeffrey knew the thrill of a father.

That evening Matthew taught him all about sushi, wasabi, and using chopsticks. And after the second call from the private investigator interrupted their dinner, Jeffrey simply turned his phone off altogether.

———

Even though she had asked for the meeting, Elizabeth had to drag herself to dinner with Ainsley Parker. At least she had dictated the environment—Tristan's on Market Street, a place she felt comfortable.

It would be a late dinner, around eight o'clock, because Hazel Moses's son, Willie, had time to talk with Elizabeth after he got home from work at six. A conversation with him would give her even more information to share with Ainsley and, she was certain, more questions to ask.

Tristan's was hidden in a corner on Market Street, one of the oldest and most historic streets on the eastern seaboard. But this street held more recent memories for Elizabeth. When Mary Catherine was engrossed in theater, acting in plays during the Spoleto Festival, Elizabeth served as babysitter and chauffer. She'd take her across the street to the row of brick buildings and walk her to what they called the "Gourmetisserie." Years later they would learn it was just a fancy

name for a "food court." But for them it was a smorgasbord of foreign fare. Foods from everywhere—China, Japan, Greece, Mexico.
Elizabeth could get Mary Catherine to eat anything if she thought it
came from some exotic faraway place even when she was ten.

Elizabeth had always been the "old soul," as Mother called her.
Mary Catherine had always been the adventurer. The memory of
that child made Elizabeth smile. She still wasn't sure how the chasm
had grown so wide.

A voice broke into her musings. "Three months down. More to
be discovered."

Elizabeth stopped in the middle of the street between the two out-
door markets. An elderly black gentleman sat there, his fingers twining
dried sea grass into a beautiful handmade basket. She'd only seen one
man making baskets here before, and that was years ago . . .

"Excuse me? Did you say something to me?"

He looked up at her and smiled, then focused once more on the
fluid movements of his fingers.

At that moment a horse-drawn carriage came to a stop right in
front of her, blocking her view of the basket weaver. She stepped
back. The horse eyed her. Fortunately, the tour guide flicked the
reins, and the horse continued his slow saunter up the street.

The weaver had vanished. There was nothing there. Not a man.
Not a chair. Not a basket. Not a piece of sea grass.

She felt her pulse increase, and she quickened her pace to cross
the street.

Inside Tristan's, the hostess eyed her curiously.

"Ms. Wilcott, are you okay?"

Elizabeth gave one more glance behind her into the street. There
was no one there. She turned back to the hostess and straightened
her posture. "I'm fine. Fine. Has Ainsley Parker arrived yet?"

"No, ma'am. You're here first."

"Well, let me know when she gets here."

Rumor had it that Tristan's was opened because the megarich of
Charleston didn't think there was a restaurant that truly met their
dining standards. Elizabeth usually ate here at lunchtime when they

had a fixed price menu for around fifteen dollars. The offerings were much more expensive in the evening, but the cuisine was well worth it. The food was magnificent and the ambience elegant.

Until Ainsley Parker showed up anyway.

"Did you get a load of those sinks in the bathroom?" Ainsley declared in full voice before she was halfway to the table.

Elizabeth didn't respond. She refused to acknowledge Ainsley until she sat down and actually came close enough for conversation.

"I've never seen a sink like that in my life! The entire thing is tilted so that all the water falls into that silver trough on the floor. I need to know who their designer is. Remind me to ask before I leave."

"I'm sure they already know you're interested."

"Well, good evening to you, Elizabeth. Waste no time in being a smart aleck, now do you?"

Elizabeth's jaw pulsed. "How about we just get to work? I've got quite a few questions so I can make sure I proceed correctly."

"Now, isn't this a fine turn of events. Elizabeth Wilcott having to ask me for advice." She turned to the server. "Oh, no lime or lemon, thanks very much, young man. I'll have some tea, and none of that sweet stuff either. We like it hard and straight in my neck of the woods."

The server eyed her curiously as they ordered and then left the table to retrieve her tea. "So, shoot. What do you need my help with?"

Elizabeth reviewed her conversations with Hazel Moses. Ainsley matter-of-factly walked Elizabeth through the course of action as their meal came and they ate. Several times Ainsley tried to change the subject, but Elizabeth kept pointing her back to the matters at hand.

At last dinner was finished, the dessert dishes had been removed, and the necessary business completed. Ainsley leaned back in the booth and raised her coffee cup. "So tell me, Elizabeth, why is it that a beautiful, albeit tightly strung, woman like yourself has never hitched herself to a man and rode off into the sunset?"

Elizabeth glanced at the check, placed her credit card inside, and returned her gaze to Ainsley. "I don't bring my personal life into the workplace."

"That's a bunch of malarkey if I've ever heard it."

Elizabeth shifted in her seat.

"You know, Elizabeth, you just need to loosen up. Get out there and have a life. Meet someone. Have a couple of babies."

"This is coming from a woman with no children?"

Ainsley's expression shifted slightly, but only for a moment. "Well, you wait long enough and you won't have to worry about it."

"Are you always so tactless?" Elizabeth folded her napkin and laid it beside her plate. "You have no right to judge me or my life or my choices. I'm not married because I *choose* not to be married. And if I wanted children, I would have them. But I won't sit here and listen to someone like you tell me who and what I should be." Elizabeth took the check and her credit card from the young server's hand. She signed it quickly and stood up from her chair.

"And quit looking at me like you're the judge and jury of my life," she went on. "Like you're so much better than I am, like you have it all together and I'm some anchorless ship drifting around in the darkness. I have an amazing and lucrative law practice. I have happy clients. I have a beautiful home. I have provided well for my employees. I have everything I need."

"I didn't hear the word *friend* in there anywhere, Elizabeth. Do you have even one friend?"

Elizabeth leaned down into Ainsley's space. "I don't need friends."

Without looking back she left Ainsley sitting there and stalked out into the cool night. The nerve of that woman! Elizabeth had friends. She had plenty of friends. She had Aaron, and she had . . . and she had . . . well, she had Aaron. She hadn't spent much time with him lately, but—

She'd call him right now and prove he was her friend.

He didn't answer.

She ran through the numbers on her BlackBerry.

"Hello? Cynthia?"

"Sorry, you must have the wrong number. There's no one here by that name."

"Oh, really? Well, that's odd, I just talked to her—" She searched her memory banks, but couldn't recall the last time they had spoken.

She found another name. The phone rang. A male's voice answered.

"Yes, hello. Is Diane there?"

"Who is this?" The voice grew slightly irritated.

"This is Elizabeth. Elizabeth Wilcott."

"Diane and I divorced over a year ago. She doesn't live here any-more."

"Oh. Sorry about—"

The line went dead in her ear. "So we obviously haven't talked in a while," she muttered. "But she could have used a good divorce attorney, if he got the house."

She'd find a friend before the night was over. Of that Ainsley Parker could be certain.

———

Matthew's warm weight nestled against Jeffrey as the credits for *Spider-Man* ran up the screen. He had never known what the real presence of a child felt like, until now. Tears burned at his eyes. He had lived for years with no emotions at all except selfish ones. Now he felt as if something had been unplugged inside of him and he couldn't stop the feelings from leaking out.

He leaned over and smelled Matthew's head. Claire had always told him that nothing smelled better than a baby, but he had never stopped long enough to discover if it was true. Tonight he breathed in the aroma of Matthew's hair, so clean and fresh from the shower. He kissed his son's head gently and laid his cheek on top of it, feel-ing the silkiness underneath his skin. His senses had somehow come keenly alive.

Jeffrey shifted Matthew's head to the pillow on his lap, stretched the boy's curled legs out from underneath him, and covered him with an afghan. And somewhere in the early hours of the morning, after he had memorized every freckle and angle and curve of his little boy's face, he leaned his head back and fell asleep.

chapter twenty-three

Terrance's mother and father were the first to arrive Thursday morning for their parent-teacher conference with Mary Catherine. They were, as Charmaine had indicated, warm and engaging and very intent on their son's academic success. She talked with them about Terrance's lack of focus, which produced grades far below his capabilities. They assured her they would address the issue, and his attention would improve come Monday. And they left her feeling as if she might actually be a teacher after all.

Not so with Nicole's mother. When Mary Catherine had called to set up their appointment, the woman promised only that she'd "see what she had going on that day." Mary Catherine had scheduled her for an appointment and hoped for the best.

About forty-five minutes into the designated hour, the door swung open. The body was about thirty years old; the face fifty; the clothes seventeen. The woman's skirt barely reached midthigh, and her blouse showed far too much cleavage and bare belly. Her hair was bleached blonde and overprocessed, and a cigarette dangled from her heavily painted pink lips.

"You Nikki's teacher?" She flicked her ashes onto the floor.

Mary Catherine wondered if holding out the trash can would elicit the same reaction from Nicole's mother. She didn't figure it would.

She stretched out her hand. "Yes, I am. I'm Mary Catherine Bean. I suppose you're Nicole's mother, Annette."

The woman stared at the hand as if it were intruding into her space. Mary Catherine withdrew it. The woman pulled up a chair, sat down, and crossed her legs, letting the heel of her shoe flap madly against her swinging foot. She held her cigarette out from her body. "So, what you got to tell me about Nikki that I don't already know?"

Mary Catherine retreated to the chair behind her desk. Now she knew where Nicole got her intimidating and brassy manner. "Well . . ." She cleared her throat. "Your daughter, Nicole, I believe, has a lot of potential."

The woman gave a mocking laugh. "You don't know my Nikki. Nikki ain't got no potential. That child is going to end up just like her mama, playing lap dog to anyone who is willing to pay next month's rent. She don't need no more than that anyway. This education stuff is nothing but a load of crap. She's only here because the law says I have to send her to school. The real education she'll get is out there in the world."

Mary Catherine tried to keep her face expressionless, but it obviously didn't work.

"What? You think there's something more? You sittin' here all high and mighty in your fancy shoes and your fancy little dress. You don't know nothin' 'bout women like me or my daughter. So unless you got real stuff to tell me 'bout my daughter, you don't need to be wastin' no more of my time."

Three months ago, Mary Catherine would have climbed under the desk and pretended she was checking for chewing gum. But teaching had given her a backbone. There would be no hiding today.

"Do you know that Nicole comes late to class every day? Do you know that she refused to take her test yesterday?" She stood up and came out from behind the desk. "Nicole is one of the smartest kids I've come across. Her IQ is higher than anyone else's in this school. She could make something of herself if you'd start helping her think she could do more in life than spend it on her back."

The woman flicked more ashes on the floor.

Anger rose up in Mary Catherine, and she advanced on the woman a little more aggressively than she had even intended. "Maybe the life you've chosen works for you. I would beg to differ, but that's beside the point. Nicole is twelve years old. She deserves to be a child, and there isn't anything childlike in her eyes, in her demeanor, or in her spirit. If you want to destroy yourself, that's your problem. But if you decide to take Nicole down with you, that becomes my problem as well."

"You threatening me, lady?"

"It's not a threat. I simply promise to do everything in my power to educate your child for more than dog duty. I have a dog, by the way, and from everything I can see, she makes out far better than Nicole."

They stared each other down for a moment. Then, without a word, the woman exited the room.

———

On his way into the hospital, Jeffrey checked the messages on his phone. Littleton, the private investigator, had called. "You'll want to hear what I found out. You're going to be ecstatic."

"To delete this message, press seven," the mechanized feminine voice instructed. Without a second thought, Jeffrey pressed the button to delete and closed the phone. He never returned the call.

Dr. Nadu was in the boardroom when Jeffrey arrived. "Is something wrong with your face?"

Jeffrey closed the door. "What do you mean?"

"In all the time you've been here, I've never seen you smile. A grimace now and then, occasionally a sarcastic laugh, but never once a real genuine smile. And trust me, I know the difference. Did you get good news on your son today?"

"Actually, I haven't heard the latest on Jacob. I'm going to check in on him now. Is there anything you need me to do before I go?"

"No, we can discuss the rounds when you get back. Go check on your boy."

The bells of the elevator chimed his ascent while his mind tried to recall the last time he'd really smiled. He smiled at Pamela whenever she walked through the door. But he didn't figure that was what Dr. Nadu had seen.

He hadn't heard from Pamela in a while. Few women he had

known were like her, using him pretty much the way he used her. The realization brought with it an unsettling feeling—shame, he thought. Or maybe guilt. He had so little experience with either.

Jeffrey pushed the thought aside and turned his mind instead to Matthew and their time together last night. He woke up this morning feeling truly alive. He hadn't felt that way since . . . since . . .

He rounded the corner and pushed through the doors into ICU.

"Claire's not here," his lookout nurse informed him. "But she won't be gone long. Some friends made her go downstairs for a few minutes to get a cup of coffee. No one can get her to eat."

Jeffrey went into Jacob's room. The boy's inert body still lay there, hooked up to monitors and machines and IVs. Flowers were not allowed in ICU wards, but there must have been at least a hundred get-well cards taped on the wall directly in front of Jacob's bed. There were pictures of Claire and Jacob and Bobo too, and he wondered briefly if she had kept those at her office or if she had managed to salvage them from the fire.

He leaned over slowly and let his face touch the edge of the gauze that surrounded the face of his son. "I'm so sorry, Jacob," he whispered. "I'm so sorry for not being there for you."

He tried to brush the tears away, but a few landed on Jacob's pillow, spreading as they hit. The chart dangled from the foot of the bed, and Jeffrey took it instinctively. They had upped his morphine in the middle of the night, and they had scraped his scabs. That explained the morphine; the necessary scraping caused excruciating pain for a burn victim. He could only imagine how Claire's night had been.

He replaced the chart and stood for a few more moments at the edge of his son's bed. His *son's* bed. *His* son's bed. Either way he said it, it reminded him of what a miserable failure he had been at being a father.

His lookout gave him a smile as he left. He returned it.

Unfortunately, he should have posted someone at the elevator door as well. Because when the doors opened, Claire stood in front of him, arm in arm with a strange woman.

She looked so tired. Not like the picture he had found back at the house—no, this was a different kind of weariness. He had seen it often enough during his years of residency, particularly in ICU. People with no sleep, little hope, and no control.

And yet she shouldn't be this way. She should have had him by her side, carrying the load. He should have protected her. Held her. Helped her.

Her fire toward him was gone. "What are you doing here, Jeffrey?"

"I went in to see Jacob, Claire. It's important for me to know how he's doing." The words sounded false and pathetic in light of his absent years.

"So you can rid yourself of guilt?"

Her friend walked down the hall to offer them a little privacy. He was grateful. "Maybe."

She gave a mock laugh. "I didn't think you were capable of feeling guilt."

"I can feel guilt." He felt his indignation rise, then recalled the unfamiliar emotion he had felt earlier that morning—one that had not visited him in thirty years. "Well, anyway, whether I have in the past or not, I'm feeling some now, and I don't know what to do with it. I just want to come and see him, Claire. Can you at least give me that?"

"Give *you* that?" A light kindled in her dull eyes, a tiny flicker of an ember. "This isn't about *you*, Jeffrey. Or are you incapable of thinking about yourself for one moment?"

His old defenses kicked in. "Is this about money, Claire? I know this has to be hard for you. Don't worry about these hospital bills. I'll take care of all of them. And where are you living after the fire? I'll give you money so you can pay your bills and get back on your feet."

The ember became a blaze. "You self-righteous jerk! I've never wanted your money. I've never asked for your money. And I don't need your money now."

The emotion died as suddenly as it had come. "All we needed was a husband and a father," she said wearily. "It was never about your money. It was always just about you."

When the alarm clock went off, Elizabeth pulled the pillow over her head and let out a moan. No. She couldn't do it. Not today. Not any day. She'd rather take a leap from one of Charleston's many bridges than have to go anywhere near Ainsley Parker and her incessant condescension and judgment.

She dragged herself out of bed and into the shower, and while the hot water ran over her, she formulated a plan to keep herself out of the office for the day. She had a meeting with Hazel, some research to do, and a number of phone calls to make. That could constitute a day of activities outside of the office. Then she'd have the weekend.

The weekend. Oh, God help us, the weekend. "I can't do Sunday. I can't do another lunch with my family."

She leaned her head against the stone shower wall, hoping the water could pound out the frustration in the pit of her gut. There were padded cells for people who felt like this. They sat in front of the TV watching *The Price Is Right*, babbling and drooling. The frightening thing was that it almost felt like a better option.

Aaron assured her that her clients were happy, that everything was running smoothly, that she would be able to walk back into that office and never even know that she had spent a year away. She didn't believe him.

Besides, he didn't know what she was being forced to do. Ever since the morning Wade Bennett dropped Hazel Moses's case into her lap, she had been trying to formulate a plan to get herself out of this without losing her inheritance or her mind.

Every morning she had to fight the urge to laugh in Ainsley's face and return to *her* job. Every morning she had to remind herself that she had two other siblings who continued to show up at their new positions every day. And every day they showed up, it became easier for them to show up the next day.

She got out of the shower, toweled off, and pressed the new number on her speed dial. The new PI, the one she hired to replace the inept Cavanaugh.

She got his voice mail and didn't even bother to identify herself. "Tell me you've found something, Mike. Give me some kind of good news. And for the record, if you can't come up with anything by Monday morning, consider yourself replaced."

She hung up the phone. At least there was one place in her life where she was still in control.

———

Elizabeth watched from the sidewalk as Hazel Moses pushed the broom across the front sidewalk.

The old woman turned in her direction and smiled. "I didn't know I was going to get the pleasure of your company again so soon."

"Well, I have a few papers I need to get you to sign. Looks like you're having a fun morning."

"Oh yes. I try to make it look presentable the best I can. I may not repair the house until I get all of this settled, but I can certainly keep it clean around here." Hazel flitted the broom in front of her, smiling. "Could I offer you some tea?"

"No, thank you. I wish I could, but I just came by to get these papers signed."

"Well, let's get them signed then."

Elizabeth followed Hazel up onto the front porch, where the old woman rested the broom against the door frame and sank into one of the rockers. "What do we have here?"

"Just a power of attorney—it gives me the right to ask questions and get information on your behalf." She pulled the documents out of her briefcase and waited as Hazel read through the pages.

Elizabeth reached out a hand and leaned it against the edge of the door frame, next to the broom. Beneath her fingers she could feel tiny grooves in the wood. "I bet you'll be glad to get rid of all of this decaying wood around here."

Hazel looked up and smiled. "Are you talking about that piece of wood underneath your hand?"

"Well, I just noticed all of these notches in the door frame. You think you might have termites or something?"

Hazel chuckled, the creases around her eyes growing deeper. "Look closer."

Elizabeth leaned in. Beside each notch she saw small letters. She squinted and focused. Names began to come into view, followed by dates, scratched into the wood.

"That is where we kept track of my babies and their growth. Each one has a notch for each year. Look how far up they go."

Elizabeth's head tilted upward, all the way to the top of the door frame.

"I have some tall children."

"I'd say you do."

"If I lost this house, I think I'd have to take that door frame with me." Her voice shook slightly.

Elizabeth looked at the old woman and saw tears gathering at the edges of her amber eyes. Hazel signed the paper and handed it back to Elizabeth. She felt inadequate to respond.

"I'll be in touch with you soon."

"I believe we're going to win this battle, Elizabeth. I know you're not here by accident. Not by accident at all."

———

Will leaned over the counter at the registrar's office. He had slept at the frat house after they took his car and was still dressed in his rumpled clothes from last night. "Lucy, beautiful Lucy," he crooned in what he hoped was a charming singsong. "Got it all taken care of today?"

She did not smile. "Will, it's been three months. I honestly don't think it's going to *get* resolved. This semester is almost over anyway. Why don't you just quit worrying about it, go do something with your time, get a job or something? Maybe you can get this fixed over the Christmas holidays."

He gave her his best smile. "Just a little hiccup, that's all," he assured her. "I'll come back Monday, and this will all be straightened out, you'll see."

chapter twenty-four

Jeffrey tipped the young man who delivered the filets mignons and baked potatoes in plastic containers. He never knew you could get steaks delivered, but Matthew had taught him all kinds of things.

He grabbed a couple of glasses of sweet tea and some silverware from the cafeteria and carried the two sacks of dinner up to Jacob's room. His spy-nurse stopped him as he came around the corner.

"Dr. Wilcott, she's in there right now."

"That's okay. I want to see her, actually."

She shrugged her shoulders and gave him a look that said he had been warned. He spotted Claire through the glass, curled up in the lounge chair, sound asleep.

Jacob's lungs were getting stronger, and the doctors had removed the intubation tube, but it had still been a traumatic day.

He set the bags and drinks on the rolling table and studied Claire's face. So delicate, yet so strong. He really had loved her—at least as much as he had been capable of loving.

She had resisted him at first. But once she had finally let him in, she had returned his love with something deep and fierce and totally different from anything he had ever experienced.

He reached over and nudged her softly. "Claire."

She shifted in her seat.

"Claire, wake up."

Her eyes opened. Deep eyes. Dark. Almost black. When she saw him, she closed them again. Tightly. "Leave me alone."

"Claire, I brought you dinner. Come on, you need to eat. The nurse said you haven't eaten anything since you've been here. That all you do is get up long enough to go to the bathroom and get something to drink. And I know she's telling the truth, because you're never gone for more than five minutes."

She rubbed her eyes and glared at him.

"I'm not here to fight. Honestly. Please, I just want you to eat something."

She straightened up in the chair and crossed her legs underneath her. Her dark green sweater complemented her dark brown hair, still pulled back in a rubber band. He brought the rolling tray from the side of the room, wheeled it in front of her, and opened one of the plastic containers. The rich aroma of the steak permeated the air. She breathed in deeply.

"Why are you here?" She shifted in her seat but kept her eyes glued on the steak.

"I'm taking care of you tonight. You can't survive on adrenaline, Claire, or you're going to end up in a bed down the hall." He laid out the silverware and began to fix her baked potato. He loaded it with butter, salt, and pepper, and laid the sour cream aside.

Her brown eyes studied him curiously. "How did you remember that?"

"Remember what?"

"That I only like butter and not sour cream."

He looked down at her potato. He hadn't even thought about it until now. "I don't know. I guess it was locked up in my subconscious somewhere." He laughed, remembering more. "And you hate it for no other reason than the fact that it's called *sour* cream." He shook his head. "Now eat."

She cut into her steak without hesitation. He sat down next to her, watching as she devoured everything on her plate. She didn't speak again until the last bite was gone. When she finished, she wiped her mouth and looked up at him. "It was good." She blushed slightly. "Thank you."

"You're welcome." He took another bite of his steak.

"So what do I owe you for dinner?"

"Claire, don't be ridiculous. This is about me wanting to make sure you eat."

When she spoke again, the familiar accusation behind her words was gone, and her tone was simply matter-of-fact. "Where have you been, Jeffrey? How could you just vacate your son's life for ten years?" Her brown eyes bored into him.

He laid his fork down. "So much for small talk, huh?" He wiped his mouth with his paper napkin and folded it neatly beside his plate. She had every right to ask. And he had an answer. "Selfishness."

Her eyes widened slightly. This was obviously not the response she had expected.

"Self-absorption. Stupidity. I could stop here."

"Why?"

"Why stop?"

She rolled her eyes. "No, why self-absorption? Why stupidity? You were a grown man."

"I might have been grown, but I wasn't a man."

An expression of surprise passed briefly across her face.

"I never realized that being a parent could actually be fulfilling. To be perfectly honest, I thought it was trivial."

"Honesty would be a nice thing from you, Jeffrey, but not something I've come to expect."

"Well, I am being honest now. I thought children were something men gave to their wives to keep them satisfied, so they could just go on with their own lives, but . . ."

He paused as his mind conjured up images of this past week with Matthew: the hot dogs, the cokes, the movies, the laughter.

"But I've done so much and I've missed so much," he went on. "And I don't want to miss any more of my children's lives." He replaced the lid on his dinner and set it aside.

"I need you to forgive me, Claire. I need you to forgive me for the way I deserted you years ago. For the way I vanished out of Jacob's life and left you to take care of everything and be both parents. I need you to forgive me. If you can. Especially now, because I know all of this—" He motioned toward the hospital bed. "All of this is my fault."

Burning tears rose up and threatened to spill over. He tried to fight them, but he wasn't sure it was any use. Wasn't even sure he wanted to. "The dog. The fire. All these years. All my fault."

Claire's frown softened. "Jeffrey Wilcott, in all the years I've known you, I've never seen you cry."

He reached a hand up and swiped at the tears. "In all the years I've known me, I've never seen it either. But I've been doing it a lot lately. I've turned into a freak. I don't even recognize myself."

She laughed slightly, then pulled her knees up against her chest and wrapped her arms around them. "Jeffrey, it's not your fault. I was just angry. All of this has made me so afraid."

She pushed herself up from her chair and walked to the glass, staring out toward the nurses' station. Nurse Lookout turned back to her paperwork as if she hadn't been spying on them the whole time.

"I don't hate you, Jeffrey, despite the things I've said over the last couple of days. That's just my world lying there." She turned toward Jacob's bed. "And if anything—" Her voice broke. She couldn't finish. Her shoulders began to sag and shake as she sobbed.

Instinctively, Jeffrey stood up and took her in his arms. She let him. He held her tightly, gently. She should have felt like a stranger in his arms, but she felt so . . . familiar.

She recovered her composure and released herself from his arms. "Jeffrey, I forgave you years ago. When I left you, I'll be honest, I did hate you then. For two years I let that bitterness steal from me even more than you stole from me during our marriage. It stole friendships. It stole any joy I had in living. It even stole my ability to enjoy my son. And then one day I looked at him and assured him that he'd never have to lose another day of his mother to her own bitterness. That was the day I forgave you, Jeffrey. I'm a different person from the one that you married."

He smiled at her and ventured a joke. "Well, there were a couple of scenes at the elevator."

"Touché." She laughed, running her hands over the top of her head. "There's still that fire in me," she said. "But I'm different. My

life is different. My choices are different. I got to the place where I
so desperately needed to *be* forgiven that I could finally *forgive.* It
released me. And I released you."

"So all these years you haven't hated me?'

"What? Disappointed?"

He shook his head. "No, relieved. I wouldn't blame you, don't
get me wrong. But I thought you hated me, and if seeing me here
added one more thing to what you're already going through then I
will walk away. But it's not what I want to do."

Her eyes darkened, and she set her jaw. "Just don't play with us,
Jeffrey. Neither of us deserves that. If you want to be here and check
on Jacob, that's fine, but if you really don't care, don't pretend. Jacob
has lived without a father for a long time. He doesn't need false
hope."

"You don't have to trust me right now, Claire. I'm not even sure
what has happened to me, or why I've been able to see things in a
different way over the last few days. All I know is that when this boy
wakes up—"

He watched as her gaze shifted back to her son and her eyes filled
with tears. "And he *will* wake up, Claire—completely, and not just
in screaming pain. He will. And when he does, I'll be there. I'll do
whatever I need to do, be whatever I need to be."

"Right now we just need a good doctor."

"Dr. Moss and Dr. Nadu are the best," Jeffrey responded. "The
absolute best."

"I thought you were the best."

"Yeah, I did too." He ducked his head. "I might have been wrong."

———

The rain was falling in a gentle mist as Mary Catherine sat in the
small booth catty-cornered to the large window at 39 Rue de Jean.
The mirrored wall across from her revealed all she needed to know.
One glass of wine, one bowl of soup, one Mary Catherine. Not
another soul but her.

She almost felt as if she were in Paris. The mist outside, the darkening evening, the scents around her. Over the last few months, she had found a growing enjoyment of the city she had never really discovered. She had toured gardens, ridden trolley cars, talked to strangers, and come alive, even while so much of the life she had known was dying. And for the most part she had done it alone.

Bits and pieces of her day came floating back to her: the parent-teacher conferences, and the disturbing fact that Charmaine's mother had not come. Surely with a daughter as intelligent as that, a parent would be vitally interested in her academic progress. But the woman had never shown up, never even called back.

Nate hadn't called back either. When he hadn't answered his cell phone, she had left a message for him to meet her here. This little Parisian bistro had always been one of their favorite places for an intimate dinner.

But he hadn't come. Hadn't called.

The conversation from the women across the way arrested her attention. They were enjoying a night of freedom from husbands and children, over wine, bread, and much laughter.

In the far booth, two older women were dolled up and shamelessly flirting with the young waiter. She watched as one of the women giggled and put her hand to her chest in an *I do declare!* gesture. As if she were a lady.

"Shameless hussy," Mary Catherine muttered.

"Excuse me?" the waiter said as he reached to refill her wine glass.

She felt her face redden. "Oh, nothing. Just chattering to myself. I teach kids all day, so I always have to talk over them to get them quiet, and sometimes I just forget I'm alone." She stopped. "You don't care about any of this, do you?"

He laughed. "It's okay, ma'am. I'll be happy to listen if you want to talk."

She forced a smile. "I'm fine. Just fine. I'm just going to sit here *quietly* and enjoy my soup."

"Let me know if I can get you anything else."

Mary Catherine waited until he was safely out of sight, then leaned over her bowl and took a long deep sniff of her soup. For one moment she let the aroma transport her to a tiny café in Provence, where she and Nate had the most amazing onion soup.

Music and laughter drifted in from the bar. She ate her soup quietly and studied the lines that ran through the aged mirror on the wall across from her.

She thought of Nate and tried not to cry.

chapter twenty-five

ey, Dad, stop! Stop!" Matthew yelled.

Jeffrey's foot connected with the brakes. "What? What is it?" They were on Edisto Island, driving past the Presbyterian Church, heading to the plantation for Sunday dinner.

"You've got to see this! Really, stop!"

Jeffrey pulled the car over into the grass parking lot. Matthew jerked off his seat belt, flung the door open, and ran toward the church, slamming the door until the car shook. Jeffrey made a mental note that they needed to talk about the proper care and shutting of his car door.

The tiny white building sat almost in the center of the tombstones that scattered the graveyard, a small clapboard building reminiscent of a life-size dollhouse. Matthew dashed up the green metal steps and opened the door. Jeffrey followed.

It was a perfect November day. The morning had been cool, but now the afternoon sun warmed the air to a balmy seventy. Jeffrey's eyes took in the hand-painted sign above the door: "Prayer Chapel, Open to the Public."

Jeffrey entered through the open door and felt a sharp drop in temperature. A tiny cross hung above the window opposite him. Two old pews lined the side walls, along with a wooden bench for three in the center of the room. There was just enough room for seven or eight people to gather—to pray, to reflect. Or, apparently on a day like today, to hear the memories of an eight-year-old boy.

"Granddaddy use to bring me up here when I'd come visit. He

said this was where he liked to come at night when he was lonely. Said he'd just sit here and talk to God. He's the one that taught me how, you know?"

"Taught you how to sneak out of the house at night?" Jeffrey was only half listening. On a bulletin board, ragged scraps of paper held the hand-scrawled prayer requests of strangers. Small wooden display cases hung along the walls, displaying a variety of tracts and religious literature.

"No, Dad! Pray. Aren't you listening?"

"Yeah, I'm listening." Jeffrey sat down on one of the wooden pews and turned his full attention on Matthew.

"You ever prayed, Dad?"

"Yeah," he answered instinctively. "I've prayed . . . you know."

"When?" Matthew walked over to Jeffrey and lifted his weight up, bringing it down on top of Jeffrey's leg. He wiggled his sharp little tailbone until he got perfectly comfortable. "When did you pray?"

Jeffrey placed a hand across Matthew's legs. He couldn't remember having a child on his lap in years. "Well, for your information, young man, I use to say my prayers every night when my mother would come to tuck me in."

"So you haven't said your prayers since you've been old?"

Jeffrey laughed. "You calling me old?" He poked Matthew in the ribs and began tickling him.

Matthew laughed the belly laugh of a child, composing himself only after he'd squirmed out of his father's reach and sat down on the pew beside him. "Yeah, I called you old. And quit changing the subject."

Jeffrey looked down at him. He laid his arm along the back of the pew and then dropped it over Matthew's shoulder. He had developed an odd need to touch this child. "How did you get so smart?"

"You always said *you* were brilliant."

"Yeah. Right."

"So you don't pray anymore?" the boy persisted.

Jeffrey's eyes rested on the top of Matthew's sun-streaked head. "You know, Matthew, I don't. I haven't prayed in years, and to be honest, if you knew my track record, you'd know that God probably wouldn't listen to me anyway."

"You'd be surprised. Granddaddy said he used to be a scoundrel too, but one day after Grandmother died, he realized he didn't want to be a scoundrel anymore. And you know what else, Dad?"

"What else?"

"He said the one thing he wished he could do over was how he raised his children. I would have told you that a long time ago, but you and I never really talked much."

Jeffrey felt his eyes sting. He reached down and took Matthew's face in his hands and turned it up toward his own. "Matthew, can you ever forgive me for being such a jerk?"

"I forgive you, Dad." He patted Jeffrey's knee softly. "I forgive you."

The silenced lingered in the small prayer chapel, but it didn't feel odd, or weird, or uncomfortable. It was just silent.

Jeffrey finally broke it. "So, how exactly did Granddaddy say he prayed?"

"Said he just sat here and talked to God."

"You ever do it with him?"

"Well, not *with* him, but whenever he would go outside to check on Grandmother's grave, I would talk to God in here by myself."

"Really? Like what would you say?"

"Oh, I just told him how I was feeling. Talked to him kind of like you and I are talking now. And then I'd ask him stuff."

"Like what? What kind of stuff?"

"Stuff like—" He shrugged. "Well, kind of like what's happening today, you know, with you and me."

Jeffrey tilted his head. "What do you mean?"

"I asked God to help you to love me, that's all. You know, like you do now. So I guess he was listening. I always thought he was. It was like I could feel him, inside me or something. But now it's real. Now I *know* he listens."

"You believed I didn't love you?"

"Dad, you never even talked to me."

"I was horrible."

"Yes, you were," Matthew said with absolute candor. "But you're great now. Just talk to God. It's amazing what can happen!"

And with that he jumped off the pew and headed out the open door.

Jeffrey sat in the silence of the small room, not even trying to wipe the tears as they fell. A presence seemed to fill up the vacant places inside of him

It's just like talking, Matthew had said.

"God, it's me, Jeffrey Wilcott," he murmured. "I'm not real good at this, and I'm not even sure if you remember me. I've been pretty pathetic for quite a while now."

His voice echoed against the wooden walls and floor of the chapel. He stopped, feeling self-conscious. After a moment of silence, he forced himself to go on. "So, anyway, if you're listening, I was just wondering if maybe we could start talking again. You know, whenever you're free."

A breeze swept through the window, and Jeffrey opened his eyes. "I've been a poor excuse for a father. Not to mention an even worse excuse for a husband, and a horrible son."

His voice faltered. "I know I've got some other people I need to talk to about this, but I figure you're the most important. If you can find any way to forgive me—and help my dad to forgive me, if you can—I really would appreciate it. And I don't want to ask you for anything other than that, but there is this one big thing. My son, his name's Jacob. He got badly burned, and he really needs a miracle. If you could help us with that, I'd appreciate it."

Jeffrey stood up from the pew slowly, then remembered something else and sat down again. "Oh, and thanks very much, I guess," he amended. "And, uh . . . amen."

As he closed the door of the chapel behind him, Jeffrey felt as if he'd left something of himself behind. The heavy part. He felt lighter, freer.

He saw Matthew over by his parents' graves and headed in that direction.

"I miss him," Matthew said, wiping his eyes. "He and I had a really good time."

"Yeah, I know, son. I miss him too." The truth was, he had missed his father for most of his life. And now, for the first time, he was willing to admit it to himself.

———

Elizabeth could have sworn that was Jeffrey's car in front of her, and it had just pulled out from the church.

"There's no way," she muttered to herself. "Jeffrey Wilcott's the last person they'd let into a church." The thought made her laugh, and she hadn't laughed in a while.

Elizabeth dreaded this day, as she dreaded its arrival each month. But every month it seemed to get more and more torturous, like everything else in her life.

The dust stirred behind her car. She pulled up to the front of the house, where the wisteria had now lost its blossoms to autumn and to the cooler temperatures. She watched as a young boy got out of Jeffrey's car. *You coward,* she thought. *Having to bring one of your kids here just to get through the day.*

Esau stepped out onto the front porch. The boy let out a shout and ran into Esau's arms. It was something Elizabeth hadn't seen in years. A child being loved.

Elizabeth had never understood how someone like Jeffrey could have so many children. He wasn't a father; he was a sperm donor. Surely there ought to be some deity upstairs controlling how children were divvied out: three to a good home here, two to a good home there. Some people didn't deserve children at all. But then, her father had sired four of his own. Obviously no God in heaven cared.

———

Jeffrey watched Elizabeth as she exited the car. She looked tired, similar to the way Claire did in the birthday photo. For the first time in years, Jeffrey felt sorry for Elizabeth.

For most of their adult life, he had simply avoided her, because avoiding her allowed him to avoid his own shame. But today he didn't want to avoid her. Today, seeing Elizabeth's face the way he saw it now, he wanted to apologize to her. Gone was the hatred, the bitterness. All he felt was an overwhelming sympathy for this woman who was his sister.

⁓

Elizabeth's hand froze on the door handle of the car. Jeffrey was talking to her. To *her*.

She hadn't registered the words. "Excuse me?"

"I said, I was wondering if you and I could find some time today to talk. Just the two of us."

She looked into Jeffrey's face. Something there had shifted, changed, distorted. His expression was open, expectant, even vulnerable. Instinctively she knew what he wanted to talk about. All the feelings came back in a rush. An old fear swept over her, the fear of a thirteen-year-old girl.

She did the only thing she knew to do. She ran. Calling Esau's name, she ran to the porch and hugged him. "Esau! It's so good to see you! And oh my goodness, is this Matthew?"

"Hey, Aunt Elizabeth," Matthew replied. "I haven't seen you in forever."

"It's been too long. Entirely too long." She wrapped her arm around him and led him inside, never looking back into Jeffrey's eyes.

⁓

Mary Catherine pulled up in front of the house; her mind had already tuned out Will's incessant droning. She climbed out of the car leaving him to entertain himself. She noticed the wisteria had all but bid adeiu until next year. She ran her fingers across one of its limp leaves and looked forward to when spring would bring it back to life. Maybe she'd be back to her life by then too.

———

Esau always cooked the night before, because he never worked on the Lord's day. He would set the table, put out the food, and put the left-overs away when they were done. That was the extent of Esau's labor on Sunday. But he certainly outdid himself on Saturday.

"This is great," Will said, digging into a piece of ham. He had shown up with Mary Catherine and hadn't yet volunteered what happened to his Porsche. Jeffrey had his suspicions.

"Put your fork down, Will. Nobody's even said grace."

Will chewed slowly and nodded, finally placing his fork down on the edge of his plate. Jeffrey tried to catch Elizabeth's eye, but she avoided his gaze

"Can I pray, Esau?"

"Go, sweet boy."

Jeffrey braced himself for "God is great, God is good." But his son surprised him. "Dear Lord, thank you for this wonderful meal we are about to receive. Thank you for the hands that prepared it. And thank you that we are together as a family, even though Granddaddy can't be with us. Amen."

"Amen," Esau offered.

"Amen," Jeffrey said softly.

———

Elizabeth busied herself with passing the ham and vegetables and resolutely avoided her older brother's attempts to get her attention.

"Where'd you learn to pray like that, little bro?" Will asked as he headed back to his ham.

"I heard a lot of praying around here, whenever I'd come over."

Elizabeth gave a sarcastic little grunt. "I always remember hear-ing you pray, Esau, but I don't ever remember hearing Dad pray."

"I heard him pray every now and then over those last few years," Mary Catherine said. "I just figured he wanted to make sure he made it wherever Mother was going."

"What are you insinuating, that you were the only one around here taking care of him?"

"Elizabeth—" Jeffrey's voice held a note of warning.

"Leave it alone, Jeffrey. Everybody at this table knows you brought your child along because you're too much of a coward to face us alone."

"Yeah, Jeffrey," Mary Catherine said. "Why did you get to bring Matthew? Isn't that against the rules? I could have brought Nate."

Elizabeth gave a mocking laugh.

"What?" Mary Catherine demanded. "You have a problem with Nate?"

"Mary Catherine, you're the only one who *doesn't* have a problem with that freeloader. He doesn't want anything but your father's money. I'm surprised you've even been able to keep him around, since he is having to wait a year to get his hands on it."

Mary Catherine's bottom lip began to quake. "You are *mean*, Elizabeth. Mean and bitter and sad!" She pushed her chair out and stood up, staring across the table at Elizabeth. "Nate never did anything to you, and he loves me! He loves me!"

"Now, I'll not have it," Esau interrupted. "Mary Catherine, go on and get to sittin' yourself down, heah. Matthew, go fetch the pitcher of sweet tea out the refrigerator."

Matthew obeyed immediately.

"Now, no more disgracin' this house or your parents' legacy any more than you already have," Esau went on, glaring at the lot of them. "You'll each one of you sit down and not speak if you can't speak with kindness to one another. I won't have none of it. I won't let you back through that there door no matter what you've been told you have to do. You heah?"

"Yeah," Will said. "Y'all need to straighten up, because I only get food like this once a month." He reached for the butter beans.

Mary Catherine excused herself and headed for the back door, not bothering to keep it from slamming as she exited.

Matthew returned with the tea. "Fill 'em up, son," Esau said.

He walked around the room and filled up each glass. When he

got to Jeffrey, Jeffrey gave him a wink and a soft smile, and touched him lightly on the shoulder. Elizabeth noticed and found the whole interchange very telling. Jeffrey thought he was winning and was flaunting it. She ate nothing else and simply sat smoldering in silence.

When Will finally laid his fork down, Esau looked at him. "Dessert, Will?"

"Oh yeah, Esau, bring it on!"

Without a word she got up and left and didn't even say good-bye.

She had almost made her getaway when Matthew's voice arrested her. "Aunt Elizabeth?"

She turned toward the strikingly beautiful young boy. She saw elements of Jeffrey in him. The rest must have been his mother, but she couldn't even remember what the woman looked like.

Matthew didn't deserve her rage. She stifled it. "Yes, Matthew?"

"I'm really sorry you had such a lousy time today. Maybe the next time I see you, you'll be feeling better."

"Sometimes adults just have lousy days."

"Yeah, well, my dad's had lousy years, but he's been different lately."

"Different?"

"Yeah, he's just been being, like, a real dad. We've been spending a whole bunch of time together, doing stuff. It's been very cool. So maybe whatever has been happening to him can happen to you, and you'll feel better."

She touched the top of his head. She hardly knew this child, wouldn't have recognized him on the street if she'd passed him. "Maybe, Matthew. Maybe."

"I hope so."

Elizabeth inhaled sharply. He was too observant for his own good. For *her* own good.

"You ever going to have any kids, Aunt Elizabeth?"

She felt the bristling beneath the surface of her skin. She'd never been rude to an eight-year-old. Never had the desire until now. She took the only escape she could think of—a lame one, but an option nevertheless. She jerked her watch upward toward her face. "Oh, look at the time! Well, great to see you, Matthew. But I've got to get going."

She reached for the door, but he got to her first. He grabbed her by the waist and held her tightly. She patted him awkwardly, and when he finally let go, she climbed into her car and left them all behind.

———

Mary Catherine walked through the back gardens, inhaling the salt air and trying to let it wash away her anger. The flowers were dormant now, and she wished that her sister would go into hibernation as well. Instead, she just got more irritating.

She headed past the old barn and down to the long wooden bridge that led to a dock sitting in the saltwater marsh. This place was just as beautiful as any of the other historical places Charleston offered. Yet this one held *her* history.

She looked out over the marsh, the reeds swaying against the breeze. One reed among the others was bent down and hanging as if it were holding on. That's how she felt, so many times, in the face of Elizabeth's demanding attitude and Jeffrey's arrogance.

From somewhere deep inside, a memory surfaced: *A bruised reed, he will not break.* She couldn't remember where the words had come from, but she let them resonate as she watched the reed swaying in the wind, its head bowed down. She could only hope the same for herself. To bend, but not to break.

———

Esau had loaded Will up with the leftovers and put them into Mary Catherine's car.

"Jeffrey, you got twenty dollars I can borrow?"

"Borrow?"

"Okay, have?"

"Where's your money, Will?"

"It's all gone crazy. I can't get to my money, and they just took my car."

"And you still think this whole thing is a joke?"

Will slugged Jeffrey on his arm. "You still think this whole will thing is *real*?"

Esau sat down in the rocking chair and took Matthew in his lap as the sounds of Will's laughter drifted back from Mary Catherine's departing convertible. Jeffrey sat on the porch and rocked awhile, and then the two of them left as well.

Esau waited a good thirty minutes after Jeffrey drove away before he reached for the telephone. "I know you were probably watchin', but they all showed up again."

"I honestly didn't expect as much from them."

Esau stared out the back windows of the kitchen, where light from the setting sun poured in like liquid gold. "You underestimate their wills. Their father counted on 'em."

"We'll see if he counted correctly. I left some money in your hiding place outside. You really should let me get you a safety deposit box."

"I don't need no safe deposit box. That money doesn't stay in these ole hands long enough to need one."

"It's still not safe."

"It's safer than a bank. They'd trace this money quicker than you could get to high tailin' it out of Charleston. And with the tempers flaring around this dinner table, there is honestly no telling what they'd do to either one of us."

"All right, Esau. I defer to your wisdom. Spend wisely."

"Will spend as needed, you rest assured."

chapter twenty-six

Mary Catherine dropped Will off and gave him a hundred dollars out of her grocery money. He had asked her to go buy him a car, but apparently he had forgotten that she couldn't touch any money except for necessities—*her* necessities. She told him to get himself a bus pass. He laughed.

"Hey, baby girl," she said as she greeted Coco and set her bag on the kitchen counter. "Nate! Nate!"

Nate didn't answer.

"You know, that's it. I am sick and tired of him not being home." She flung open the French doors overlooking the backyard and the pool and took the stairs two by two until she hit the beach. Coco followed with delight.

As she walked, Mary Catherine scanned the beach for any sign of him. His car was in the garage, but he was nowhere to be found. She returned to the house and sat on the bottom step, watching as Coco played in the ocean. If she was a smarter woman, she'd admit to herself that something was up in the land of wedded bliss, and it sure wasn't bliss.

"I *am* a smart woman," she murmured to herself. "I'm a very smart woman. I'm so smart, I'm going to let him enjoy an evening on the sidewalk until he decides to tell me where it is he's been."

She picked up the phone and dialed. The locksmith was there in an hour. Nate wasn't. Too bad for Nate.

When Elizabeth got home, she went straight to her phone, praying the red light would be blinking. Praying. Even though she didn't believe a God existed.

She wanted a message, *any* message, that the Executor had been located. She had hoped her threat to fire the private investigator had been incentive enough to get him off his duff. She had already fired one. She'd have no problem doing it again.

No red flashing light. No message.

She sighed, picked up her keys, and left again.

A few minutes later she pulled into the parking lot of Hominy Grill, with its large mural of a smiling woman painted on the side of the building. This was the best place in Charleston for comfort food. And right now, Elizabeth needed comforting.

She took a seat at a wooden table and waited for Aaron. He entered a few minutes later, clean shaven, wearing camouflage pants and a black sweatshirt.

"Why'd you shave? It's Sunday."

"I shave because I go to church on Sunday."

"You go to *church*?"

He shook his head at her. "Yes, Elizabeth. I've gone to church for the last eight years."

"I never knew that."

"You never ask."

What did that mean? She pushed aside the possibilities. She had her own agenda here. "I have friends, don't I?"

Aaron frowned at her. "What?"

"Friends. You know, buddies. People you hang out with, talk to. *Friends*. I have them, don't I?"

"No," he replied.

"*No*? Are you telling me I don't have friends?"

"Can you think of any? Besides me, that is?"

"Yes, there's . . . well, there was Diane."

Aaron laughed. The server appeared, and he ordered the fried green tomato BLT and a Coke. Elizabeth asked for two eggs over light, grits, bacon, and wheat toast, with orange juice.

Aaron raised his eyebrows. "What happened to the Bran Queen?"

Elizabeth sneered. "What are you, the breakfast police? Never mind the snide comments. Answer my question."

"Diane was never your friend," Aaron said. "She couldn't stand you. She thought her husband liked you, remember?"

"Really? I didn't remember that. Well, maybe that's why they got a divorce, if he had a fondness for women other than Diane."

"They're divorced?"

"Yeah, I found that out on Friday when I tried to call her."

They sat in silence for a while. The waitress brought Aaron's Coke and her orange juice. She took a long sip and contemplated the pulp clinging to the inside of the glass. "So really, you don't think I have any friends?"

"You have to make yourself friendly to be a friend, Elizabeth. It's not one of your strong suits."

The waitress came back with their meals, and she lowered her voice. "Now you're saying I'm not even friendly."

He picked up his sandwich to take a bite. "Pretty much."

"You know that's just sad," she retorted.

"You're right. It is sad."

"Not *me*, Aaron. It's sad that you and Ainsley Parker and my entire family judge me the way you do. You all look at me as some pathetic creature because I'm not married or don't have children. But that is what I *choose*."

"Good for you. But nobody's judging, just observing."

Elizabeth pawed through her grits in the same way she was pawing through her thoughts. None of it was coming out too pretty.

"Ainsley had the audacity to tell me I was bitter. Mary Catherine told me I was mean. What would you like to say, Aaron? Go on, get it off your chest. Surely there is some pronouncement you would like to make over me."

"You need to tone it down, Elizabeth."

She knew he was right, but she couldn't seem to help herself. "What? Am I embarrassing you, Aaron?"

He leaned over and placed his hand on top of hers. "You either quiet down, or you're going to finish this meal by yourself. I don't know what is happening with you, but you're getting completely out of control."

Elizabeth felt the hairs on the back of her neck stand up. Her father use to scold her, and she hated it. In her opinion, you only had a right to scold people if you were willing to be there when they needed you. And no one had been willing to do that.

"If I'm so out of control, why don't you just leave?" she seethed through her clenched teeth.

Aaron removed his hand from on top of hers, picked up his napkin, and calmly wiped his mouth. He signaled to the waitress. "Can I get a to-go box?"

She brought the box in record time.

He packed up his sandwich and took another drink of his Coke. "This is why you don't have friends, Elizabeth, because your entire life is about nothing but *you*. If you'd stop thinking about yourself long enough, you'd realize maybe someone else actually has something to offer. Ainsley Parker is not a bad person. People around this city do nothing but talk about what a difference she has made with that program and how great she is to work with. You just never get pleasant enough for anybody to like you, let alone love you. I'm probably your only friend, Elizabeth, and sometimes even that is questionable. But it's nobody's fault but your own."

chapter twenty-seven

It had been a nearly flawless day, but Jeffrey couldn't expect it to last. One phone call, one voice mail message, and reality came crashing in again. Jacob had developed an infection.

"I'm sorry, son," he said for the third time as he pulled on a clean shirt and rummaged in the closet for a jacket. "But I have to go to the hospital."

"It's okay, Dad." Matthew watched him with solemn eyes.

"I called Gretchen. She'll be over in just a few minutes."

"I can stay by myself, Dad. I have before."

"Yeah, but you shouldn't have." Jeffrey tousled the boy's brown hair. "You'll be all right until she gets here?"

"*Yes*, Dad."

"Okay." He kissed his son on the top of the head. "I—I love you," he stammered.

"Love you too, Dad," Matthew replied, as if it were the most natural thing in the world.

All the way to the hospital Jeffrey's mind lurched back and forth between Jacob and Matthew. Except for Elizabeth's icy reception and sudden departure, the day at the plantation could not have been better. After dinner Jeffrey and Esau had taken Matthew down to paddle around the marsh. Matthew and Esau had picked out every pelican, loggerhead sea turtle, wood stork, and heron—and a few odd creatures they just made up names for.

He had forgotten how much he loved the place. How he and his friends use to row out to the ocean and spend hours catching fish, swimming, laughing. Jeffrey felt as if he were starting to learn how to live again.

"We've worn you out, I'm sure," Jeffrey told Esau as they tied up the boat and headed back to the house.

"I've missed the company, son."

The wistfulness in his tone had stopped Jeffrey cold. "Esau, I'm so sorry. I hadn't even stopped to think how you must be hurting over our father's death."

Esau's weathered face crinkled up. "Your daddy was my closest friend."

"We'll come by more often. I promise. I'll bring Matthew. He loves it here. Forgive me, please, for forgetting you."

The memory of Esau's face caused Jeffrey a deep pang of remorse. He had let down so many people in his life. Including his eldest son, Jacob.

He heard the screams coming from ICU before he even rounded the corner, and he broke into a run. Now that the intubation tube had been removed, Jacob's groans had turned to wails, and with every scream Jeffrey felt a stabbing pain in his own chest.

One of the doctors turned as Jeffrey entered. "We need to scrape the burns, Dr. Wilcott," she said in a low voice. "But the boy's mother won't leave."

He went to Claire and put an arm around her shoulder. "Come on, Claire, just wait out here. Let them do what they need to do."

The duty nurse, Jeffrey's spy, watched as they came out of the room. "She never leaves, Dr. Wilcott. I try to make her; really I do. But she won't even take a break."

"I know, Doris. It's okay. But I do want you to get me a cot for his room. I want her to have a place to lie down. No more sleeping in a chair, okay?"

"I'll have them get it right away."

Jeffrey settled Claire in a chair in the family waiting room and got her a cup of coffee from the machine. Then he called home. "Gretchen, I need you to stay there with Matthew tonight. I have a situation here at the hospital that I just don't feel like I can leave this evening." He could tell she didn't believe him, but he promised her weekend pay. She agreed, and he hung up.

The doctors were finished treating Jacob, and an additional shot of morphine had put him out for a while. Jeffrey settled Claire back down in the chair next to Jacob's bed until the cot arrived.

Dr. Moss exited the room, and Jeffrey walked out with him.

"What have you been able to find?"

"He's got a Staphylococcus infection. It's produced a high fever, which isn't good for any of this. But right now we have his blood pressure steady. We've upped his electrolytes, given him a higher powered antibiotic. His breathing is still good, so we haven't felt the need to intubate him again. He doesn't need that additional stress right now."

Jeffrey blinked back tears.

"I'm really sorry. We're doing everything we can. We just didn't need something additional to have to deal with."

"Does Claire know?"

"She knows there is an infection, yes. She's made it clear she wants us being completely honest with her."

"I'm sure she did." Jeffrey turned and looked at her through the glass window. The resignation on her face made it pretty clear to him that she knew it wasn't going as well as any of them hoped. He turned back around and patted the doctor on the shoulder. "Thanks. I appreciate it."

"We'll keep plowing away, Jeffrey. Just hang in there. I'll be here all night checking in on him. And you."

When Jeffrey entered the room, he saw a small cot situated on the other side of the bed. Good. At least Claire could get a little sleep.

She looked up at him. "He's such a good kid, you know."

He didn't know.

"He always makes straight As. He is an amazing baseball player. The girls love him. I always tell him that's because he is so kind and smart and—"

"I'm still that," Jacob said.

Claire jumped up and walked over to the side of the bed. "Hey, baby, can you see Mom?" She wiped her tears with the back of her hand.

"Yeah, and I can hear you too." His voice slurred from the drugs.

She laughed softly and sniffed. "There's someone here to see you." She reached a hand in Jeffrey's direction.

Jeffrey shook his head. He couldn't do it. He didn't even know what to say. Claire smiled and nodded, encouraging him. He walked slowly over to the edge of the bed and positioned himself in Jacob's view.

"Hey, Jacob."

Claire leaned over the bed. "Do you know who this is, Jacob?"

Jacob's eyes shifted from her face back to Jeffrey's. "He looks kind of like me."

Claire laughed softly again. "Yeah, he does, doesn't he? It's your father, Jacob."

Jacob's eyes opened wider, taking in Jeffrey's face. A faint light seemed to come on inside him. "Dad?"

Jeffrey swallowed down his own tears. "Yeah, son. It's me. It's your father."

"It's about time," Jacob said.

Claire and Jeffrey both laughed together. "You're right. It's way past time." Jeffrey reached down and gently laid his hand underneath Jacob's bandaged arm and bent down close to him. "Son, I need to ask your forgiveness. I'm so sorry for not being there. For not seeing you grow up. For not being a father to you. Please forgive me."

"I've already done that, Dad." Jacob's frail voice filled the room. His eyes grew heavier and closed.

"You rest now, son. Your mother and I will be right here when you wake up."

Claire reached out and touched him on the shoulder. "That's the first time he's spoken, Jeffrey. He hasn't done anything but scream and moan since all of this happened. It's a miracle. It honestly is a miracle."

Jeffrey gazed down at the boy's ravaged face. There was so much to say. So much he wanted to know. So much he wanted to learn. He prayed for one more moment. Just one more moment. "With as much morphine as he is on, it *is* a miracle. And that's a word doctors are seldom willing to use."

"I'm going to walk outside and make a few phone calls now that he's settled. My phone won't work in here. Would you mind staying with him until I get back?"

"Not at all. I want to be with him, as long as you don't mind." Claire shook her head and left him there with his son. In the deepest part of his soul, he ached to take his son in his arms and hold him and kiss him and tell him how much he loved him. He felt that somehow, if he could only do that, it would all be okay. He leaned his body down over Jacob's, trying to get as close to him as possible yet not wanting to cause him any more pain.

"I love you, son. I love you with all of my heart."

And then over the noise of the heart and blood pressure monitors came Jacob's words, slow and deliberate. "I love you too, Dad. I've always loved you."

Without warning, the monitors began to go wild. Alarms sounded. The numbers on the BP monitor began dropping rapidly.

In a rush and a scramble, Jeffrey found himself shuttled out of the room. Doctors and nurses swarmed around his son's bedside, shouting orders, taking no notice of the burns. They had only one concern—saving his life.

And then he heard it. The sound he dreaded. The droning tone of a heart monitor flatlining.

He looked around and realized Claire hadn't returned. He didn't want her here. Not to see this. Not to witness how their son had to be pounded and shocked. But she'd hate him forever if he didn't get her.

He started off in a daze down the hall. Jabbed the down button on the elevator, then cursed its delay and tore down the stairs, adrenaline pumping wildly. She could be anywhere. He burst through the front automatic doors and turned in every direction, hoping to find her on the sidewalk. She wasn't there.

He ran back up to the ICU, and at last he saw her, outside on a patio beyond the waiting room. He tore through the door.

One look at his face was enough to tell her everything. She ran toward him, tried to push past. He grabbed her. "You don't want to go in there, Claire."

"Let me go, Jeffrey! That's my baby!"

"Claire, Claire," he murmured. "Listen to me. Listen to me."

She had already started sobbing. "What? What happened?"

"His blood pressure crashed, and he went into cardiac arrest. Trust me, they are doing everything they possibly can. But you don't want to see what they're having to do." He spoke this last sentence so softly, so compassionately, that it sounded like someone else, even to his own ears.

Her words were barely discernible through her tears. "Just let me get to him."

"I will. You just have to know you can't go in the room."

Back in the ICU someone had closed the door and all of the curtains to Jacob's room, but it was evident they were still working feverishly.

Claire paced, her lips moving with each step. Jeffrey was certain she was praying. Thirty minutes passed. Jeffrey knew that with each minute his son was getting farther and farther away. He wanted to crawl in the corner and weep. He wanted to scream. But Claire deserved his sanity.

Finally, Dr. Moss opened the door. His face said it all. Their boy was gone.

"I'm so sorry," he said. "We did everything we could." He turned to Jeffrey. "Give the nurses a few minutes, okay?"

Jeffrey knew what he meant. Claire didn't need this as the last image of their son.

He went to her, wrapping his arms around her. She stayed in his embrace, standing there completely silent, for almost fifteen minutes. She never moved. She didn't cry. She just let him hold her.

Two nurses finally came through the door, and before they could stop her, she removed herself from Jeffrey's arms and went straight through the door.

He let her go. And he let her go alone. She had raised him all by herself. She deserved to say good-bye by herself.

‎ ~

Jeffrey had finally talked Claire into letting her friends take her home. At last Jeffrey was alone with his son.

He walked to the bed. All the noise had ceased; the monitors were gone. Silence hovered over him like a shroud.

Jeffrey had few memories of Jacob's life—disconnected images, like scenes from a movie he had never seen all the way through. He was so grateful he had at least shown up for the ending.

He pushed the iron bed rail down and leaned over his son, reaching his hands underneath the gauze-wrapped body. At last, Jeffrey held his son. He gripped him tightly and lavished his bandaged face with the kisses of a father. He let his tears fall, knowing they would not hurt now; they would only heal.

There on that hospital bed, Jeffrey held his son for the first time in years, just as he had prayed for the opportunity to do.

part 3

February

chapter twenty-eight

The cold air burned Elizabeth's lungs as she ran. She could smell wood smoke from the chimneys in the homes along the Battery. The scent brought a wave of nostalgia surging up in her. Real wood-burning fireplaces, like the ones at the plantation. She tried to stifle the thought.

As dawn broke she thought how her entire life had changed. She was running in the morning hours now, because sheer exhaustion kept her home in the evenings. But getting out of bed to run was becoming increasingly difficult.

The research and deposition of Hazel Moses's family members, tracing their genealogy back to the times of slaves, had proven even more taxing than her law school years. The frustrating part was that she couldn't contact Everett and Associates directly to try to reassure Mr. Everett that she really was working on his behalf. She wasn't sure he'd believe her anyway, but the stipulations of the will made it clear she was to have no contact regarding her business. And even though he had chosen another law firm to represent him, so as not to cause a conflict of interests, she still couldn't risk it. She had already lost a small fortune on this case simply because he had taken his business to another firm. She couldn't risk losing her entire inheritance on a technicality. And right now, playing along was still her only option.

For once she wished she would run into a brick wall. But when it came to Hazel, every door seemed to fling itself open, daring her to enter. And one thing she'd never been good at was declining a dare. But she knew to survive she had to find some way to blow this case to smithereens, but so far she hadn't come up with anything that would sabotage Hazel's claim to the property.

She had spoken with a cousin of Hazel's, twice removed, who lived in Savannah. She was going to see him in the next couple of days, and from her initial conversation with him on the telephone, she hoped he might be the key. He didn't seem inclined to do anything that would help Hazel Moses. Yet in spite of her hard edges, she had a soft spot for Hazel. And she didn't want her caught in the crossfire.

She dragged herself home and got in the shower, then stood in front of her closet staring numbly at the choices. Picking out clothes had become a burden, much like talking to Aaron.

He still called her with weekly updates, but ever since their fiasco dinner, she had refused to talk to him. He'd leave her a message and she'd listen to it, but she never called him back. She rationalized her coldness, told herself she wanted him to think about his actions and realize what a good friend she really was. But deep inside she knew he was right, and she was embarrassed.

Elizabeth pulled up to the curb in front of the office, sipped at her Starbucks, and closed her eyes, trying to gear herself up to go inside. She was still sitting behind the wheel when Ainsley jerked open the passenger's door and climbed into the Jeep. "Don't get out. Let's go eat."

"Ainsley, I've really got a lot of work to do. I don't have time—"

"Elizabeth, the only work you have is what I give you to do, and today I'm giving you the work of taking me to breakfast. Besides, I've got some things I need you to help me with."

"Like you need my help."

"You'd be surprised." Ainsley patted her arm. "Ooh, suede. Nice." She stroked the sleeve of Elizabeth's coat. "So, how about we go up the street to the Waffle House?"

"The what?"

Ainsley's head darted in Elizabeth's direction. "Don't tell me you've never been to the Waffle House."

"I've had waffles," Elizabeth hedged, her defensiveness rising.

"You've *never* been to the Waffle House? You *are* a spoiled brat. The Waffle House, for your information, is that restaurant with the yellow and black sign, you know, that you see off the interstate all the time." She laughed. "Oh, that's right, you don't see a lot of that from your private jet, do you?"

Ainsley pointed her in the direction of the Waffle House. When Elizabeth finally parked the car, she stared at the tiny rectangular building. "Come on. You'll love it."

"I don't eat grease."

"The grease will love you, I promise." Ainsley climbed out of the car. Elizabeth watched the back of Ainsley's black coat as she made her way to the building. Only witches wore black all the time.

Elizabeth exited the car reluctantly. She looked down at her own black trousers and wished she had put on beige instead. Ainsley held the door opened for her and they were greeted by the sound of sizzle. "Do you know they sell more hash browns, eggs, and grits than waffles?" Ainsley asked as she walked in behind her.

"No, I can't say I was aware of such trivia."

Ainsley slid herself into a booth. "And they have amazing coffee, I might add."

Elizabeth followed her. She jumped slightly when a copper-headed waitress appeared like a genie from behind a plastic partition. "What'll it be, ladies?"

Elizabeth eyed the long menu in front of her. "This menu has pictures." She fingered the edge of the menu and flipped it over quickly, as if that might shield her from the film of grease on the plastic cover.

Ainsley jerked the menu from Elizabeth and handed it to the waitress along with her own. "We'll have two eggs, scrambled," Ainsley began.

"Over light," Elizabeth interjected.

The waitress bit her eraser. Ainsley continued, undaunted, "Okay, two eggs scrambled, and two eggs over light, two sides of grits with cheese—"

"Ah, no cheese on my grits, please."

Ainsley raised her right eyebrow. "Okay, like I said, one side of grits with cheese and one without, two orders of bacon, two helpings of your hash browns, scattered, smothered, and covered—"

"No hash browns," Elizabeth interrupted.

"Would you hush and just let me order? You've never even been here before. Could you just trust someone for one second?"

"The menu has *pictures*," Elizabeth reminded her, as if she might not have heard the first time.

She turned back to the waitress. "Two orders of hash browns, and a waffle for each of us, with pecans, please. And two cups of coffee, black." She grinned at Elizabeth. "Now, was that so difficult?"

"I'm not sure. I'll let you know when my food arrives."

Elizabeth jumped again as the waitress yelled their order back toward the kitchen. She presumed it was their order anyway, although it was completely incomprehensible to mere mortals.

"It's their special language," Ainsley informed her.

"Oh, I'm not surprised that you would need a special language for a place like this."

The waitress smacked two mugs of coffee down in front of them.

"Oh my word. They are not. I know they are not."

"What?" Ainsley looked over her shoulder in the direction of Elizabeth's gaze.

"Those children are drinking the half-and-half cups."

"You're a snob, you know that?" Ainsley said flatly. "If it doesn't fit into your tiny way of life, you just pooh-pooh it."

"I don't pooh-pooh anything," Elizabeth muttered, her words lost beneath the yelling of the waitress.

"You pooh-pooh everything."

Elizabeth stirred her coffee with a vengeance. "Why am I here?"

"You're here because I have some questions."

The waitress dropped two plates down in front of her and then returned with two matching plates for Elizabeth.

"How in the world does anyone eat this much food?"

"It won't go to waste, I assure you."

"It's noisy in here too. Why do you come here?"

"Shut up and eat. You're more attractive that way."

Elizabeth's instinct was to stick her tongue out, but she repressed the desire. Instead she forked up a bit of the hash browns and tasted them cautiously. Ainsley watched her with a smirk.

"Oh my . . ."

"Good, aren't they? They're better like this." Ainsley grabbed up the ketchup bottle and squeezed a circle next to Elizabeth's potatoes.

Elizabeth stuck her fork back in the hash browns and dipped them lightly in the ketchup. "What all is in here? These are delicious."

"I told you," Ainsley said, taking a bite of her own. "Onions and cheese."

"How long has this place been here?"

Ainsley rolled her eyes. "Over fifty years."

Elizabeth drenched her waffle in syrup and took a huge bite. "Oh wow," she said with her mouth full. A bit of the waffle came out, and syrup dribbled down her chin. She started to laugh.

"What? Why are you laughing?"

But Elizabeth couldn't answer, couldn't get control of herself. Before Ainsley knew it, she was laughing with her, not even knowing what was so funny.

"Ooh, ooh," Elizabeth said, trying to talk again. "Who would have ever thought I would be sitting in the Waffle House with Ainsley Parker, snarfing down lard and loving every minute of it?"

They continued laughing and eating until every morsel of food was gone from their plates. Elizabeth finally set her fork down and leaned back into the vinyl cushion, sighing heavily. "I cannot believe I ate all that."

"Loved it, didn't you?" Ainsley replied, wiping her mouth.

"Every bite." Then they both laughed again. At last Elizabeth regained her composure and signaled the waitress for more coffee. "So, what was it you needed help with?"

"Just bringing your walls down."

"Excuse me?"

"I just wanted you to let your walls come down, and I've never found a cookie I couldn't break by taking them to the Waffle House."

"So you brought me here just to make me laugh?"

"For no other reason. It was worth the ten bucks I'm going to have to pay."

"This only cost ten dollars?" Elizabeth started to laugh again.

Ainsley nodded. "For *both* of us."

The waitress refilled their mugs, sloshing coffee onto the Formica tabletop. Elizabeth soaked up the mess with her napkin. "Why do you care about my walls, Ainsley?"

"Because believe it or not, Elizabeth, I care about *you*."

Elizabeth grunted. "You care about one-upping me, and I know it."

"You don't know all you think you know, Elizabeth Wilcott."

"I know that from the first moment I came, you had it all planned out how you were going to make me your little minion, and it all started with my initiation."

"I initiate everyone that way."

Elizabeth blew her off. "Yeah, right."

"Ask them. Every single person in my staff learned how to operate the phones all by themselves. It's the best way for people to figure everything out quickly. Throw them in the fire. Then you know if they really want to be there."

Elizabeth cocked her head, still not wanting to believe her. "You do that to *everybody*?"

"Everybody."

"It wasn't just because you wanted to torture me?"

"If that was my goal, I would have come up with a far better method, I assure you."

"That's one of the reasons I stayed. Because I hated you so much that day, I wasn't about to let you have the last word." Elizabeth almost regretted what she was revealing.

Ainsley placing her stubby fingers on the tabletop. "I know."

"You knew?"

"Yeah, I knew. I knew that if you hated me enough, you wouldn't dare leave. You'd be too proud to let me win. And eventually, what

you discovered about the job, and the people, and maybe even yourself, might keep you here for the rest of the year."

Elizabeth shook her head. "You're good."

"I know." Ainsley gave a smug little grin. "And just for the
record, Elizabeth, I never hated you. Not even in school. It was never
about competing for competing sake. You always made me pull the
best out of myself. And you may not want to admit it, but I helped
pull the best out of you."

"You infuriate me."

"I make you dig deep."

"You make me crazy."

"You were already crazy."

That made them both laugh.

"I could be your friend, you know. You'd like me if you'd stop
hating me long enough. And stop this charade, whatever it is, that
brought you here. Let yourself actually enjoy what you're doing. Find
some fulfillment in it."

Elizabeth paused and studied the sincerity in Ainsley's face. "I
don't know how to not hate you. It's what I've always done. And I
told you why I'm here. I'm here to learn."

"That's a load of crap, but you're obviously not ready to concede
that territory. So regarding hating me, how has that worked for you?"

Elizabeth pondered this question, and Mary Catherine's words
reverberated in her head. "Not too well," she said at last. "Apparently
I'm mean and bitter and sad."

"Well, honesty is the first step to recovery."

"I do have friends, you know," Elizabeth interjected.

"No, you don't."

Elizabeth turned her gaze down to her syrupy plate. "You're
right. I don't have any." She paused. "I did have one though." She
held up her index finger as if that would solidify the statement. "I
didn't even deserve him."

"Everybody deserves at least one friend, Elizabeth. But you could
have more than that if you'd just learn to be nice."

"I am horrible, aren't I?"

"Insufferable," Ainsley said, straight-faced.

Elizabeth smiled. "I don't know how to be friendly."

"I'll help you. The smiling is good. Just keep trying it." Ainsley slid out of the vinyl booth. "Come on, let's go help people. That always takes your thoughts off yourself."

Elizabeth sat staring up from the booth. "Why do you care what happens to me, Ainsley?"

"I don't know, Elizabeth. I really don't. Truth be told, you're one of the craziest people I've ever met. Downright certifiable. And you're not even very charming. But I like you. For some odd reason, I like you."

Elizabeth stood up from the booth. "You're too honest. You need to learn to edit."

"If I edited, you'd still hate me for no reason."

"Oh, I still hate you."

"Good. I wouldn't want this to be too easy. I've always loved a challenge."

chapter twenty-nine

Jeffrey pulled down the driveway and stopped to grab the mail. He had been so busy with checking in on Claire and hanging out with Matthew over the weekend that he had forgotten to pick it up on Saturday.

The large white envelope on top arrested his attention. It was from a law firm, and his mind immediately latched on to the possibility of malpractice. Who would want to sue him? With his abrupt departure from his clinic, the options could be limitless.

That one woman—he couldn't remember her name—hadn't been happy with the nose job he gave her last year. She wanted to go from looking like Barbra Streisand to Cindy Crawford, and there were just some things even he wasn't capable of doing.

He put the car in park and ripped the envelope open. It was a petition for divorce.

Jeffrey drove on out through the gates past the golf course, thinking about Jennifer. If he were being completely honest, he had never loved her. And it wasn't her fault. He had been selfish and arrogant.

He had called her a few times to try to get her to talk, but she refused.

Still, he felt obligated to try to work out their marriage, even though his heart wasn't in it. But he knew it was a commitment he needed to try to keep. And he desperately wanted to see their daughter, Jessica. He didn't want another Jacob experience on his hands, a child he never knew.

Jennifer had never returned a single call, but simply had her attorney deal with his attorney. He wasn't sure what the problem was, since she had signed a prenup, but he would find out sooner or later. It didn't matter. He would be fair with her, regardless of what she asked for. All he wanted was to be a father to his daughter.

Jennifer would never in a million years believe that. Why should she? The only wife he had truly cared about was Claire, and even she had fared no better with his self-centeredness. Three broken families washed up in the wake of his egotism.

He thought briefly of Pamela. He hadn't seen her or spoken to her since he canceled the *Charleston Magazine* cover. He hadn't missed her. Apparently she hadn't missed him either.

He picked up the phone and dialed Jennifer's cell number. It had been disconnected. He'd call his attorney later and talk through the papers. But with the graffiti on the garage door just recently painted, he'd do whatever he could to lessen her anger. Maybe letting her go would somehow release her from her hatred. He could only hope.

Dr. Nadu met him in the hallway of the hospital. "Are you ready to be a part of something extraordinary?"

Jeffrey nodded. "I'm ready to help someone, if that is on the agenda for the day."

"Helping is always on our agenda. Follow me, please." They turned the corner and headed toward the surgery holding area.

"So, are you going to tell me who we're going to see?"

"We're going to see a young boy who has no chance of a normal life without us."

"What's his name?"

Dr. Nadu pulled back the thin curtain. "I'll let him tell you."

A young African boy, perhaps eight or nine years old, sat upright in the bed surrounded by a cluster of interns and residents. He turned his head to look at them when they entered the room. A large tumor protruded from the left side of his neck, making that entire side of his face pull. When his eyes lit on Dr. Nadu, he managed a lopsided grin.

"Tell this doctor with me who you are."

"I'm Selemani," the child announced with more power than Jeffrey expected.

"That's Swahili for Solomon," Dr. Nadu informed the room. He walked over and patted the young man on the back. "Today is Selemani's day to get rid of this old friend he's been carrying around."

"He's not my friend."

Everyone laughed.

"All right, here we go." Dr. Nadu unlocked the wheels and rolled Selemani's bed toward the operating room.

Jeffrey wasn't sure he'd ever seen a doctor wheel his own patient to surgery. But Dr. Nadu guided the bed, talking to the child as they went. He leaned over the little boy's face as the anesthesiologist induced sweet dreams. "Sleep well, my sweet friend. And when you wake up, we'll all have some ice cream."

Jeffrey assisted in the surgery. The tumor ran much deeper than he would have thought, and its mass had been slowly decreasing Selemani's ability to swallow. Friends and family members had motivated the entire country to help him come to the Medical University to have this procedure.

He watched as Dr. Nadu began to make his final stitches—such precision, as if every stitch had been planned even before the surgery began. Dr. Nadu tied off the final stitch and stood back, examining the young child's neck as an artist would survey his canvas. He nodded his approval and walked from the room.

Jeffrey lingered behind for a moment, thinking of his own surgeries. The true artistry of his occupation had been lost long ago, buried in the mundane routine of facelifts and liposuction.

But Dr. Nadu was a master. There was nothing about him or this surgery that even bordered on the mundane.

It made Jeffrey question why he had thought himself so wonderful for so long.

———

Will's buddies dropped him off back at his condo. He rode the elevator up to the third floor, and even before he got off, he saw the uniformed man standing by his front door.

"Are you William Wilcott?" the tall, lanky officer asked before Will even made it to the front door.

"You're looking at him. I'm not in trouble with the law or something, am I?"

"I'm here with an Order of Eviction. I have to escort you off the premises."

Will laughed out loud. "Okay, the joke's over. I'm tired of all this. Who put you up to it?"

The officer didn't laugh. Didn't even smile. "We can do this the easy way or the hard way, son. I'd prefer the easy way. Would you open the door, please? You can get some personal items, and we'll make preparations for the furnishings to be picked up."

Thirty minutes later Will was standing in the hall, a duffel bag at his feet and a padlock on the door behind him.

chapter thirty

Mary Catherine was on her last nerve as she drove from North Charleston toward the Isle of Palms. Yesterday she had given another test, and again Nicole had refused to take it. There had been a showdown, a battle of wills exactly like the first one. But this time Mary Catherine was prepared. She had brought food—both lunch and dinner—and the two of them sat there for hours. The standoff ended with Nicole finally completing the test, but only because she had to go to the bathroom and was too proud to pee in her seat.

It wasn't much of a victory, and it left Mary Catherine exhausted. On top of that, Nate had come in at God knows what hour last night and passed out on the sofa. When she got up this morning, he was lying there looking like a bum.

Apparently changing the locks affected his behavior for exactly one week. Then he went back to his "late hours" and "busy schedule." She was tired, she was cranky, and she was suspicious. For her, not a healthy combination.

Mary Catherine dug in her bag for her cell phone and punched in his speed-dial number.

"You've reached Nate Bean. Don't bother leaving a message. I don't return them anyway."

That message had always driven her insane. "Nate!" she shouted into the phone. "All I have to say is, you better get your behind home before I get there. Because mama ain't happy!"

When she got home, the driveway was empty. She didn't even bother pulling in. Instead, she drove down the coast looking for the red and black Jeep. She had bought it for him for a wedding gift. He had loved it and loved her in it. But that was a long time ago. He hadn't paid any attention to her in months, and she was way past the point of being anxious or worried. Now she was mad.

She pulled into the sandy parking lot at the beach access where Nate spent most of his time, even though there was no sign of his Jeep. She could see the neon tips of surfboards and heads bobbing in the ocean.

"Where is he?" she hollered as she approached the water. Heads turned, and one surfer began to paddle his way to shore.

"Where is he, Tanner? Don't lie. Don't even think about lying. Tell me where he is—now!"

He reached an arm out in her direction.

She jerked her elbow away. "Don't touch me. Tell me."

"You really want to know?"

She had always hated Nate's friends. Ever since they had showed up at the wedding in different shades of Hawaiian swim trunks, she had hated them. It was the picture of *them* that made it to the society page. She glared at him with the same look she used on Nicole. "You will regret not telling me."

"He spends most of his time lately down at a beach house owned by one of the island's new residents."

"A woman?"

"A beautiful woman." He smirked.

She bit her lip and narrowed her eyes. "Where is it?"

"It's the white one." He nodded down the beach from them. "The one with all the glass."

She turned and headed back to her car.

"While you're being so high and mighty about honesty," Tanner called to her retreating back, "why don't you find out *why* he married you in the first place?"

She kept walking until she reached the car and then sped off in a cloud of sandy dust.

Nate's Jeep was parked in the driveway, in full view of the street. He wasn't even *trying* to hide. That made her even angrier. She pulled her VW to a whining halt on the other side of the street and got out, heading to the front entry.

"Nate Bean, you better get your sorry behind out here *now*!" She pounded on the French doors and tried to peer in, but sheer curtains blocked her view. She heard movement inside. She jiggled the door handle. More movement—a thud, a bang.

She had envisioned this scenario in her mind so many times, even though she hadn't wanted to admit it. Behind that door, her husband was hopping around on one foot, trying to pull his pants up, and everything Elizabeth had ever said about him was true.

The door opened a crack and a pair of fake green eyes stared out. A halo of bleached blonde hair stirred in the evening breeze.

"Open the door now!" Mary Catherine demanded.

"I'm sorry, but I don't know who you think you are, coming to my house, carrying on—"

"I said open the door, sister!" Mary Catherine shoved. The door smacked the bimbo in the nose, and she let out a screech.

Mary Catherine careened past her. "Don't worry. I've got a brother who can fix that when you go in to have your next boob job." She never missed a beat. "Nate Bean, get your sorry butt out here!"

She looked around. The room was all white, shabby chic. Mary Catherine detested shabby chic.

A door closed in the other room. She ran through the great room and flung open the door to the bedroom. French doors leading to the ocean lay wide open with the sheers blowing in the wind. Nate was trying to sneak down the stairs of the back porch.

She ran full throttle and launched herself onto his back. The force of her momentum brought both of them to the ground.

"Mary Catherine, wait. Please, just listen to me."

"Shut up, you creep! Just get in the car!" She jerked him up and shoved him around the side of the house.

"I'm not going with you like—"

"Get in the car *now*!" She held out a hand, palm up. "Give me your keys."

He complied, and she got into the driver's seat of his Jeep. She left her VW on the street outside the bimbo's house and roared off before he could get the passenger door closed. "You are a horrible excuse for a man," she raged. "In fact, you're not a man; you're a worm! No, you're worse than a worm; you're the muck that lives inside of a worm!"

He reached out and tried to touch her. "Baby, this is nothing like what you—"

"Get your nasty paws off of me!" She swatted at him with both hands. "You've hoodwinked me for the last time!"

A horn honked. Mary Catherine looked up to see a sedan coming straight for them. She placed both hands on the steering wheel and jerked it hard back into her lane. Nate's head hit the window. She didn't care.

"You used me!" she cried.

"No, baby, I didn't—"

"Don't talk!" she said. "You cannot talk! You can never talk again! As of today, you are officially banned from ever speaking to me again!"

Somehow she managed to find the house, but left the Jeep parked with two wheels on the front yard. She got out of the car and slammed the door. He followed.

By the time she got to the top of the front steps, a steady calm had returned to her. "You will not come into *my* house." She turned and put out a hand to stop him. "You will stay right here."

A moment later she came back with an armful of his clothes. She threw them out the door and went back into the house. For the next fifteen minutes she made multiple trips, and when she was through, every remnant of Nate Bean was lying in a heap at the bottom of the steps.

"How long, Nate?" she said. "How long were you going to pretend you loved me? Just until I got the money? Is that it?"

He stood there, clearly afraid to speak.

"Talk, you jerk." Her calmness remained.

He tried to advance toward her. She extended her hand, and he stopped in his tracks. "I never pretended—"

"Shut up. At least now you could tell the truth. At least now."

She headed back up the stairs, then stopped and looked at him one last time. "I did love *you*, Nate. With all my heart. You remember that, okay? One day when you learn how to become a man, remember that you took advantage of a really wonderful woman."

And with that, Mary Catherine Wilcott stuck his car keys inside the top of her shirt and left the pitiful man to cart what he owned in this world away on foot.

It was the least she could do.

⌇

Elizabeth studied the stacks of depositions in front of her. She had traveled all over the South acquiring signatures and statements from Hazel Moses's extended family. She had heard more childhood stories than anyone should ever have to endure. And not one member of the Moses' clan opposed Hazel's right to the house. Which was odd, considering her first conversation with Hazel. When the family received Hazel's initial request for them to sign over all legal rights of the property to her, many of them had refused. They smelled the money of some rich developer, and they wanted their share of it.

Yet now they had all readily complied when Elizabeth had sat down with them. Maybe it was fear of an attorney, but Elizabeth sensed it was something else, something beyond her understanding. *Someone* else even. Someone who wanted Hazel to win. Someone who knew how to speak to hearts.

She couldn't even believe she was thinking such a thing.

She pushed the idea aside. Hazel's own deposition was scheduled for the end of the week, and Mr. Everett would be there, along with his lawyer. It was the one deposition they were adamant about being a part of. She stashed the papers she needed for her meeting tomorrow inside her briefcase.

Tomorrow was her last chance. She was going to interview this final cousin, twice removed, in Savannah. It was her last opportunity to get something—anything—that would serve the cause of Everett and Associates.

But as she looked at the piles of paperwork on her desk, part of her hoped that, against all odds, Hazel would prevail.

———

Will saw Olivia coming out of the library as he was heading back to the fraternity house for a late game of poker. He was currently over five thousand dollars in the red, but he assured the guys they'd get their money.

"Hey, Olivia, wait up and I'll walk you back to your dorm."

She turned and gave him a cursory glance, then kept on walking.

He caught up with her and fell into stride next to her. "Why is someone as beautiful as you walking all alone?"

"Hello, Will."

"She speaks."

She didn't respond.

"So, if we're speaking, does that mean that you want to go out with me Friday night?"

She crossed the street and came to a stop at the edge of the side-walk in front of her dorm. "Will, I don't know how else to say this to you. I'm not interested. You're not my type."

"What type could you possibly have that I'm not?" He posi-tioned himself between her and the door and gave her his most charming grin.

"Will, get out of the way. Just let me go inside."

"No, I want to know. What is your type? You're the only girl around here who doesn't turn her head twice when I walk by. Tell me why?"

"You really want to know?"

"I'm asking. So, yeah, I want to know."

"Okay. First, you're presumptuous and arrogant. Second, you're an alcoholic. And third"—her gaze softened—"you're the biggest waste of potential I've ever met. Here is a guy with every privilege, every opportunity to succeed, and you don't give a flip whether you accomplish anything. You have no character. And that, Will, doesn't interest me in the least. The only reason you think you're interested in me is because I don't fawn all over you when you cruise past me in your expensive sports car, or try to win me over with that beautiful, albeit egotistical, smile."

"Did you just call my smile beautiful?"

She shook her head and groaned. "Good night, Will."

"So, Friday?"

She didn't even bother responding.

He watched her as she slipped inside. Waste of potential? He was nothing *but* potential. The girl had no clue.

As he walked back toward the frat house, he tried to think of an argument that would convince her, a mental list of his accomplishments over the last four years. It was a short list. Shorter than he expected.

chapter thirty-one

As he put the car in drive, Jeffrey felt a tugging in his gut. His divorce from Jennifer had been granted—with a reprimand to her for destroying property, a healthy financial settlement, and visitation rights for Jeffrey. The request had surprised her, enraged her. Clearly she thought he intended to use visitation just to get back at her. Time would tell the real story.

He was now free. He had given Gretchen the morning off, dropped Matthew at school, and called the hospital to tell them he'd be in a little later today. There were no surgeries scheduled this morning and no trauma patients, so unless something came through emergency and they paged him, he would have the morning to himself.

Jeffrey didn't like golf and had never understood why he bought the house on Kiawah Island, but now he realized how much of a sanctuary the resort really was. Jasmine Porch was the perfect place for a quiet breakfast. He ate at a window overlooking the ocean, spoke briefly with a few other Kiawah residents, and read the paper while he downed three cups of coffee and a plate of eggs, grits, and crisp bacon.

He took his time driving, simply enjoying the leisurely pace of the morning.

Jeffrey had been over to Claire's rental house only a couple of times since the funeral. She was doing remarkably well, all things considered—better than he was, he thought. He studied the pansies along the walkway. They were holding on diligently through the cold winter. The yard and planting beds were immaculately kept. He could see Claire's artistic hand everywhere. Even though she'd only be here until her house was rebuilt, she had already put her touch on the place.

He rang the doorbell and waited.

"Jeffrey? What are you doing here?"

"Sorry I didn't call, but I was hoping to surprise you."

Her bare feet stepped back inside the house. "Well, you succeeded. Come in. It's freezing out there."

"Hope I didn't catch you at a bad time."

She closed the door behind him and led him to the sunporch at the back of the house, where a paintbrush and palette lay on the table next to a large canvas on a wooden easel.

"Were you working?"

"Trying to."

He walked over to the canvas and studied the dark, abstract landscape. "It's beautiful."

"You're kind."

"No, I'm serious. It's absolutely stunning. Where is it going?"

"Oh, a gallery on King Street has requested two pieces. I'm hoping they will sell quickly and for a lot of money." She chuckled.

"I'm sure they will."

He turned back to her, and they stared at each other awkwardly.

"So, why are you here?"

His face flushed slightly. A woman hadn't made him blush since—well, he couldn't remember when. "I have an invitation for you," he said, the words rushing out like a sixth grader asking his first girl to the middle-school dance.

She shook her head. "What kind of invitation?"

"I know. You love jeans and sweat suits and comfortable stuff. But I have a rather swanky affair Thursday night—a party for the contributors and board of the Home and Garden Tour. My father was head of the board for years, and Wisteria Plantation has been on the tour forever. I have to go. It's fabulous food, wonderful dancing, and"—he pointed to himself—"very amicable company. Besides, you need to get out."

"How do you know I haven't gotten out?"

He stuttered slightly. "Well, I don't, but I just assumed that maybe you've been in here working a lot, and I just wanted to give you a really nice evening. A nice evening for both of us."

"I'm not sure, Jeffrey. I've always hated crowds."

"Me too."

She arched her eyebrows. "You are so full of it. You love these things. You're in your element."

He shrugged. "Okay, so I enjoy the occasional to-do. But I'd enjoy this one a lot more if you were there with me."

"I don't need anything complicating my life right now, Jeffrey."

He edged closer to her, his hands in the pockets of his cashmere coat. "Trust me, Claire, I'm not here to complicate things. I just thought we could have a nice evening out. Two friends, a little dinner, a little dancing—"

She bit the inside of her jaw, a gesture he recognized as her thinking pose. "When did you say this was?"

He sensed her warming to the idea. "Thursday night. I could pick you up around six thirty."

"I don't have anything to wear to a *swanky* affair."

"Another reason to get you out. And you can spend money on you."

She shifted her weight on her bare feet. "Okay, but it's not a date." She pursed her lips and shook her finger at him.

Jeffrey grinned. "Of course not. I don't even really like you."

"Yeah, yeah, good-bye." She pushed him toward the door, laughing. "See you Thursday."

"I'm crazy," she said as she closed the door behind him.

If being crazy meant she was coming, he would be grateful for crazy.

———

"You look like crap."

"Good morning to you too," Mary Catherine retorted as Mr. McClain held the front door open for her. She stalked toward her classroom, head down, trying to stifle her sniffles. He followed.

"You have more to say?"

"Just want to make sure you're okay."

"I'm fine," she lied.

"Things bad at home?"

She turned toward him abruptly. "How do you know things are bad at home? Maybe I spilled coffee all over myself on the way to work and burned the tar out of myself and I'm crying from the pain."

He scanned her denim skirt and brown wool V-neck sweater. "I see no coffee stains."

"Well, maybe I slammed my hand in the car door and I'm still recovering."

"Your hand is fine. I saw you pull up."

"Well . . . well . . ." Tears rushed to the surface. "How do you know it's something at home?"

"Listen, Mary Catherine, I'm sorry. I'm probably way out of line, anyway."

"Too late for that," she retorted. "You've already inserted your nosy self."

He gave a brief half smile. "Yes, you're right. I deserve that. It's just—well, that one time I met him—ah, your husband, that is—when he came by to bring you some new throw pillows, I think it was. Well, I just didn't have a good feeling about him."

"A good feeling? You met him for all of two seconds. How do you have any feeling at all about a person in two seconds?"

"You're right. I'm sorry I asked. Please forgive me." He began to walk past her.

"He cheated on me." She said it quietly, but in the hallway of metal lockers and tile floors, it carried straight to him.

Mr. McClain turned back around. "Why don't we go to my office for a minute?"

Mary Catherine followed him down the hall and through the door to his office. She didn't wait for an invitation to sit.

She fumbled with the strap of her brown handbag. "How did you know?"

"I was married before. To a woman with the same look and the same smooth way of talking. I just sensed in my gut he was up to no good." Mr. McClain sat down behind his desk. "You know, Mary Catherine, I still don't know the real reason why you're here at all."

"Money." The word flew out of her mouth before she could catch it.

Mr. McClain laughed. "Honey, I know you're not here for the money. You're not making any. I've never understood that either, why you came to work for us for free."

She changed the subject quickly as she turned her gaze out the window. "Never mind. It's just—well, I never expected to be the betrayed wife."

"You're a lucky woman to discover this so early."

She turned her eyes back in his direction. "You call this lucky?"

He got up from his desk and walked around to sit in front of her on the desk's edge. "You know, the day I found out my first wife was not what she had pretended to be, I thought my world was over. Everything I had ever believed seemed like a lie."

She watched him, her tears falling freely. She swiped at them and motioned for him to continue.

"But when I met the amazing woman I'm married to now, I realized our paths would have never crossed if I had not gone through that pain."

"Where did you meet her? In therapy?"

He laughed. "No, in church, actually. Amazing where a little heartbreak can drive you. Mine drove me to my knees."

She glanced his way. "My mother was religious. I really enjoyed that when I was little. But I just found it's never worked for me. You know, since I've grown up."

"I'm not talking about religion, Mary Catherine. I'm talking about faith. Believing in something that can change your life."

She brushed at her tears again.

"And when my life changed, I was able to become the man I was meant to be. So, who is Mary Catherine meant to be? Separate from her stuff?"

He had apparently pegged her pretty well. She sat silent for what seemed like a minute. "I don't know."

"Well, you can be sure Nate would never have been able to answer that question for you. There is only one who can do that."

She dabbed at her cheeks with the back of her hand and stood up from her chair. "I better get to class."

"You're doing a great job, you know," he said as she was walking out the door.

"I'm surviving."

But even amid the present turmoil, she knew she was doing far more than that.

———

Elizabeth pulled up to the small house on the outskirts of Savannah. She had never liked Savannah. It tried to flaunt itself as the consummate Southern city, but to her it was a weak imitation of Charleston.

Hazel's cousin sat in one of four lawn chairs—but which one, Elizabeth didn't know. Apparently three of his friends had joined him to check out the "Charleston attorney." The four of them were bundled up in trench coats and hats reminiscent of Humphrey Bogart.

Wrapping her thick shawl around her, she got out of the car and left her briefcase lying in the seat.

"Mr. Wilson?"

Four pairs of coal-black eyes bore down on her as if they'd never seen a white woman in their lives. She waited, trying not to fidget under their stares.

"I'm George Wilson," the frailest of the gentlemen said at last. She noticed a hint of gold in his mouth as he spoke.

"Mr. Wilson, I'm Elizabeth Wilcott, Hazel Moses's attorney. Is there somewhere you and I can speak privately?"

"Ain't no need for privacy. These here's my brothers. They knows everything needs to be knowed 'bout me. So Hazel tryin' to go and take what ain't rightfully hers, huh?"

Elizabeth shifted her stance to get more comfortable. Obviously this meeting was going to transpire right here, whether she liked it or not. "Well, I don't think that—"

"Don't go tryin' to defend her. She's always acted so high and mighty, like because she was a teacher she got somethin' to teach the rest of us. Well, I don't need to be taught nothin'. And she ain't got nothin' I need to learn anyway."

Much to Elizabeth's surprise, his accusation against Hazel seemed to ignite some deeply buried indignation inside of her. She tried to stifle it. She wasn't supposed to care what happened to Hazel. This was about helping her business. She had come here hoping he would refuse to sign the papers.

That was the plan anyway.

"I think we might be talking about two different Hazels."

"Don't try to get me all flustered with your legal mumbo jumbo. That's what my friends told me you was gonna try and do. Ain't got no time for that." He stood up, and his faithful followers followed.

She was being dismissed. Elizabeth hated being dismissed.

"Mr. Wilson, have you ever even *been* to Hazel Moses's house?"

"Humph," he said. Elizabeth hated being "humphed" at even more than she hated being dismissed. In a flash she passed all four men and made her way to the top step of the porch before they got there.

Everything she did was in perfect control—in perfect control for an incensed woman, that is. Fifteen minutes later she was back in her car with her documents signed. Hazel had permission from every necessary member of the family, granting the rights to the property to her alone.

Elizabeth had won. And she had also hammered the final nail into her own coffin and effectively buried her career.

chapter thirty-two

Elizabeth's new Nike running shoes hit the pavement in a perfect rhythm. With her early trip to Savannah, she hadn't had time to run this morning, so she forced herself to make time this evening. The February air ripped through her lungs as she made her way to the Battery and stopped to catch her breath.

The abduction over six months ago still had her looking over her shoulder. She ran a gloved hand along the cannon, feeling the deep cold that permeated from the iron.

The Battery was part of her own personal history. She used to play here as a child with her best friend, Bernadette. Bernie, as everyone called her, lived in one of the condos of the Fort Sumter House, which until 1974 was the Fort Sumter Hotel. The Battery was Bernie's front yard, and Elizabeth, so in love with Charleston, wanted it to be hers as well.

She wanted her daddy to move away from Edisto, get them off that island and into the city. She wanted to get away from the country, away from the memories. He told her that Wisteria Plantation was and would always be their family home. It made her want to spend even more time at Bernie's.

Her thoughts were interrupted by footsteps—a dark figure was coming down the walk, headed in her direction with deliberate intent. "Who's there?"

"It's me, Lizzy." Aaron's face came into view underneath the street lamp.

She tried to steady her weak knees. "Lord have mercy, Aaron, you almost scared me to death."

"Sorry," he said. "But you seem to be hard to catch by telephone. I figured I might as well track you down."

"Did something happen at the office?"

"No, this has nothing to do with the business and everything to do with the fact that you've been ignoring me for three months, and it's time you quit acting like a child."

"It's time for you to quit acting like you're my father."

"I only wish I was half the man your father was."

"You don't know everything there is to know, Aaron, despite what you might think."

"I know enough about you, Lizzy. I know you're angry about something that happened a long time ago. I know that you won't let anyone into your little shell. If you were being honest, you'd admit you like it that way, because then you stay in control. And I know that your father loved you very much, but you obviously can't forgive him for whatever he did or didn't do when you were younger. How am I doing so far?"

"You should just go, Aaron." She tried to push past him, but he grabbed her by the arm and swung her around.

"I'm not going anywhere until I say what needs to be said."

"Do you enjoy airing your feelings in public?"

"At least I *have* feelings, Lizzy. You've kept yours bottled up for so long you don't even know how to feel anything—except anger. Oh, you love to be angry. The problem is, you're mostly angry with yourself, and that's the one person you can't push away."

She tugged her arm out of his grasp. She'd never disliked him more than she did at this moment. "You don't know everything about me."

He stepped closer to her. "I know you're a woman who won't let anyone love her. Even your dad tried to love you, Elizabeth. I know he pushed you, but especially those last years, he so tried to love you."

She felt her jaw beginning to pulse and fought to control her anger.

He stepped in closer again.

"And you know what else? I've tried to love you, Lizzy. I've tried to love you for the last ten years. I've been so stupid, thinking I could break through that hard exterior and get in there and find a way to get you to love me back. But I'm letting you go, Lizzy. I'm letting you go so I can figure out how to have someone in my life who can love me in return."

His words registered like a brick to the gut. She tried to laugh it off. "Aaron, you're not serious."

"I've never been more serious. I'm letting you go, Lizzy. I'm letting you go to be bitter, to be angry, and to be whatever else it is you want to be. I can't spend another day aching over you, or praying that you will come to your senses and realize you don't need to throw away any more of your life feeling sorry for yourself."

She opened her mouth to reply. Nothing came out. Absolutely nothing.

"I don't know what happened to you, Lizzy, but I didn't do it. And if you were being honest, you'd know that you love me too. You're just too blinded by yourself to admit you need anyone. I don't mean someone to run your business; I mean someone to *love* you."

He ran his hands across the bill of his baseball cap. "I'm tired, Lizzy. I'll finish running your office until the year is over, and after that our relationship—if you want to call it that—can remain strictly business."

The expression in his eyes made it clear that he meant every word he said. "No more midnight phone calls, Lizzy. No more crying on my shoulder or bending my ear. I have to get on with my life and see if there is someone out there for me to love. Because the woman I've longed to love has worn me out."

And with that he left her standing in the middle of the Battery, where wars hadn't been fought in years, but where the cries of desperate souls could still be heard.

———

Elizabeth never got drunk, even when she did drink. It was her brothers' weakness, not hers. And she wasn't weak.

She misjudged the distance to the table, and the empty wine bottle toppled to the floor. She picked up the phone. "You sleep?" she slurred.

"You drunk?" Ainsley's voice came from the other end.

"Does a bottle of wine make you drunk?" She rubbed at her bloodshot eyes.

"Just tell me you're not driving."

"I'm not driving."

"Tell me you're at home."

"I'm at home."

"Tell me . . ."

"What is this, *Jeopardy*? I'm drunk, not illiterate. So, is your husband home?"

"Elizabeth, are you wanting me to come over because you're drunk and sad? If so, forget it. Besides, you told me you weren't a drinker. And if you're starting now, then apparently sunshine's got some problems."

"I hate you; you know that."

"Yes, I know. You've confirmed that more often than is actually necessary. Now, go get a cup of coffee. Put on a CD of somebody singing something happy, and then sleep it off. I don't want to see you until noon, if at all. Now, hang up the phone, and quit terrorizing tired people."

"Ainsley, I love you."

"Yes, I know, Elizabeth. Go get sober, and we'll deal with your multiple personality issues tomorrow."

"Thank you," Elizabeth slobbered into the phone.

"You're welcome."

When the line went dead, Elizabeth stumbled into the kitchen, fixed a pot of coffee, and drank it all. By the time she was finished, she was buzzed on caffeine, so wired there was no hope of sleep. She put on Bette Midler's CD of Rosemary Clooney classics, proving she was wasted, and spent the next three hours cleaning her house, until she finally collapsed on the sofa, not to awaken until two the following afternoon.

At three thirty on Wednesday she walked into the office, sat down in her chair, and stared at the computer screen through the darkest sunglasses she could find.

Hazel's deposition was tomorrow.

"Death becomes her," Ainsley said as she passed by Elizabeth's desk.

"Yeah, yeah."

Everyone left her alone. When only she and Ainsley were left in the office, she went to the door and pushed it ajar. "Did I make a complete horse's behind of myself last night?"

Ainsley's red spikes shifted as she raised her head. "Complete? Is there such a thing as a *partial* horse's behind?"

"Did I call you last night wanting you to be my friend?"

"I'm not sure. Do you usually seek out friends only during drunken stupors?"

She walked over and plopped down into the chair in front of Ainsley's desk.

Ainsley raised an eyebrow. "How rude of me. Please, do sit down."

Elizabeth ignored her. "I've never called a woman before."

"Excuse me?"

"Called a woman. You know, like I did last night. I've never called a woman before when I needed something. I always call men." She paused. "Actually, that's not quite accurate. I always call *Aaron*."

"Oh, yeah, the guy you're madly in love with and that you remain in complete denial over."

Elizabeth shot a darting look at Ainsley.

"Oh my word, you're acting as if this is something new?" Ainsley shook her head. "Is there *anything* in your life you're actually willing to admit?"

"I know myself very well, thank you." Elizabeth turned in her seat.

"So having no friends, having no life, refusing to admit you're in love with this guy—you've admitted all that to yourself. And the fact that you're an angry little snit too."

"I am *not* angry!"

Ainsley rolled her eyes.

"I'm not—" She stopped herself. "I'm completely angry, aren't I?"

"Well, thank the Lord. There is officially a God in heaven if Elizabeth Wilcott is willing to admit she's angry."

"You shouldn't gloat."

"I'm not gloating, I'm rejoicing. Honestly. Someone should be singing the 'Hallelujah Chorus.'"

Despite herself, Elizabeth smiled. "Why am I angry though? Why do I live so much of my life angry?"

Ainsley left her desk and seated herself in the leather chair opposite Elizabeth. "Only you can figure that out, sunshine. You might not like the journey getting there, but once you get past it, you might find the trip has changed your life."

"What do you know about anger?"

"A woman who has been falsely accused of embezzlement has every right to be angry."

Her candor surprised Elizabeth.

"But far worse than that, a woman who has had three miscarriages knows a lot about anger. She blames whoever is willing to stay in the room long enough to be blamed. Shoot, I probably blamed you at some point." She laughed. "But one day I realized that the rage that was inside of me was destroying the life that wanted to be lived. And I finally admitted it wasn't my fault, it wasn't my husband's fault, and it wasn't God's fault. I was left with the realization that if I was willing, the experience could make me into a different person—a better person, if that's possible."

"I'm sorry, Ainsley. I had no idea."

"I didn't tell you that for your pity, Elizabeth. I told you for your healing. A healing you had better find before the man you love gets away."

Elizabeth stood up and headed for the door. "I may be angry, but I'm not in love with Aaron."

"Right. And you've got a boatload of friends too, don't you?" Ainsley sighed. "And I thought we were getting somewhere."

Mary Catherine pulled her coat tighter around her neck. The wind off the sea could be brutal in winter. She walked around the familiar church. It was the only place she could think of to come.

She had gone home to let Coco out, but she couldn't bring herself to stay there. It got dark so early; the last thing she wanted to do was to sit in the dark for five hours hoping to fall asleep. Despite what people thought about Nate, she loved him, and she thought she had finally found a man who loved her in return. They had traveled together, laughed together, made plans together. Maybe she should have been able to see through him. But she was so busy falling into him, that she didn't see the gaping chasm that awaited her.

She walked toward her mother's and father's grave.

"Are you lost?" A voice came from the darkness.

Mary Catherine jumped. "Oh my heavens, you scared me nearly half to death."

"Well, unfortunately, we only house the *fully* dead here," the man said as he stepped in closer. "I didn't mean to frighten you."

"Oh, no, I just came to check on my parent's grave site."

"And your parents are?"

"Rena and Clayton Wilcott. They're buried right over here."

He followed. "Clayton Wilcott was your father?"

"Yeah, that's my dad."

"He was a wonderful man."

"You knew my father?"

"Yes, he came here every Sunday for five years."

She laughed. "You've got the wrong man, mister. My dad didn't go to church. He wouldn't be caught dead—" She stopped and gave a nervous laugh. "I better not say that in a graveyard, huh?"

The man gave a little chuckle. "There are, in fact, some *living* people here, about to have a covered-dish dinner. I'm sure they would love to get acquainted with you, if you're hungry. We could talk a little more about your father."

Mary Catherine did want to know more, but she didn't want company. Especially strangers. "Oh, well, no. I . . . I really need to get home."

He trailed her back toward her car. "These folks fix every imaginable kind of Jell-O salad."

She turned back to eye him. "How do you know my father? Really?"

"I'm Mitch Young, the pastor here. I met your father five years ago, right over there in that little prayer chapel. He came in late one night, and as I was locking up the church, I heard someone weeping."

Mary Catherine studied his face in the dim light. "You don't know my father," she said. "He doesn't weep."

"Your father, Elijah Clayton Wilcott II, lived up the road at Wisteria Plantation. He had four children: Jeffrey, Elizabeth, Mary Catherine—you, I presume—and his baby boy, Will, who caused him the most concern and heartache. Esau was his right-hand man, and one fabulous cook, I might add. And your father *did* weep. He wept over the time he never had with his children."

Mary Catherine found herself surprisingly speechless.

He laughed. "Now, we'd really love to have you join us for dinner. They make enough food for the whole island. And I'll answer any more questions you have."

She puckered her nose. "But I *hate* Jell-O salad."

"Me too," he whispered. "But they make some mean fried chicken too."

"Ooh, now you're talking."

Mary Catherine was fawned over and given extra helpings of rice and gravy and Jell-O salads in every color. She met people who knew her father and shared stories about her dad that she never knew. And they made her laugh, made her forget for a moment or two the heartbreak that would be waiting at the door when she got home.

As they were clearing the dishes, she sneaked off into the quiet sanctuary. She went to the second pew on the left, where Mitch Young said her father sat every Sunday. She rubbed her hands across the rich wood, wishing his warmth remained. Slowly she laid her head down in the pew, as she had when she was a little girl. Her tears began to fall and puddle on the wood beneath her cheek.

She squeezed her eyes shut to stop the tears, only to find her mother waiting in her memory. "Just tell him, sweetheart. Tell Jesus how you feel. What you need."

Mary Catherine opened her eyes. "I've been so selfish," she whispered into the darkened sanctuary. "I've forgotten how to love, how to give. I've forgotten so much."

She gripped the back of the first pew and laid her head against her hands. "The stuff took over. My wants. My things. My life. It didn't leave any room for anything else, anyone else. Not even you. And now look at the mess I've made."

Something began to happen, although Mary Catherine couldn't really explain what it was. A warmth, a presence, something living and real and loving and vaguely familiar.

Nothing had changed, not really. Nate had still betrayed her; the pain was still there. But something *had* happened. And tonight that was enough.

chapter thirty-three

Elizabeth had been dreading this day for weeks. It was the day of Hazel's deposition, and it was being held in the offices of a prestigious Charleston attorney who had been trying to steal development contracts from her for years. He would only be too glad to see her.

She pulled the car up in front of an impressive stone house on Church Street—one of the many old residences that now housed law practices—and turned to look at Hazel. Wrapped in a soft brown coat that matched her eyes, the woman looked peaceful, composed.

"You okay?"

Hazel's mouth turned up in a sweet smile. "I'm perfect. It's going to be a good day, Elizabeth. I can feel it in my bones. It's going to be a really good day."

Elizabeth didn't want to break it to her that the men inside that imposing stone house were determined to take her down. They would fight this as far as they needed to. And they could afford it.

Wade gave a slight snorting noise from the backseat. Elizabeth had almost forgotten she had brought him along.

She was glad no one asked *her* if she were okay, but at this point it didn't matter. She had no other choice but to follow this through, and she had too much pride to do a bad job, even if she did want to lose.

But did she? She wasn't even sure of that anymore.

They climbed from the car, with Wade trailing behind, lugging a large brown file box—all the depositions she had taken over the last few months. Elizabeth paused on the front porch and smoothed her hair, straightened her coat, whatever she could find to do that would let her stall for a minute. Wade steadied the box against the stone and rang the buzzer. The secretary pushed a button of her own, allowing them to enter.

The old house smelled of stale cigars, expensive cologne, and old money. As they entered the foyer, Roy Townsend came through the pocket doors into the front room "Elizabeth! So good to see you!"

She extended her hand to him as he barreled toward her. His hair was pure white, but the skin of his face was stretched taut and his blue eyes were enhanced by brilliant contacts. He was probably one of Jeffrey's pincushions.

He shook her hand furiously. "Come, come. We're in the board-room waiting on you. All of you."

"Roy, I'd like you to meet my client, Hazel Moses."

Southern charm oozed from him suddenly, as if somebody had turned on a tap. "What a pleasure to meet you, ma'am." He engulfed her small hand in his big paw and leaned over her graciously. "Come inside here and let's sit down and get comfortable."

"Thank the Lord," Wade mumbled. He lumbered past them, bent beneath the weight of the box, and set it heavily on the table. Elizabeth glared at him. They would have a discussion about office etiquette when this was over.

"Shelby, could you bring our visitors something to drink, please?" Roy said as they followed Wade into the boardroom.

Elizabeth entered the dark paneled room with its coffered ceiling and found herself slightly overwhelmed at the large gathering of suits around the table. But she knew from years of experience how to enter a room. She assumed the appropriate facial expression. Confident. Completely confident.

Mr. Everett rose from his chair on the other side of the table. "Elizabeth. Good to see you."

"Would you like something to drink, ma'am?" the secretary interrupted.

Elizabeth turned her head sharply. "Coffee. Black." She returned her attention to Mr. Everett. "Good to see you too, sir." She offered her hand and realized it was damp with sweat.

"I'm looking forward to seeing how today will transpire."

The secretary handed Elizabeth her coffee. She resisted the urge to chug it down in one gulp and instead held it in her hands and offered Mr. Everett a smile. A confident one, she was certain.

Roy Townsend helped Hazel off with her coat and seated her in a large burgundy leather armchair. Elizabeth sat down beside her, opening her briefcase and removing the files necessary for this morning's deposition. Wade took a seat behind them.

Elizabeth studied the opulent boardroom, and a momentary anger flared up in her. It was the old pressure ploy, the psychology of intimidation. She had played that card herself a thousand times. Bring clients to an environment that makes them uncomfortable and see what kind of leverage can be gained in a battle of wills. Seeing it from this side of the boardroom table, however, made her realize how crass and vulgar the whole thing was.

Of course they wanted this deposition on their own turf. Bullies always did.

But then, they'd never met Hazel.

The court reporter at the end of the table signaled that she was ready to begin. Elizabeth opened the large file in front of her and pulled out the yellow legal pad with her questions.

Roy Townsend wasted no time. Once Hazel was sworn in, he shucked off the Southern gentleman persona like a dirty shirt and launched into an immediate barrage of questions.

Elizabeth's training and experience kicked in, and everything else faded into the background. She was Hazel's attorney. The niceties were history.

"Do you at this moment possess the deed to your home?"

Hazel straightened her tiny frame in her chair and placed her hands on the table in front of her. "Well, no, but I—"

Roy cut her off curtly. "Yes or no is all we're asking for here."

Elizabeth eyed him.

"Do you at this moment have any legal rights to the property on Smith Street where you currently reside?"

"It depends what you consider rights."

Elizabeth wanted to smile at Hazel and slap Roy.

But he kept on, battering her with questions, his arrogant superiority obvious in every move, in the tone of his voice, in his facial expressions, in his body language. Question after question. Elizabeth raised objections multiple times, but still Hazel was required to answer each one.

Then, in the middle of the barrage, Hazel raised a small brown hand. "Could you give me just one moment, Mr. Townsend?" Hazel asked, shushing him like a schoolchild. "Just one moment, sir."

Roy started to cut her off, but Mr. Everett touched his arm to silence him. "Yes, ma'am," Everett said. "We'll give you a moment."

Roy spoke to the reporter. "Note my objection for the record."

"It's your *client* giving permission," Elizabeth reminded him.

"Note my objection anyway."

Hazel waited. When she had their attention, she began to speak. "This home has been occupied by members of my family since the Emancipation. I grew up in this home. My children grew up in this home. I've lived my entire life contributing to my community. Not taking one thing, but giving. I probably taught some of your children, if they went to public school. I taught my own children. Out of five children, three of them own their own businesses, and two are teachers now themselves. My husband worked his fingers to the bone until the day he died. We've never asked anybody for anything. And yet today, because your company wants to make a tiny profit, a little drop in your great big bucket, you want to uproot the seeds of my heritage, and you expect me to just answer yes or no, say thank you and take the money."

The court reporter sniffed. Roy glared at her.

"Well, I'm sorry," Hazel continued, "but some things aren't about money. Some things are about what you remember. Every memory my family and I have lies within those walls and on that little patch of land. So, if all the other developments you own don't turn enough profit for you, I'm certain that the piddling amount you make on destroying my home won't matter either. So now *I'm* going to ask a question, Mr. Townsend."

Roy Townsend's face went red—as red as the tall amaryllis that stood in a terracotta pot on the table behind him.

Elizabeth glanced at Mr. Everett. His eyes were fixed on Hazel.

"Is this about having it all?" Hazel asked. "Or about having what you need?" She gazed at Townsend with an open, guileless expression. "Don't get me wrong. I believe in progress. I believe in growth. I believe in giving families a place for new memories. But you don't give one family new memories by taking away those of another." She turned her attention to Elizabeth and nodded. "Sorry, Elizabeth, but I just needed to speak my piece."

Elizabeth bit her bottom lip but couldn't completely stifle the smile. "It's okay, Hazel." She turned her attention back to Roy. "Any more questions, Mr. Townsend, before I begin to ask a few?"

"Well, yes. That was a shameless—"

Mr. Everett reached over and placed a tanned hand across the arm of Roy Townsend's thousand-dollar pinstriped suit. "There will be no more questions needed by anyone."

Roy gaped at him. "But, Mr.—"

"I said, no more questions."

Had Elizabeth not known Everett so well, she would have protested about not being able to have her questions answered. But she knew what he meant.

The court reporter pulled out a tissue and blew her nose.

"Thank you for your time." Elizabeth stood up. Wade followed.

Hazel looked up at Elizabeth. "That's all?"

Elizabeth offered a hand and helped her out of her chair. "That's all."

In silence the three of them walked out the leaded glass door to the car.

"I hope I didn't mess anything up in there," Hazel said.

"You were perfect," Elizabeth said. "You can't mess up what's in your heart."

"Elizabeth!" She turned. Mr. Everett was coming down the steps toward her. She met him at the bottom step, out of earshot of the car.

"Why are you doing this? Working for the Benefactor's Group? I mean, *really* working there?"

"It's a long story, Mr. Everett. But I can tell you that my expectation of what this experience would afford me and my clients isn't . . ."

"You don't even have to say it. It's obvious." He placed a hand under Elizabeth's elbow and leaned in close. "You know, we really do have all the property we need."

She sighed. "Thank you, Mr. Everett."

He gave her a wink. "You're still the best attorney I've ever met. If I'm going to lose to anybody, I'd want it to be you."

She winked back. "I'd want it to be to Hazel."

chapter thirty-four

A re you all right? You've been fidgeting all day." Dr. Nadu's eyes darted from his charts to Jeffrey's face. "I'm glad we didn't have surgery scheduled. I would have had to put you up in the observation booth."

"I'm fine. Just have a big formal dinner shindig tonight."

"I can't imagine you being nervous about something like that. I would expect you to be quite at home at a—what was your word?— *shindig.*"

"It's not the shindig; it's the company."

Dr. Nadu raised his eyebrows. "Ah, a new woman. I see." He closed the file and tapped it on the palm of his hand. "Rather soon, isn't it? Not that I wish to pry."

"You're not prying. And actually, it's not a new woman. Well, she's not an old woman, but she's old to me."

"You might not want to tell *her* that." Dr. Nadu chuckled.

"It's my ex-wife, Claire. She's going out with me tonight."

Dr. Nadu removed his glasses. "Jacob's mother? Is that a good idea, do you think? Is she ready to date so soon after such a loss?"

"No, honestly I'm not sure it's a good idea at all," Jeffrey said. "But it's not a date."

"Ball gowns, tuxedos, fine wine, dinner, and dancing," Nadu mused. "No, of course not. That does not sound like a date at all."

Jeffrey stood up and walked to the window, placed his fingers between the slats, and looked out at the last remnants of daylight. "Oh my word, I'm going on a date."

"A word of warning, Jeffrey, if I may. A woman who has lost her son in such a terrible way can be very fragile." Dr. Nadu patted Jeffrey on the shoulder. "And so can a father."

⌒

If he hadn't been a doctor, Jeffrey would have been certain he was having a heart attack. He sat in the car in Claire's driveway, breathing deeply, trying to regain control of his racing pulse. Finally he calmed himself and took the bouquet of cream-colored roses from the passenger's seat and forced himself up the walk to the front door.

What was he thinking? Was this not the stupidest thing he had done in the last decade? Claire was going through so much; the last thing she needed was him bringing more confusion to her train wreck.

The door opened. "Were you going to stand there all night or ring the bell?"

Every racing thought came to a screeching halt. His mouth went dry, and he couldn't speak.

She looked . . . stunning. Magnificent. Her slim figure fit perfectly into her dress, and her olive skin blended beautifully with the champagne color. Her dark shoulder-length hair was pulled back on the sides and lifted from her face. Every flawless feature was visible.

"Can you speak?" she asked, smiling as she held the door open.

"Uh-uh," he stammered.

She looked at the flowers. "Are those for me?"

He stuck out his hand. "Uh-huh."

"Jeffrey Wilcott, the one thing you have never been is speechless around a woman."

"I know. It's crazy." He swallowed hard and tried to shake off his momentary paralysis. "You look absolutely amazing."

"Not too bad for a thirty-eight-year-old, huh?" She took the roses from his hand and walked toward the kitchen. Their aroma moved with her. "These smell wonderful."

"I'm glad."

She pulled a vase from the cabinet. "You did very well." She arranged them neatly, placing each one with care. She took them out to the sunroom and set them on a table by the sofa. "Now I can enjoy them all day."

He tried to pretend he wasn't staring. "Are you ready to be wined and dined?"

"Let's go. I'm starving."

"You always did like to eat."

She grinned at him. "Some things even age doesn't change."

———

All eyes followed Claire and Jeffrey as they entered the historic house on Edisto Island. Claire noticed the attention they were receiving, but she was more interested in absorbing every detail of the stately mansion. A massive crystal chandelier hung in the center of the majestic foyer, and a sweeping staircase curved around the wall as if Scarlett O'Hara herself might descend it. She had left this kind of extravagance behind when she had left Jeffrey.

A buxom woman glittering with sequins and diamonds descended on Jeffrey. "Jeffrey darling, so wonderful to see you." She gave him an overenthusiastic kiss on the cheek and put a pudgy, gem-encrusted hand to her heaving cleavage. "I haven't seen you since your father's funeral. We've missed him so much on the island, you know."

"Thank you, Bernice."

"Who is this lovely lady with you?"

"This is Claire Webber. Claire, meet Bernice Pageant, our hostess for this evening."

Claire removed her arm from Jeffrey's and shook Mrs. Pageant's hand.

"Claire's an old friend of mine."

"She's too lovely to be an *old* friend, Jeffrey." They all laughed.

"I'll rephrase that before I introduce her again."

"You'll have the plantation ready for the tour, won't you?"

"I wouldn't think of missing it. It was one of my father's passions."

Jeffrey extricated Claire from Bernice's grasp and ushered her into the main parlor. Whispers and stares followed in their wake.

Jeffrey steered Claire through the crowd, introducing her to colleagues and acquaintances and a few friends. But after studying them again he realized he really didn't have any friends. A lot of women through the years, but never any friends. Claire had been the only real friend he'd ever had. He watched her as she charmed the women and intrigued the men. How could she smile and be so enchanting, he wondered, after all she'd been through? After all he'd put her through.

She tugged at the sleeve of his tuxedo. "I thought this was a party."

"It is."

"You're not smiling."

"Sorry, my mind just drifted for a minute."

"Mine's been drifting to the food. Can we get some?"

He raised one eyebrow and took her arm. "Let's feed that beast, shall we?"

They ate and talked and then moved outside into the magnificent garden dominated by a lighted white tent. A big band was playing songs of the forties.

"Come on. This is the best dance music in the world." He took her hand and tugged her toward the dance floor.

"Jeffrey, you know I can't dance."

"You could dance if you were willing to let me lead." He gave her a wink.

"You remember I wasn't so good at that, huh?"

"I remember a lot more than you might think."

The lead singer crooned out the words: *I'll be seeing you in all the old familiar places . . .* Jeffrey took her in his arms and rested his cheek against the top of her head. And for the first time—ever—she actually followed his lead.

When the music ended, he ushered her to a bench at the edge of the tent. "I'm going to get us something to drink, okay? I'll be right back."

"I'll wait right here."

Jeffrey made his way through the crowd and toward the open bar. "Two Perriers, please."

"Dr. Wilcott! I heard you might be here."

Jeffrey turned toward the soft feminine voice. The blonde twenty-something gave him a smile, the edge of her arm brushing up against his sleeve.

"I'm sorry, have we met?" He diverted his attention back to the bartender.

Her voice oozed awareness of her own sex appeal. "I went to your office to see you and found that you had taken a leave of absence for a while."

He took the two green glass bottles from the bartender's hands and looked at her. "You came to my office?"

"Yes." She turned her body into his, allowing it to brush against him.

For a moment, just a brief second or two, Jeffrey felt something awaken inside him. All the habits and desires that had been submerged to months of crisis and anxiety came surging to the surface. This young woman—this *girl*—wanted him, and he liked the way that made him feel.

But when he turned back to her, there was something in her face that startled him. He'd seen that same look on many women before through the years. Someone else's date or mistress or wife, it didn't matter. If they desired him, they made it known.

And in that moment he wondered what it was they saw in him that made it okay. Was he a man who might as well be selling his body on some sleazy street corner or running an escort service or wearing a sign around his neck that said, "Available and Cheap?"

"Would you excuse me, please?" He set the bottles down on the bar and headed quickly to where Claire waited in the tent.

"You all right?" Claire asked as she took the handkerchief out of his breast pocket and dabbed at his forehead. "You're perspiring."

"I have had a discovery tonight." He took her arm and steered her toward the patio.

She tugged at him, forcing him to stop outside the double French doors that led back into the house. "What have you discovered?"

"That I hate these things."

She leaned back and looked into his face. "Want to get out of here?"

"Please." He bent down and kissed her softly on the cheek. "Let's ditch this joint."

Giggling like schoolchildren, they retrieved their coats and stepped out into the frigid winter air. Claire pulled the collar of her long velvet coat up around her neck as they walked back to the car.

He reached for the car door. "No, let's walk," she said.

"It's not too cold for you?"

"No, I like it. My coat's plenty warm."

They strolled in silence for a few minutes, down the long driveway. "How are you doing?" Jeffrey asked at last. "I mean, *really* doing?"

Claire heard the faint sound of an ambulance siren and waited to speak until it passed. "How am I doing? I'm not sure. I just get up each morning hoping I can breathe and praying that one day the pain will go away. You know, I heard somebody say that grief never goes away, it just explodes less often. I'm praying for the less often."

"Well, you seem to be doing remarkably well. Your strength amazes me. Almost superhuman, somehow."

She laughed. "You know, Jeffrey, when you left—"

"I know, Claire." He gazed out over the lights reflecting in the water. "I'm so sorry. I hope someday you'll forgive me for how I left you and Jacob."

She squeezed his arm. "Hush, no more apologies. When you left, I was forced to figure out how to survive. And I did. I came to terms with myself. I realized that what you said back there was true."

"What did I say?"

"That I never learned to let you lead. And I didn't. I was so self-sufficient. I thought I could do it on my own. Why wouldn't you look for someone that needed you?"

"You can't blame my affair on yourself."

"I don't," she said flatly. "Trust me on that one. But I did learn there were things in me that needed to change. Things in my heart. Things in my head. So, one day, driving in my car on the way to work, I made some decisions."

"Decisions?"

"Yeah. Decisions about my life. And decisions about you. For the first time, I surrendered. I gave up the illusion that I was in control. I gave up the notion that I knew how to run my own life—or yours."

"Yeah, but *somebody* needed to run my life," Jeffrey admitted. "I was a spoiled young kid who thought he was going to be a big-time doctor and have the entire city of Charleston bowing to the god of his scalpel."

"How'd that work for you?"

"We're still working out the spoiled part. I'm not so sure I'm a big-time doctor, but plenty of people—mostly women—have worshiped at the shrine of my surgical prowess."

"Make you feel powerful?"

He lowered his head. "Yes, it has, if you want me to be completely honest."

"I like you being honest."

"A lot of doctors think they're gods, you know. They heal. They mend. They hold knowledge that only the chosen possess. But so many of them are bankrupt, and I'm not talking about their finances."

Claire smiled gently. "You know what I've learned, Jeffrey? We're all bankrupt in some regard. We're all broken. We all need to seek out the only one capable of truly fixing us."

Her eyes followed the movement of the light from the street lamps that lined the driveway. "I have grieved so much over Jacob. I've screamed. I've cried. I've beaten the ground until my fists were bruised. But then something comes over me, a peace, a place of comfort that I can't conjure up. A place that only heaven can bring to earth." She shook her head. "I'm not superhuman, Jeffrey. But somehow I managed to get through to the next day. And then one day I found myself smiling. And then one day I actually laughed. And one day—someday—I'm going to feel alive again. I know it. I just know it."

"I know it too." Jeffrey stopped, turned to her, and touched the tip of her nose. It was frigid beneath his finger. "But you might not live to see tomorrow if I don't get you warmed up."

When they pulled up in front of her house, Jeffrey got out of the car and walked around to open her door.

"Thank you for the wonderful evening, for the food and the dancing and the conversation," she said. Her heels clicked on the concrete walkway.

"Can I ask you a question, Claire?"

"Sure."

"Why did you never remarry?"

She stood there pondering in the moonlight. "I'm not sure. Probably because I wanted to raise Jacob without being preoccupied with someone else and his needs. And now that I realize I had so short a time with him . . ." Her voice caught. She turned the key in the lock. "Well, let's just say I'm grateful for the decision I made."

"You are an extraordinary mother."

The tears spilled over and coursed down her face. He reached down with both hands and wiped them away. "Thank you for the evening."

"Thank you for helping me feel alive."

chapter thirty-five

M ary Catherine had felt strangely alive the last few days. Even though Nate was hounding her with phone calls, serenading her outside her window, and pledging undying devotion through love notes stuck on her car, she remained unmoved. She had done a search of his e-mails only to discover that he had been playing this charade for months. One or two of them hinted that he might have loved her at some point, but greed and duplicity had clouded and ultimately destroyed what could have been a happy life. She almost wished now she had never been born to wealth. Maybe a nest egg, but not a multimillion-dollar inheritance.

She stumbled into the hallway, shook off her umbrella, and squeaked her way down the hall to the classroom, shivering as she went.

Charmaine was there early, as usual, wiping off the dry-erase board. She had stayed late a couple of evenings and helped Mary Catherine decorate the class for Thanksgiving. And once Thanksgiving was over, no doubt she'd help decorate for Christmas too.

"Ooh, it's so nasty out there." Mary Catherine shook off her heavy raincoat and hung it on the hook by the door.

Charmaine set down the eraser. "How was your evening?"

"How was my evening?" Mary Catherine frowned. "My evening was as perfectly boring as the last six months of evenings. Coco and I ate cereal for dinner, watched HGTV for three solid hours, and then we went to bed. And how was your evening?"

"Oh, you know—same old, same old." Charmaine shrugged.

Mary Catherine sat down in her chair. "And what does the same old, same old look like at Charmaine's house?"

The girl fidgeted with her hair and straightened her skirt. "Oh, nothing that would be of interest to either one of us. So what are you doing for Thanksgiving?"

"Oh, I doubt Thanksgiving will be much of anything special. I might go out and spend it with Esau at my family's plantation."

"You have a *plantation*?" Charmaine's eyes grew round.

Mary Catherine felt herself flush. "Well, sort of. It was my father's house—it's been in the family for years. Anyway, Esau takes care of the place. He always cooks a big meal for any of us who want to come. I suspect my freeloading brother will be wanting me to take him. It's a free meal, after all."

"You have a freeloading brother?"

Mary Catherine laughed. "Let's just say he's slightly misguided. So, what are you doing for Thanksgiving?"

Charmaine shuffled her foot. "Ah, not much. My grandparents died a couple of years ago, and my mother is going somewhere with her boyfriend, I think."

Mary Catherine felt her concern rise. "And your father?"

Charmaine laughed. "My *father*? Mrs. Bean, I've never met my father. Truth be told, I'd be surprised if my mother even knows who he is."

Mary Catherine reached over to take Charmaine's hand. "I'm sorry, sweetie. I had no idea."

"It's no big deal," she said. "So, I bet Esau makes some great turkey and dressing."

Mary Catherine knew where this was going. She stood up and walked over to the board to write out the day's lessons. "You know, he makes so much more than we can eat. You think maybe you'd want to go with us?"

"Oh, I wouldn't want to intrude on your Thanksgiving, Mrs. Bean. I know those are really special family times."

"Well, if you insist . . ."

"But I really would love to."

Mary Catherine turned around. "Then it's settled. You, Charmaine, will be spending Thanksgiving with me. Now, I can't promise it will be uneventful. My family has a way of making events happen."

"I love eventful." Charmaine almost danced.

Mary Catherine couldn't help but laugh. "Lucky for you."

———

Jeffrey drove to work through a driving rain but barely noticed. His evening with Claire still lingered in his thoughts. Even with the tragedy of Jacob's death, these last few months held their own kind of sweetness. The changes he had been making in his life had brought him a freedom he'd never known before.

And last night had been another turning point. He had recognized, finally, the fatal flaw that had plagued his whole life—the ego, the narcissism. And although the awareness shamed him, it brought him a certain comfort as well. At least he knew now that wherever he was headed, it was away from where he'd been.

Jeffrey walked into the office to get the rundown for the day's patients. "Nice evening?" Dr. Nadu asked.

"Yes, it was, actually."

"I am delighted to hear it. You both deserved a nice evening after the last six months you've had." Dr. Nadu left the room, closing the door behind him.

"*I* don't deserve anything," Jeffrey said to the silence.

Jeffrey heard the door open again and turned around, expecting Dr. Nadu. "What have you forgotten?"

"Look at what that butcher of yours did to me!"

It wasn't Dr. Nadu. It was Penelope Jackson, one of his clients. One of his most *dependable* clients. "Penelope, hi. Uh, what's wrong?"

She lifted up her top and exposed two rather large yet lopsided breasts. "This is what's wrong! See anything odd?!"

The sudden exposure left him speechless for a moment. Then his doctor instinct kicked in, and he studied the damage more intently. "Who did this surgery?"

"If you had been there, it would have been you. But *no*, you apparently had to come off and save the world instead of taking care of your faithful clients. This was that Jordan lady. You'd think a woman would know how to make another woman's breasts the appropriate size."

"Jordan isn't supposed to do surgeries."

"What? She told me Dr. Frederick was booked, and I told her I couldn't wait, so she agreed to do it for me."

"You should have waited," he said flatly.

She started to cry.

"Calm down." Jeffrey manipulated her right breast, trying to determine why it had drooped so much lower than the other one.

She stood diligently, holding her blouse over her head, her body heaving slightly from her sobs. The door opened again.

"Jeffrey, Dr. Nadu told me that—oh, excuse me." The female voice made Jeffrey's heart lurch. He leaned around Penelope.

It was Claire. Of all the people who could have come into this office at this moment . . .

"Claire, I—"

Her face drained of all emotion. "Excuse me. I didn't mean to *interrupt*." She closed the door quietly behind her.

"Claire!" Jeffrey headed for the door.

Penelope turned around, hands still in the air. "Where do you think you're going, Jeffrey?"

"I'm going to get that woman."

"You better not leave here before you tell me what you're going to do about my breasts!" she demanded.

"There are more important things in life than your breasts, Penelope."

"What about lawsuits?" She threw her hands down. "You got something more important than that?!"

He grabbed the door handle and jerked the door open. "Yeah, Penelope, I do." He sprinted off down the hall toward Claire's disappearing shadow. "Claire, wait! Wait! Please! This is not what you think!"

She was already halfway to the parking garage. He raced after her, through the crosswalk, panting hard. "Claire, please! Will you stop just for a moment! I promise it's not what you think!"

She turned around, and he could see that she was biting her jaw to control the swimming tears. "You're right. It's not what I thought. I thought that maybe, just maybe, you weren't the same man I knew all those years ago. That maybe you had changed. That you weren't the perverted, selfish Jeffrey you always had been." She reached for her car door. "I was wrong."

He grabbed her arm and turned her around. "She was a *patient*, Claire. That's all. She got a bad breast enhancement by the doctor who replaced me."

"Sure. And you were checking it out to make sure everything was okay. Because after all, *she's your patient*. Does that line sound famil-iar? It's the one you always gave me: 'She's just a patient.' Well, enjoy your patients, Jeffrey." She climbed into her car and slammed the door, leaving him standing in the parking lot.

———

Will sat on the edge of his bed in the fraternity house, his head in his hands. Three of his frat brothers—officers—stood awkwardly in a semi-circle around him. "We're sorry, Will. It's just that you're not technically a student anymore, so you can't be the president of the fraternity."

"What about un-technically? I never liked technically anyway."

"It's what our advisor told us. You've got to go, Will. You can't stay here."

"Yeah, man. And we're really sorry about it and all, but they've voted me for president, and now this gets to be my room."

Will stood up and slapped one of them on the back. "You know, you guys are good. I'll have to give you props for how you've pulled this year off. I still don't know how you've done it all, but it's the best prank ever."

They rolled their eyes at each other. "You want us to help you get your stuff?'

"Nah, you guys go ahead. I'll get it."

"We—ah, we're supposed to help you. You have to go—now."

Ten minutes later, Will found himself on the damp sidewalk with two duffel bags of clothes at his feet. He had heard about that déjà-vu stuff, and if this wasn't it, he didn't know what was. The rest of his stuff he had never even bothered to retrieve from the storage room at his condo. He picked up his bags and began to walk, wishing now that he had bothered to get that coat out of storage, but very grateful it had stopped raining.

⁓

Elizabeth bolted upright in the bed. She glanced over at the alarm clock across the room. But a glance didn't work anymore. She rubbed her eyes as if that might bring the numbers into focus. It didn't help. She needed glasses, and this confirmed it. She got up and walked over, bending down to glare at the numbers. Two a.m. "Who in the world is ringing my doorbell at this time of the morning?"

She clumped down the stairs. The doorbell continued to chime incessantly, followed by the brass door knocker. "Whoever it is, they are insane."

She peered through the peephole. She'd recognize that shaggy head anywhere. "Will, what in the world are you doing here at this time of the night?"

"Hey, Sis. What time is it?" He slipped past her into the house.

"It's 2 a.m. And don't call me Sis. Do you not have a watch?"

He looked down at his shirtsleeve and shifted it up. His wrist was bare. "No. No watch. I had to give it to the cab driver. Sorry, I hope I didn't wake you." He dropped his duffel bags on the couch and headed toward the kitchen.

Why did every man who entered her house go straight to the kitchen? "No, Will. I'm always up at 2 a.m. It's when I do most of my thinking and best work actually."

The sarcasm eluded him entirely. "That's what I figured, with you being a lawyer and all." He opened up the refrigerator and peered inside.

"You want to tell me why you're here?"

"I just need a place to crash for a couple days, if you don't mind. There's been some crazy mix-up at the school that I can't seem to get resolved." He pulled out a container of yogurt and rummaged through the drawers looking for a spoon. "Everything has been whacked since Dad died," he said with his mouth full. "I can't get into my apartment. They won't give me my car back."

"You still don't get it, do you?"

"What? You're saying all this is part of that will charade?" He pushed himself up and sat on the counter. Men didn't seem to realize she had a table either. "I wouldn't be surprised if you and Jeffrey were doing all this yourself, trying to get me to believe that pile of bull. Anyway, I figured I'd just come hang with you for a while until we get this settled. If you get tired of me, maybe you'll give me my car back or something."

"Or something," she mumbled. This was no time to expect Will to get any wiser.

He tossed the empty yogurt container and spoon into the sink, then stuck his head back into the refrigerator as if a five-course meal might miraculously appear. "Do you ever *eat*, Sis?"

She ignored the question. "So what are you planning on doing now?"

He retrieved a bottle of water and headed back into the hall. "Thought I'd just crash here for the evening. Grab some z's."

She only had his disappearing figure to respond to. "Sure, Will. Grab you some z's."

Elizabeth had never understood Will. Maybe she had never tried, if she were being honest. He was just a baby when their mother had died. It was all sad, really, but pathetic as he might be, he still annoyed the blazes out of her.

How could four children from the same parents have absolutely nothing in common? They were strangers to each other. She probably understood Ainsley Parker better than she did those who shared her gene pool.

Elizabeth went back upstairs to her room, where the overhead light was still on. She heard Will before she saw him, snoring and slobbering all over *her* pillow.

She stifled a bellow of rage and resigned herself to the guest room.

chapter thirty-six

Jeffrey slipped into the pew of the church at Edisto. He and
Matthew came every Sunday now; they picked Esau up and took
him to church and then went down to the Gullah restaurant for
lunch. Just as Esau and his father had done every week.

He and Matthew acted like two little boys on these Sunday
excursions—rowing in the marsh, swinging from trees. Jeffrey had
felt more alive over the last three months than he had felt in his
entire life.

The only problem with finally being alive was that you could
feel. He had found himself forced to endure the pain of Jacob's death
and Claire's misunderstanding. But at least he could feel the pleasant
moments as well.

He sat in the pew listening to the choir, with Matthew's little
hand resting on his knee. He reached down and covered it with his
own, and as he turned he caught sight of Mary Catherine sitting in
the back row. Again.

He had seen her quite a few times over the last couple of weeks,
but today, sitting there, he realized he didn't even know her.

Well, he knew what he had come to *believe* about her—that she
wasn't the sharpest knife in the drawer, even though his father had a
keen affection for her. He knew she had pitiful taste in men . . .

As soon as the thought came to him, he recognized the irony.
Mothers had probably said the same thing about *him* when their
daughters brought him home.

"We're so glad you're here with us today," the minister began as he approached the pulpit. The man's name was Mitch Young, and Jeffrey thought that ironic too. Ministers were supposed to be old, with greased hair and black suits. This one was in his thirties, maybe, with unruly blond curls and a baby blue tie.

But when he began to preach, the youthful appearance gave way to a powerful wisdom. The sermon today was about family, commitment, morally corrupt affections, and forgiveness. And here Jeffrey sat, with an estranged sister just a few rows behind him, three former wives who hated him, a string of adulterous affairs, a son who had died without ever knowing him, and another he was just beginning to connect with. Not to mention a nearly year-and-a-half-old baby who bawled her eyes out every time Jeffrey tried to hold her.

Hot tears ran down his face, and he tried to brush them away. But Matthew squeezed his hand and nodded as if he understood it all. Sometimes Jeffrey thought there was a little ninety-year-old man wrapped up inside that eight-year-old body.

The organist played the postlude, and they walked out quietly as the music wafted through the open doors.

"It was good to see Aunt Mary Catherine there again today," Matthew said.

"I 'spect that young pastor we got us is probably very relatable to her. You, too, for that matter." Esau grinned back at Matthew.

Today was the monthly family dinner at the plantation, so they followed Mary Catherine back along the road and down the driveway.

"We saw you at church again, Aunt Mary Catherine," Matthew hollered as he jumped out of the backseat.

"Oh, you did, did you?"

Jeffrey watched as she bent down and gave him a kiss on the cheek; then he ran off to help Esau get dinner out on the table. The child was always starving.

Jeffrey got out of the car next to one of the pruned wisteria plants. Esau refused to let the defiant vine get out of control. He fell into step beside Mary Catherine, and they walked toward the house in an awkward silence. "We haven't really talked about seeing each other at church," he said at last.

"No, we haven't."

"What brought you there?"

She shrugged. "Just nostalgia, I guess."

"Are you missing Dad?"

"I've been missing a lot," she muttered.

"How's everything else?"

She turned sharply in his direction. "What do you mean, how's everything else?"

He took a step back and held up both hands. "Just wondering about your job and Nate and your life. Just trying to have a conversation."

"Why? You've never tried to have a conversation with me before."

"Touché." He dug his hands into the pockets of his coat. "I'm sorry about that, Mary Catherine. I'm sorry about being so self-absorbed all these years. You know, not really being a brother. I feel like I know some people in my office better than I know my own family."

She paused on the second porch step. "You *have* been a sorry excuse for a brother," she confirmed. "But you know what? I think I attract sorry men."

Jeffrey looked at her in amazement. Maybe she wasn't as dense as he had always thought.

"Not that I attracted *you*, of course. You just came with the territory. But Nate, now, Nate's a different story. We're getting a divorce, you know."

"No, Mary Catherine, I had no idea."

She sat down on the top step, and he joined her. "Why would you? You don't know anything about me. All you know is what you want to know. I see the way you look at me, Jeffrey. Like I'm one bean shy of a bushel."

He stifled a grin. Not exactly the way he would have put it, but true nevertheless. "I didn't mean to."

"Yes, you did. You've always had that condescending, arrogant demeanor. Elizabeth is mean, and you're a jerk. Maybe you can't help it. Maybe it's just in your cell structure. But whatever it is, it sure has made for an unpleasant family life." She caught his gaze and held it. "You know, when you and Elizabeth left, it was just me and Will. We had some wonderful times. But now I feel like I'm an orphan. You and Elizabeth aren't even enjoyable company. And Will—well, Will is almost as pitiful as Nate."

"I should respond to all of that, but I'm not quite sure what the response should be."

She nudged him with her shoulder. "Well, what do you know? Mr. Know-It-All has nothing to say."

He nudged her back. "Any chance for reconciliation?"

"With you or with Nate?"

"Either."

"Not with Nate. You don't reconcile with the devil. But you?" She got to her feet and looked down at him. "You have a lot of making up to do."

———

"Do you *ever* shut up?" Elizabeth asked Will as she pulled into the driveway for her monthly Sunday affliction.

"You are a very tightly wound woman, Elizabeth Wilcott. Has anybody ever informed you of that?"

"You are a mooch. Has anyone ever informed *you* of that?"

He laughed, that same annoying laugh she had been forced to endure for almost three days. She brought the car to a screeching halt and slammed the car door as she exited.

With the leaves now gone from most of the trees in the backyard, the pitch of the old barn roof could be seen. She averted her eyes immediately, but she couldn't as easily divert her memories. She pounded up the steps, shivering from the chill of winter and her hovering demons. The pruned wisteria seemed to shiver as she passed. Will slouched along behind her.

Esau opened the door. Elizabeth paused, and Will ran into her from behind. "Get off my tail," she growled.

"Good to see you too," Esau said.

She jerked off her coat and threw it across a chair. She smelled dinner, so fortunately she had been late enough to avoid the small talk.

Will headed straight to the table, patting Esau's narrow shoulders enthusiastically as he passed. "Esau, my man, can't wait to see what kind of feast you've made us today." Esau stumbled forward slightly.

And a feast it was. Fried chicken, potato salad, baked beans, collard greens, and peach cobbler for dessert. Will sat down and immediately tried to snatch a piece of chicken. Esau slapped his hand as he passed. "You will wait for us to pray."

"Oh, yeah, sure. Y'all come on so we can pray."

From the direction of the kitchen, Matthew bounded into the dining room holding a basket full of rolls, and Mary Catherine and Jeffrey came in from the parlor, both smiling. Elizabeth found that both odd and irritating.

Esau stood behind his chair and bowed his head. "Lord, we thank you for another day to partake of your great bounty. May each time we're together remind us of the treasure of family. We pray these things in your precious name. Amen."

"Amen!" Matthew echoed, and Jeffrey laughed.

They all filled their plates, and for a while the dining room was quiet except for the clinking of silverware against the antique china.

Mary Catherine finally broke the silence. "I have an announcement to make." She set her tea glass down by her plate. "I've already told Jeffrey, but the rest of you probably need to know that Nate and I are getting a divorce."

Jeffrey watched the others. Elizabeth cast him a knowing smirk. Will simply kept eating.

"Oh, Mary Catherine, I am so sorry to hear that." Esau laid down his fork to give her his full attention.

Jeffrey sat at the end of the table, wondering for a moment if this was how the conversations had been around the tables of his ex-wives and their families when his indiscretions were exposed. He'd like to think their families had been more sympathetic, but somehow he doubted it.

"Thanks, Esau. It's really hard." Mary Catherine's voice started to quiver.

Esau turned in his chair to console her with a touch. "What happened?"

"He was having an affair." Tears streamed down her face. "But he was just using me, I think."

"And how long did it take you to figure *that* out?" Elizabeth's words dripped with sarcasm.

"Elizabeth!" Jeffrey said. "Can't you have an ounce of empathy?"

"Excuse me? This coming from one of the most accomplished adulterers of the modern world? What, Jeffrey, are you seeing a little too much of your own life here?" She dropped her fork, and it clanged against the side of her plate.

"Do you have something you need to say to me, Elizabeth? If so, maybe we need to go into the other room so we can talk." Jeffrey pushed his chair back.

"You have a problem with everyone here knowing the truth?"

By this time even Will had stopped eating.

"Don't try to show up and be the big brother now, Jeffrey!" Elizabeth shouted. She had fire in her eyes, and she turned the blaze fully upon him. "I know you were there that day! You saw what was done to me, and you did nothing about it! That's why I hate this place! That's why I hate you! And that's why if you get every last dime of the inheritance, I don't care. Because I will *never* come here again!" She pushed back from the table with such force that the chair fell crashing to the floor.

Elizabeth dashed for the front door, grabbing her coat and purse from the chair in the foyer. She flung the door open so forcefully that it crashed into the wall.

Jeffrey ran after her and reached just as she was unlocking her Jeep. "Elizabeth, please! You've got to listen to me!"

"No, Jeffrey, I don't have to listen to you! I heard you once! I heard you run! You ran away when you could have helped me! You could have stopped him, Jeffrey!"

She leaned with her back against the car, doubled over, gasping.

"You could have stopped him from raping me just by coming in the barn! But you didn't! You ran! And Dad never came to help me either! What was it? Your little secret?!" Her body began to heave with the force of her sobs.

Jeffrey reached out and grabbed her by the arms. She beat against his chest. "No! Leave me alone!" She tried to break free from his grip, but he wouldn't let go. He wasn't going to leave. Not this time.

"Listen to me, Elizabeth," he said in what he hoped was a calming voice. "Please, just listen to me. You're right. You're absolutely right. I left you in that barn to be raped by a man we both trusted. A man our father trusted. I should have tried to help. I should have screamed and ran and done anything. But he was too big; I knew I couldn't stop him. And I was afraid to leave you. So I sat outside the barn just making sure he left. I didn't know what else to do. And when he finally came out of the barn, I started running toward the house to tell Dad. But he chased me down and told me that if I ever told a soul, he would do it again, and that he'd kill our father if he ever found out we had told him."

Jeffrey was crying too, now, hot blinding tears. "I didn't know what to do, Elizabeth. I didn't know what to do."

"You never told Dad?" Her body heaved.

He slumped his shoulders. "No, no, I never told Dad. He said he would kill him. And I believed him. I was so afraid. I was so afraid."

Elizabeth dropped to the cold, packed ground. Jeffrey sank down beside her.

"It hurt so bad."

"I know." He drew her into his arms, running his hands over her hair. "I can't imagine what you've carried, and I'm so sorry. Please forgive me, Elizabeth. I should have told! I should have told Dad, but he was his right-hand man on the plantation, and I just didn't know what to do. And then when he died that next year, I knew at least that you were safe."

She leaned back in his arms. "But he's been here ever since." She reached up with a forefinger and pounded it against her temple.

"And that moment has been here." He pointed to his heart.

"I didn't know he threatened you."

"I didn't want you to know I had even been there."

"I saw your shoes and heard you run past the barn. Through the crack under the door."

"But I would never have left you. I couldn't leave you. Not until I knew he was out of there."

"I've hated you since that day. I've hated both of you." She wiped her nose with the sleeve of her coat. It was one of the most unladylike things she had ever done, and it made Jeffrey smile.

"I know you have. I've hated me too. Maybe that's why I became the man I was. All the horrible choices. Maybe I didn't think I was capable of being a real man. The kind who sticks in there and makes it work. I became a runner."

"It's haunted me all these years, Jeffrey. Not just what he did to me, but what I thought about you and about Dad. I thought you didn't care. I thought nobody cared."

Jeffrey reached up and brushed back the brown curls from around her face. "Can you ever forgive me?"

"I could have forgiven you long ago if I had just known. I didn't know you had stayed."

"I couldn't leave."

"I'm sorry you had to experience what you went through too." She dabbed at her face with the palms of her hands. "I spent all those years hating Dad too."

Jeffrey reached down and held her face in his hands. "But he loved you so much."

Her tears seeped through his fingers. "But I still hate it here. I've hated this place ever since that day, because every time I come, I have to see that barn."

"You've got to let it go, Elizabeth. Somehow you've got to find a way to let it go."

"I don't know how."

"I didn't either. But I'm learning."

"I'm stubborn."

"No, you're mean, remember?" They laughed together as Jeffrey let his hands fall to his side. He felt a chill run through him, and he shuddered.

"We're going to freeze to death out here."

He looked at her and grinned. "Not if we had a campfire."

⌒

For the first time in years, Elizabeth looked at her brother. Really looked at him. There was an odd expression on his face, a strange light in his eyes. A look of triumph. He stood to his feet and took her hand. "I need you to trust me."

She should have laughed at such a statement. But she didn't. "What?"

"Just trust me," he said as he led her through the back gardens to the fence line.

She pulled back. "Jeffrey, no." She wasn't ready. Not now. Not ever.

"It's all right," he said gently. "You're not alone this time."

She felt her very insides tremble as she entered the cold, musty barn. She thought she might throw up, but she could feel Jeffrey's presence, right beside her, taking every step that she took.

"It was right there," she said, pointing a shaking finger at the far corner of the last stall. "That's where it happened." She swallowed down the bile that had lurched up into her throat. "Every day, all my life, I've seen it. Seen *him*."

"But look, Elizabeth, he's not there now," Jeffrey said. "He's gone. He's dead."

She knew he was right. But tell that to her brain and her gut, where he still remained, where everything still remained—the sounds, the smells, the pain, the fear. The barn might have been empty except for a few rusty old tools and some moldy hay bales, but it was full of every demon she had fought for the last twenty years.

The scream started in the very soul of her, low at first, but building into a primal rage that shattered the quiet of the barn. "No!" she shouted. "No, no, NO!!"

She lunged forward, out of Jeffrey's grasp, and grabbed up a pitchfork that leaned against the barn wall. She plunged it into a pile of hay in the corner of the stall, over and over again, screaming out her anger and pain with every thrust. She would end this, once and for all. Right here. Right now.

Much to her relief, Jeffrey didn't try to stop her. He just waited quietly until she was finished and finally sank, empty and spent, on the floor of the barn.

Almost an hour of silence passed between them before she finally spoke. "Thank you," she said. "Thank you for being here."

"Got anything left in you?" he asked.

And he pulled a pack of matches from his pocket.

The smoke from the fire was still thick in the night air when Jeffrey and Matthew finally left. Esau made his way outside, bent over the cast-iron flowerpot, and lifted it up by its edge. The white envelope was there, just as it was every month. There was no need to count it.

A day with the kids always left him drained. But he knew that, especially with what had transpired between Elizabeth and Jeffrey today, the playing field had shifted completely.

There was so little time left. He sat down on the teak bench underneath the covered porch and pondered—quietly, solemnly, hopefully. He'd know in three months if it had worked. It was all out of his hands now.

part 4

May

chapter thirty-seven

Mary Catherine sat back in her chair and looked across at Terrance's parents, Mr. and Mrs. Johnson. "I think you should be extremely proud of Terrance this year. He did a complete turnaround since our first meeting. If he can maintain this attitude through the remainder of middle school, he will see amazing things happen." Mrs. Johnson smiled across at her husband. "Terrance told us just the other day that you had made all the difference for him. I told him, 'Well, Terrance, you need to tell Mrs. Bean that.' He looked at me with that look he has, you know?"

"Oh yes, I know." Mary Catherine chuckled.

"And he said, 'Mama, if I told Mrs. Bean I liked her, she would advertise me like Shrimp Lover's Tuesday at Red Lobster'!"

"Well, we'll keep his admiration our little secret."

Mr. Johnson opened the door. "It's no secret to us what a wonderful job you have done. We couldn't be more grateful for the attention you've given our son. He may never have another teacher like you, but he will always know what a good one was."

As they started out the door, Mrs. Johnson turned. "Did we tell you we had a son in the fifth grade? Terrell."

Mary Catherine felt her knees go weak. "No . . . ah, no, you never told me about Terrell."

She heard them laughing as they walked up the hall.

She walked back into the classroom and looked down her list of parents' names. She had gotten a few more than last time, but Charmaine's mother was still a no-show.

She closed her lesson book and gave a satisfied sigh. Only four more days until school was out.

As she climbed into her car, she felt a tug in her gut. Only a few times in her life had she felt such a compulsion, this *knowing*. Once was shortly before her mother died—even as young as she was, she had an overwhelming desire to spend the entire day with her mother. They painted their toenails, braided each other's hair, and giggled with Elizabeth over an old movie. She'd felt the same sense of urgency the week before her father passed away, and again the night she had gone to Edisto Island to sit in the church.

She knew she had to do it, whatever the outcome. She turned the car in the direction of the North Charleston projects, one of the few low-income housing projects that remained since the revitalization of the North Charleston area.

She found the address she was looking for and pulled over to the curb. It wasn't until she was halfway up the walk that the vulgar remarks began from across the street. She quickened her steps and opened the ripped screen door. The hallway smelled of marijuana and stale urine.

A drunk lay passed out across the stairs with no clue anyone else was on the premises. Mary Catherine scanned the darkened corridor for Charmaine's apartment number, then realized it must be upstairs. She skirted over the drunk and made her way up the metal steps, trying to keep from touching either the rusted railing or the graffiti-covered gray wall.

The smell of pot was stronger here, mixed with some other strange odors she didn't recognize. At last she found the right apartment number and knocked tentatively on the dented door. It opened slightly against her touch, and she froze. Terror seized her: go in and die, or run and possibly survive the last three months to even see your inheritance.

She stood there vacillating between possible death and a comfortable life. Finally she tapped on the door lightly once more. It shifted open even farther. She reached up and pushed against it.

It took a minute for her eyes to adjust to the darkness. The tiny apartment was full of . . . bodies. Two lay sprawled across the sofa half-dressed. One was scooping up white powder off of the floor. One sat in the corner smoking a crack pipe and singing children's songs. Two more lay on a filthy mattress in the middle of the kitchen. They weren't dead, but they might as well be. Not one of them even acknowledged that there was someone else in the room.

Then she caught sight of a slight shaft of light coming from underneath a door down the hall. Against her better judgment, she stepped inside farther. The woman with the crack pipe stopped singing and gazed at her oddly but made no move to stop her.

The door had three separate dead bolts and a peephole. Mary Catherine raised a trembling hand and knocked.

A shadow passed behind the peephole. Locks flipped, and a black arm reached out and jerked her inside.

She squinted in the sudden, bright light, and as her eyes adjusted, she had the strange sensation of falling down the rabbit hole into another world.

It was a typical teenager's room. A single bed occupied one wall, with a bright pink bedspread and accompanying pink pillows. In one corner sat a small wooden desk with a lamp and a stack of schoolbooks on top. The walls were covered with posters. Everything in the room was neatly and perfectly arranged.

Charmaine still had her by the arm and shook her. "Mrs. Bean, what in the world are you doing here? You could have been killed. Lord knows you better get back out there, or your car will be stripped—or gone completely."

"Charmaine?" Mary Catherine whispered.

"Mrs. Bean, you don't have to keep your voice down. There's not a crackhead out there that can hear you or would care what you had to say if they did."

Mary Catherine grabbed the girl and pulled her down on the edge of the bed. "Charmaine, how long have you lived like this?"

The girl shrugged. "I've lived this way most of my life. But don't worry about it. I'm perfectly fine. I've got food." She nodded toward the corner of the windowless room. Behind a makeshift curtain of brightly colored beads stood a small refrigerator, along with a toaster and a stack of plastic plates and cups.

"It's so clean."

"I'm a neat freak. You should know that about me by now."

Mary Catherine shook her head in disbelief. "But how do you get money for food, and for your school uniforms?"

"Getting money isn't hard. You can always find money in a crack house. When you're addicted to crack, there are only two things you ever think about—when do I get my next fix, and where do I get the money for my next fix? I know where my mother keeps her stash, and I pull out a twenty here and a twenty there. I figure it's not really stealing, considering that parents are supposed to feed their children."

Mary Catherine grabbed Charmaine and pulled her to her chest, holding on as if arms might reach from underneath the bed and snatch her away.

"Mrs. Bean, I can't breathe."

"Oh, honey, I'm sorry." Mary Catherine was still whispering. "Now, you listen to me, we are going to pack your bags right now. You are getting out of here today, and you're never coming back."

"Mrs. Bean, that's a nice thought, but I don't have anywhere to go, and this is my home."

She looked around at the young girl's room and felt a lump grow in her throat. "Okay, here's what we'll do. How about you come home with me for now? We'll take everything we can carry, we'll lock up your room, and I'll get someone to come over here and get all of your stuff."

Charmaine turned her dark eyes on Mary Catherine. "I can't leave my mama."

Mary Catherine stood up and ran her hands through her hair. She started pacing. Why should the girl even care? She studied the adult concern on Charmaine's childlike face. It didn't matter whether she *should* care. The fact was, she *did* care.

"I will get someone to help your mother, okay? That will be my responsibility." She sat back down on the bed and took Charmaine by the shoulders. "I'm not sure how we'll work all this out, but you can't stay here. Not another day. Now get up, and let's get you packed."

The corner of Charmaine's face turned up in a smile. "Mrs. Bean, are you sure about this?"

"Honey, you can't live this way. No one can live this way! I don't have any idea how you've managed. Now, get to stepping!"

In five minutes they had stowed most of Charmaine's things in a couple of big black trash bags. She locked the door behind her, and as they made their way through the party room, Charmaine went over to the woman with the crack pipe and kissed her on the cheek.

"I love you, Mama," she said. The woman turned vacant eyes to the ceiling and resumed singing.

Mary Catherine caught the burning tears but not before they momentarily blinded her. "Let's go, honey."

They climbed over the drunk and made their way out the door only to find four men sitting on Mary Catherine's car. In that moment every ounce of anger, fear, and outrage came into focus, and when she opened her mouth, it all came out in a terrifying scream. The men took off as if the devil himself was on their heels.

"You're crazy, Mrs. Bean." Charmaine opened the car door and put her bags in the backseat. "I'm not saying that's a bad thing, but you are crazy."

———

"I'm glad you called." Jeffrey held open the door to Poogan's Porch restaurant so Elizabeth could enter.

"I'm glad you were available."

A young blonde woman nearly collided with Elizabeth in the doorway. "Oh, excuse me."

Elizabeth stepped back to let the woman pass. She was beautiful, tall and elegant in a navy sleeveless dress.

Then Jeffrey spoke from behind her. "Aaron!"

Elizabeth turned, and Aaron nodded in her direction. "Hello, Elizabeth. Jeffrey." He extended a hand in Jeffrey's direction, and

Jeffrey let go of the door, which banged into Elizabeth's protruding knee.

"Ouch!"

"Sorry." Jeffrey released Aaron's hand to grab the door again. "It's great to see you. It's been a long time."

"Yes, it has been awhile."

"I hear things are going wonderful with Dad's company under your care. I know he always trusted you."

"Well, he was a very special man to me."

"I think you've proven that."

Elizabeth and the blonde stood there eyeing each other. In a split second, Elizabeth came to a conclusion: the woman was a bimbo.

"Oh, excuse me," Aaron said hastily. "Erica, this is Elizabeth and Jeffrey Wilcott. Their father owns—well, actually *they* own the company I work for."

Elizabeth lifted her chin slightly.

"A pleasure to meet you," the bimbo said.

"How are you, Elizabeth?" Aaron asked.

"Me? Oh, never better. Couldn't be more perfect, actually. Totally fine. Peachy, actually." She gave a fake laugh and cringed inwardly. Apparently she was quite capable of sounding like an idiot. It had never happened before.

"Erica here is an attorney with Avant, Taylor, and Dunham. Elizabeth is an attorney as well."

"Oh really? What type of law do you practice?"

"Well, I do a lot of different things. Real estate development, closings, titles, things of that nature. And you?"

"I'm a child protection advocate. I've fought for the cause of children my entire life."

Okay, Elizabeth thought, *maybe she isn't a bimbo.* But she had to be a retired beauty queen, at least, because that certainly sounded like a canned pageant speech. She probably wanted world peace too.

"That's a very noble career," Elizabeth replied. "Well, if you'll excuse us."

Aaron took the hint. "Sure. It was wonderful to see you though." He caught Elizabeth's eye. "Both of you."

She gave a forced nod.

"Maybe we'll see each other again," Bimbo Beauty Queen said.

"That would be lovely." Elizabeth went on into the restaurant, looking down at her black pants and making a mental note to go buy herself a nice dress.

"That would be *lovely*?" Jeffrey mocked.

The host pulled a chair out for Elizabeth and handed her a napkin. "What?"

"I have never heard you use the word *lovely*."

"I say *lovely*." She shook her napkin out for emphasis. "In fact, *lovely* is one of my favorite words."

He hid his face behind the menu, but she knew he was laughing. "I'll have to remember that."

They both ordered seafood—Elizabeth the pan-seared scallops, and Jeffrey one of the house specialties, the peanut-crusted catfish. When you grow up in the Low Country, you acknowledge seafood as one of the main food groups. Their mother could do a Low Country boil better than anyone they knew, and Esau knew all her tricks. If they went to the plantation on any other day than Sunday, he might actually cook it for them.

Jeffrey picked up his knife and slathered his cornbread with butter.

"I never told you how truly sorry I was about Jacob," Elizabeth said.

"Thank you. I appreciate that." He took a bite of the cornbread. "So why aren't you two together?"

"What two?"

"You and Aaron. You know he's crazy about you. Always has been."

"Why would you say that?"

"Elizabeth Wilcott, you are one of the smartest women I know. How could you not know that Aaron was in love with you? You nailed Nate Bean with a single glance, but you couldn't figure this out?"

"It's complicated."

He laid down the cornbread. "The rape?"

She shrugged. "It just messed up everything."

"How are you doing? We haven't talked about it since, well, since that day."

They both quieted as the waiter sat their meals down in front of them.

"I've been going to a therapist."

"Is that helping?"

She cut a scallop in two with her fork. "For a hundred and fifty dollars an hour, it better be helping something. Of course, since I'm making such big bucks at the Benefactor's Group, I don't really need to worry."

Jeffrey laughed. "Yeah, this hasn't been the most financially lucrative year, has it? But you're changing the subject."

"What was the subject?" She bit into a scallop and rolled her eyes.

He took a bite of his collard greens. "How you're doing."

"Well, you're going to think this is crazy."

"After this year? I doubt it."

"Well, I have a *friend.*"

"No!"

She laughed. "Yes. I, Elizabeth Wilcott, actually have a *friend.* She's rude, obnoxious, and just as stubborn as I am."

"The perfect pair. Who is it?"

"Ainsley Parker."

"The girl you hated in law school?"

"That's the one. She's my boss. But there's something different about her. She's had some really tough stuff in her life too, but she's happy. She has a great marriage. She's great at her job. People really respect her. And I don't know, she's just fun. It's insane, I know." She placed a slice of zucchini in her mouth.

"It doesn't sound insane to me. I think this entire experience has both of us doing things we should have been doing for a long time."

She reached down and wiped away a streak of condensation on her water glass. "You know, I never thanked you."

"Thanked me for what?"

"For torching the barn. I never knew how healing that would be."

He reached across the table and took her hand. "If I had known, I would have done it years ago."

Just as they finished their dinner and left the restaurant, Elizabeth's phone began to vibrate in her purse. "Hang on," she said to Jeffrey. "Let me get this."

"Elizabeth, you're going to love this," the voice on the other end said. "I've finally gotten a break regarding the Executor you've been looking for. He actually—"

Elizabeth looked at her brother, who was studying her expression intently. "Um, listen . . . listen. Wait a minute. I appreciate your work, but you know what?" Her gaze never left Jeffrey's face. "It doesn't matter anymore."

"What are you saying?" the befuddled response came from the other end.

"Send me a bill for your services, but call off the dogs and destroy your records. We're done. It simply doesn't matter." And she closed the phone.

"Dare I ask?" Jeffrey said as they continued walking up the sidewalk.

She grinned at him. "Wrong number."

———

Jeffrey loved Charleston in May. Well, he loved it now anyway, because now he noticed things. The dogwoods and Bradford pears had already gone from white to green. He turned his head back toward the street to see Elizabeth climb in her car.

That's when the memory returned. A familiar scent.

His mind scrambled to place it. In the doorway, with the blonde woman.

Aaron's cologne. And suddenly he remembered where he had smelled that scent before. The night of their abduction.

His heart stopped. It couldn't be. Surely all of this wasn't Aaron's doing. Not the way he loved Elizabeth.

But if anyone had had their father's ear, it was Aaron. His father loved him like a son—too much like a son, Jeffrey had often thought. More than he loved his own flesh and blood.

It would make perfect sense. Aaron could easily have influenced his father to change the will. Maybe Aaron was the one who would get everything if they didn't complete this year.

Elizabeth passed him in her Jeep. She smiled and waved as she drove by. She was just starting to live. He could see it in her face. The lines had softened, the smile came more readily. She had a friend. She was beginning to heal. If she found out Aaron had done all of this, she would retreat back into her bitter shell and never come out again.

Jeffrey had stood back and let her be abused once. He wouldn't let it happen again.

chapter thirty-eight

Jeffrey sat inside his car in the parking lot in front of his father's office building. He had been there for an hour, just to make sure he didn't miss Aaron. He would have gone to his house last night, but he didn't know where he lived. And he wasn't about to call Elizabeth to find out.

A dark green Land Rover pulled into the parking place next to Jeffrey. The moment he stepped out of the car, Jeffrey was on him immediately.

He grabbed Aaron by the arm and flung him against the side of his truck, his face just inches away. "This was all your doing, wasn't it? You masterminded all of this by manipulating our father!"

For a moment Aaron stared at him, speechless. Then, in a flash, he jerked his arm free and pinned Jeffrey up against his own car. "You better explain what you're talking about, and you better explain it quickly."

Jeffrey's cheek was mashed against the roof of his own Mercedes. "You know what I'm talking about." He struggled, trying to free himself, but Aaron pinned his arm more firmly behind his back.

"I have no idea what you're talking about, but if you'll act like a normal person instead of a crazy man, I'll let you go and we can discuss this like two adults."

Jeffrey nodded. Aaron dropped his arm, and Jeffrey spun back around to face him. "I know what you've done!"

Aaron straightened the collar of his suit coat. "What do you think I've done?"

"My father's will. This challenge. It was all your doing, wasn't it?

You manipulated my father so you could try to steal the inheritance from our family. You have played us, and you've used your fondness for Elizabeth to try to mask your deceit."

"You are not serious." Aaron shook his head and turned his back on Jeffrey.

"Don't walk away from me."

"I'm not walking away," Aaron said. He faced Jeffrey again. "I'm just trying to figure out why in the world you would think I had something to do with your father's will. I didn't even know anything had changed until Elizabeth called me the night after all of you had been kidnapped."

"Elizabeth called you?"

"Yes, she called me as soon as she got back home, I guess. I went straight over. This is crazy, Jeffrey! Why would you think this was me?"

"Your cologne. I recognized the cologne my kidnapper was wearing. I didn't realize it until yesterday, at the restaurant, when I smelled it again."

"You're accusing me because of *cologne*?"

Jeffrey frowned. Now that Aaron was saying it, it did sound absurd.

"Where were you kidnapped from, Jeffrey?"

"From my office parking garage. What does that have to do with anything?"

"I was at home when Elizabeth called me. She called me on my home phone. How would I kidnap you and be able to be home when Elizabeth called me?"

Jeffrey began to play the logistics out in his mind. "I don't even know where you live."

"I live on Water Street. Could I have dropped you off and made it home in time to answer Elizabeth's call?"

Jeffrey really wasn't sure. He wasn't sure of anything. "I was dropped off at my office downtown. You could have had plenty of time. You—you could have had it all planned out with the other kidnappers."

"This is insane! You're getting all of this from a cologne? And how many people wear this cologne, Jeffrey?"

Jeffrey didn't answer.

Aaron shook his head. "Do you know how much I cared for your father? I was there. I helped Esau take care of him when none of his own children even called."

Jeffrey gave one last attempt. "All the more reason he would have listened to you."

"If he had listened to me, Jeffrey, he would have started being a father to Elizabeth and the rest of you much earlier."

That was when Jeffrey saw it. The look in Aaron's eyes. A love like that, like the one he had for Elizabeth, could never harm her or take advantage of her. He dropped his head. "I'm sorry, Aaron. The whole idea was stupid."

Aaron felt his anger rising. "You're right. It is stupid. I've served your father for over ten years. And I've loved your sister for about as long. But if this is what you think of me, then here are my keys." He fumbled with his key chain.

"No, Aaron, I don't want your keys. Listen, I'm sorry. Really, I'm sorry. I don't know what I was thinking. It's just Elizabeth, you know, she's been the walking wounded for so long. And I just thought if you hurt her too, she might never recover."

Aaron gave a short, bitter laugh. "Your sister wouldn't care what I did."

Jeffrey shook his head. "That's where you're wrong. She may not admit it, but she loves you. She just doesn't know how to love. Promise me you'll fight for her, Aaron. No one has ever really fought for her before."

"You can't fight for someone who won't let you love them."

"She's coming around. I promise. Just try one more time. And again, I'm really sorry. This whole thing was stupid." Jeffrey extended his hand. "Truce?"

Aaron reciprocated. "Truce."

———

Aaron watched as Jeffrey drove away. He walked into the office and headed upstairs, his footsteps creaking heavily against the old wooden stairs. Once in his office, he sank into the chair and opened the bottom file drawer on his desk.

In the back of the drawer lay a tiny box—an antique diamond ring that caught the morning light with its brilliant facets. His grandmother had given it to him, to place upon the finger of the woman who stole his heart.

His heart had been stolen for a long time—kidnapped and held for ransom. He had just begun to get it back again. And now Jeffrey wanted him to open himself up again, to make himself vulnerable to Elizabeth's apathy.

He, too, was just beginning to heal. The wounds were barely closed, still raw and painful. He snapped the box shut and put it back into the file drawer.

He couldn't risk getting his heart torn out again.

Not this time.

The blue lights of the patrol car turned into the projects off of Rivers Avenue into a ghost town. At the first sign of the police, all the drunks and crackheads scurried for cover like cockroaches. Mary Catherine had called in a substitute for the day so she could make sure that not one of Charmaine's possessions was mishandled. It was the last week of school so all the substitute had to do was control the bedlam anyway. And Mr. McClain had clearly understood.

The first thing she had done when she got home with Charmaine was to call Child Protective Services. Charmaine begged her not to do it.

"I have no choice, Charmaine," Mary Catherine had explained. "As a teacher I am required by law to report this. Technically I shouldn't have taken you out of there without official permission." Fortunately the social worker had understood and agreed to allow Charmaine to remain in Mary Catherine's custody temporarily instead of shuttling her off to a foster home.

"I'm afraid they'll arrest my mother."

"They'll get help for your mother," Mary Catherine assured her. "And they're going to send a policeman with me to get the rest of your things tomorrow. We'll store them in my garage for the time being."

The patrolman, when he showed up, turned out to be a boy she knew in college. "So you came here all by yourself last night?" he asked.

"I've been called crazy recently."

"I can understand why. Most of Charleston's finest don't even want to come down here."

The movers she had hired for the morning had to be goosed an extra two hundred dollars, even with the police escort. But nothing was stirring in the projects; the place looked completely deserted. Even the drunk on the stairs had found another place to sleep it off.

Charmaine's mother and her friends had been taken into custody during a raid the previous night. Mary Catherine had already spoken with a friend who was a lawyer to help get her in a rehabilitation facility in Columbia, away from anything familiar.

In less than an hour Charmaine's bed, desk, books, and all her personal treasures had been boxed up, loaded into the small U-Haul truck, and taken to Mary Catherine's. By the time she left to pick Charmaine up from school, the girl's entire room had been re-created in Mary Catherine's guest bedroom.

———

Elizabeth pulled up to the front of Hazel's house. Hazel was waiting on the front porch with her best blue Sunday dress on and her black patent leather purse strapped across her dainty wrist.

"Are you not going to tell me where you're taking me?"

"Hazel, how many times in life do people actually get a real surprise?"

"Well, I had five of them."

Elizabeth laughed. "Your children don't count." She closed the car door, and they drove in silence to the market area off King Street, pulling to a stop at the door of Tristan's restaurant.

"Ooh, this is a might fancy restaurant, Elizabeth."

"Well, you look so beautiful you deserve a mighty fancy restaurant."

Elizabeth led Hazel into the restaurant and through frosted glass doors into a private seating area. The room erupted with applause. All five of her children, along with some of the staff from the Benefactor's Group, were seated around a large table.

Ainsley slipped a file of papers into Elizabeth's hands and turned up her nose. "Are you wearing a *dress*?"

"I wear dresses." She glared at Ainsley and returned her attention to the moment. The crowd hushed. "Hazel Moses," she said, "it is my great honor to present to you the official deed to your home." She pulled the title from the file.

Hazel's hands flew to her mouth and tears welled up in her eyes. "Elizabeth! You can't be telling this old woman the truth!"

"I'm telling you the gospel truth," Elizabeth retorted.

Everyone laughed and chattered and hugged everybody else. The waiter came and took their orders and brought them all drinks. And at last the food arrived.

"Now before we receive this fine meal, we need to thank our good Lord for all that he has done for us today," Hazel said. All of her children clasped hands and bowed their heads instinctively. They had obviously done this before.

Elizabeth cast her gaze in Ainsley's direction, but her head was already bowed. Elizabeth followed suit. She felt Ainsley reach out and grasp her hand.

"Dear Lord, we can't thank you enough for what you've done for us today. You've parted waters as great as those that you parted for the children of Israel."

"Yes, you have, Lord," came a response from across the table. Other affirmations followed: "Yes, Lord. Yes."

"And, Lord, I pray today for those family members that allowed us to have our home. I pray you bless them. And I pray for the men who tried to take it from us. May their business be blessed. And, Lord, for our home that you've given us, may it be used all the days of our lives to bring you glory. To feed the hungry, house the lonely, raise godly grandchildren, and pass on a heritage for the world to come."

"Oh, make it so, Lord, make it so." Elizabeth cocked one eye open to see one of Hazel's daughters talking to the ceiling.

"And, Lord, about Elizabeth here—"

Elizabeth heard the falter in Hazel's voice. She clenched her eyes tighter.

"Lord, I don't know why you blessed me with such an angel to take on my case, but I don't believe that any of this would have happened without her. I pray that somehow she would see how mightily and wisely she allowed herself to be used on my behalf."

Ainsley squeezed Elizabeth's hand. Elizabeth let go and swiped at the tears on her face.

"Amen," Hazel finished.

"Amen," everyone responded—including Elizabeth.

"Now let's eat some of this wonderful food."

Elizabeth watched the love that emanated from Hazel to her children—indeed, to everyone in the room. She wondered briefly if she should introduce Hazel to Esau. She laughed to herself, then sat back and enjoyed this surprisingly rewarding moment.

———

"Come walk with me," Dr. Nadu said as Jeffrey walked through the door.

"Do you want to tell me where we're going?" Jeffrey's tennis shoes squeaked on the tile as he tried to keep up.

"And take away the mystery? Certainly not."

"I didn't figure you would."

The gold vinyl chairs of the emergency waiting area came into view. Jeffrey felt his heart lurch slightly. Every time he came near the emergency room, he saw his son lying on the table.

Dr. Nadu leaned closer. "You can handle this, Jeffrey, I assure you."

The double doors to the emergency room opened. Dr. Moss,

who had treated Jacob, was waiting for them as they rounded the corner. He handed the chart to Dr. Nadu.

"No, give this one to Dr. Wilcott."

The surgeon hesitated momentarily, then placed the chart in Jeffrey's hands. "We have a seven-year-old girl with severe burns to both legs caused by a motorcycle engine."

Jeffrey turned to Dr. Nadu and shoved the chart in his direction. "I can't do this. You know I can't do this."

Dr. Nadu stood his ground and never even reached for the chart. "Dr. Wilcott, we do not travel along the paths of our lives so that we can pretend they never happened. We travel them so that when we encounter others on the same journey, we can comfort and help them. You've experienced the most difficult of losses. Now it is your turn to comfort. You are an extraordinary physician. You know what to do."

Jeffrey's arms fell numbly to his sides. "I'm not ready."

"We are never completely ready, Jeffrey. But we must always be available. This is your moment."

Jeffrey studied the face of his mentor. The nine months with Dr. Nadu had brought a respect. A respect no one had ever held in his life. Unfortunately, not even his father, at least while he was alive.

"Are you coming?" asked Dr. Moss.

Dr. Nadu crossed his arms and gave Jeffrey a reassuring nod.

Jeffrey turned toward the bed where the little girl lay. "Let's see what we have here."

Later that afternoon Dr. Nadu walked into Jeffrey's makeshift office. "You did a wonderful job with that family today."

"You're a sink-or-swim kind of teacher."

"You swim well." Dr. Nadu sat down and tented his fingers together. "Jeffrey, when I agreed to take you on for a year, I thought it was a mistake. A rather large mistake, I might add. But now—" He paused. "I am still uncertain as to why you wanted to work with me. But I would be honored if you would consider becoming a partner in my practice."

Jeffrey stared at him, overwhelmed by the enormity of the request, by its weight and privilege.

Dr. Nadu raised his head and turned it slightly. "Jeffrey Wilcott is speechless. Amazing." He smiled broadly, his teeth white and even against the brown of his skin. "You are an exceptional doctor, Jeffrey. You came in here arrogant, ready to teach me something, but you have in the long run proved to be teachable. And you have faced your greatest tragedy and yet survived."

He stood up. "I know you have your own practice, but no matter what decision you make, I just wanted you to know that I've found it an interesting journey these past months, and I could see us making a fine team."

Jeffrey still sat silent.

Dr. Nadu opened the door and peered back over his shoulder at Jeffrey. "Many doctors have come to me here asking for such a position. You should know this is the first time I have ever offered it." He closed the door behind him.

———

Mary Catherine passed out report cards as each student left on Friday. Some gave her smiles, a few brought her cookies from home. Terrance brought her a picture of himself. Nicole slipped out past her without speaking.

She walked into the hall and peered down the corridor, just catching a glimpse of Nicole's pink pants.

"Nicole!" she called out.

Nicole didn't turn around.

"Stop this minute!" she demanded.

Half the students in the hallway froze, and so did Nicole. Mary Catherine caught up to her and stood in front of her, holding out her report card. "You forgot this."

"I didn't forget it." Nicole stood, arms folded across her chest.

"You don't care that you made all As except for the one semester you refused to take my test?"

Nicole shifted slightly.

"You're not stupid, Nicole. If I didn't know better, I'd say you know how smart you are. There are other worlds than your mother's, and you know it."

Nicole's eyes blazed red-hot at the mention of her mother.

Mary Catherine chose her words carefully. "You're not lost potential, Nicole. You're just misguided potential. Now take your report card so you will always know how gifted you really are."

Nicole snatched the report card from Mary Catherine's hand. "Are you finished?"

Mary Catherine stepped aside. "Yes, I'm finished."

Nicole pushed past her and continued down the hall, tossing her report card in the trash can as she went by.

———

Jeffrey opened the car door on Friday evening and collapsed into the seat. His habitual remedy to relieve the stress of the week would have been to crawl into the arms of a woman. Didn't really matter which woman. But the young girl with the burns had dominated Jeffrey's thoughts and absorbed his time and attention. He simply found it hard to leave.

His mind had ached all week over the load that Claire must have endured. He watched these parents with a different keenness, a different level of compassion than he had otherwise known.

When he pulled up in front of the house, Claire was outside with a small trowel in one hand and a Gerber daisy in the other. He watched her for a moment. She didn't hear him approach, and once he saw the iPod earphones, he understood why.

"Claire," Jeffrey said.

There was no response. She dropped the Gerber daisy into the shallow hole she had dug and patted the earth around it.

He squatted on the sidewalk next to her. "Claire!"

She jerked around and grabbed her chest. "Jeffrey, what in the world are you doing here?" She pulled the earphones out and jumped to her feet.

He stood up. "I just thought you had ignored me long enough."

She got to her feet and headed to the house, removing her gardening gloves as she walked. "I intended to ignore you forever."

"That was what I figured."

She slipped off her rubber clogs at the front door, dropped the gloves on top of them, and let herself into the foyer. Jeffrey followed.

"You can't stay mad at me forever."

She turned and looked at him. "Jeffrey, I don't waste my energy being angry. And trust me, if that was the land I wanted to live in, I'd be far more angry over the fact that my son died at the age of thirteen than over the fact that my ex-husband, after almost twenty years, still has no self-control with women."

"But it wasn't what you think."

She chuckled as she opened the refrigerator door and pulled out her tea pitcher. "It was never what I thought, was it?"

"Okay, you're right. You have every reason in the world not to trust me—to hate me even. I wouldn't blame you. To be honest, it still amazes me that you ever allowed me into Jacob's room, much less into your life."

She poured some tea into a glass but didn't bother to offer him any.

"I don't claim to know how you feel, or how you've dealt with all of this. But the one thing I do know is this: whether you want to admit it or not, you were willing to open your heart up to me. You probably won't believe me, but that woman in the boardroom with me *was* a patient—an irate patient who had a botched breast augmentation and wanted me to see how poorly it had been done."

Claire raised her right eyebrow. He could tell she was having difficulty preventing herself from rolling her eyes.

"I admit, there have been multiple women who have come through my office that attracted me."

This time she did roll her eyes. "No kidding."

"I've been stupid. I've been careless, and I've let my desires rule me most of my life. That's why what I'm about to tell you may sound like the craziest thing you've ever heard."

"I'm used to crazy. Try me."

"I love you, Claire. You are the only woman I've ever truly loved."

"Well, if that's how—"

"I know. If that is how I love somebody, you'd hate to see what I'd do to the woman I don't love. Well, there are two other wives who could tell you all about that. And because I love you so much, I'm going to leave you alone until the old Jeffrey is gone. Completely and totally gone."

He inched in closer to her.

"I have never known how to love well. I've never thought of anyone other than myself. I've never cared that my actions had repercussions for anyone else. But I do know this: as much as I was ever capable of loving, Claire, I loved you."

She didn't speak, but the expression on her face told him she knew it was true.

"I never fought for you before. I've never fought for *anyone*. But I want to learn to love you. I want to learn to love you the right way. The way you deserve. I'm not the same man I was, Claire. But I'm not what you deserve yet either." He shrugged. "I will be. I promise. And when I am, I'm coming back here, and I hope you'll let me love you well."

He leaned over and kissed her warm cheek. He wanted to linger there, just pressed against her skin, but she didn't deserve to be toyed with. She was still leaning motionless against the countertop when he let himself out.

He slid behind the steering wheel and leaned on it, exhaling a sigh of relief. He had no idea when he'd return, or if she'd even answer the door when did. Now he could only hope and pray.

Maybe he'd ask Matthew to pray. He was still much better at it than Jeffrey was.

———

Jeffrey had to call information to get the number. He pulled over to the side of the road and put it into his speed-dial list, then punched it up on the drive home. "I hear you have a new live-in."

"Who told you?" Mary Catherine asked.

"Elizabeth. She said Will told her."

"That boy can't keep his trap shut."

"Want to bring her over to watch a movie?"

Mary Catherine's voice went up an octave. "Excuse me?"

"I said," he repeated slowly, "do . . . you . . . want . . . to . . . bring—"

"Like, come to your house?"

"Yeah, like come to my house."

"Are you drunk?"

"Not lately, no."

"I don't even know where you live."

With a shock he realized he didn't know where she lived either. He knew she was on the Isle of Palms, but he had no idea where. "You're right, Mary Catherine. I hadn't even thought about that. Sad, isn't it?"

"Dreadfully."

"So, do you want to come?"

"You ordering pizza?"

He laughed.

"This kid is about to eat me out of house and home."

"I know, I have one. I'll get pizza. Plus, Matthew will love her."

"She likes adventure movies."

"Then I know he'll love her."

———

Elizabeth walked into the backyard, the steam from her coffee cup rising into the early morning air. She walked around the edge of the pool and dipped her toes into the cool water. Walk, dip, walk, dip. The bottom edge of her pajama leg came up wet, so that the strawberries printed across the green fabric looked fresh and washed and ready for eating.

The morning was warm, the water perfect. But just as she was heading back in for her swimsuit, the back gate opened.

She saw his brown curls first. He closed the gate behind him and walked determinedly in her direction.

"Aaron, what are you—"

He was standing in front of her before she could finish her sentence. "No, you're not to talk. You're to listen."

He took the coffee cup from her hands and set it on the small stone table between two lounge chairs that flanked the edge of the pool.

"You know I love you, Elizabeth Wilcott. And I know you love me, although whether you've admitted it to yourself is another matter. Now, I can't take away all your demons. You'll have to work through those somehow. But I'm not living like this. Apart from you. Away from you. You're not running from me anymore."

He wrapped his tanned arms around her waist. He had never been so close before. The warmth of his breath washed over her face. Her pulse quickened. She knew him so well, yet seeing him this way felt so strange.

He opened his mouth to say something else, but before he could speak, she leaned into him and kissed him—a deep, slow, passionate kiss. The kiss she had wanted for years without realizing it.

At last he pulled away and came up for air. "Well, I didn't expect you to make the first move."

She felt her face flush, and she leaned against him. "I didn't expect that either." Then she laughed. "But I am a control freak, you know."

"Ah," he said, "but you don't get to decide everything." And to prove his point he kissed her again—a kiss that left her wishing she had given up control sooner. Much sooner.

the
second
will

August
One Year Later

chapter thirty-nine

Elizabeth didn't know how it would arrive. She was just hoping that there wouldn't be a need for a midnight abduction and a black bag over her head.

The request was delivered by a man in a three-piece black suit who looked as if he had just left his position as the local funeral home director. With a stiff and formal silence, he handed over an elegant invitation engraved with gold lettering:

Your presence is requested this evening at Wisteria Plantation at half past six for the reading of the will of Elijah Clayton Wilcott II. Immediate family only, please.

As Elizabeth drove up the dirt road, she took in the tranquil beauty of the plantation. Since Jeffrey burned down the barn, she was able to enjoy this place for the first time in years. This home. Her home.

She wished she had told him sooner. She wished she hadn't let that one moment of terror and pain rob her of so many years. But she would waste no more time wishing. Today she would be grateful for the stillness in her soul.

Some people in life experienced instant miracles: a cancer cured, a marriage mended, a life rescued. But it hadn't been that way for her. Instead, it had been a process. She had healed a little that morning at the Waffle House with Ainsley Parker—the healing of simple laughter and friendship. And a little more when Hazel had hugged her and prayed for her. Still more over a nice dinner with a brother she was finally getting to know.

And allowing Aaron to love her, allowing herself to love him in return, had restored so much of the ground she thought she had lost. Whatever was to come in the future, she believed, would also be used to complete her recovery.

But as Wisteria Plantation came into view, something else struck her as strangely healing. Assuming this entire thing wasn't a hoax, she was only moments away from receiving her inheritance. But she could just as readily turn the car back around and drive away without ever knowing what inheritance might have been hers. It didn't matter. What mattered was the life she had created—or the one that had re-created her—over the course of the past year. The one her father had known would be for her good.

A sense of freedom, of liberation, surged through Elizabeth's veins. At the curve of the driveway she caught a glimpse of something expansive and purple and brilliant. Her father's wisteria, its flowers draping like bunches of grapes.

Little vines spread out from the tops of the sculpted plants, connecting one plant to the next, encircling the entire driveway.

Encircling her.

Embracing her.

Elizabeth leaned her head back against her headrest and took in every graceful arch of the dark green vine, every lush and magnificent cluster of purple flower.

All her life it had been there, growing, multiplying, blossoming with wild abandon, yet beautifully molded, and she had never really seen it before. She resisted the urge to shout for sheer exhilaration. She hummed softly instead, knowing that, for the first time in her life, there wasn't a sound she could make that wouldn't be heard.

———

It was a magnificent day. Jeffrey drove with the top down and inhaled deeply of the fragrant wisteria as he approached his family home. His heart had been opened in so many ways over the last year. And now he could not just see things but appreciate them as well, things like an amazing South Carolina afternoon, the familiar smell of his heritage and family. His family. This year had given him the rare opportunity to learn what family really meant. He had never truly known before.

For thirty-eight years, Jeffrey Wilcott had thought of nothing except Jeffrey Wilcott. And yet over the last six months, he had discovered that he was actually capable of more. Much more. Real feelings. Feelings that weren't wrapped up in selfish desires, but emotions uncontaminated by self-centeredness. Feelings that were simply right.

Jacob's death had been the catalyst. Opening himself to Jacob meant opening himself to heartache. And that vulnerability brought gifts he had never imagined. The softness of Matthew's skin. The awareness of his own failures. The newly awakened love for Claire. Pain, compassion, joy, sorrow, loss, and shame. And most importantly, forgiveness.

He thought about his brother and sisters. Jeffrey still did not know if Elizabeth had orchestrated this entire year, but he didn't really care. He only wanted to know and grow and learn from each member of his family. He wanted to be a good brother to them. A real brother.

He felt especially concerned for Will. But he didn't know how to reach someone who seemed so irretrievably broken.

The irony did not escape him. He had been perceived that way for many years—as irretrievably broken. But he had been retrieved. He had been rescued. He had been mended.

He pulled up next to Elizabeth and watched her for a moment as she sat with her head thrown back. He laid his head back as well and looked up. The purple of the wisteria mesmerized him. He studied the stubborn vine, amazed at how it had been pruned and woven in directions it would never have gone on its own. It was pliable, and because it could bend, it had become all the more beautiful.

Jeffrey smiled. For so many different reasons, he smiled. But mostly because, for the first time in his life, someone would actually care if he hadn't come home.

⌒

The live oaks stood over the driveway of Wisteria Plantation in regal splendor, the moss draping down as if bowing. Welcoming royalty, Mary Catherine thought.

She had felt anything but royal over the last year. She'd endured a radical change in lifestyle, the annulment of her marriage to a man she loved, a job that tried her to the limits, and sudden parenthood to a teenager in puberty. But she'd never been happier. She'd never been saner. She'd never been more at peace, with life, with herself, with her past, with her future.

And she was coming home, to the place that held her inheritance. Not the money, but the memories. The love of a man and woman, a father who did his best, and even in the end tried to make up for what he had left undone.

As she pulled up to the circular drive, she parked next to Jeffrey. The wisteria blossoms draped across the hood of her car, the lilac blooms nodding to her as if she had been expected. She nodded back and paused, a prayer forming softly on her lips, thanking God for what had transpired this year, for what was about to happen. A prayer for Jeffrey, for Elizabeth, and for Will. Especially for Will.

And this time, unlike a year ago, she knew why she was praying.

⌒

Elizabeth watched as a small red sports car came careening up the driveway, going so fast that the dust churned by its wheels couldn't catch up. Will's head was sticking out of the sunroof. The owner was most likely the sun-drenched beauty behind the wheel.

"Who is *she*?" Elizabeth muttered to Jeffrey.

"His latest girlfriend, I expect. Ever since he left your place, he's been bouncing around from one to the next, staying until they kick him out."

Elizabeth raised an eyebrow. "How do you know this?"

Jeffrey shrugged. "He's my brother. I keep an eye on him."

The sports car came to a screeching halt in front of the house. Will bounded out of the car, visibly inebriated. The girl climbed out as well.

Jeffrey walked around to the driver's side. "I'm sorry. No one but our family is allowed into the house."

"But Will said—"

"I apologize for whatever misinformation Will might have given you, but it might be best if you go for a drive and come back in an hour or two."

She turned her false eyelashes in Will's direction and fluttered them. Elizabeth was almost certain she could feel the breeze.

"Come on, Jeffrey, don't be such a hard—"

Jeffrey turned and looked at Will. "Will, you heard what I said. There is no negotiation."

Will stumbled to her side of the car and gave her a sloppy kiss in front of all of them.

"After seeing that, I'm going to postpone dating for at least five years," Mary Catherine whispered.

Will kissed her again. "I'll be right back, baby," he slurred. "Right back with all the money your little heart could desire."

Jeffrey stood holding the car door open for her. "You need to leave now. Will can call you on your cell phone when we're finished here."

She roared away in a cloud of dust. Will headed for the porch and stumbled on the first step. Jeffrey came around and tried to help him, but Will shook him off.

Esau was there, dressed in a white shirt and bow tie. Elizabeth saw him clutching a copy of the gilded invitation in his hand. Of course. Esau would be part of this too. Whatever the terms of her father's will, he would take care of his old friend.

They all stood in the middle of the grand foyer, waiting for something to happen.

"Got any food?" Will's request broke the silence.

"There's some cold fried chicken in the refrigerator," Esau said.

But the ringing of the doorbell stopped even Will. "Let's get this ridiculous thing over with," he said, changing directions from the kitchen to the front door. He opened it so hard it bounced against the wall.

The Executor reached out and stopped it before it could slam in his face.

"May I come in?"

Will stepped back and bowed.

The Executor entered the foyer, opened his briefcase, and drew out a gold-colored folder. "Shall we?" He motioned to the study at the other end of the foyer, across from the drawing room.

Elizabeth felt a tingle run up her spine. She almost wished she had taken that last call from the private investigator. Despite whether Jeffrey had anything to do with this or not, she still wanted to know *who* this character was.

The mahogany paneling of their father's study glowed red in the setting light of the August sun. Despite the humidity, the room was cool. A ceiling fan whirred softly overhead.

The Executor seated himself in their father's aged leather chair and propped his elbows on the desk. Elizabeth and Mary Catherine pulled Esau down on the sofa with them. Jeffrey and Will sat down in the two leather club chairs across from the desk. Will slapped Jeffrey on the arm and then rubbed his hands together as if they were two fraternity brothers about to enjoy a round of poker.

Elizabeth watched the interchange between them. It was evident that Will thought this reading was somehow more legitimate than the last, and equally evident that Jeffrey was both annoyed with him and concerned about him. Even from this distance, she could tell Will had been drinking most of the day.

The Executor cleared his throat and began to speak. "As you know, it has been a year since we last met. Over this past year your actions have been closely monitored. We have watched to make sure that each of you has followed the guidelines set for you. Three of you did, and one of you did not." He eyed Will.

Will shifted slightly in his seat. For the first time, he seemed to be getting the message that this might actually be serious.

"Esau, we know that you are just becoming a part of this reading," the Executor continued. "However, I will belabor the point no longer."

They watched as the Executor's long index finger reached underneath the lip of the envelope and undid the clasp. He pulled a large document out from inside, laid it on the table, and began to read.

"I, Elijah Clayton Wilcott II, being of sound mind and body . . ."

He read through the preliminaries without pausing. When he got to the personal part, he slowed his speech.

"To my children. Years ago, when your mother and I inherited this piece of land, I found an unruly vine of wisteria. Wisteria is a stubborn specimen, and if it is not trained in the direction you want it to take, it will eventually take over the entire yard. And so Esau and I planted stakes and began to tell the wisteria where we wanted it to grow. We gave it direction and trained it into something so beautiful that this place became known for it."

Mary Catherine was already dabbing at her eyes. Esau took one hand, and Elizabeth reached for the other.

"The challenge of this past year has been very similar. For years, in my ignorance, I let you grow wild and untamed. I did not give you direction, instead simply gave you advice, forgetting that my primary responsibility was to be your father and not your friend. I watched as four beautiful children became so unruly and self-directed that they threatened to ruin their own future happiness and success."

"He calling us wisteria?" Will asked.

"Just listen, Will," Jeffrey said.

"Jeffrey, I can only hope that somehow this past year has changed you. There has always been an insatiable need in you

to be loved and approved, making it ever so clear to me that you never felt those things from me. I hope somehow you have found the love and approval your heart has so longed for. And I hope that you can forgive me for not supplying you with the complete assurance of my love for you."

The Executor shifted his glasses on his nose.

"If the Executor is reading this part, then you have success-fully completed your year's journey. I can only say how proud I am of you. My hope, however, is that it was not merely a change of occupation, but a change of lifestyle and of values. I leave to you one-third of my estate, approximately three hundred and fifty million dollars, to be distributed in one lump sum when all of my assets, except my company and the plantation, are liqui-dated. You will also serve as one-third partner of the company I spent years developing. I pray this is worth the sacrifice you have made this year. But more than that, I hope you have learned how to love well."

"Did you understand all of that, Jeffrey?" the Executor asked.

Jeffrey was having trouble catching his breath, and it wasn't because of the staggering amount of money he had just been be-queathed. In thirty-eight years he had only heard his father tell him that he loved him one time, and never that he was proud. He tried to hold back the tears. "Yes," he choked out. "Uh, yes, I'm fine."

"Woo-hoo!" Will shouted, bouncing up and down in the seat. "Keep it coming, man!"

"To my daughter Elizabeth. What an amazing woman you have become! I only hope that the hostility you had toward me has been put to rest since my death. You are so like your mother—headstrong, passionate, and my right-hand girl despite the feelings you had toward me. The day you left my company, I grieved so desperately for you. But I knew you had to learn how to fly on

*your own, and fly you have. I hope you know that I loved you
with all my heart."*

The Executor turned the page.

*"You have spent your year doing what I asked of you. I trust
that in giving yourself to pro bono work, you have experienced
a side of life I was never capable of showing you—a life where
obstacles are common, prejudices are numerous, and opportunities are limited. I hope you have come to realize that to whom
much is given, much is required. You have within you gifts that
are capable of turning the tide for others.*

*"Every life needs a tide turner. Some people are capable of
turning their own tides by sheer faith or determination, but others need a mediator, a mouthpiece. You have the ability to give
a voice to the voiceless, to be an advocate for those who need one.
I only hope that this experience has revealed a part of you that
has surprised even you. And finally, my sweet, strong girl, I hope
this year has helped you banish the fears you have been harbor-
ing all your life."*

Elizabeth let out a soft cry. The Executor paused for a moment,
and then continued to read.

*"I know that something happened to you, Elizabeth. Some-
thing you would never speak of. And I have prayed that the God
of this Universe would reach into your soul and heal your deepest places. That freedom would be the greatest endowment you
could possibly have.*

*"But as for your inheritance, I leave to you one-third of all
of my fortune, approximately three hundred and fifty million
dollars, to be distributed to you in one lump sum once all of my
assets except my company and the plantation are liquidated. You
will also serve as one-third partner of my company. I pray this is
worth the sacrifice you have made this year."*

Elizabeth's shoulders slumped as her tears took over. Jeffrey got up and knelt in front of her. "You okay?"

She nodded.

"Come on, Elizabeth. He needs to keep going," Will interrupted. "This is getting good!"

"You can wait, Will!" Jeffrey snapped. He turned his attention back to Elizabeth, who was trying to compose herself.

"I'm fine. I'm fine." She patted her eyes with the handkerchief Esau had given to her.

Jeffrey went back to his chair, and the Executor continued.

"To my precious Mary Catherine, my baby girl. You have been so good to me. You cared for me after your mother died. You genuinely loved me, and you will never know how special those moments were that we shared over the last couple of years. You have a true heart of gold, Mary Catherine, even if it has gotten clouded by your priorities.

"But if the Executor is reading this, then you have spent the last year using that education I paid for. I hoped you would spend the year teaching, because 'teaching teaches the teacher' just as 'parenting teaches the parent.'"

Mary Catherine gasped. Elizabeth gripped her hand more tightly, and saw that Esau did the same.

"But no matter what you chose to do, I hope you discovered something about yourself. I hope you've discovered the deep well of talent that has been inside of you untapped for so many years. I hope that you've become confident in your abilities, realizing that people don't have to be bought, simply appreciated. And I hope that you've come to understand the love I had for you."

"I did, Daddy, I did." Mary Catherine's tears overflowed and fell onto her linen skirt, spreading as they landed.

"As I did for the others, I leave to you one-third of all of my fortune, approximately three hundred and fifty million dollars, to be distributed to you in one lump sum. You will receive your money once all of my assets except my company and the plantation are liquidated. You will also serve as one-third partner of the company that I spent years developing. I pray this is worth the sacrifice you have made this year. But more than that, I hope you will change someone's life with the gifts you've been given."

The Executor paused to study Mary Catherine as she steadied her chin. Then he turned his gaze to Will. "Are you sure you are ready for this, son?"

"I've been ready for this charade to be over for a year."

Elizabeth cringed when she saw him turn and give Jeffrey an exaggerated wink. In his alcohol-induced stupor, he had not yet realized that three-thirds equals one. "Bring it on."

"To my baby boy, Will. If I questioned how I raised any of my children, Will, it is you. You received a father's old age and apathy. Forgive me. It wasn't until you started college that I realized how far off the path you had strayed, and by then I didn't know how to get you back. All I can do now is remind you of what I know is inside you—greatness, humor, the ability to lead. Wherever you go, people follow.

"I am grateful I am not there to witness this moment, because even writing this, thinking that you did not complete your task, I feel as if my heart will break. I had hoped you would spend a year serving in some capacity, because a good leader must first know how to serve.

"Yet you have chosen not to serve, but instead to continue on a path of self-centeredness and self-destruction. At this point, son, the only person who can help you is you. So it is with great sorrow that I tell you, you will receive no inheritance."

Will laughed. "Come on, man. Quit trying to play me. I'm not falling for it."

The Executor gazed at him with an expression of great sorrow. "I'm afraid this is real, Will. And there is more."

Jeffrey put his head in his hands, and Mary Catherine cried softly. Elizabeth felt her heart slowly crack inside her chest.

"Everything I had put aside for you has been equally divided among your siblings. You will have no part in the family company. Furthermore, your siblings are instructed not to help you financially in any way other than the following: They may offer you a job suitable to your education and experience at a salary commensurate for the position, and they may pay for any rehabilitation treatment you need to help you recover from your self-destructive habits and become the man you were created to be. But, Will—"

The Executor stopped to make sure this was sinking in. Elizabeth, like the rest of them, was watching Will closely. His skin had gone pale and clammy, and he looked as if he might throw up. But his expression had changed. It was both sober and stunned. He had finally gotten it. Unfortunately, it was too late.

The Executor continued.

"You need to realize that no matter what you do from this point on, the inheritance you would have received will no longer be available to you. You have made your choice. I gave you ample warning and opportunity. You chose to heed neither. I can only pray that at some point that you will come face-to-face with yourself and your need. Your real need."

Will slumped back in the leather chair. The Executor heaved a sigh and read on:

"And to my fine friend Esau. No one has cared more for me or this plantation than you. You have been my constant friend and true companion on life's journey. I ask you to reside on this property until our Maker takes you home as well. You will receive a cash

inheritance of a million dollars. It is yours to do with as you like. You can travel to all the places you and I wanted to see and eat all the home cooking your heart desires. An account has been set up to provide for the continued upkeep of this home. None of the money needed to care for this property will come out of your inheritance.

"And, Esau, I want you to know that I'm saving a really good seat for you.

"Finally, to my son Jeffrey, I leave Wisteria Plantation, in the hopes that he will make it a home for himself and my grandson Matthew. Matthew has always had a special connection to this place, and I would like for it to be his one day.

"I love each of you, my dear children, and I am confident I will see you again. All my love, your father."

No one moved. The Executor stood from his chair and walked toward the door, then turned back. "Might I say one thing?"

"Sure," Jeffrey said.

"I'm really surprised that none of you pressed through to find me. I understand your men got really close."

Elizabeth laughed softly to herself, and much to her surprise she heard Jeffrey do the same. Then she truly knew. The Executor's heels clicked against the hardwood floors, and he was gone.

Jeffrey moved first and went to stand in front of Will's chair. "Will, listen, I need you to listen to me."

Will's glazed eyes shifted slightly in Jeffrey's direction. "We can get you help. Dad told us we can at least do that. We can get you into a treatment facility. We can get you whatever you need, and then we can get you a job."

Mary Catherine nodded. "We can, Will. You need this. You need to get help. You can't keep living this way."

Elizabeth went to join them, intending to comfort her younger brother, but Will jumped from his seat and fled for the front door. They all ran to the door after him and watched as Will kicked up dust like Forrest Gump down the long dirt driveway, screaming as he ran.

"Run, Forrest, run . . ." Jeffrey muttered.

"You think he'll ever stop?" Mary Catherine asked.

"I don't know," Elizabeth said. "He's been running all his life."

"We'll get him. Somehow we'll get to him," Jeffrey said. His eyes still searched the driveway.

"There's nothing we can do about him right now," Esau said. "Anybody for some food? It's not Sunday, you know."

Mary Catherine turned around. "Low Country boil?"

"Shrimp, crawfish, lobster tails, and crab legs ready to go in the pot."

"Matthew will be devastated," Jeffrey said.

"We'll never tell him." Esau grinned and disappeared into the kitchen.

Esau walked down to the marsh. The Executor was sitting in the boat, watching the water as it lapped beneath the dock.

"Is Jeffrey moving in?" The British accent was gone, replaced by a deep Southern drawl.

"Yes, sir. Probably next weekend. He told me he wouldn't be bringing much; said he was sick of all that white furniture. It will be nice having life back in the house."

"You won't miss the quiet?"

"I never wanted quiet."

"How'd you do it, Esau? How'd you talk Mr. Wilcott into changing his will? You honestly thought it would work?" He slid an oar into the water, and the movement ruffled the surface, breaking the light into slivers.

"I felt it was the final hope. He didn't know how to reach them—*really* reach them. I told him maybe he could accomplish in death what he hadn't been able to do in life. That was when I got the idea of changing the will."

"You could have inherited everything, if none of them stayed to their task."

Esau sat down on the edge of the dock. He slipped his rubber shoes off, rolled up his thin khaki pants, and dipped his feet in.

"I never wanted the money. All I ever wanted was for them to be a family. Me and Bernice had a family. A good family. These kids never, until this very moment, knew what a real family was—even when their mother was alive, God rest her soul. Money can't buy it, you know.

"Anyway, I knew there was enough competitiveness in them to stick it out, especially Jeffrey and Elizabeth. Just to make sure the other didn't win."

"Did you count on Mary Catherine?"

"No, I prayed for Mary Catherine."

"What did you expect from Will?"

"I didn't know. I am glad his father didn't live to see it."

"Well, I'm glad he didn't either. It would have broken his heart, I'm sure." He arched his bushy eyebrows. "So, promise me you'll get you a bank account now, and I can stop leaving money under a flowerpot."

"It worked, didn't it? But thank you for doing it. And for keeping it safe. Mr. Clayton didn't want a big transfer into my account even if it was for the upkeep of the house and the land. He wasn't sure where the kids would search."

"Does this mean we can go back to our Friday night bingo nights?"

"I'll try to steal away. I still don't think Jeffrey needs to know about you quite yet."

The Executor pressed his oar up against the dock and pushed off.

"Are you going to tell me where you got your thugs?"

"I have eight grandsons. They all have a nice inheritance of their own coming as long as they keep their silence. And they've met Will. Trust me, they're liable to die mutes."

Esau laughed. "See you soon, my friend." He kept his feet dangling in the cool water and watched as his friend rowed up the marsh to his house a quarter mile up the way.

epilogue three months later

"So, this is where the rich people work?" Ainsley said as she opened the door to Elizabeth's office at Wilcott Enterprises.

Elizabeth put on her best snooty rich girl voice. "Oh, certainly, my dear. Do come inside and experience the finer things of life." She greeted Ainsley with a hug. "You miss me so much, don't you?"

Ainsley patted her back. "Miss you? Not a chance. Why would I miss having the place stunk up with those ridiculous candles of yours?"

"Sit, sit." Elizabeth said. She pointed to the brown leather tufted sofa.

Ainsley fell into the sofa and stroked the soft leather. She looked down at the thick Oriental rug and up at the ornate coffered ceiling. "Ever going to give this room a feminine touch?"

Elizabeth sat down beside her and propped her elbow up on the back edge of the sofa. "I don't know. It makes me feel close to him, you know. My dad. Being here with his stuff, his books, and his pictures."

"So he trusted you to run this place?"

"Aaron really runs the place. I run the trust. Jeffrey and Mary Catherine agreed I was the best one for that job."

"And how are the two of them doing?"

Elizabeth smiled to herself. She was having a conversation, an actual conversation, with a friend. It was like they were catching up. It was so . . . normal.

"Jeffrey's fine. He and Matthew have moved out to the plantation, and Jeffrey's taken on a new partnership with Dr. Nadu at the

Medical University. Mary Catherine's still teaching, although she used some of her trust money to paint and do landscaping at the school. She says that if you send children to a school that looks like a prison, they'll act like criminals."

Ainsley laughed. "Smart woman."

"She's actually taking Charmaine to see her mother today. The woman has been in rehab for three months and apparently is making real progress."

"And Will?"

Elizabeth looked down and fiddled with one of the buttons on the sofa. "Will is—" She shrugged. "We'll keep trying. We're not giving up on him. But our father was right. Will has to stand on his own feet."

Ainsley nodded. "We all do." She tilted her head and gave Elizabeth a piercing look. "You know, what you did was exceptionally vulgar."

"You could just say thank you." Elizabeth nudged her and smiled.

Ainsley slapped at her hand. "All right, I'm thanking you. What that money from the trust will do for us is—well, it's something the Benefactor's Group couldn't have accomplished in years of fund-raising."

"It's our pleasure. Now, let's go. I'm taking you somewhere extravagant for lunch!" Elizabeth bounded off of the sofa. "You can get it smothered, covered, and dunked for all I care."

She opened the door to see Aaron standing there with his hand raised, preparing to knock. "I was just about to ask if you wanted to get a bite to eat. But I see that you're busy."

Ainsley was on her feet in a flash.

"Ainsley Parker," he said, giving her his most charming grin. "A pleasure to finally meet you. I've heard all kinds of things about you."

Ainsley shouldered Elizabeth out of the way and reached out her hand, bangles clanging at her wrist. He shook it, and she held on, surveying him from top to bottom. "Oh my, oh my. A pleasure to meet you too, you most charming specimen of a man."

His face flushed slightly. He turned back to Elizabeth. "You've got plans. I'll go."

Elizabeth pulled him back, brushing an imaginary piece of lint off his shoulder for an excuse to touch him. "I'm free for dinner."

"Dinner it is, then," he said, his voice low and smooth.

"Do you two need to get a room?"

Elizabeth turned. Ainsley was standing there with her hands on her hips, grinning like a Cheshire cat.

"No, we don't," she said curtly. "You and I are going to lunch."

"Let's go, then," Ainsley said. "Preferably today."

"She thinks she's still my boss," Elizabeth told Aaron.

"Somebody needs to keep you in line," Ainsley said. "And I'll tell you one thing: if you don't marry this man, you are sadder than I thought."

Elizabeth laughed.

Ainsley pushed her way past both of them, leaving them standing in the doorway.

"Now!" she yelled from the front door. "I'm not getting any younger here!"

"You wanted a friend," Aaron said with a chuckle.

"I've already got the best one." Elizabeth said, reaching her left hand up to his cheek. The antique diamond caught a shaft of light from the window and sparkled shamelessly as she leaned in and kissed him.

———

A well-dressed gentleman got out of his car and picked his way across the site of the new Habitat for Humanity house in downtown Charleston. "How long has he been here?" he asked the foreman.

The supervisor removed his hard hat and took out his handkerchief, wiping the sweat from his brow. "Two weeks."

"Has he been beating nails like that this entire time?"

"Sir, he could probably build this house by himself."

"What's that he's saying?"

"Not really sure, but he's been mumbling it since he got here. Something about work."

"Do you know who he is?"

"Yeah. Name's Wilcott. His brother comes by here every evening just to check on him."

"Odd."

"Very."

The two men walked out to the truck that held the latest delivery of lumber. The young man, the subject of their speculations, knelt on the plywood pounding nails as fast and as hard as he could.

And with every nail he repeated the same words, over and over again. "This has got to work. This has got to work. This has got to work."

acknowledgments

On the beautiful backroads that I often travel from Charleston, back to my hometown of Camden, South Carolina, the lilac wisteria hangs in many of the trees that line those country roads. Like kudzu, you're not sure where it starts, and you definitely have no idea where it will end. As I made this trip recently, I was reminded once again of the power of something that is left unchecked, uncontrolled, unbridled. It will eventually take over, and the true beauty of what it could be is tainted by what it has become.

I've never written books because I thought I was an amazing writer. To be honest, I often read other people's work and wish I could write like them. I even come home sometimes and try to create these beautiful, eloquent, rhythmic words, like my good friend Charles Martin, only to find my narrative running along in typical Denise fashion. But the one thing I do believe the Lord has gifted me to do is to take the human relationship and strip it down to the place we all live. That is what I have tried to do with these characters. In all their realness and rawness, I have tried to give each of us a glimpse of ourselves.

I've struggled over the last year with the "whys" of life: the "why" of sickness, the "why" of loss, the "why" of victimization. And I believe I've discovered something amazing about our gentle Pruner. Much of life is the result of a fallen world. A divine plan that man abandoned, by a will that man was given. Because of man's choices, all the inhumanity of this world was allowed. Yet in the middle of the "stuff" of life, God sets us up for victory. He surrounds each of us with everything necessary to win. Whether it is people, talents, or opportunities, he places in our path everything we would ever need to shape even the ornery places of our will into something that can clearly express what we were truly created to be. Each of us will taste "life." It's inevitable. But each of us has been given every necessary tool for our refining, our taming, our potential.

I've had a tough year. And there are so many people that I need to thank and acknowledge for making this book what it has become. But this time, I'm only giving written acknowledgment to one. I'm acknowledging the one who so graciously and lovingly took this stubborn, sinful, needy will of mine and surrounded it with everything needed for its victory. Jesus, may you bridle me as needed. May you check me even in my most unlovely places. And at the end of the day, may what I produce be a testament of your great grace, extreme care, and gentle hand. I trust you with my life. Thank you for trusting me with this story.

reading group guide

1. In the opening of *The Will of Wisteria*, each sibling is defined by what they do. Are you defined by what you do or by who you are?

2. Clayton Wilcott has manipulated his children's futures from beyond the grave. Has anyone ever tried to manipulate your future? Have you ever tried to manipulate someone else's? Did you have good intentions? Does that matter?

3. Each sibling wrestles with the decision of whether to play along with what could be a game or—even worse—a plot. Yet the risk of not obeying is too great if it turns out to be real. Was there ever a time when you participated in something, but didn't know for certain if it was what it appeared to be?

4. Aaron is able to see something in Elizabeth that she refuses to admit to herself: her fear. Who in your life is able to see into the deep places of you?

5. When Jeffrey sees his son Jacob for the first time in years, he was forced to confront the man he has become. Have you had an event occur that ended up revealing to you the person you've become? Were you surprised?

6. Mary-Catherine is responsible for leading her students with a respect that is earned, not a respect that is freely given. Do you have people in your life that have made you earn their respect? How did that make you feel? What did you do to gain that respect? Do you give respect freely?

7. In Elizabeth's dealings with Ainsley Parker, her college nemesis, she finds herself reluctantly enjoying her company. Has there ever been someone in your life that you decided you didn't like only to have them become one of your favorite people?

8. Elizabeth and Jeffrey come to a critical climax over a secret from their past—a secret that had severed their relationship because of things they *thought* rather than things that actually *were*. Has there been a situation or relationship in your life where years were spent in bitterness and anger only to find out that what you thought was true was not what actually happened?

9. Forgiveness seems to be a part of each character's ability to move forward. Is there a place in your own life where your inability to forgive has incapacitated your progress?

10. Wisteria is a stubborn vine, yet it is a vine that can—if someone is willing to take the care attention necessary—even be shaped into a tree. Do you have instances when you've let go of your stubbornness and allowed yourself to be moldable? What was the outcome?

11. Esau had only one desire for these four children: that they become all they were created to be. He was even willing to encourage their father to redirect the course of their lives. He took a huge risk; a risk that if discovered could have, at one point, destroyed any potential to achieve his goal. Have you ever taken a risk on some-one who had potential but were incapable of seeing it themselves?

What did you do? What would it have cost had they discovered your motive before they were ready?

12. In the end, Will was trying to achieve something that was no longer achievable; his chance had passed. What character traits are needed to make sure that we don't miss the most important opportunities, even if they are challenging, in our lives?